Praise for *THE LAST PATIENT*

"*The Last Patient* is a beautifully written, absorbing account of one family's life in Romania under Communism. Focusing on the father, a noted surgeon, this novel shows the forces that drive even those who love their homeland to leave it and start their lives over. A moving story populated with rigorously delineated characters, *The Last Patient* is an especially important book now, when immigration to the United States is increasingly misunderstood."

—J. WYNN ROUSUCK, author of *Please Write: A Novel in Letters* and award-winning Theater Critic at WYPR, Baltimore's NPR Affiliate

"Tudor Alexander's *The Last Patient* offers a vivid, often poignant portrait of one family enduring and emerging from the dark period of Ceausescu's regime in Romania. At once intimate and sweeping in scope, the novel evokes the specifics of time and place through deeply atmospheric prose and dialogue that rings utterly true. With both clarity and compassion, Alexander depicts the dreams and desires, strengths and frailties of each of his characters. As they navigate the convolutions of Communist rule and the even greater complexities of the heart, they variously cling to and relinquish hopes and expectations, and make tenuous deals with others, and with themselves."

—LAUREN GOODSMITH, Founder, Intercultural Counseling Connection; author, *The Children of Mauritania*, *The Path of the Sun*

"*The Last Patient* is a beautifully written story set in post-war Eastern Europe…blending historical fiction with personal conflict. Alexander captures the era's essence with vivid realism… bringing history to life through detailed descriptions and well-developed characters. The novel's strength lies in its complex characters and emotional depth… exploring political ideology's impact on personal lives and moral compromises under oppressive regimes. Thought-provoking and deeply relevant, *The Last Patient* masterfully combines history and drama. Educational, engaging, and unforgettable."

—CAROL THOMPSON for Readers' Favorite, 5-star review

the

LAST
PATIENT

TUDOR ALEXANDER

Boyle
&
Dalton

Book Design & Production:
Boyle & Dalton
www.BoyleandDalton.com

Copyright © 2025 by
Tudor Alexander
LCCN: 2025900890

Paperback ISBN: 978-1-63337-884-1
Hardback ISBN: 978-1-63337-887-2
E-book ISBN: 978-1-63337-885-8

Printed in the United States of America
1 3 5 7 9 10 8 6 4 2

To the memory of my parents and grandparents.

To Vio.

Even in Siberia there is happiness.
ANTON CHEKHOV

To watch over mouth and tongue is to keep out of trouble.
PROVERBS 21.23

Prologue

Maryland, 1993

An oxygen bottle lay next to the hospital bed in the middle of the living room. The nurse was supposed to connect it when she came by later. Kostea was asked not to smoke. He didn't like to be told what to do in his own house. When Toddy arrived, Kostea went down to the parking lot to have a cigarette.

Alone, Toddy looked at his mother's body, a knocked-down tree, her legs broken branches sticking out from under her pale blanket to touch the cold metal railing. Her eyes were closed, and the light that always shone in her face was extinguished. Her colorless hair, glued to one side of her forehead, covered her temple and revealed an oversized ear, white like a seashell thrown on the shore by last night's tempest.

There was a rattle in her chest, her breath a harsh noise, a useless struggle.

When Kostea returned, Toddy left for work. He said he'd call at lunchtime.

Kostea brought two mugs of tea and set them down on the coffee table near the bed. "Clara."

She didn't answer.

He pulled up a chair, put on his glasses, and opened his poetry book.

His foot rested on the oxygen bottle. "You'll like this poem I found last night. It's by Marcel Breslaşu. It doesn't have a title, and it is very short."

Don't fear dying, my dear
Beginnings and endings are one and are near
A short night untangles the engagement between us
Thereafter, death eternal together will bring us.

He set the book in his lap. "This will be our poem, Clara. Do you like it? We are together in this—just us. Two people without a title."

BOOK I

EVERYTHING IN THE
NEW WORLD WAS RED

Mostly Bucharest, the 1950s and earlier

CHAPTER I

Class Struggle

March 1950

"It gets worse by the day," Kostea said.

"We're small potatoes," Clara said. "I don't think they would touch us."

"The Soviets are here to stay. I'm afraid they'll touch everybody." Kostea removed a strand of blond hair from his face and walked to the dark window. The bare bulb in the ceiling was spreading a dull yellow light in the kitchen. Old furniture lay scattered everywhere. "Uncle Sebastian," he said. "I just heard that they gave him twelve years."

Clara shrugged.

"I practically grew up with the man," Kostea continued, a melancholy smile on his face. "You know he's Eugene's uncle."

"I don't understand what he did that was so terrible."

"Nothing," Kostea said. "He buried twelve stupid gold coins in the backyard. Somebody saw him and informed the authorities. That person was being vigilant. Vigilant, get it? The new lexicon, the word of the day. Everything is a class struggle. The war ended five years ago, yet we're still fighting. Uncle Sebastian tried to hide twelve coins of his prewar family fortune, and they gave him twelve years."

"They are setting an example."

"Poor man. Poor us. Poor everybody." Kostea was on a roll, his eyes steely. "You're right: We are small potatoes, but it doesn't matter. What started at the top extends now to everybody. Simply put, it's terror."

"Kostea, don't scare me. I'm tired." Seated, Clara rested her head on the kitchen table and looked at her husband sideways. As she twisted, her belly protruded forward like an oversized melon. She was nine months pregnant, still worked, and had spent that entire day at Elias Hospital where both she and Kostea were employed as interns.

"Sure you are," Kostea said. He kneeled next to her, brought her hand to his lips, and kissed it. "Any time now, you might go into labor."

"And the baby room isn't ready."

"I'll take care of it. Don't worry."

Just then, there were loud knocks on the door and male voices. Kostea jumped to his feet. "You stay here."

A man, a woman, and a child escorted by a policeman in uniform stood by the front door.

"Comrade Bardu, your apartment has been subdivided," the policeman informed Kostea, handing him an authorization with the emblem of the precinct. "These are Comrades Sorin and Marta Ionescu, and their five-year-old son, Radu. Your second bedroom was assigned to them, with access to your kitchen and bathroom."

Kostea paled. Haltingly, Clara had followed him, and he heard her breathing behind him. He turned and pointed at her rounded belly. "There must be a mistake. We need the space. We're expecting a baby."

The policeman shrugged. "I'm merely executing an order. You know there is an acute housing shortage after the war. All of us make sacrifices."

For a few seconds the Ionescus stayed silent. Then Sorin Ionescu asked to inspect the premises. He led with a heavy step, Marta, Radu, and the policeman trailing. "We'll be here tomorrow with a truck full of furniture," he announced with a sweeping arm gesture. "And we expect our room to be empty."

"We need you to make space in the bathroom and kitchen," added Marta Ionescu.

In the days that followed, the Ionescus became noisier and more assertive. A few times Kostea was on the verge of confronting them, Clara managing each time to calm him down and preserve a precarious balance. During the day, Sorin went to work, as did Kostea and Clara. Marta stayed home with little Radu. Sorin proudly informed Kostea that he was a communist activist at a major Bucharest manufacturing shop called Red Grivița.

Everything in the new communist world was red. Everything.

———————

Clara shook Kostea and told him that her water had broken. Sweat formed on his forehead. The doctor in him took over, and he brought towels and helped her get dressed. The Demetriades in the apartment two levels above had a phone. It was four in the morning, so Kostea knocked hard on their door. The chances of getting a cab or an ambulance were practically nonexistent, and he called Professor Dinescu, who sent over his government-issue Pobeda sedan and his driver. Both Clara and Kostea had been his students in medical school, and he had kept in touch with them with an eye toward influencing their future careers. Weeks earlier, he had told Kostea, "When Clara's labor begins, don't hesitate. Day or night, call me."

That was the type of man the professor was—helpful and calculating.

As Clara waddled down the front steps to the dark street, holding on to the handrail with one hand and Kostea's arm with the other, the Ionescus showed up in the doorway.

"You made such a ruckus I feared the Americans had landed," Marta yelled at them, her robe half unbuttoned. "Don't you know our *baby* is sleeping?"

Kostea's first impulse was to tell her to shove it, but he was too preoccupied with Clara and ignored her.

Despite the early hour, the car ride to Elias Hospital took a full twenty minutes. As the contractions came and went, Clara panted and moaned, her tearful green eyes filled with fear. Her dark-brown hair was disheveled, and beads of perspiration ran down her forehead. She squeezed Kostea's hand.

At the hospital, Clara's obstetrician, Dr. Pop, determined they had a while longer to wait and assigned them a private room. The fact that they worked there assured them special treatment.

Propped up by pillows, Clara tried to breathe and relax. Her hair fanned over her shoulders. She rested her bare arms on her belly, and Kostea imagined their baby curled up inside, getting ready for the big journey.

"Kostea," Clara said, "my mother doesn't know I am here."

Kostea nodded and went to the nurses' station. It was a few minutes before six, and the night shift was ending. He saw a familiar face among the tired nurses getting ready to leave. "Good morning, Monica," he said, sounding deliberately positive.

The nurse waved as she adjusted her overcoat.

"It's happening," Kostea said. "Clara's in labor."

"I know, and good luck to you both," Monica said. She smiled. "I'm out of here till my next shift."

"Listen. Could you do Clara a favor?"

"I'll try. Anything for your beautiful wife, Dr. Bardu."

"You live in the same neighborhood as Clara's mother. Stop by her place and ask her to come here."

Monica hesitated. Kostea took a large bill from his wallet and offered it to her.

"No," Monica said, looking around at the other nurses, who didn't seem to be paying attention.

"Yes," Kostea said. "You're here after a sleepless night and under no obligation to help us."

"This is too much," Monica said, reaching for the money.

"If you think it's too much, I'll ask you for something else. Go by my friend's place two streets down from my mother-in-law's and give him the same information. Tell him that if I can, I'll see him later at the Garden." Kostea went to the dispatch table and wrote the names and addresses on a piece of paper.

Monica nodded, placed the paper in her purse, and left the hospital.

———————

As soon as Clara's mother arrived, Kostea hugged Clara, threw on his doctor's coat, and joined the team of interns on their morning rounds. He didn't want to leave his wife, but her mother was there, and he was a doctor. Duty called, and he knew that for the moment there was nothing more he could do for Clara. She was in good hands, he'd be close by, and the time would pass faster if he kept busy.

At lunchtime, Professor Dinescu took a break in his schedule and stopped by Elias Hospital. His voice assured, he spoke to Dr. Pop while absentmindedly patting Clara's hand. Her status was unchanged. Hearing that the professor was there, Kostea left the interns and came back to the room to meet him.

Professor Dinescu stood and grabbed his gray fedora. "Walk out with me, Kostea."

"Is it all right if I stop by the Garden?" Kostea asked Clara. "The guys might be there."

Silently, Clara nodded.

Kostea turned to his mother-in-law. "If it's time, tell a nurse. They know where to find me."

He removed his doctor's coat and stepped into the balmy spring air with the professor. The older man walked a half step ahead of his former student, looking tall and elegant in his dark overcoat and fedora. Kostea kept his eyes down, out of respect and slight apprehension. If the professor wanted to walk with him, he might have something new to offer, and it was wise to be patient.

The guard at the hospital gate stood at attention, his fingers pointed at his cap in a military-style salute. "My honor, Comrade Professor, sir! And you too, Comrade Doctor." His burning cigarette rolled on the ground. He squashed it under his boot and opened the personnel door to the street. "Dr. Bardu," he added with a smile, "I guess congratulations are in order."

"Not yet," said Kostea. "They're estimating a few more hours, so I'm going to kill some time at the Garden."

"Sure thing," the guard said. "What's a man to do but drink while he waits for his wife to deliver."

"Smart-ass," Kostea said. "They'll send somebody for me when she's ready."

"When I saw your missus so big this morning, I said to myself the baby would come out in no time. But maybe you'll have twins, Dr. Bardu."

Kostea shrugged and followed the professor into the street. The Pobeda was waiting, engine running.

"I have to go now," Professor Dinescu said as he leaned forward to enter his car, the white silhouette of the Triumphal Arch looming behind him. "I hope to hear from you very soon, Kostea. Remember, the world is changing. Come work for me, and Clara can come work for me also. Honestly, you'd be a fool to reject my offer."

———

The wide, tree-lined Kiseleff Boulevard leading up to the Triumphal Arch split and went around either side of the monument. There was no traffic, and Kostea crossed the boulevard at a leisurely pace. That was it, he said to himself. Nothing new from Dinescu except a repeat of his job offer, which was a very good thing. And the fact that Clara could work there also. Yeah, right, Clara. Clearly, Dinescu liked her. But Clara was Kostea's wife, and Kostea tried hard not to be jealous.

At the base of the arch, a dozen men in striped inmate uniforms tilled a flowerbed. Three soldiers sat quietly on the curb, their bayonetted rifles on the pavement next to them, watching the inmates and smoking. The inmates were political detainees, weak and scared representatives of the former ruling class, presenting no flight risk whatsoever. The soldiers showed no interest in Kostea. They were very young, boys really.

As he walked, Kostea thought of a time years ago, when he was as young as these soldiers. He was just returning to Bucharest after being discharged from his army surgical unit, and he'd written to tell Clara he was coming home. They had been apart for more than a year, and he was eager to hold her in his arms. Fighting was still going on in western Romania, and the train, full of soldiers returning from Moldova, was delayed again and again. Kostea didn't dare hope to find Clara waiting for him. But after his train arrived and the platform cleared of soldiers, there she was, sitting on a metal bench at the end of the tracks, wearing a bright summer dress, clasping her little purse, a smile on her beautiful, tired face.

This happened in late August 1944. It was March 1950 now—a lifetime. Clara and Kostea had graduated medical school and gotten married. The king was exiled, the pro-Soviet government had taken over, and the purges had begun. People spied on each other. They behaved one way at home and with friends and in a different way on the phone and in public.

Now Clara was giving birth. Their apartment had been subdivided. And he had to decide on his job. It was a lot, and he needed to stay calm and collected. Whatever the future held, he had to ensure his wife and child were protected.

CHAPTER 2

A Good Father and Husband

The Garden was in an old stucco villa, not even a hundred yards from the Triumphal Arch. A sign over the metal gate carried the name of the restaurant in warped, rusty letters. The place, now closed, would open later for dinner. A long narrow path, covered by the remnants of an old vine hanging from a trellis, led to the back door. Tiny buds dotted the dry branches.

"Good news? Are you a father?" Igor said as soon as Kostea entered the small hallway behind the oversized pantry and kitchen.

"Not yet," said Kostea. "How did you hear?"

"Eugene told me. He said you rushed Clara to the hospital this morning and sent word with a nurse. He's here, and Marin, also." Igor winked. "You're in for a treat. Marin's brought us some sturgeon from Sulina."

Igor used to own this place. Now he only managed it and kept it open for his friends, no matter the hour. They often met for lunch—no reservations required. Given the shortages, it was customary to bring food for Igor to prepare—hard-to-find beef or pork or even an entire chicken. But give it to Marin: a sturgeon! This was something else altogether. The last time Kostea had tasted this delicacy was in high school.

"How is she?" Igor said.

Kostea took his arm. "Let's go inside, and I'll tell everybody."

The restaurant was L-shaped, with the long wall opposite the windows covered by a full-length mirror to give an impression of openness. Kostea's two friends were at a table in the center of the empty room, each holding a bottle of beer, which they raised when they saw Kostea.

"Hey," Eugene yelled, "here comes the new father!"

"Not yet," said Kostea. "It's our first, and it'll take longer."

"You left Clara?" asked Eugene. He had a wide face with big round brown eyes and a straight nose that flattened at the tip, as if it had been punched and broken in a fistfight.

Kostea pushed a tall glass vase with branches of sunny forsythia out of his way and sat at the table. "Yeah, I did," he said, shaking his head in mock annoyance. "There is nothing I can do for her now. Nothing."

"You could *be* with her, dummy. It's important," Eugene said.

"When your daughter was born, did you stay with Norma?"

"They wouldn't let me because I'm not a doctor. But you are."

"That's right, I'm a doctor," said Kostea, patting his chest. "And I know what I'm doing." He grabbed Eugene's bottle and took a long swig.

Igor dragged a chair over from another table, turned it around, and sat on it backward. With his mane of softly curled chestnut hair, kind brown eyes, straight nose, and full lips, he looked like a Hollywood star. When they drank, he liked to play the guitar, his velvety voice traveling over the strum of his strings, bittersweet and full of passion. "Kostea," he said. "Tell us."

"She's in labor," said Kostea, "and her obstetrician is very experienced. Clara didn't want me to stick around, second-guessing her doctor and getting all sentimental."

"And you believed her," Eugene said. "Buddy, you have no clue what women want, and your Clara's a saint and a sweetheart."

"You've always had a soft spot for her, haven't you, Eugenius? Maybe I should have a word with Norma." Kostea knew that Eugene didn't like to be called Eugenius, and that amused him. They had competed for Clara's attention since middle school, and even though Clara had married Kostea, in Kostea's mind, that competition was still on. He grabbed Eugene's beer bottle again and took another long swig, then leaned toward his friend. "I was sorry about Uncle Sebastian." His voice sounded mellow, the change from aggressive to compassionate as sudden and natural as switching on the light in a room.

Eugene hesitated. "Is it safe to talk here?"

"We're the only ones in the restaurant," Igor said. "Not to worry."

"If you find out where they took him," Marin said, "I'll try to arrange for you to send him food packages."

"Thank you. My family would be grateful."

"Clara's not alone at the hospital," Kostea said. "My mother-in-law is with her, and when the time comes, they'll send a nurse to get me."

"Ina Georgievna," Eugene said, stressing the patronymic. Unlike Kostea and most people whose families had come to Bucharest from Kishinev after the Second World War, he didn't speak Russian. "I've known her since we were boys, and she likes me."

"She likes me also," Kostea said, laughing.

Marin smacked his lips. "What's going on with the fish? I'm hungry."

"Vera's fixing the roe," Igor said. "Give her a few more minutes, and better tell us about your trip to Sulina."

"The trip was good," Marin said. "The fish was a gift. Didn't have time to go fishing."

Igor seemed disappointed. He was a hunter and fisherman, and to him, sturgeons were a treat as much for the thrill of catching them as for their taste. "Why didn't you go fishing? No point in being in a place like Sulina if you don't go fishing."

"I didn't have time. Period."

"What else is there to do?" Igor insisted. "Why did you even go to Sulina?"

Eugene passed a pack of Select unfiltered cigarettes around the table, and Kostea watched the smoke rising like a mist in the mirror. Igor's inability to understand that curiosity had limits, annoyed him. There were things one talked about and things one didn't. No point in pestering Marin. He couldn't speak openly about his trip, but he had confided its real purpose in Kostea: a delicate Party mission to Sulina, the last urban outpost on the shores of the Danube Delta. From that marshy terrain, guerillas armed by foreign powers were sabotaging the pro-Soviet communist government recently installed in Romania. Marin had been sent to organize a brigade to quash the resistance. As his Russian counterpart had said, he had to do this *za rodinu*—for the homeland.

"Hey, Igor!" Kostea said. He took a drag of his cigarette and nodded to Marin. "Nobody cares why Marin didn't go fishing." In the mirror, he saw Vera come out of the kitchen carrying a large tray at shoulder height.

"Here you go, food for everybody," Vera announced. She was a striking Russian beauty who had married her first husband—an officer in the Soviet Army, stationed in Bucharest—at nineteen and had cheated on him with Igor at twenty-one. To Igor's delight, she got divorced and married him later.

"Grab a chair and come sit with us, Vera," beckoned Eugene. "You know you have a special place in my heart, don't you, honey?"

Vera rolled her eyes and placed her hand on Igor's shoulder.

"Shut up, Eugenius," said Kostea.

Igor raised two fingers. "Fellows, let me run to the pantry and grab something that goes best with this fish—you know, my special plum brandy." Food shortages notwithstanding, he was still in control of his liquor.

Vera followed him to the kitchen.

A few seconds later, Igor returned with an unmarked one-liter bottle and four shot glasses.

"Za rodinu!" yelled Marin and lifted his shot glass.

"Fuck rodinu," said Kostea.

They all laughed, downed their drinks, refilled the glasses, emptied them one more time, and chased the hard liquor down with beer.

The aroma of fresh bread tickled Kostea's nostrils. He hadn't eaten anything since the previous evening. The fish meat was white and flaky, the fried skin crispy with salt and pepper. Fat, sautéed spinach, and tidbits of cucumber salad dropped on his shirt. The plum brandy took its toll, and a mellow happiness descended over him.

"Marin," he said suddenly. "Dinescu brought up again his job offer this morning. He had promised before that with my talent and the right level of effort, I'd have a path to chief surgeon—and an opportunity for an assistantship at the school of medicine."

"Well, will you take it?"

"I'm tempted."

"Listen to me," Marin said. "No matter what you choose, and before anything else, join the Party."

Kostea was a practical man. He had witnessed Marin's rise in the Party and could sense the direction in which the political wind was blowing. "That's what Dinescu had told me."

"It's the right thing for a young man starting his career." Marin's eyes sparkled.

"Of course," Eugene said. "Only the best for Kostea."

There was noise at the back door, and Vera burst into the room. "Kostea! The guard from the hospital came. You have to go. Quickly!"

Kostea nodded, dipped his bread into the bowl of pearly gray and black caviar, and stuffed his mouth—one last bite. Then he gulped down his beer and ran out through the narrow backyard, vines clinging to his clothes.

———

TUDOR ALEXANDER

At the hospital nurses' station, Kostea approached the head nurse. "Where are they?"

"In the delivery room."

"Which one? I'm going in," he said, panting.

"Not like this you don't, Comrade Doctor," the nurse said. "First, you go to the bathroom and wash your face and hands. Then you change. I'll contact Dr. Pop, and I'll tell her you're here."

Kostea's first impulse was to say that as a doctor he didn't have to listen to a nurse, but he refrained. "Where's my mother-in-law?" he asked.

"Waiting in Mrs. Bardu's room. She's a nervous wreck."

Kostea looked at the high ceiling and his world spun. "Sure."

Ina was sitting on the edge of her chair, next to the empty hospital bed. She held a closed book in her hands. Her face was white and crumpled, like the sheets on the bed where Clara had labored for so many hours. Even when seated, it was obvious she was heavy and short. Kostea remembered an old photo of her taken when she was in her twenties. There she was fresh, pretty, and slim. Delicate. Unchanged from her youth were her expressive eyes. Widowed when Clara was four, life had been difficult for her and her little girl—but then, in those times, who had it easy? She had worked first as a math teacher and later as a bookkeeper to make ends meet, and she was now a part-time accountant for some government agency.

"Finally," she exclaimed when she saw Kostea. "You took your time, for sure."

"What are you talking about? I came running."

"You were drinking." Ina checked her wristwatch, her long white braid shifting as she moved. "It's been at least half an hour."

"They took Clara half an hour ago? Can't be. I left as soon as the guard came—and, by the way, why did you send him? I specifically said a nurse."

"None were around."

"Well, let's get something straight," Kostea said, feeling like he was on a slippery slope and unable to help it. "You're in a hospital now, and I'm a doctor. Mama, if I tell you to do something, you do it."

He called her Mama sometimes, and every time he did that, Ina took it as a warning. Her book fell to the floor. She raised her eyes and looked at him as if she despised him. "You've been drinking," she repeated, her tone heavier.

He'd had a few drinks, so what? Rushing to be present at the birth of his child, he had felt elated. Now he had to contend with this woman. She had a way of getting under his skin, always reproaching him for drinking, knowing full well that her reprimands irritated him. It wasn't his fault her dead husband had been a drunk. "It's none of your business," he told her.

"Look at you," Ina said. "Go and wash your face, quickly."

"I know what to do," he snapped and walked out.

The doctors' locker room was down the corridor. There were two faucets over each sink but no hot water. Thankfully, he was alone. He closed his eyes and splashed his face. His skin felt rough from the day's stubble. If he let his beard grow, it would be red and curly, while the hair on his head, combed backward, was slightly wavy, light blond, nearly white in the sun. His face resembled his mother's, except for his eyes, which were blue.

He turned his head left and right, frowning and grimacing, playfully wondering if he was better looking than his friends—although he knew it wasn't important. He would be a father soon, and that was what mattered. Poor Clara. There was nothing he could do to help, just wait around while she suffered.

Water dripped on his shirt. His doctor's coat was hanging in his locker.

His mom and dad should have been here, not Ina. They'd have been so happy and supportive. But they were stuck in Bistriţa, at the other end of the country.

He was drying his hands when the nurse spoke to him through the door. "Dr. Pop asked me to tell you that everything's under control, but it's taking longer. Today you're a worried dad expecting his first child, not a doctor. Just go to the waiting room and be patient. The visiting hours haven't started, so it's quiet in there. I'll bring you some tea in a few minutes."

Kostea took off his shirt, then put on his white doctor's coat directly over his undershirt and buttoned it up all the way. In the waiting room, he closed his eyes and allowed his thoughts to race freely.

Clara and the baby would come home, strong and healthy. He'd be good to them, a good father and husband. He'd have Ina come live with them and help with the baby. They'd get along fine—if he wanted to, he could be nice and civil. And maybe, if by some miracle the Ionescus moved out in spite of the housing shortage, he'd have more space for his family. In addition to teaching at the medical school, Professor Dinescu was head of a hospital called Speranța—a reputable place meaning *hope* in Romanian. There, Kostea hoped, if he accepted the position, his career would take off like a rocket. Kostea's father, Alexander, or Sasha at home, was a surgeon. His mother, Marie—Mimi—was a pediatrician. Kostea had wanted to be a doctor since he was little. In middle school, with his rudimentary French, he had become fascinated by the charts and instructions of H. Rouvière's *Anatomie Humaine Descriptive*, second edition. In the summertime, he had helped in his father's hospital. In his mind, he could visualize his father's hands—a surgeon's hands, with nimble fingers and trimmed nails, parchment-dry from too much washing. Kostea had grown up in his father's shadow.

When he opened his eyes, Ina was sitting next to him, her small sweaty hand holding his across the armrest. Two cups of tea waited on the side table.

"Comrade Doctor, you have a healthy baby boy. Congratulations!" Nurse Monica said. She had started her night shift already.

"Oh my God! How is Clara?"

"Exhausted but doing well. They're moving her to her room right now."

"Was it hard?"

"It was. Dr. Pop just left, but she'll tell you herself tomorrow. If you're ready, I'll take you to see the baby."

Kostea sprang to his feet. Ina stood as well. In the nursery, behind a large glass wall, there were several rows of bassinets, the babies wrapped in identical white blankets.

"Which one is my itsy-bitsy tadpole?" asked Kostea.

The nurse looked amused. "Right in front of you, Doctor. Your wife, that poor soul, is a hero. No wonder the delivery took so long. He's the largest tadpole we've seen in a while—almost five kilos."

CHAPTER 3

My Boy

May 1950

They baptized him Alexander, in a small ceremony at the old Saint Elefterie Church, several blocks from their apartment, and asked Eugene to be the godfather. He showed up in a gray three-piece suit, a burgundy tie, and gold cuff links, determined to play his part properly. At Clara's request he made the necessary arrangements with the bearded priest and the much younger deacon. Eugene's wife, Norma, studied the smoke-darkened Byzantine icons that decorated the walls.

Wrapped in a white christening gown, the baby slept in Clara's arms. She handed him gently to Eugene, who gasped and whispered in Clara's ear, "Your eyes shine like emeralds in this light." Clara nodded, slightly embarrassed. Next to them, Kostea pranced like a peacock.

"If you want to join the Party, being in church is not the greatest idea," Marin had forewarned Kostea in response to being invited to the ceremony. "The communists frown at religion."

Clara happened to be present when Marin gave that warning, and at the time, Kostea had thrown her a glance, begging for reinforcement. "Marin," she had said. "None of us is religious. Christening is the acknowledgment of our roots. What our parents did, and before them, our parents' parents."

21

"It's our son we're talking about," Kostea had added. "The communists can kiss my ass with their frowning."

"Suit yourself," Marin had concluded, then asked, "What time is the celebration starting at your place? I'll catch up with you there."

The baby cried during the oiling and screamed while being dunked in the baptismal font, which was filled with lukewarm holy water. "The servant of God, Alexander, is baptized in the name of the Father, and of the Son, and of the Holy Spirit," the priest chanted at the top of his lungs to ensure his voice rose above that of the crying child.

Kostea turned to his guests. "My boy," he whispered, his pride like a hushed draft running from the nave to the altar.

Everyone made the sign of the cross.

When it was over, relieved she could comfort Alexander, Clara took him in her arms, kissed his face, and wrapped him in his christening gown. She shivered. Eugene went behind the altar and paid the priest for the service. Then all of them left for the apartment, including the priest and the deacon.

"Why are they walking with us?" Kostea whispered to Clara.

"I asked them to bless our home. Easter is near."

"And who says I care?" Kostea hissed, but he didn't say anything else, and their little procession continued.

At the apartment, the priest said another prayer, swinging his thurible by its chain back and forth to fill the rooms with the smell of incense, and sprinkled the doorways and walls with holy water. In the kitchen, Ina wrapped up some of the food they had prepared for the guests and gave it to the deacon. As soon as the two disappeared, Marin, accompanied by an unknown young woman, showed up with a demijohn of wine.

Clara observed Marta Ionescu watching the scene through the half-opened door to her room.

———

While the party was going on, Clara retreated to nurse Alexander. Sleep-deprived and bone-tired, she was also profoundly happy as his small hand reached up to her shoulder, gently pushing and scratching at her uncovered skin. His trust was disarming.

Under his closed lids, his eyes were dark blue, like most babies, but turning greener by the day. Her eyes! They would announce to the world that he was hers, that he belonged to his mother. A thin layer of black hair grew over the pink of his skull. White skin, black hair, green eyes—what a marvelous combination. How girls would fall for him when he was a young man, strong and healthy. Nursing him now—or at night, or at the crack of dawn—no matter how exhausted she was, calmness overtook her, calmness such as she had never experienced before. With him at her bosom, her life was full of purpose.

Kostea claimed he understood how she felt, but how could he? He just offered practical suggestions. He had not carried Alexander inside his womb, had not felt him grow, kick, and turn. The umbilical cord had tied her, not him, to the baby, and he wasn't the one providing Alexander with milk now, enshrining the bond between child and mother.

On the day of Alexander's birth, that long, difficult day she would rather forget, Kostea had gone drinking and taking care of business. She didn't blame him, but she knew that he only possessed an outsider's appreciation for the gut-wrenching pain of delivery, the overpowering emotion of bringing life into the world. The baby had been too big, and they had pulled him out by the head with forceps. That's why his head was squashed, like an oblong melon. He had two depressions, one above each ear. Dr. Pop assured them the depressions would disappear under the hair, and the skull would regain its full-moon shape before the baby's first birthday.

In a couple of weeks, her maternity leave would come to an end, and Ina would take over. Kostea suggested—insisted even—that Ina move in with them and help them take care of Alexander. Clara trusted Ina completely but feared that both Ina and Kostea were opinionated and short-tempered, and their continuous proximity would create opportunities for Kostea to badly hurt Ina's feelings. At the time, Ina lived with Uncle Leo, her brother, and his family, but she said she would move in with them in an instant. She was wasting her time at that boring government job, and what joy it would be to help raise her grandson.

Through his connections, Kostea obtained a health certificate documenting Ina's mild rheumatism, and she retired from her job with a small medical disability pension. The official retirement age for women was fifty-five. Ina was turning fifty-two in June of that year.

"By the way," Ina had said, "Alexander is too long a name and too pompous for someone so little and precious. It's beautiful—don't get me wrong—but for later. We need a nickname right now, something sweet and easy. And I don't like Alex or Alec or Al, and for sure not Sasha, like his grandfather. No, he deserves a name that rolls off your tongue along with a lullaby and with soft children's verses. How about Tad, from tadpole, as Kostea had called him the day he was born? Tad, Toddy—you think about it. He'll be able to say it himself by the time he starts cooing."

The parents looked at one another and shrugged, and the nickname survived: Toddy.

The apartment became more cramped. It had been perfect for Kostea when he came to Bucharest as a student and lived there alone. Now he had a wife and a baby, the Ionescus were there, and Ina was soon moving in. Kostea and Clara were left with their bedroom, furnished with a twin bed, a mirrored armoire, and a chestnut linen trunk filled with soft blankets and converted into a crib—they couldn't find a new crib in the stores. Their former living room was slightly larger than the bedroom, with a rectangular oak table in the middle, six upholstered chairs, a bookshelf, a radio on its stand, and a tufted sofa covered in wine-red velvet. Behind the bookshelf was a locked door, which used to open into the room now occupied by the Ionescus. Ina had agreed that when she moved in, she'd sleep on the sofa and drag the makeshift crib next to her, to be able to pick up the baby at night and feed him his bottle.

As for Kostea, he had decided to take the job at Speranţa. The hospital specialized in urology but also treated internal medicine, oncology, and heart disease cases. Kostea had said that Professor Dinescu believed that the best surgeons must be first-rate generalists. "He sounds like my father," said Kostea. "And I'll have to start my postgraduate work right away, keeping me on my toes for several years." Clara understood him and trusted he would enjoy a successful career. She would see to it, guide his steps, and put out his fires. He had been a brilliant student. And to give him the freedom to pursue his ambitions, she ignored Dinescu's offer and opted to join the Municipal Public Health Lab as a microbiologist. It was interesting work, and she'd be home every night with her son and her mother.

Now, she changed Alexander and tenderly rocked him in her arms until he was sound asleep. She lowered him into the linen trunk and rearranged her dress in the mirror. The noise of many people talking at once came through the walls. She glanced again at Toddy. He was asleep like an angel, his lips moist, his lashes feathery. Slipping out through the door, she made sure it was firmly closed behind her before rejoining the party.

In the kitchen, Ina was preparing a second round of open-faced sandwiches. Dora, Ina's sister-in-law, was spreading chocolate icing on the cake she had baked for the occasion. Marta Ionescu was there as well, watching Radu, who was sitting at the table and eating white bread smeared with jam and cut into small squares. Pissu, a scrawny cat the Ionescus had picked up from the streets, rubbed against Ina's legs, waiting for scraps. Cigarette smoke wafted in through the open door from the hallway.

"So," Ina asked, "is Toddy asleep?"

"Toddy?" said Marta.

"Toddy is Alexander's nickname," Ina explained.

"Cute," Marta said. "Like when we call our Radu Răducu, because he is little."

Radu's mouth, smeared with strawberry jam, parted in a crooked grin. He liked being called Răducu.

Kostea stormed into the kitchen holding the demijohn. He had left his jacket somewhere, and his white shirt was open at the collar. "What's going on with the food? People are hungry."

"If you're in a hurry, come help us," Ina challenged him.

"That's your job," Kostea said without missing a bit. Then he yelled through the open door at his guests, "Anybody out there needs a drink?" and disappeared.

"Men," said Marta.

Ina rolled her eyes. She cut a slice of ham and threw it to the cat. "Here you go, Pussy, Pussy."

"Her name is Pissu, not Pussy," said Marta. "Pissu, pronounced 'pee-sou,' is a popular name for cats around here."

"Pussy is popular also," answered Ina, grinning. "Pronounced 'poo-see.'"

Clara smiled. Ina was right: cats were commonly called Pussy also. Give it to her mother. Always direct, often argumentative, like a few seconds earlier when she told Kostea to come help in the kitchen. That comment was meant to irritate him, clearly, and while Clara loved Ina for it, therein lay the problem. Ina needed to learn to suppress her instincts and strike the right balance with their neighbors and Kostea.

Radu pushed the empty plate away and jumped off his chair.

"Wait, Răducu," Marta said. "Let me wipe your face. And I have to fix something for your father. He's so hungry when he comes home from the factory."

"He's working on Sunday?" asked Clara.

"Saturday, Sunday, Monday, it doesn't matter. He works all the time. You know how men are. Everything for the Party."

"Marta, we have plenty of food," Clara said. As much as she disliked having to share the apartment, she didn't abhor Marta as a person and was motivated to find a modus vivendi and serve as example to both Ina and Kostea. Her soft approach was always an invitation. "You and your husband are welcome to join in our celebration. I'm afraid you won't be able to rest anyway. It will be noisy."

"How long will this last?" asked Ina, always concerned with Clara's tiredness and well-being.

"As long as the people are enjoying themselves, Mama."

"Sometimes you need to think of yourself, Clarushka."

———

Clara sat at a corner of the dinner table. The people around her seemed to be there for the long haul. The neighbor, Sorin Ionescu, had had a few drinks. Marta and Radu were nowhere to be seen, and the cat had also disappeared. Ina had cleared the food and retreated to the kitchen, but not before repeating out loud that Clara was very tired.

Marin's girlfriend, Miranda, stood at the close end of the table, next to Eugene, who was standing also. Marin watched from behind them.

"This man knows no limits," Miranda told Eugene, pointing back at Marin with her head. Her long black hair bounced playfully over the dark skin of her shoulders. Under her red dress, she was wearing no bra. "We met at this boring Party function three nights ago, barely exchanged a few words, and he had the gall to invite me to dinner. And you know what? I was silly enough to accept."

"Why silly?" Marin said. "Miranda, you got a free dinner out of me."

Miranda was pretty, even though there was something rapacious about the way her lips curved down like the mouth of a shark when she was silent.

"That's how he talks to me." Miranda laughed, turning, braiding her hands around Marin's neck and kissing him. "Tell me, Eugene, the two of us, do you think we have a future together?"

"Do you mean you and Marin?" Eugene asked, playfully.

"Yes! Who else could I mean, silly?"

Eugene shrugged.

"Let's have another drink," Marin suggested.

They'd already had plenty. The table was littered with bottles, wine-glasses, shot glasses, and ashtrays full of cigarette butts. The demijohn sat under a chair. Clara was sure it was empty. The window was now closed, the sun had set, and it was chilly outside. Cigarette smoke floated around them and gathered below the ceiling.

Ina's brother, Uncle Leo, was hanging on. His hands were crossed in his lap, the left one resting on top. Clara knew he had lost the middle finger on his right hand in a work accident, at the same factory where Sorin Ionescu worked, Red Grivița. Even though many years had gone by, Uncle Leo was always hiding his injury.

"She's a keeper," Kostea said, winking at Marin and pointing to Miranda.

"You're telling me!" said Marin as he filled four shot glasses with plum brandy and brought one to his mouth. "Za rodinu!"

"Za rodinu," answered Kostea.

Ionescu lifted his glass too. "Long live Comrade Stalin."

"Spoken like a true Stakhanovite," Eugene said.

"So, I'm a hard worker. Do you have a problem with that?" Ionescu inquired.

"No. Why would I have a problem?" Eugene said, looking around. "It's good being a Stakhanovite, isn't it?"

"I don't know what's good and what's bad with you religious people," Ionescu said, got up, and walked toward Eugene, whose face turned crimson.

"Now, what's *that* supposed to mean?" asked Kostea.

"I'm surprised that you, Comrade Doctor, have chosen to baptize your son."

"Haven't you heard of tradition, Comrade Ionescu? Easter is around the corner. How are you going to celebrate?"

"I'm not," Ionescu declared. "That's what our Party is striving to eradicate—legends with resurrections and old Jewish kings born in mangers. They were invented to keep the working people in darkness. But we are building a new world order, Comrade Doctor."

"Comrade Ionescu belongs to the Party Committee at my factory," said Uncle Leo, as if that fact excused Ionescu's comment.

"I had no idea," Kostea said. "Comrade Ionescu, do you know Uncle Leo?"

Ionescu looked at Leo and nodded. "Yes, he looks familiar, although there are thousands of us working there. It's impossible to know everybody."

"I've seen him with the higher-ups," Leo told Kostea. "Comrade Ionescu is in charge of propaganda."

"And you're not a higher up," Kostea told Leo. His eyes were bloodshot, and his forehead covered by a thin layer of sweat.

"How about manners?" Marin asked, taking a step toward Ionescu. "In addition to religious stories, is the Party eradicating good manners? Comrade Ionescu, I see you here, sitting at Comrade Doctor's table, enjoying the camaraderie of his friends, drinking his wine, and eating his food."

"I live here," said Ionescu.

"Hey, Uncle Leo," Igor said from across the table. "Can you give Comrade Ionescu from the Party Committee the middle finger?"

Leo leaned back in his chair and lifted his right arm. His index and ring fingers extended straight up, but there was a space like a gap-toothed grin where his middle finger had been. Most burst out laughing.

Kostea didn't laugh. "You might live here, but this is not your home. Ionescu, let me show you the shortest way out of here." He took him by his lapels and pushed him toward the door. Unprepared, Ionescu stumbled, and while searching to regain his step, he grabbed at the tablecloth. Bottles and glasses tumbled. A heavy ashtray fell with a thump to the floor.

Clara let out a scream.

Marin tapped Kostea's shoulder. "Easy now, Kostea, easy."

Kostea relented.

"Comrade Ionescu, do you know who I am?" Marin asked.

Ionescu regained his control instantly. "Yes, you're Comrade Sabac, from the Bucharest Central Committee."

"That's right. And I'm acquainted with your direct boss at Red Grivița."

Ionescu flattened his lapels. "Comrade Sabac, what I said to Comrade Doctor was a friendly warning. Other people—bad people—might take things like these out of context and use them against him. Not me." He looked at Kostea. "Comrade Doctor, please, I didn't mean any harm. Believe me."

"I like that," Marin said. "Kostea, join us and let us have that drink in honor of Comrade Stalin."

CHAPTER 4

Didn't Run Far Enough

July 1950

In the middle of the summer, a heat wave swept over the city. Ina was constantly covered in a film of sweat. She breathed heavily, pinned her braid to her head to expose her neck, and patted her red cheeks and forehead with her embroidered cotton handkerchief. Toddy slept naked except for his diaper, while Ina tried to keep him cool with a fan she crimped out of writing paper.

When she opened the windows, flies filled the apartment. Annoyed, Ina purchased several packets of Muscamor, then put the red poisonous disks in small plates of water and placed them on the windowsills and tables.

Marta objected. The cat, like a small hungry tiger, was likely to lick the sweet poison.

"The Muscamor is off the floor," Ina argued.

"Cats jump."

"Keep your cat off our kitchen table."

"Your table? How is it yours? This is shared territory," Marta said, towering over Ina as she spoke. "Pissu has jumped on this table many times in the past, and you haven't complained about it."

"Now I am," Ina shot back, "and I don't want your Pussy on our table."

"Her name is Pissu."

"Pussy, Pissu, who cares? I'm tired of flies everywhere. They land on my face when I doze off, and they're in the crib with the baby. It's not hygienic."

"Then don't open the windows."

"It's too hot, Marta. Don't tell me it doesn't bother you."

"It doesn't. It's summer, and that's what summer feels like," said Marta.

When Kostea came home that evening, Ina wheeled Toddy in his carriage into the kitchen. She had a green salad and a roast with potatoes ready for dinner.

Kostea cleared his plate. "Can I have some more salad?"

"Leave the salad for Clara," Ina said and pushed the roast closer to Kostea. "Here, eat more meat and potatoes."

"Mama, I want some salad. Look here, I might need to go on a diet." Kostea tapped his stomach.

"Nonsense. You're not fat, and for a man your age, it's all right to sport a small belly."

"I'm not even thirty."

She measured him head to toe with her gaze. He looked like a slender teenager. "Right," she said. "But you're not alone, and you have to think of your family."

"I think of my family all the time. And I want more salad."

In his carriage, Toddy started cooing. Ina leaned over him, and her face opened like a flower. "Who is my little baby? Who is awake? My little Toddy. Toddy wants to play with his grandmother."

Kostea watched the softening of her face, the warm smile, the creases deepening around her eyes. Then he reached inside the carriage, picked up his son, and lifted him onto his chest. The boy burped, and drool ran down Kostea's shirt. "Hey, Tadpole, is that how you greet your daddy?" Kostea laughed and started walking back and forth in the small kitchen, rocking the boy and singing the first line of a lullaby, the only one he knew, over and over. "Mama," he said, "is it me, or it is very hot here? Open the window."

Ina told him about her conversation with Marta.

"Well, she has a point."

"Sure, don't take my side. Why would you?"

"And what do you want me to do? Kill Pissu?"

"You're the head of the household. You should talk this over with the Ionescus."

"I have an idea," Kostea said. "If you bring the food to my bedroom, I'll eat there, and I'll be able to open my windows."

"Carry your own food. You have two perfectly good hands, and you're young and healthy."

"Mama, I never liked eating in the kitchen like a servant. I can choose where I eat in my own house, can't I?"

"Your house, sure." Ina sat at the kitchen table, fighting back her frustration.

Kostea felt a pang of guilt. He had promised Clara. He could be nicer to Ina, and Ina was right—he could take his own food to his room. Still, in this world there was an order, and he was merely following it: women had their place, and men theirs. He didn't create the order, and he didn't question it. He liked it. Seemingly, Ina liked it also, because nobody was forcing her to call him the head of the household or wait for him every night with the dinner ready.

He reached over and touched her hand on the table. She pulled it away, stood up, and without looking at him, walked away.

Kostea took his time. He grabbed a plate from the cupboard, found some bread, cut a few slices, and spread the butter. He had to control his temper and pay attention to the way he treated people. He had this tendency to jump from one thing to the next, oscillate between extremes, and be moody. At the top of the world one moment, he could find himself down on his knees the next—and the busier and more frustrated he got, the more significant the extremes. He upset Clara often, and Eugene, unintentionally. He had to especially watch himself at work, where it really mattered.

———————

"This is nice," Kostea told Clara. "You and I at the Garden. It feels like we own the restaurant."

Igor brought their lunch and withdrew discreetly.

They were the only patrons. Clara checked her reflection in the large mirror: a young woman with sparkling eyes, looking tired. She straightened her neck and lifted a strand of hair off her forehead.

"Your mother told me last night that I need to take better care of my family," Kostea said.

"She thinks you don't?"

"You tell me. She's your mother." He started eating.

Clara laughed and started eating too. "The cheese is good. Ask Igor where he buys it."

"I'm sure it's rationed and sold under the table."

He spread butter on a piece of bread and topped it with cheese, ham, and slices of cucumber.

Igor came out of the kitchen. "Anything else your hearts desire?"

"Thank you. No," Kostea said, and as soon as his friend disappeared, he leaned over the table and lowered his voice. "Igor lost this restaurant, right? It was nationalized. Knowing there was nothing they could do, his mother and brother walked away from the business. He did not. And he doesn't complain, but do you think he is happy?"

"He should be. He could be behind bars, like Uncle Sebastian."

Kostea nodded and looked around. "At least here we could talk without being overheard by nosey neighbors."

"I was enjoying myself," Clara said. "What's the matter?"

"I have to join the Communist Party."

She searched his face. "You don't have a political bone in your body."

"My beliefs are not the issue. Look at Marin. He's become an important Party operative. He has a nice apartment and a network of contacts."

"All you want is to be a great doctor. You have always wanted that. In high school, while I was shooting the breeze, you worked at your father's hospital."

"But my attention was on you. You were in high demand, missus."

"Well, that fight is over. In the end, you succeeded."

"I like to get what I want," said Kostea. "I love you."

"I love you, also."

"Joining the Party will only help my career. Marin says it is time for me to jump on the wagon."

"Then jump! But don't expect me to join."

"Clara, I'm serious. Dinescu said the same thing, and he is a Party member. Eugene is talking of joining. Our apartment was subdivided because someone in the Party decided we occupy too much space. They could come after us for no reason, twist my words, interpret them as subversive. Sorin Ionescu could say I'm religious. I really wanted to smash his face the other night. Good thing Marin was there."

"If by joining you could get rid of Ionescu, I'm for it. Remember how they complained when we first brought Toddy home from the hospital? Like their Răducu didn't cry as a baby."

Kostea shrugged. He looked at himself in the restaurant mirror. He looked at Clara. "In the past, I've never thought of my family history," he said. "But in the eyes of the current regime, we are bourgeois, Clara. My father was a doctor in Kishinev, and so was my mother. We had a house— an entire one, mind you, on the grounds of the hospital. And your mother and father were teachers."

"My father was a drunk," said Clara.

"He served in the White Tsarist Army and fought the Bolsheviks. How long do you think it would take someone who hates us to hold it against us?" Kostea put his hand over Clara's. "I was a year old when we fled the Soviets in Odessa and settled in Kishinev. My mother was heartbroken, having left my grandma behind, a widow, too frail to travel." He kept on about how later, before the Soviets arrived in Kishinev at the end of the Second World War, his parents had to run again and hide in Bistriţa, a small town in the middle of Transylvania. How with time, their fear of the Soviets diminished, but as much as possible, they insisted on keeping their origin secret. "I must protect all of us," Kostea added. "You, Toddy, as well as my parents. There is a saying in my family that the only smart Bardu is Uncle Misha, my father's brother, who left Russia before the revolution, ran all the way to Paris, and became a stockbroker. The rest of us didn't run far enough, Clara."

———————

The meeting to debate Comrade Kostea Bardu's request to join the Communist Party was scheduled for Tuesday afternoon. On Friday the week prior, Professor Dinescu summoned Kostea to his office.

"There is an objection against your admission," he said in the dreary tone of someone who intends to remain neutral on the issue. He started gathering papers from his desk and shoving them into a brown leather briefcase.

"On what grounds?" asked Kostea.

Dinescu looked up. "There was an anonymous complaint. Something with your religion. I shouldn't even bring it up with you. You understand me, Kostea."

It couldn't be. Sweat ran under Kostea's shirt down to his bellybutton. How dared he? Ionescu. The bastard. The mixture of anger and nervousness overcame Kostea. He wanted to apologize and explain himself to Dinescu, but right at that moment Ileana, Dinescu's assistant, walked into the office.

"Professor, your car is ready."

"I'm going to Sinaia over the weekend," Dinescu told Kostea. "To work on my articles." Sinaia was a picturesque place in the Southern Carpathians, two hours by car from Bucharest. Until a few years ago, the king and his entourage had summer residences there. Now the Party faithful and personalities like the professor occupied the palaces and the villas.

The professor turned to Ileana. "You're coming with me, right?" he asked her.

"Right," she said and remained standing.

The professor had recommended Kostea to the Party committee, and would attend next Tuesday's meeting, but that was the extent of his involvement. He wasn't the man to stick his neck out for others unless absolutely necessary. Kostea realized that telling him about the baptizing would not change much. As to whether the professor's wife was also going with him to Sinaia, that was not Kostea's business. Their discussion was over.

Kostea left the professor's office and decided not to tell Clara. An entire weekend and a day had to fly by before the meeting. Why get her worried? He should have smacked Ionescu. Punched him in the nose and brought him to the floor, unconscious. But no, Marin had stopped him.

Slowly, Kostea's anger was replaced by shame, as if he had failed a test, as if suddenly he became less valuable. Applying to join the Party and being rejected would be worse than not having applied at all. It drew attention to himself and rendered him vulnerable. If the Party rejected him, people would know. They would laugh at him and attack him. As he had told Clara the other day, they could come at him for no reason. Call him a traitor. Reassign him as a country doctor or send him for "reeducation" at the Danube–Black Sea Canal, the extermination camp where people dug soil and rocks by hand every day and died by the dozen.

But then again, maybe they won't reject him. He had Marin. All was not lost, for sure. More than anyone else, Marin had been the one to convince him to join the Party. He had pushed him into it, and now Kostea was in a bad spot. Marin owed him.

Kostea went into the doctors' room, called Marin, and was told that Marin was out on assignment. They did not know when he'd be back and took a message. Kostea thought about reaching Miranda but couldn't remember her surname and gave up on the idea.

———————

In the spring of 1944, as the Soviet army advanced toward Odessa, Kostea's medical unit left ahead of the retreating Axis forces. A young corporal was brought in with a fresh wave of wounded soldiers from the Second Romanian Armored Division. A piece of shrapnel had grazed his ribcage, ricocheted into his left arm, and lodged itself into the soft tissue of his biceps. In the triage area, Kostea yanked out the shrapnel with a pair of surgical pliers, then cleaned and sutured the wound—all without anesthesia.

During the days that followed, the young medic and the corporal, whose name was Marin Sabac, took a liking to each other and spent every free second together. The wound healed quickly. Kostea knew that Marin would have to go back to his unit, a move the corporal dreaded. Human losses were huge. Before Marin's release from his medical care, Kostea put him through a test.

"Raise your left arm above your head," he asked.

Marin did.

"Now raise your right arm and stretch both arms as far up as you can."

Again, Marin complied. There was no difference.

"Clear," Kostea concluded. He drafted and signed a certificate attesting that, as a consequence of injuries received while in heroic service for the country, the left arm of Corporal Sabac remained weak and with a limited range of motion. Return to active duty was not recommended.

The corporal was reassigned to an administrative position.

The meeting was taking place at the Party headquarters of the Eighth Bucharest Precinct where Kostea lived and Speranța Hospital was located. Kostea's weekend had been long and torturous. He did his rounds at the hospital each day and checked the telephone switchboard often but received no messages from Marin. At home he slept a lot and was uncharacteristically quiet. He played with Toddy more than usual. Even Ina wondered if something was amiss. Monday was busy at work. He went to the barber shop. Ileana told him Professor Dinescu was unavailable.

That was that, and now it was Tuesday.

Kostea walked to the Party headquarters, and when he saw Professor Dinescu's Pobeda sedan parked in front of the building, he wondered if things were bad enough for the professor to avoid him.

A red cloth covered the presidium table opposite the audience. Red carnations in a tall vase stood next to a full water pitcher and five glasses. Of the five metal chairs behind the table, only two were occupied: one by the Secretary of the Party cell, the other by Professor Dinescu. Portraits of Lenin, Stalin, and Gheorghe Gheorghiu-Dej, the leader of the Romanian Communist Party, hung on the wall behind them. There were two doors to the corridor, one behind the presidium table, the other in the back.

Kostea sat in the first row, away from the others. He asked himself if his nervousness was obvious. A narrow line of white skin showed along his sideburns and at the back of his neck, where his hair had been cropped for the occasion.

Slowly, the room filled with doctors and medical staff—about fifty in total—from several Bucharest hospitals. Cigarette smoke curled to the ceiling.

The first item on the agenda was Comrade Doctor Kostea Bardu's admission to the Communist Party.

Kostea stood and turned to the audience. His red tie pressed against the starched collar of his shirt, embedding it into his chin and contributing to his discomfort. He had not wanted a tie, but Clara had insisted.

"Dr. Bardu comes with the highest recommendations," the secretary said. He opened a folder and extracted several pieces of paper. "We have a recommendation from Professor Dinescu, a person who commands our utmost respect, and a second one from Comrade Marin Sabac of the Central Committee, a young Party leader who needs no introductions."

The secretary paused to let that information sink in, and added, "But I'd be remiss if I didn't mention a complaint we received recently. It seems that Doctor Bardu chose to baptize his newborn son at the old Saint Elefterie Church. It goes without saying that the Party does not condone such backward behavior."

A hush traveled through the audience. Kostea felt jitters in his knees and his belly. He was alone, and this was his Achilles' heel, the moment he feared. He had to react, now or never.

He turned and looked at Dinescu, who averted his eyes. He faced the secretary. "Comrade, please share with me the name of the complainant."

"I can't. The complaint is anonymous."

Someone in the back stood and exited the room.

"Then let me explain," Kostea said and took a tiny step forward. It was an involuntary gesture, lacking aggression. "I am not a believer."

The door behind the presidium table sprang open, and Marin stepped inside, followed by Miranda and a man dressed in a business suit and wearing a perfect red tie, just like Kostea's. "I hope we're not late," Marin said. "Comrade Secretary, I'll take it from here."

The audience emitted a second hush, slightly louder.

"Comrade Sabac, you came," the secretary said. "This is an honor. Welcome. To you, and to your associates, Comrade Nedelcu and . . . and . . . I don't know your name," he added, addressing Miranda. "I am sorry."

"Comrade Miranda," Marin said. "We work together."

Kostea had never met Nedelcu, but like everyone else in the room, he knew who the man was: the Bucharest mayor. As for Miranda, her introduction was meant to disguise, no doubt about it. In the parlance of communist gatherings, people addressed each other by their surnames, like in the military. Withholding it could mean only one thing: the person worked undercover.

Nedelcu and Miranda advanced to the presidium table and sat. The audience fell quiet.

"Let's see," Marin started. "What do we have here? On one hand, two very strong recommendations for an accomplished young professional, and on the other, an inconclusive complaint from someone who didn't even have the courage to state his name for the record. Comrades, let me surprise you: I was invited to Comrade Bardu's son's christening, so I know about it firsthand. I didn't go to the church—I went to his apartment afterward, and we celebrated the joyous occasion. Earlier that day I'd had a discussion about this very issue with Comrade Bardu—mind you, he wasn't a Party member then—and he explained that he was doing it for his mother-in-law, whom he loves and respects and who had worked hard to raise his wife as a single mother. Recently, his mother-in-law retired on account of a medical condition, and Comrade Bardu has taken her in to ensure that she lives surrounded by family. She had been a widow for decades, and during the old regime, like countless others, her only solace had been her daughter and her religion.

"Comrades, we now understand that religion is the opiate of the masses. But that doesn't mean that we can eradicate the past by chopping it off with a hatchet. On the contrary, we need to be sensitive and understanding, like Comrade Bardu. Don't blame him for being human! Comrade Bardu saved my life during the war. I've known him ever since, and I can tell you that he is hardworking, competent, and loyal—in other words, exactly the type of person our Party should accept without hesitation. Let's cast our votes in his favor."

During Marin's speech, Kostea remained standing. All eyes were on him, and he kept his head high, trying to look confident. But he continued to be concerned, even though he managed to make eye contact with Miranda, and even Dinescu.

When Marin finished, the secretary turned to Dinescu, "Anything you would want to add, Comrade Professor?"

"I agree with Comrade Marin Sabac one hundred percent. I vote for Dr. Bardu to become a member of the Party."

"In that case, all in favor, please raise your hand," the secretary said, and hands shut up, followed by applause.

Outside the meeting room, on their way to the exit, Marin placed his arm around Kostea's shoulder. "You made it."

"Boy, this was close." Kostea was beaming. "I say I was lucky. You showed up at the very last minute."

"There was no luck," Marin said. "It was all by design." He looked at Miranda and nodded.

"We had our mole in the room," Miranda explained. "He signaled us when to enter."

"Here, here," said Comrade Nedelcu.

"Besides, Comrade Nedelcu helped us take care of your buddy, Sorin Ionescu." Marin winked. "You're welcome."

Professor Dinescu approached the small group. "Kostea, congratulations. I'm going back to the hospital. Join me. The car is waiting."

Sorin Ionescu received a new Party assignment in a town north of the Carpathians. Huffing and cursing, Marta Ionescu collected her belongings and threw them into the pickup parked by the curb. Sorin tied down the mattress. Then Marta grabbed Răducu and Pissu the cat and walked out without saying goodbye.

Well, Ina thought, some people just don't have manners.

CHAPTER 5

This Wasn't Hard

Early spring, 1954

Kostea went to work early each morning, seven days a week. Clara left about an hour later. She did not work on Sundays. On her way out, she stopped by Ina's half-open door and looked inside. The room was the one previously occupied by the Ionescus. If Ina noticed Clara, she blew her a silent goodbye kiss. If not, Clara would linger and sometimes observe her mother looking at herself in the round mirror above the dresser. Ina's face was soft and smooth, her eyes flooded with morning sunshine. From the doorway Clara couldn't see the stubborn crow's feet around Ina's eyes, but she knew they were there, a sign of distinction rather than the passing of time. She admired Ina's long white hair, which Ina brushed until it crackled with static and shone like fresh snow, reaching the small of her back. Clara watched her weave it slowly into a thick braid, which she gathered on top of her head or at the back of her neck and secured in place with pearl-and-onyx teardrop hairpins.

If Toddy made the slightest noise, Ina immediately rushed to his crib. It was obvious he was her joy, the light of her days. Of that, Clara had no doubt. Whatever Ina had lacked in her life was now in front of her, within reach. Ina watched over Toddy, fed him, bathed him, played with him, and read Pushkin's *Ruslan and Lyudmila* to him. At naptime and bedtime, she sang to him:

Spi mladienets moi prekrasny
Tolyko krepko spi.
Bayushki bayu.

Ina wasn't musical, and her notes often went astray, but Toddy didn't seem to mind. Charmed by his grandmother's voice, whose timbre was softened by new hope and old sorrow, the boy's arms and legs relaxed, his eyelids fluttered, his face mellowed, and he happily passed into the realm of dreams. It seemed to Clara that Toddy knew, in that secret way in which all children know, that listening to his grandmother's song was hearing the sound of love.

Since Kostea started his work before Clara, on the days he didn't have difficult cases at the hospital, didn't attend Party meetings, and wasn't on night duty, he returned home first. Ina told Clara that even after three years of living in the same apartment with Kostea, her edginess in his presence had not diminished. For Clara's sake, she was willing to accept a truce of sorts. When she served Kostea dinner, she spoke little and tried to stay out of his way. She liked to grab Toddy and retreat with him to the bedroom they shared. This wasn't always easy, because Toddy loved to greet his father and play with him and because Kostea was in the habit of opening doors without knocking. And when Toddy climbed on his father's knees, Ina felt a pang of envy she often confused with concern.

Kostea confessed to Clara he felt tense in Ina's presence as well. He understood he held the advantage of youth over her, often reminding her that he had been the one who had asked Ina to come live with them and help them raise Toddy, over time becoming convinced he was doing her a favor by giving her a family and a sense of purpose.

Both Ina and Kostea relaxed when Clara arrived home, and they eagerly solicited her attention. Toddy also ran to his mother. Clara listened to the three of them while putting down her heavy bags of groceries. She hugged them, played with Toddy, and rewarded each of them with warmth and understanding, no matter how intense her own day had been or how tired she was.

"Toddy had a tummy ache," Ina said as soon as Clara came in the front door. The boy stood a few paces behind her. Kostea was in his bedroom.

Clara dropped her string grocery bag on the floor and rubbed her reddened palms. She reached for Toddy. "What happened, baby?" She picked him up.

"I went up high on the snow pile."

"Oh," Clara said, "you went sledding."

"Nice carrots and potatoes," Ina said, looking in the string bag.

"Put them on the kitchen table," Clara said and lowered Toddy to the floor. "Boy, when did you get so heavy?" She took Toddy's hand, and together they followed Ina into the kitchen.

"He complained of a tummy ache, and I gave him the hot-water bottle. He's better now."

"What's going on?" Kostea appeared in the kitchen doorway in his undershirt and boxers.

Ina started stowing away the potatoes.

"Toddy had a tummy ache," Clara said.

Kostea frowned. "I've been home for two hours. Mama, you didn't tell me. Why?"

Ina brushed aside a strand of white hair. "There was nothing to tell."

"That's not the first time," Kostea said.

"I know."

"I'm a doctor. Do you know that?"

"You never fail to remind me."

"And I'm his father, too."

"Kostea," Clara said and took a small step in his direction, blocking his access to her mother. She knew Kostea would never get physical, but she could sense the tension. "Of course you're his father. His tummy hurt, my mother helped, and now he is better. All right?"

"Mama," Kostea said, "did the boy go to the bathroom today?"

"He did."

"Are you sure?"

Ina had raised Clara by herself and had taken care of Toddy since he was a newborn. She wasn't a dimwit. She was sure, of course. Full of annoyance, she said, "He went to the bathroom, and he ate like always."

"Maybe he exerted himself playing outside in the snow," offered Kostea. "You know, like when you run too much, and your spleen starts hurting."

"It wasn't his spleen," she shot back. "And he didn't run much. Or fast. The other children were faster than him."

"Are you saying he's slow?"

"I didn't say that. You came home, and you were tired, as usual."

"Did I say I was tired?" Kostea asked.

Toddy waited with his head slightly lowered, his cheeks crimson, and his eyes darting from one adult to the other. He knew they were talking about him but couldn't understand what the deal was.

"Come here, Toddy," Kostea said. "Let Daddy examine you." The boy approached his father, and Kostea lifted Toddy's woolen sweater, undid his checkered shirt, and lifted the white undershirt. "You're dressed in layers," he said.

"It's winter," Ina said.

Kostea touched Toddy's tummy. "Hold on, sonny, my fingers might feel cold. Do you like cold fingers? Does it hurt?"

"No," Toddy said.

"No to the first or to the second question?"

Confused, Toddy looked at his mother.

"Take a deep breath," Kostea said, laughing. "Like this." He inhaled and released the air noisily to show Toddy how to do it.

The boy imitated him.

"I'd rather him be hot than cold," Ina said. "People don't get sick from overdressing."

"They don't." Kostea patted Toddy on the buttocks. "You're all right. Run."

Toddy darted out of the kitchen, and Ina went after him.

Kostea dropped on a chair. With his elbow, he pushed the carrots out of the way. "Your mother's a riddle," he said.

Clara understood but asked, "Why?"

"Why wouldn't she tell me? I need to know and examine Toddy. She knows how much I love him. This is not the first time."

"I don't believe you're jealous," she said.

"Jealous is not the right word. Why doesn't she trust me? This is clearly out of whack. She is your mother and she makes it so hard." He reached for Clara's hand and pulled her onto his lap.

She sat, closed her eyes, and lowered her head on his shoulder. Like a tempest, thoughts swirled in her head. This wasn't hard. She remembered another time, during the war, when everything was truly out of whack and hard.

CHAPTER 6

Life Is a Game of Chess

1935–1944

Clara was in Bucharest during the war. She had moved there from Kishinev to study medicine, and lived with Uncle Leo, his wife, Dora, and three-year-old Toni. The classes were suspended. Food was scarce and Clara spent hours standing in line at the grocer's and the baker's, her ration tickets in hand. There were sudden shortages of sugar, flour, and sunflower oil. One day you could buy them, and then you could not. Everything for the front, the slogans said. Meat was a luxury. Clara managed to buy a live chicken at the Matache Market, near the North Railway Station. She rushed home, carrying the chicken in her shopping bag, proud of her achievement.

Dora stepped into the street with a knife and offered a passerby a few coins to chop the bird's head off. Blood spouted all over the sidewalk. The two women plucked feathers side by side into the kitchen sink. There was a wet, organic smell. Toni sat on the floor. He looked ashen.

"Anemic," Dora said.

"Give him the chicken liver," Clara said.

Toni didn't want to touch the liver. He didn't want any meat. He wanted to ride his tricycle on the sidewalk, avoiding the fresh blood stains.

Clara wanted to visit Ina in Kishinev, but the trains were too danger-ous, and Uncle Leo said no. Kostea was away with his medical unit. He had written to her every day, but recently his letters had stopped.

On a sunny spring day, Clara found potatoes at the Matache Market. She found a jar of honey, yellow as gold, and bread, white and fresh, with a nice heavy crust. She put everything in her string bag and started toward home at a leisurely pace. Turn-of-the-century stone houses with shady fenced-in yards lined the streets. The lilacs were in bloom. People waited for the electric tram.

Sirens ripped through the air.

Clara had never heard the air defense warning system before. She saw people running. Someone screamed: "Airplanes!" Then the sirens stopped, and it was quiet. She ran like everybody else but was not sure where to go. She was afraid and she wasn't, and things seemed to be happening in a parallel world. A low-frequency whistle began and ended with a huge blast. The ground shook, and a wave of warm air swept along the street like a storm. Lilac petals swirled around her. Suddenly there were planes overhead, more than she could count, and the sky seemed to turn totally black. Everything was vibrating and shaking with the roar of the engines. She heard another explosion, and another one, closer and louder each time. On her lips she felt dust.

A man in blue overalls and a newspaper cone on his head rushed from his yard, followed by a woman in a white apron, holding a child in her arms. The child could have been five or six, too big to be carried, but the woman didn't seem to mind. The child must have been scared to death when his mother picked him up. No time to explain or argue with him.

"Run! The shelter is in the bank building on Plevnei Street," the man yelled.

Clara followed them.

The basement smelled of sweat and mildew. People whispered. There were maybe fifty of them. A few electric bulbs hung from the unfinished ceiling. When bombs exploded above, the lights flickered. Plaster and paint flakes floated like snow. Cobwebs darkened the corners. Most people stood, but gradually they claimed their spaces and sat on the floor. One older man fished out a pack of cigarettes and passed them around. Several men lit up.

Clara sat on the cold floor across from the man in blue overalls. His newspaper cone fell off his head. His shoulders were covered with dust. The woman and the child sat next to him. The mother cleaned the child's nose with her apron and held him tight. The child looked at a large cobweb and winced.

"He doesn't like spiders," the mother said to Clara, like an excuse.

"Who does?" Clara shrugged.

"We should be afraid of the bombs, not of spiders," a man standing next to Clara said.

"He doesn't understand what's going on," the mother tried to explain.

"No one does," the man said.

"I beg to differ," the man in blue overalls jumped in. "It's the Americans—they're coming after us."

"When they bombed the refineries last year, they had six hundred planes," the man said.

"One seventy-eight," the man in blue overalls corrected. "If one of those American bombs falls on this building, we are kaput. *Fertig*. This shelter's a joke."

Everyone looked at the ceiling.

"Let's pray," somebody said.

"What's your name?" Clara asked the child, who buried his head in his mother's lap.

"Val," the mother said. "His name is Val, after his grandfather who owns land in Dobruja." She waved away a strand of hair that covered her eyes.

The man in blue overalls laughed. "What good does it do us now, that land?"

"He's my brother. He's painting my house," she said to Clara, point-ing at the man in blue overalls. "My husband's at war."

Clara thought of Kostea. "Val's a beautiful name for a boy," she said.

"We were having lunch when I heard the sirens. Never finished eat-ing," the woman said.

Clara felt sorry for the little boy. She lifted her string bag and showed him the honey in the jar. "Would you like some of this?"

Val didn't answer, but his face lit up.

"Let's see," Clara said and took out the loaf of bread and the jar. The lid to the jar was stuck.

Someone produced a pocketknife. "Here, this has several blades, a corkscrew, and a little spoon."

The man in blue overalls pried the jar open with the pocketknife. He flattened his fallen newspaper coif, set the loaf on it, and sliced off the heel of the bread. He drizzled honey on it with the spoon. The boy eagerly ate the whole piece.

"Would you like another slice?" Clara asked, and Val nodded.

There was a loud explosion, and the lights blinked. The men stubbed out their cigarette butts. Now Clara was scared. She didn't know what to do and suddenly wondered why Kostea's letters had stopped. Thinking of Kostea was helpful. There was so much going on.

———————

As teenagers in Kishinev, they dated on and off. Kostea often picked up Clara at her one-story brick house tucked inside a fenced yard under shady cherry and plum trees. He'd knock at the door and ask Ina if Clara was ready.

Ina would always fake surprise. "Clara, Kostea's here!" she would call and allow Kostea to enter in the foyer and stop at the edge of the woolen carpet. A properly behaved young man, Kostea would stand there patiently, shifting his weight from one leg to the other, his hands to his sides, his lips stretched in a forced and timid smile.

Clara would soon cross the living room and foyer like a bolt of lightning and stop in front of Kostea. "Let's get out of here! Mama, goodbye, and see you later."

"Hope not too late," Ina would invariably reply and mumble, "You have plenty of studying left for tomorrow."

Clara would roll her eyes or laugh, and the two of them would dart out the door, run past the trees in the yard, and slow down once they were in the street. They'd walk to the corner, and if nobody was around, Clara would plant a quick little kiss on Kostea's lips. She was an attractive girl, her body curvy and full, her skin light, her eyes intelligent, and her hair the color of shiny chestnuts. There was a joyful clumsiness about her, timid yet playful.

When they were both nineteen years old, they traveled to Bucharest several months apart to attend medical school and ran into each other on a late summer afternoon. Clara was a woman by then, stylish and enchanting, with the unmistakable air of determination on her face. She realized that, in seeing her, Kostea was moonstruck. They walked toward the main study hall on a path flanked by white, yellow, and red rosebushes, their chance encounter setting their world on fire.

Unfortunately, around them the world was already burning. The year before, Hitler had occupied Poland, and France and the United Kingdom had declared war on Germany.

Bucharest hosted a large German army presence, and the gray building of the Military Circle was brightly lit every night. Water fountains sprayed jets in the colors of the Romanian flag. Young officers in spiffy uniforms rode in military jeeps, champagne at the ready, up and down the Elisabeta and Brătianu Boulevards. The parties at Capşa, the Athénee Palace Hotel, and the open-air restaurants on Kiseleff Boulevard lasted through the wee hours. The Iron Guard joined the Antonescu government and was then suppressed. Jews were persecuted and killed in Bucharest and Kishinev. During the summer and fall of 1941, close to 18,000 soldiers perished in the Siege of Odessa. The young officers had good reasons to get drunk every night.

Clara and Kostea refrained from politics. They tried hard to look the other way, live their lives, and ignore the war. Medical school kept them busy. After the long hours of study, they explored their new city. They walked the parks and the boulevards and rounded the squares, admiring the equestrian statues of King Carl and Michael the Brave. They stopped for beer and coffee and laughed with colleagues in noisy, smoke-filled restaurants. In the winter, they skated on the frozen pond in Cișmigiu. Kostea was a good skater—he had played hockey in high school—and Clara leaned on his strong arms and allowed herself to spin and slide and be supported by him, her hair full of snowflakes, her mind filled with the love songs playing on the loudspeakers. In the spring and summer, they walked along the rose-rimmed alleys of Herăstrău Park and went rowing on the ring of lakes north of the city.

Never before had they tasted the freedom they now enjoyed. Their parents were far away. As a student, Kostea's military service was temporarily deferred. While Clara lived with Uncle Leo, Kostea lived alone in his three-room apartment.

Besides Kostea, Clara didn't have any close friends in Bucharest. She loved him. Of that she was sure, as she was sure he loved her as well. She had read somewhere that in a relationship, one partner loves more, and the other consents to be loved, and she thought that she was the one who consented. It wasn't their emotional bond she wanted to comprehend but his desire for sex.

She understood him physiologically, and her body said yes all the time. Kostea was charming and desirable. He could be unpredictable, brash, but all in all, he was a good man. Yet she resisted, for reasons that didn't make sense to her . . . or didn't make *total* sense.

With freedom came responsibility, the adage went. What responsibility?

Pregnancy was a concern, but she and Kostea were students of medicine who knew a few tricks. God and society weren't the reason. She had already decided that if God were out there, he'd have more important things on his mind. And society was unraveling everywhere. Boys were sent to their deaths, and girls with painted eyes and open lips, many younger than Clara, were chasing them through the city before they left. Tomorrow held no value and promised nothing: it was all a matter of now. Yet having sex with Kostea was to Clara a line in the sand, a border between her childhood and the rest of her life she hadn't known existed. Once crossed, there was no going back, and Clara was playing for time.

They always ended up in this game in Kostea's bedroom. Kostea kissed her, and she kissed him back. He took off his shirt. She kissed his neck, his earlobes, his clavicles, his chest. He whispered to her. He told her he loved her, and he undid her blouse. Or she got to her feet and allowed her dress to fall off. In the winter, she was wearing a girdle. Socks in the summer. Her pubic hair showed through her cotton underwear. He removed her bra, brought his face to her breasts, and circled her large nipples with his lips. His lips were hot. His breath was hot. His hands touched her body. Up and down. She shuddered. She glued herself to him. When he reached for her underwear, she said no, every time.

"Why? Clara, I love you."

"I love you too."

"If you loved me, you'd want this as well."

"I do, but I'm not ready." She felt him all eager and tense. There was a power to her resistance as well—a feeling she didn't enjoy.

"Will you ever be ready? I don't understand. Clara, don't string me along."

"Give me time."

"Let's get married," he said once. "We love each other, and I want to make love to you. Why this torture? Our marriage would make it official. In front of your family, society, God."

"No. People get married when they're ready to spend their lives together, not when they're eager to screw."

"That's all you think I'm after?" Red in the face, he paced the room. "At least you're not mincing your words."

"Marriage is a big deal. Kostea, there's a war going on."

"You always say no." No stopping him now. "I'm a man. I have needs. I can't be like you—switch myself on and off. But if you want me to wait, you know, there are all kinds of girls. Just don't be surprised when you hear the rumors."

"What's this? A threat?" Clara cried. "That isn't right. Do that and never come back."

Sometimes he came close and caressed her tears away. Other times he held his own. He got dressed and walked Clara home, quiet like the night, or exploding with fury and ripping leaves off tree branches, kicking stones. To Clara, his anger was less upsetting than his obstinate silence, and when he kept silent, she refused to see him again the next day.

At that time, Eugene was enrolled in officers' school on the outskirts of town. He had come to Bucharest from Kishinev. Years earlier, he had asked Clara out a few times. Kostea had been jealous of him. He still was but was now better at hiding it. In Kostea's presence, Eugene was careful how he looked at Clara and how he talked to her. When they were alone, a smile lit up his face, as if he knew something that Clara knew, as if they shared a secret.

One day, he bragged to Clara that on the previous night he and Kostea had visited Stone Cross, an area near the Old Armenian Quarter where red lanterns shone in the shop windows. Clara pretended she couldn't care less, but pain shot through her heart like arrows.

Then the school of medicine closed, and Kostea was drafted to join a mobile surgical unit. They had a few nights left to say goodbye. Anguished, Clara considered giving herself to him, and then again, she changed her mind. He would be back. He wouldn't be killed. It wasn't a goodbye forever.

This time, Kostea didn't push. He was gentle and subdued. They could no longer pretend that their life was normal and unscathed by the destruction happening around them.

She went with him to the North Railway Station and stayed in his arms until right before the train left.

It was raining on the way home. Beggars lined the sidewalks, their wet rags spread around them like the wings of blackbirds foretelling a curse.

Months flew by, and Clara's chagrin settled over her like a layer of dust. Most of her colleagues, who had come to Bucharest to attend medical school, had returned home. Eugene was moved east.

The bombing stopped an hour later, as suddenly as it started. Clara rushed home wondering what she would find. She ran past houses in ruin, women wailing and tearing at their hair; ambulances and fire engines sped beside her through rubble-filled streets. In front of the post office, she saw a dead horse.

Her uncle's house was standing, and the street was untouched. That evening, they had bread and honey with tea. Toni's delighted expression made Clara think of Val. They read in the paper the Allies had targeted the North Railway Station and the marshaling yard. Hundreds of buildings had been destroyed and over five thousand people killed or maimed. Countless old poplar trees in the botanical garden, not far from Kostea's apartment, had been uprooted.

Alone in her room, Clara felt terrified. She missed Ina and asked herself how alone her mother must be in Kishinev. She reread Kostea's letters, one by one. Why did he stop writing? She curled up crying. Her legs turned to lead. On the other side of the door, Uncle Leo walked on tiptoes. He never knocked. She would have liked him to come in, to speak to her like a father and ask her about Kostea. She could have used his hugs, his body heat.

When Clara finally stepped out of her room, Leo poured two shots of vodka and set up his game of chess. They drank, and he started explaining the moves to her: the bishop, the rook, the queen.

"Do you think my mother is safe in Kishinev?" Clara asked.

"I don't know," Leo said. "Life is like a game of chess. You do your best in anticipating your next move." Toni came over and, with a swipe of his little hand, sent all the chess pieces flying. Leo looked at him and frowned. "Then somebody comes along and throws everything out of whack."

CHAPTER 7

You Disappeared. Remember?

August 1954 and earlier

The tenth anniversary of the August 1944 Insurrection was a huge event and a national holiday. Over one hundred thousand people—workers, farmers, and soldiers, civilians young and old—were expected to march through Victoria Square in front of the Party leaders. The parade took the better part of the day, with celebrations continuing into the evening. Food stands, military bands, and a medical emergency center were set up in Herăstrău Park, next to the Triumphal Arch and one long block north from the square.

Kostea was dispatched—or as the Party put it, volunteered—to the medical center, a white tent with a huge red cross on it, pitched between the Island of Roses and the Sculpture Garden. The center was outfitted with an examination table, two folding beds and six chairs, stretchers, medical supplies, a telephone, and running water. An ambulance was parked near the tent entrance.

Bored, Kostea watched the continuous flow of young people strolling along the lakeshore. He treated a woman with symptoms of food poisoning and a man with a sprained ankle. He stepped outside, walked a few paces away from the tent to the lakeshore, and lit a cigarette.

It had been one month since Toddy was rushed to Speranţa Hospital with acute appendicitis. How Kostea had missed the earlier warning symptoms was, to say the least, surprising. Kostea could not forgive himself and could not stop thinking of it. Dinescu had performed the surgery, and everything had turned out all right, but Dinescu had kicked Kostea out of the operating theater. That, too, bothered Kostea greatly.

Now the nurse called him back to the tent. "Doctor, a Russian woman is looking for you."

"Russian? What's wrong with her?"

"I don't speak Russian."

Kostea inhaled the smell of the muddy shore and stagnant water. He crushed the cigarette under his shoe and walked back slowly, a sense of foreboding overcoming him.

The single electric bulb inside the tent illuminated the woman. Her figure was heavier and her blond hair longer than Kostea remembered. He gasped. "Katya?"

She nodded and answered him with a smile, clutching her purse with both hands.

He walked to the examination table and leaned on it. "How did you find me?" he asked in Russian. Then he became aware of the nurse and turned to her. "Give us a moment, would you?"

"Of course, Dr. Bardu." The nurse left the tent, and the door flaps closed behind her.

"*Dr.* Bardu?" Katya repeated after the nurse, a twinkle in her eyes; the word "doctor" was the same in Romanian and Russian. "You made it." Her voice dropped and the light in her eyes extinguished. "You promised to take me with you to Bucharest. Remember?"

"Katya, you disappeared. Remember?"

She looked around the tent and took a small step in his direction. "I had no choice." She took his hand. "It's good to see you, Kostea."

The moment he felt her touch, the past hit him like a wave. It lifted him, and it turned him around until it seemed he was drowning. His world filled with the memory of her—the taste of her lips and skin, her legs high on his hips, her sighs, her breathing.

He had to say something to pull himself back to the present. "I am married now. I have a child, a four-year-old boy, Alexander."

"Beautiful," Katya said. "Did you marry Clara?"

"I did."

"I'm glad for you. Congratulations." Her voice sounded hollow.

Kostea looked away. "How is your boyfriend?" he asked.

Katya shook her head, and Kostea spoke again, as if he had anticipated her answer. "You have a lot to explain. Let's walk out of here."

She leaned her head to one side, as if she found his expectation reasonable. "Please, lead the way. It's your city."

Outside the tent, the nurse was watching the throngs of people moving back and forth along the lakeshore. The light was dying.

Kostea left Katya behind and walked up to the nurse. "I'm taking my guest to the nearest taxi stand and will try to be right back. Cover for me until then, will you?" Kostea glanced back at Katya. In her blue-and-white polka-dot dress, she looked very pretty.

The nurse nodded. "Our shift ends in less than twenty minutes. I'll wait until the evening doctor and nurse arrive and let them take over."

Kostea had never seen this nurse before. Perhaps he would never run into her again, but he could imagine her telling people at work, God knew where, about a mysterious Russian woman who had paid a visit to a married doctor from Speranța Hospital, and the story circulating in the medical community and reaching Clara. "I met this woman during the war," he said to the nurse, feeling the need to explain. "She's here with a Soviet delegation. She wanted to say hello and bring me news about some people we both know."

"I understand," the nurse said. "Don't worry."

Kostea signaled Katya to follow him, and they disappeared among the people. They walked fast in the direction of the nearest park exit, side by side, without touching or talking. Afraid he would run into someone he knew, Kostea kept scrutinizing faces. He felt trapped, lusting for Katya, his desire sudden and paralyzing. He felt as if she had snapped her fingers, and he had come running back to her like a puppy. It was a mistake. He shouldn't have left the Red Cross tent with her.

On Kiseleff Boulevard, the crowds thinned. By the time they reached the Triumphal Arch, they found themselves alone on the sidewalk.

"Look there," Kostea said into the awkward silence. "Our Triumphal Arch was copied after the one in Paris."

"Oh, yes, Paris. I go there often." She laughed. Her eyes met his. They held a promise.

As they crossed the large intersection, Katya took his arm and leaned on him gently. He inhaled her delicate fragrance, remembering it from Odessa.

He couldn't take her to the Garden—too many people he knew might be there—but not far was another restaurant in a mansion with a spacious outdoor terrace. The evening was pleasant. They were on the verge of going in when he noticed a group of youths horsing around under a streetlamp on the opposite sidewalk. Near them, he recognized Eugene. Quickly, he led Katya into the restaurant and closed the door behind them.

In 1944, Kostea's medical unit was stationed in a military compound on the north edge of Odessa. As a child, he had often heard his parents talk about Odessa, had seen glimpses of it in family photographs, and had read some of his grandmother's letters. He expected that Odessa, his birthplace, would be familiar to him, a homecoming. His grandmother lived in the city's center, and he had written to her about his imminent arrival, but he had not received a reply. She had seen him only as a baby, and the anticipation of their reunion after two decades filled Kostea with a sweet nervousness, a mixture of curiosity and nostalgia.

On his first free afternoon in Odessa, he put on a fresh shirt under his long military winter overcoat, grabbed his brown military cap, cigarettes, and his medical badge, and set out on foot toward the center. The February weather was mild, and he soon took off his gloves and shoved them in his pockets. He smoked as he walked along the shoreline. The surf was breaking like the breath of a tired monster. His grandmother's name was Aneta.

Her house was a three-story limestone building with a carriage gate and a rather muddy inside courtyard. She had lived in the same small apartment since he was born and his parents, Mimi and Sasha, fled Odessa. In front of her door on the second floor, he waited a few seconds to calm his emotion. The buzzer had an annoying sound, like rocks scraping on metal. He heard movement, and the door sprung open.

"Kostea," an old woman said. She threw her hands around his neck and hugged him tightly. At his chest she felt light and small. Leading him by his hand, she pulled him quickly inside the room to the window. "Let me see you." She looked hard at his face and touched it with her fingers. "Good-looking young man. My daughter is in your features," she said and started crying.

Kostea smiled, removed his coat, and hung it on the back of a chair.

It turned out she was expecting him. She had received his letter, and one from his parents, and had replied to both, but her replies had never reached them.

They sat down at the table covered with a round embroidered doily. Aneta asked him about Mimi and listened dreamily. She cried for as long as he talked, dabbing her eyes and trembling lips with a small white handkerchief. Her gray hair fell in disarray over her face and forehead. She was wearing a black dress with buttons down the front and a silver pendant around her neck. Her face was wrinkled.

Kostea took out his cigarettes. She accepted one from him, and they smoked silently for a while.

"Tell me more," she pleaded. "But not about everyday things. Those I know from her letters. Talk to me about feelings. How is my daughter's heart? Is she happy?"

"Yes," he said. "She's happy. Although now there is a war going on." He wanted to say more but couldn't. He felt embarrassed. He didn't know how his mother felt, really.

Aneta got up and walked through a door into what Kostea guessed was her kitchen. "You must be hungry," she said from there.

The room he was in was filled with furniture gathered over the years, perhaps over several generations, a dignified comfort all around. Two scuffed pillows were on the floor, one near an armchair and the other one under the side table. She had two cats, he knew from her letters.

On the opposite wall, three small windows opened onto the street. The cobblestones below were wet, shimmering shades of gray. A brown military truck drove down the street. A girl or young woman appeared out of nowhere, looked both ways, waited for the truck to disappear, and crossed in a hurry. She had short blond hair and was wearing a white sweater but no coat or jacket.

"Grandmother, where are your cats?" asked Kostea.

"They're out doing what cats do, but they'll be home for dinner," came the answer as Aneta emerged carrying a tray with a loaf of white bread, an opened can of sprats, and a bottle of vodka. "Attapo always comes home first," she said, arranging the food on the table. "He meows and scratches at the door. He's the boy, and he's cuddly." She opened the armoire against the wall, releasing a passing waft of mothballs. Dresses and coats hung behind the mirrored door in one section. On the top shelves were stacks of china, rows of glasses, and silverware in open boxes. She chose two plates decorated in a fine pattern of pink roses and green buds, looked at them in the light to make sure they were clean, and placed them on the table. "I have these from my mother. Rosenthal, from Germany." She grabbed two knives, two forks, and two shot glasses and inspected them as well. One glass was chipped, and she sighed and kept it for herself. "Let's drink to you and your family."

Kostea poured the vodka. They each had a shot, then another, and ate the sprats with bread and butter.

"Matzipura is younger," she continued, referring to her other cat. "She thinks she needs to assert her independence."

Kostea lit a cigarette.

"See what you did?" she said. "You asked me about my cats, and I can talk about them forever. They're what I have left in the world—the cats and the cemetery. But I'm not complaining. I go to the cemetery twice a month, first to my dad's grave and then to your grandfather's."

"And Mila?" Kostea said. "Isn't she keeping you company?"

"After your parents left and my sister died, she was my lifeline, really. Now she's married, has a son, and is busy with her own family. But young man, eat up. We'll have tea and cookies as soon as Katyusha shows up."

"Katyusha?"

"Yeah, Katya, Katyusha, she's this neighborhood girl who helps me. She brings me milk every second afternoon from the black market." Aneta said the last words in a whisper, as if sharing a secret. "Food has always been scarce in the Soviet Union, but here in Odessa, we have managed. We've always had bread, sprats, and potatoes. And vodka. We know commerce. In the last five years before the war, it got ridiculous. That's why everybody needs a girl like Katya. Your mom and dad ran away—they had to—and they couldn't come visit. The Soviets never gave me a passport. I can't tell you how many times I tried. The distance between Kishinev and Odessa is less than two hundred kilometers, yet we have not seen each other in twenty-three years." Aneta stopped to breathe, and Kostea noticed she was crying again. He took her dry hand and squeezed it. "They keep us here, in prison, and now, under the Transnistria Governorate, it's even worse. There are fewer supplies, and they have rounded up all the Jews, so fewer people are selling groceries and other household items. We still can't travel with the war going on, plus—and don't take this the wrong way—for Odessa to be under a Romanian administration is kind of laughable."

Kostea had no reply. With 18,000 Romanian soldiers dead during the siege of Odessa two years before, and about as many fallen Russians, the advance of the Axis army seemed anything but laughable.

"This cannot last," Aneta added thoughtfully. "Nobody messes with Mother Russia. Nobody."

There was a scratch on the door, and Aneta sprang to her feet. "Here she is, Katyusha."

She was the girl in the white sweater Kostea had seen from the window. Floating through the room as if no one was sitting there, she disappeared in the kitchen. Aneta followed Katya, the sound of their animated chatter traveling through the door. Then they reappeared holding hands, Katya pirouetted and stopped in front of Kostea. "The famous grandson," she said in a teasing tone, accompanied by a deep curtsy.

Kostea rose.

Her handshake was firm, her fingers thin and still cold, he guessed, from the outside winter.

"How long are you here for . . . Kostea?"

"A few days," he said. "Who knows? Maybe a few weeks. We just arrived and are stationed near Suvorovsky. I'm with the medical unit."

"I know you're with the doctors," Katya said and smiled broadly. "Your grandmother told me. Didn't you, Aunt Aneta?" Katya turned to Aneta and hugged her. Side by side the two women looked like dolls, an old one and a very young one, stuck together. Their clothes were frayed. The sleeves of Katya's sweater were loose and dirty. In Aneta's arms, she seemed vigorous. There was beauty in her face, but one had to warm up to it like to a naughty girl with a wild streak. Her lips were full and her chin round. Short blond locks tumbled unrestrained onto her forehead.

"If you just arrived," Katya continued, "you haven't seen Odessa, and exploring Odessa's a must, even in winter. They call it the pearl of the Black Sea, but I think it's more like a diamond in the rough. You have to see through the grunge." She pulled up a chair and threw herself into it, leaning back and raising one foot. She had odd-looking shoes made of a faded brown felt. "You'll need a guide," she said quickly. "Somebody to take you places. Because you can drink rum at Lanzheron right now in the middle of the war or have any ice cream you want at Lubachevski. Bad things are going on, but we don't care."

"Why go to Lanzheron?" asked Aneta, clearly cherishing the company of the young. "We have plenty of vodka right here." She opened the armoire and returned with a third shot glass. "Let's make this afternoon memorable!"

They drank.

Katya sprung up and hugged Aneta again. "Aunt Anya, you're closer to me than my own parents." They looked at each other and talked quickly about people Kostea didn't know, and he understood that Katya's immediate family was somewhere in the countryside, behind the front line with the Soviets.

"Listen, kids," said Aneta. "I need to start the teakettle. Can I leave you alone a few seconds?"

"Aunt Aneta, what are you suggesting?" Katya threw a glance at Kostea. "Don't you trust me alone with your handsome grandson?"

"Katya," Aneta protested as she walked into the kitchen.

"I love your grandmother," Katya exclaimed. "She's been through a lot, yet she's funny and generous. But listen, I have to leave soon. More to do in the neighborhood."

He would have liked to know what it was she had to do, but she didn't say, and he didn't ask. "Will you show me Odessa?" he said instead.

"Of course. I promise."

They drank their tea and enjoyed the homemade cookies, then Katya got to her feet, chirped a rapid goodbye, and disappeared without suggesting to Kostea a time and place to get together.

He spent the rest of the visit listening to his grandmother, while trying to not think about Katya. The cats came home, Attapo first, then Matzipura.

"I'll visit again soon," he promised his grandmother before leaving.

She pulled him hard to her chest. "Thank you, Kostea."

It was dark outside, and the street was deserted. He was ready to walk across when he heard steps and sensed somebody approaching.

"Hey," Katya said. "Did I scare you?" She was still in her white sweater, but now she wore white mittens, a scarf, and a pair of ankle boots with thick, midsized heels. A faint perfume filled Kostea's nostrils. She seemed slimmer and taller, and there was something aglow in her appearance.

He mumbled something, and she laughed, satisfied with her surprise and his clumsiness.

"C'mon," she said. "Let's see Odessa."

They walked along the empty streets, talking in low voices. They were mostly alone, and Katya was weaving in and out, taking a few steps sideways and then moving toward him, almost touching. The echo of her steps followed them faithfully. He tried to take his clues from her, watching her, smiling.

On Deribasivska, humidity hung under bare linden trees and around each wrought-iron light pole in waves of green and lilac. Suddenly there were a few people around them.

"This is the heart of Odessa. Everybody comes here," she told him.

"This is everybody?" he asked and tried to imagine the city in peacetime, in the summer, crowded, people walking arm in arm under perfumed lindens and the restaurants open and welcoming. "I thought this city was lively, the way you said, but this is a ghost town."

"I said it was beautiful. How could it be lively, after what you did to the people?"

"What *we* did? What did we do?"

"Half the population left when the Soviets retreated. Of those who didn't flee, many paid a heavy price. Your army arrested and killed thousands. Especially the Jews, and you know that."

He did know. He had heard about the killings and had pushed those stories out of his mind because they made him shudder. But he didn't expect to be talking about it right now, not with this girl whom he liked but barely knew, not in this fashion. "Look," he said in frustration. "Like you, I don't like this war. I take care of the wounded, no matter who they are."

"I'm bitter. Forgive me," said Katya.

He felt awful. This was her world, and she didn't need to apologize. He wanted to say something smart, and, as he often did when he couldn't find the right words, he stuck his hand in his pocket and took out his cigarettes. She asked for one, and they walked along, smoking.

At the corner with Rishelievska, patrolmen were checking papers. He flashed his badge, and they waved them through, one of them winking and wishing him good luck in Romanian.

"What did he say?" Katya asked, and when he hesitated, she laughed. "You don't need to tell me. I know exactly what's on all your minds, you horny soldiers."

The entrance to the opera house was lit, but the street behind it was silent and shrouded in darkness, and he sensed rather than saw the sprawling buildings with people watching from behind drawn curtains, a solid presence through absence.

Katya danced happily on the sidewalk. "Look, the most beautiful opera house in Europe! It was rebuilt after a fire destroyed it in the middle of the nineteenth century. A neobaroque architectural wonder."

They reached a park and found a bench near a statue of Pushkin.

She stomped her cigarette butt with her boot. "Tell me, in Bucharest, do you have a girlfriend?"

"I do," he said, and told her about Clara.

She slid down on the bench and looked up, resting her head on the backrest. "Kostea, do you feel how damp it is? That's because of the sea. I love this moisture, and the smell of Odessa. And I like the sky, full of stars, bright like the hopes of young people."

"It's cloudy," said Kostea.

"It is now, but those shining stars are up there forever."

They got up, and she asked him, "Listen, can you come by tomorrow around six o'clock? Just show up at the corner, and I'll find you."

He took her hand. "Let me walk you home. You might get in trouble because of the curfew."

"This is my city. Trust me, I know how to be invisible."

The next day, Kostea brought his grandmother a ham and two bottles of sunflower oil, obtained and paid under the table at the officer's mess. Aneta was delighted. She could get used to seeing him every day, she said, with or without the prized provisions. They spent some time writing a letter to his parents, sipping black tea, and eating tender deep-fried *khrustyky*, the powdered sugar making Kostea lick his fingers.

As soon as it got dark, he hugged Aneta and left.

Walking slowly, he again felt people watching him from behind curtained windows. Katya hadn't told Aneta she had spent the last evening with Kostea, although, what was there to say? Nothing of note had happened: a walk in the city, a short conversation in the park, a cigarette. Back at his unit, he'd been unable to put words on paper for Clara, no matter how hard he tried.

At the corner, he waited a long time, long enough for him to get anxious. Finally, Katya arrived, and chirping in her high voice, she asked, "Were you afraid I stood you up? Really? Or did you think I got arrested last night? Kostea, don't make such a face. It's fashionable for a girl to be late, to be unpredictable."

"Yes, yes," he mumbled.

"Do you want to see where I live?"

"I'd love to."

He followed her to a building on his grandmother's street. The front door opened onto a dark and narrow staircase. A sharp smell of braised cabbage and fried onions came from above.

Katya took his arm. "No lights in the stairway," she whispered, "but I know this house like the back of my hand." She guided him up the first steps and onto the zigzagging stairs, which he climbed holding on to the metal banister. She unlocked the door and turned on the vestibule light. "We'll be alone for the evening," she said. "My landlord and his nosey wife are away. Kostea, it's perfect."

A corridor led from the vestibule to several rooms, Katya's being the first. It was smaller than his grandmother's, and it had the same feel to it, like an old imprint that could not be removed. There was a narrow bed, a desk with a single chair, an armoire, a lamp. The window was slightly open, and fresh air filled the room. The smell of cooking had disappeared, and Kostea looked down at the street corner under the feeble streetlamp.

"Aha," he said, "this is the place where you're watching what's going on in the street."

"Sometimes," said Katya. She sat on the bed and took off her boots, and then her sweater. She wore a blue-and-white plaid man's shirt underneath, over her skirt, tight on her bosom and hips. The two top buttons were undone. She patted the bed. "Come here."

He placed his cap and his overcoat on the back of the chair and, moving slowly, sat next to her. "Want a smoke?"

She took his cigarettes and matches and dropped them to the floor. Her hands joined playfully around his neck. Before he could pull away, she kissed him. He liked how she tasted, soft and fresh, slightly bitter. He reached out and brought her close to his chest. They stopped for a second and looked at each other. Then she closed her eyes and kissed him again. Their world was in there, between their lips, with lust and purpose. He reached to the front of her shirt, his fingers fumbling. Gently, she pushed him aside and pulled her shirt over her head.

Later, she put on a robe over her naked body and went to the bathroom. When she returned, he gathered her in his arms and caressed her short hair, her breasts, her thighs. "You're beautiful."

A small wooden cross dangled around her neck on a loose leather strip. He held it in his fingers.

"From my boyfriend," she said. "You have Clara, so it's only fair."

"Where is he now?" he asked.

"No longer with us."

There was apprehension and trust in her voice. He didn't ask anything else, feeling how close she was to him, how dear.

On the way back to his unit, Katya stayed on his mind. He didn't look at the streets of Odessa, the parks, or the seashore. All he saw was her image: her face and her body. He had left her only minutes ago, and he was lusting. Clara was far away. There was a war going on. What happened, happened.

Many wounded soldiers came in from the front. He stayed busy for four days and nights, tending to the soldiers' wounds and dreaming of Katya. On the fifth day, he ran to his grandmother's street and stood at the corner.

Katya showed up in a minute. "I thought you had forgotten me."

They walked through the streets until very late, and then she suggested, as if reluctantly giving in to desire, "Let's go to my place. My landlord is there, so we'll have to be very quiet." On the stairway in front of the door, she stopped him. "Wait here." She crossed the vestibule without turning on the light, checked the corridor, and waved Kostea in, a finger across her lips, laughing silently. He took his shoes off and quickly tiptoed to her room. She locked her door with the deadbolt.

He was careful not to say anything about Clara.

She did. "Don't tell her about us," she urged him.

He felt offended. "I want to be honest with her."

"Don't be. Women don't like this type of honesty."

"How do you know?"

"I'm a woman."

———

Katya took Kostea to a park. "I used to come here with my buddies when we were in high school. It's dark and very secluded."

He didn't ask what she did in the park with her buddies.

They spread his coat over the moist grass. The sky was clear.

"See?" Katya said, pointing. "The clouds have been blown away, and the stars are shining. Just like that, one day the winds of peace will chase away the war."

"When peace comes, I'll return to Bucharest to study."

"I'll be happy for you."

"I'll take you with me," said Kostea.

"Swear on a star?"

"I swear."

They were lying on his coat side by side, looking up. It was colder than it had been on other nights, or maybe the chill of the soil crept through their bodies. She raised her head and placed it on his shoulder.

"Which one?" she asked.

He pointed. "The bright one over there."

"Not that one. It's the evening star, too common. I want a star a trillion miles away that nobody else can claim. A star that's only ours." She stood. "Look at that oak. The little cluster to the west, the blinking star, the fourth one from the bottom."

He stood up and counted. She leaned against his body.

"I see it now," he whispered.

"When we're apart, each time you look at it, I'll know it."

———————

The next evening Katya didn't show up. Something might have happened to her, he thought, and asked his grandmother.

"Katyusha is a free spirit," Aneta said. "She's disappeared before."

"You're sure that nothing bad has happened to her?"

"What? Are you worried?"

He didn't want to explain and didn't answer.

A few days later, he went to Katya's apartment. "I'm looking for your tenant, Katya Ivanovna Larkov," he said when the landlord, a smallish man of about sixty, opened the door.

"She moved out," the landlord said.

"Do you know where?"

"I have no idea."

Kostea went back to the street and walked for hours. He had been certain Katya loved him, but suddenly he didn't know anymore. Had something happened to her, Aneta and Katya's landlord would have told him. Why would she run away? Why disappear?

At each street corner he hoped to make the turn and see her. He heard steps following him, but when he looked back, there was no one. His lust became a wound, his heart an anchor. Thoughts came and went and got reshuffled. When his medical unit left Odessa, he had to leave also. If he stayed behind to look for Katya or wait for her to reappear, he'd be a deserter.

They sat in a secluded corner on the restaurant terrace. After ordering wine and an appetizer, she eased into her story. "Ten years ago, I left to join my parents. They sent somebody to take me. The Soviets were approaching, and your unit was going to leave Odessa. I'm not big on goodbyes, so I decided to vanish."

"I would have come with you."

"Don't say that, Kostea."

He wanted to pull her in his arms and kiss her, assure her he wasn't lying. It would be easy.

She didn't wait. She looked at him with melancholy eyes and kept on speaking. "My former boyfriend was killed by the Germans. After the war, I didn't return to Odessa, never saw Aunt Aneta again or the opera house. In Moscow, I joined the Komsomol and became a political activist. I advanced through the ranks, got married, and then divorced. We didn't have children. When the Party asked me to participate in this year's festivities in Bucharest, I decided to try my luck and seek you out." She grinned. "My friends at the KGB, the former MGB that is, found you in no time, alive and prosperous."

"Why wouldn't I be alive?" Kostea said.

"These have been difficult years. Many people have died or disappeared."

"I guess I was lucky during the war. I have also learned to compromise, and I joined the Communist Party."

"You *were* lucky," Katya said. "Having been involved with politics for years, I saw up close their methods: random arrests, trumped-up charges. Nobody has been safe, myself included. I know it hasn't been as bad over here as in the Soviet Union, but they all learned from the same master. They love to keep the population guessing." She shrugged. "Now that Papa Stalin is dead, it might get a little better."

"If your KGB friends fed you news about me, then you must have known I'm a doctor. And that I'm married. Yet you pretended otherwise."

She took a sip of her wine. "I thought about you. Always." She looked away. "Kostea, our star is still there. On clear nights, I imagine us running into each other by chance. I talk to you in my mind over and over. Each time I do it, I hear you promise to take me to Bucharest and hold me forever."

He felt his body throbbing with desire, but he remembered. "We almost lost my son last month," he told her.

She looked aghast. "What happened?"

"Appendicitis. A routine, simple condition. But I, the famous doctor, I missed it. I waited and didn't rush him to the hospital until the last moment, until it turned acute and dangerous. He's only four—so tiny."

"But he's all right."

"He is, thank goodness." He took her hand. "He's all I have. I'm sorry."

"I'm too late," she said. "I understand, don't worry." She drew close and kissed him fast on the cheek. "It's one thing to read about you in reports, another to see you. I'm happy your son is well, and I am happy for you, Kostea. You're all right, and that's what matters."

When a waiter came by, he asked for a taxi. One must have been nearby, for in a few minutes the waiter signaled, and Kostea escorted Katya to the street. After an awkward hug, she got into the cab, Kostea shoved the door shut, and she disappeared.

CHAPTER 8

Are You Here to Stay?

As Kostea left the restaurant, he saw people milling about, on the sidewalks and in the middle of the road, talking, laughing, singing, and yelling. An occasional car advanced slowly, with flashing lights and honking. Men huddled together and followed groups of women, less numerous, men whistling after them, propositioning. The women pretended not to care or responded with flirtatious bursts of laughter and cheeky comments. The summer evening air was lustful.

Kostea walked fast and looked around with tolerant disdain. He had been there. Now he had other things on his mind, more important. He understood the forbidden fruit, and that evening, he had almost succumbed to temptation. Any fool can cheat on his wife, but the true measure of a man was to stay faithful. He was a husband, a father, a man, and he had made a commitment. That evening, he and Katya had put an end to a beautiful story. From now on, there would be just a star in the sky and a secret.

He found Clara alone in the kitchen, smoking, looking tired, her hair falling in unkempt strands. "You're home," she said when she saw him.

"Of course I am." A weight lifted off his shoulders. He took the cigarette from between her fingers and brought it to his lips. "I was working. You worried?"

"Not really. I was thinking."

He put out the cigarette, and they moved to the bedroom. "About what?" he whispered.

"Not much. You and me. Toddy's surgery. The way we almost lost him."

"It was my fault. I should have caught it earlier, even though your mom didn't help by hiding from me that Toddy experienced tummy aches," said Kostea. "And I'm still disappointed with Dinescu, who chased me out of the operating room. Just like when Dr. Pop didn't let me assist during your delivery." He knew that wasn't exactly true, but it sounded right, and he said it. He continued, "As a doctor, I know what can go wrong. Toddy's my son. Why would Dinescu kick me out? Tell me."

"Kostea, you know why. Doctors are not supposed to operate on their own, especially their children."

"Don't you think I'd be able to control my emotions? Don't you trust me?"

"I do," Clara said. "But it doesn't matter. Look, I'm tired." She kissed him good night, switched the lights off, and nestled her head on her pillow. Her thigh reached his back, seeking his warmth under the covers.

His eyes closed, he counted to ten, then counted again and tried to breathe normally. Sleep was not coming. Trust, as important as love and family, he thought. He lingered, enjoying the feeling of having his wife asleep close to him, peacefully, *trustfully*.

He'd been lucky. Tonight, he had not only resisted his basic instincts and stood by his wife and son, but he had been prudent. There was no obvious reason for Katya to show up, no matter her explanation. She said she had always loved him, and this had been her first chance. Ten years, and she suddenly found herself in Bucharest. She worked with the KGB—she was a government employee, and who knew what her real mission was? Maybe it wasn't him, or maybe there wasn't a mission, but how could he know for sure? That was the curse of the regime—one never knew, and one never trusted. Except for friends and family, of course, and even then, there were exceptions. As Katya said, the masses were kept guessing. There were no consequences, no logic—only fear. She came, they spoke, she disappeared. Beyond the romanticism of it all, he had to trust she had disappeared forever. The opposite of trust was suspicion, and jealousy that came with it, in its many forms.

He got up and, moving as silently as he could, reached the open window. His thoughts twirled. His son's surgery, Clara, the KGB, trust, jealousy.

As a teenager, his jealousy burned like hot embers when his friend Eugene bragged that he had taken Clara skating. When she went out with other boys, the ones he knew about and the ones he suspected, his thoughts dazed him, his chest tightened like in a straitjacket. He fought for Clara, competed for her love, and in the end, he succeeded. She waited for him during the long and hard years of war and chose to spend her life with him.

Kostea didn't.

His time with Katya shook him to the core. For a few confusing weeks afterward, he did not know which way was up or down or if his life made any sense. Then the memory of those days burned away, not because he wanted it erased, but because, in the turmoil of the war, feelings drifted like smoke.

One night during the war, before he returned to Bucharest, he met his parents on a train from Kishinev to Jassy, full of people escaping the advancing Soviets. Unusual as it was for Kostea to confide in his father, there was a moment when Mimi stepped out onto the crowded train platform to smoke, and Kostea did so in a whisper, without reservation. He talked about Katya, about his feelings for her, and his longing for Clara. "In the end," he said, "Clara is the one I am choosing."

"I'm happy for you," Sasha said. "I like Clara." He gazed out the window at the deserted field they were traversing. "As a young man, you were bound to run into someone like Katya. Who knows? You might have already met more young women like her. A few might make your head spin, and losing them might seem a huge disappointment. Such disappointments pass. I married late in life, and I know. Enjoy while you can. When you get to be my age, you forget most women you dated—at best, you remember a gesture, a lace blouse, a few whispered words. If you are to sleep around, do it before marriage. Don't do it later, when you have a family and a career, or you'll look like a fool. What might be a tragedy later, right now is not. Right now, this experience is good for you. Katya was good for you. She gave you knowledge."

He and Clara, Kostea knew, had survived difficult times. Clara had taken him back into her life as if he had always belonged there. No questions asked, except if he intended to stay. In a way he was glad—he didn't have to lie about Katya. But he was left with scar tissue. If it happened once, it could happen again. And if he could be disloyal, then anyone could, including Clara. He continued to wonder if Clara was hiding anything—or anyone—from him, but he dared not ask.

Jealousy.

———

Kostea returned from the war, and Clara waited for him at the railway station. In less than a week, he left again on assignment to the Sanatorium of Mangalia, a place for wounded soldiers to rest and recover. It was early fall, and the country was slowly emerging from a war still raging on its western border.

There was a restaurant in Mangalia belonging to an enterprising Tatar who knew how to obtain fresh produce, meats, and liquor in a time when such items were in short supply. On beautiful evenings, the most coveted section of the restaurant was the open-air terrace, perched high on the rocky coast. The sand on the beach below was pearl white and fine. A craggy Y-shaped pier at the entrance to the harbor allayed the surf. Flickering, the lighthouse beam, called the Genovese Beacon, cut through the night at the end of the short leg of the pier. Inland, across Steven the Great Street and the main city square, a delicate minaret rose high above the Esmahan Sultan mosque.

Along with Clara, Dr. Max, and Rodica, a nurse from the sanatorium, Kostea was enjoying a mild evening on the restaurant terrace. He was happy. Clara had arrived that morning from Bucharest and had rented a room in a fisherman's house in Mangalia.

The moon rose to the east, its color changing from gold to silver. A half-empty bottle of plum brandy stood in front of them, next to shot glasses and beer mugs.

Sailors from the naval base spent their meager allowances getting drunk on cheap cocktails of rum and cherry syrup. Young women from the Mangalia Seamstress School, which had reopened that summer, tried their luck with the sailors. A boisterous Gypsy quartet in colorful embroidered vests played ballads and horas on a dulcimer and three violins. The violinists wandered from table to table and serenaded the patrons, bowing for tips.

"A new batch of wounded has arrived from the battlefield," Max told Clara. He was a lanky man who was losing his brown hair prematurely.

"Which means we could use all the help we can muster," Kostea added, looking pointedly at Clara. He had lost weight, was tanned, and needed a haircut. His features, more mature, reflected virility and determination. His jaw was more angular, especially when he smoked, his lips chapped, his eyes burning, and his nose more prominent than before, but not in a bad way. On the contrary, it was straight, narrow, and proportional to his face. His hair, combed back as usual, was sun-bleached, almost white, cascading down on both sides of his forehead and giving him a meditative aura. "Rodica, tell Clara," Kostea urged the nurse. "Tell her about your experience here, how much you're learning. And about our beautiful sunrises."

"He's right," Rodica said, smiling at Clara. "Listen to your boyfriend."

Just then, the quartet approached their table, and music drowned their conversation.

"Let's have a drink," Kostea yelled loud enough to be heard above the sound of the violin and rushed to pour the last of the plum brandy.

Swaying slowly to the music with their girls in their arms, a few young sailors dressed in navy blue pants and striped short-sleeved shirts commandeered the dance floor. They seemed lucky to have found their partners, at least for the evening. The quartet played a romantic ballad, hardly suitable for dancing. Lost in a reverie, the men didn't care, while the girls giggled, rolled their eyes, and threw meaningful glances at each other. A group of less fortunate sailors looked on, their voices booming over the music, laughing loudly, pushing each other, and ogling the other women in the restaurant.

"Careful, you're spilling the brandy." Rodica laughed. "Hey, that's a sign of good luck," she said, dipping her fingers in the little puddle on the table and dabbing Clara's forehead. "Here, maybe somebody's getting married real soon."

"To marriage," Max said and lifted his glass.

"To Clara," said Kostea.

They drank, and Clara blushed like a schoolgirl.

Two sailors approached their table. "Would you care to dance?" the taller of the sailors asked Rodica. He touched the brim of his cap and quickly removed it, displaying a crew cut and a tall forehead that was white compared to his sunburned face.

"Sorry, no," said Rodica.

"And why not?"

"Well, I'm married," she lied, pointing at Max. "That's my guy over there."

"I don't mind if you're married," the sailor said. "It's just a dance, lady."

The other sailor nodded in agreement and approached Clara. "How about you, pretty? Or are you married also?"

Kostea jumped to his feet and in his hurry overturned his chair. "Hey! You're bothering us."

People at other tables turned around and stared.

"Take it easy, fellow," the tall sailor said. "We mean no disrespect."

"Then beat it."

The second sailor's lower lip trembled. He was missing a tooth. "She didn't answer my question."

Kostea took a step forward, and came eye to eye with him. "She said no, blockhead."

The music stopped. The surprised dancers froze like mannequins in a shop window.

"Guys, get back here!" an officer standing by the dance floor yelled.

"Yes, boss," the tall sailor said. "C'mon, George, move it."

George flashed an angry smile. "I'll be back."

"Don't you dare," said Kostea.

Max pulled at Kostea's sleeve. "Sit down, will you?"

Kostea lifted his chair off the floor. "Jerks," he mumbled. "I'm hungry. Let's get some gobies and *chebureki.*"

The bar, where the patrons ordered their food, was standing room only. The smoke was as thick as a curtain. The owner of the restaurant was completely bald, the black handlebar mustache under his flat nose his only hairy adornment. A white apron was tied over his protruding belly. "Doctors, I heard there was some commotion on the terrace," he said and patted Max on his back with a warm gesture. "I apologize. The boys are hot, but they don't mean any harm."

"No worries," Max said. He was much taller than the restaurant owner. When Max tried to catch his eyes, rather than bend forward, he flexed his knees, lowering his entire upper body and hitting Kostea in the process. He winked at the restaurant owner. "Just keep the drinks coming."

Kostea moved to the side to make room for Max, inadvertently pushing a man who was having a drink.

"So, you're the doctors from the sanatorium," the man said.

"What if we are?" asked Kostea. He lit a cigarette, and while waiting for their food, to emulate his new companion, he asked for a shot of brandy. The man at the bar tipped his head and said cheers.

The cook set their food on the counter. The seared gobies, surrounded by lemon slices, were served in a cast-iron pan that was heavy and hot, and the chebureki were wrapped in wax paper, with the bottom sagging and the fat pouring out. They had to carry the food, the utensils, and the breadbasket. The owner grabbed a pitcher of beer and, walking ahead of them, parted the crowd. The sailors watched them as they went back to their table.

The music was loud. "Maestro, could you have your boys play 'Zaraza'?" Kostea asked the leader of the Gypsy band.

Clara took a bite of the crispy, hot chebureki, and the meaty sauce ran from the corners of her mouth to her chin. "Tasty," she said happily, wiping her face.

"Told you," said Kostea. "Do as I say. Always." When the quartet played his song, he asked her to dance. "Zaraza" was a tango popular with the soldiers on the front line. Sex, love, beauty, and death expressed by words of exotic simplicity and bittersweet music poured out with a rhythmic end-of-the-world yearning.

"My fingers are sticky," Clara said.

"I love your fingers."

They danced close together, forgetting their worries, and he told her again that he loved her. When the song ended, they walked to the edge of the terrace and looked at the sea. The moon shone on the water. The people in the restaurant were less than two steps away, but it didn't matter. Clara and Kostea pressed against the handrail and kissed.

Kostea felt movement. When he looked up, he saw George.

"You danced with him. Now it's my turn," George told Clara in a hushed and coarse voice.

"Like hell it is," Clara said.

"One dance." George yanked at Clara's arm. He was blinking a lot and seemed to have trouble standing.

"Let go of her arm!" Kostea said.

The taller sailor materialized from the shadows. "Oh, yeah, *Doctor?* How are you going to stop us?"

"They're drunk," Clara said.

Kostea didn't wait. His fist landed on George's jaw with a dead thud. George let Clara's arm go, took a step back, grabbed his face, and slowly lowered himself to the ground. People at the nearby tables sprang up. The tall sailor leaned over George, picked him up by his armpits, and helped him stand. "I'll find you," he whispered to Kostea.

Back at the table, Kostea laughed and poured drinks for everybody. "Here, here," he said. "If I had to, I could have taken both of them."

The magic was gone.

"Take me home," said Clara.

No streetlights were on. Except for the moon, Mangalia had disappeared in darkness. They walked silently toward the minaret, and Kostea guided Clara down the steps to the pier. On both sides, huge boulders protected the walkway from the foam-laced waves. They could still hear the music from the restaurant. The wind was stronger than on the terrace. Clara shivered, and Kostea put an arm around her, pulling her close. They stopped at the end of the short leg of the pier on a smooth rock under the Genovese Beacon. Every minute or so, the beacon flashed over the surface of the water.

Slowly, Clara's breathing calmed down. "You scared me when you punched the sailor," she told him. "You're too fast with your fists for my liking."

"Only if I have to."

They watched the sea together. He spoke of the wounded he had encountered and treated in the war, and about his grandmother. He said, "I was unable to write to you from Odessa."

"I love you," she whispered.

They marveled at the stars straight above and at the ones over the land to the west. In his mind, he counted the fourth star from the bottom, blinking in a cluster.

At the fisherman's house, they entered her room through a door that opened directly into the yard. There was a bucket with water against the wall, and the whitewashed outhouse was in the back.

Clara switched the light on, a bulb hanging from the ceiling. Next to an oak cupboard stood a bed covered by a white freshly starched sheet, a fluffed-up pillow, and a folded blanket. A narrow jute carpet was spread on the concrete floor in front of the bed. Clara's open suitcase rested on the only chair in the room, pushed away from the desk.

Clara lowered the curtains and sat on the bed.

Kostea sat next to her.

She looked around. "I have no coffee or tea. Nothing to offer."

"But you do," he answered. He got up and turned the light off.

"I waited for you," said Clara.

"I know."

"Kostea, are you here to stay?"

"I'll be here with you. Forever."

They made love. She cried a little but only in the beginning. Kostea was so overtaken by passion that he didn't react. He didn't react later, either, and was silent when he kissed her and felt the drying tears on her face.

They made love a second and a third time that night. When the clock struck six in the morning, he rose. They stood side by side, held hands, and said goodbye.

"There are plum trees in front of my window," she said. "Just like at home, in Kishinev."

He got dressed. A dog started barking, and he left quickly, before the landlord woke up. On foot, he had to cross half of Mangalia to get back to the beach and then walk the rest of the way along the shore to the sanatorium. Morning rounds started at seven. He'd be late, and there was no time to sleep anymore, but a cold shower in the doctor's bathroom at the end of the hallway was all he needed.

He reached the bottom of the pier and felt his head spinning. Above the seawall, the restaurant was empty, silent like a ghost. If he dropped down on the sand and fell asleep, his buddies would understand. Clara! They had joked about marriage last night, and she had not said a word. She loved him for who he was, no preconditions.

He took off his shoes and socks and walked as fast as he could, his heels sinking in the sand. The surf touched his bare feet. It was cold, rejuvenating. Bursting with happiness, he bent over and washed his face with the seawater.

Over the horizon, the sky was turning red. The sun was about to rise, and rays of white light were breaking through. A translucent moon sat high up in the sky, the morning star paling near it.

In the distance he saw a silhouette, barely distinguishable, walking toward him.

He reached in his pocket. His cigarettes got wet from his wet hands. He trembled when he struck the match, but he didn't like the smell of the moist paper and threw the cigarette away. It died in the water with a fizz. When he looked up, the silhouette was closer. He recognized the white and blue uniform. He realized there were several sailors, not just one as he had initially thought, walking single file. The seawall was on his right, the sea on his left—no place to run or hide.

He didn't oppose them. After the first blow, he let himself fall to the ground.

People found him later, unconscious, and carried him to the sanatorium. They brought his shoes and his socks. There was no serious internal damage, but he had a black eye, two broken ribs, and his classical Roman nose was swollen. His colleagues cleaned him up, gave him a shot of morphine, and sent for Clara.

Kostea never said who attacked him. He was young and strong, and heliotherapy did its miracles. In a few days, he was working again. Clara had decided to take the job and stayed at the sanatorium. They tended to the recovering soldiers most mornings, and when the weather was fine, they spent the afternoons huddled together on the beach. Sometimes they retreated to the doctors' lounge, which had a lock on the door and a sofa.

In November, all medical school students returned to class. The war ended in May the following year. Kostea's parents came from Bistriţa for the wedding. Uncle Leo gave Clara away. Standing proudly behind her daughter, Ina was on the verge of tears.

CHAPTER 9

This Is Good Turkish Coffee

September to November 1954

Eugene confided in Kostea. "It all started the night when we found out Uncle Sebastian would be released from prison. Marin told us at the Garden. It was unexpected. Good and bad. I had a hard time controlling my feelings."

"I remember," said Kostea. "You said there is no room for him in your apartment. Only two rooms, with your parents, Norma, and little Elvira."

When it came to the housing shortage, people in Bucharest were being creative. Igor had found the solution. The couple who lived in the attic of their building were moving out. Eugene had just joined the Party, and he announced in a meeting that he and Norma were separating. It was a fictitious declaration to document a real need: a place for Uncle Sebastian. Understanding the urgency of finding a new place for Eugene, the Party's housing office issued him an authorization to occupy the attic. Nobody frowned at the idea that his parents would continue to live in the old apartment with his presumed estranged wife and his daughter.

On the day of the move, to prevent any issues with squatters, Eugene waited at Igor's place and walked into the attic the second the neighbors were out the door. With Igor's restaurant delivery truck, he brought a mattress, a chair, and a lamp on a wooden stand to the new place. To improve air circulation, he added a decrepit electric fan to the inventory. Then he entered his name in the residence ledger: Eugene Sarafianides.

The plan was for Eugene to spend his nights alone in the attic for two months, during which Uncle Sebastian would live at home and regain his strength after leaving the penitentiary. Eugene and Norma would attend the mandatory Party reeducation sessions and eventually declare reconciliation and return to normal married life. Uncle Sebastian would then move into the attic. The issue of the first name in the ledger would be easily correctable.

Eugene continued his tale in a rushed tone while Kostea listened, nervously wringing his fingers.

September was unseasonably warm, and at night the fan moved wafts of hot air from the small tilted window of the attic in the general direction of Eugene's mattress. His sleep was troubled by the sound of metal rubbing on metal and by erotic revelries toward the morning.

Sometimes, at the crack of dawn, he snuck back home. There, taking advantage of the morning commotion—his mother and daughter getting ready to walk to kindergarten and his father drinking black coffee and speaking conspiratorially to Uncle Sebastian in the kitchen—Eugene and Norma consummated the remnants of his nocturnal desires silently in their bedroom.

Most mornings, however, were spent alone in his attic. He would get dressed in yesterday's clothes, eat stale bread with butter, drink tap water, and smoke, while waiting for the clock to turn seven thirty, a signal for him to leave for work. He was unhappy, depressed even, counting the remaining days of his voluntary exile and thinking of the sacrifices one had to make for the harmony of one's family.

This changed the morning he happened to glance out the window and see Igor, newspaper folded under his arm, walking nonchalantly to his truck parked under an old poplar tree. Eugene felt a sudden urge for a warm cup of coffee. Leaving his untouched glass of water on the floor next to his mattress, he ran down the stairs and knocked at Igor's apartment door. After a long silence, while he was reconsidering his action, he heard steps. Vera asked who was there.

"Eugene. I have a quick question for Igor."

"Oh," Vera said, "Igor's at work." The door opened, and she appeared in a white robe thrown over what Eugene guessed was her nightgown. "C'mon in."

"I don't want to disturb you," Eugene said, walking quickly past her into the living room. "I didn't realize he leaves this early."

"He needs to get his supplies and provisions," Vera said. "He is lucky to be allowed to use the truck. I join him at about eleven, so my mornings are free and lonely."

Eugene glimpsed the unmade bed in the bedroom, which filled him with a sense of intimacy and a deeper understanding of being lonely.

"Don't just stand there," Vera added, rounding her vowels with her soft Russian accent. "Come, have a cup of coffee with me in the kitchen."

Eugene sat on one of the two stools by the table. Vera took a shiny bag from the cupboard. "This is good Turkish coffee," she said. "I got it for the restaurant from a friend. You don't find it in stores." She measured two heaping teaspoons of ground beans and dropped them into a small copper vessel with a long handle that she filled with water and placed on the stove. She sat on the stool next to Eugene. With her perfect white skin, shapely body, and light-blond hair framing her face, she looked like a nymph. "This Friday morning Igor is going pheasant hunting for two days. He says fall is the best season."

"He's a true outdoorsman, Igor is," Eugene said.

When the water came to a boil, she turned off the flame. "This is my favorite coffeepot. We should let the coffee grinds settle. It's too hot to drink anyway. Good things take a long time."

They were close enough for him to touch her. Instead, he pulled out his cigarettes. "May I smoke?"

"You can do whatever you want, dear." She bent over to reach a lower shelf in the cupboard where she kept her saucers and coffee cups. The top of her robe gaped open. She caught his stare and slowly rearranged the lapels. "It is all right to look, but don't rush for . . . the coffeepot. It might burn your fingers."

"Sorry, of course not. You're a beautiful woman."

"Men, you're all alike. Do you know that?"

"At least I'm not an outdoorsman," he said, feeling blood rush to his face.

She smiled. "The men who come to the restaurant say I speak with a foreign accent."

"It's a very slight accent."

"Do you mind it?"

"It's sexy."

The coffee was good, thick, and sweet from the sugar she added.

"Shall I tell Igor you came looking for him?" she asked when they finished.

"Don't bother. I'll catch up with him later."

"That's what I thought." Her tone was insinuating. "Friday morning, I'll pay you a visit."

———————

"I'm head over heels in love with Vera," Eugene told Kostea.

"What about Norma?"

"I love her also."

"Nonsense," said Kostea.

"In two days, I'm moving Uncle Sebastian to the attic."

"Buddy, Eugenius, this is the perfect moment to stop. Think about your wife and daughter. Think about Igor."

"Don't you think I know this?" Eugene lit a cigarette and blew the smoke through his nostrils. "Of all people, I thought you'd understand. I saw you with that woman, after the parade. I never told you."

Kostea thought for a second and remembered. "Nothing happened with that woman," he said quickly. "She was the nurse assigned to the Red Cross station, and I walked her to the bus at the end of the shift."

"I saw you enter the restaurant with her. Do you think I'm stupid?"

"You're not stupid," Kostea said, wondering how to embellish his lie further.

Luckily, Eugene turned back to his story. "Vera's moaning and thrashing about, goodness. She was so loud I feared the neighbors would hear. I turned the fan on every time I remembered. We did it in all possible ways, *Kamasutra* and *One Thousand and One Nights* combined, if you know what I'm saying."

"I can imagine."

"Are you and Clara the same?" Eugene asked and looked at his hands with attention.

"None of your business," Kostea said. "Grown men don't talk like this, and let's make one thing abundantly clear—don't tell anybody about your affair. I mean don't tell Norma or Igor and make sure that Vera keeps her mouth shut. Get it?"

"There is a problem. She's pregnant."

"No."

"Yes, pregnant."

"How can you be sure it's yours?"

"Igor can't have kids. You should know that. You are a doctor. She said she'll have an abortion. I'll pay and she'll ask Clara for help. End of story. I wanted to talk about it and she said, 'Don't be an idiot, Eugenius.' She borrowed your nickname for me, her Russian accent pathetic."

Kostea felt vexed and slightly aroused after Eugene's confession. Kamasutra, right under his nose. How was it possible? Sure, it was. Such things happened. People cheated on each other, and this way or that, the wrinkles got smoothed out in the end. The future held no direction. He decided he would never tell Norma or Igor. Why hurt them? He wouldn't be lying, just minding his own business. As for Vera relying on Clara, that was understandable. Abortions were legal, and like all medical care, they were free, except for the small or not-quite-so-small thank you one usually had to offer the doctor to ensure complete dedication to the procedure. Eugene would produce the money. Clara was kind and empathetic and knew how to keep a secret. Kostea was sure of that, and tried to guess why Eugene might be pleased that Clara would find out. In Eugene's weird mind, perhaps still longing for Clara, he would see no harm in her hearing about his getting around. Chop-chop, able to make a baby.

He had a fleeting question. Was Eugene's deed a license for Kostea to somehow do the same, smarter and more discreetly, of course, his father's advice notwithstanding?

The last time Clara spoke to Vera face to face, several days after the secret abortion, instead of being relieved, Vera came across as depressed and angry.

"Don't worry Vera, things will fall into place," Clara tried to assuage her.

"I feel terrible," Vera said. "And I don't mean physically. Of course, I was in pain in the beginning, and now I'm better. But what I feel has everything to do with Igor. How many times can I lie to him? How many fake headaches?"

Clara believed one stayed faithful in a relationship. She had never betrayed Kostea, and she trusted he had never betrayed her, and both would know how to resist temptation. Igor was Vera's second husband, and perhaps there had been other men in her life. Biting from different forbidden apples didn't seem a concern to Vera, but now she was paying the price. Yet Clara didn't judge Vera. She didn't accuse her, because in her mind, Vera didn't know how to be strong and was, truly, the victim. Then and there, Clara decided to offer Vera appeasement. "You're not the first or the last woman to have an affair. What's done is done, and what matters right now is what you'd do in the future. You still love Igor, don't you?"

"I think so. I'm not sure." Vera looked at the ground. "I want to ask for a divorce." She took a cigarette out of her pack and lit it.

"Don't do anything rash. You're angry."

"Ashamed," said Vera.

At work, Clara couldn't think about anything else: Eugene and Norma, Igor and Vera. She had to do something to bring things back into balance. She couldn't talk to Igor. She couldn't talk to Norma. Eugene, he was at work. So what? She'd call him.

"Clara," he said when he picked up. "What an unexpected pleasure."

"We'll see. I want to talk to you about Vera."

"Did something happen?"

"Maybe," Clara said. "Meet you at four p.m. at the coffee shop at Capşa?"

Eugene agreed, and when Clara arrived, he was waiting on the sidewalk. "You look lovely," he said and opened the door for her.

A waiter brought them the menus.

"I didn't think this through," Clara said. "They have excellent desserts here, but it's against the rules to have dessert before dinner."

"It's all right to break the rules sometimes."

"You know," said Clara.

When the waiter returned, she ordered a Joffre cake.

Eugene chose coffee and pistachio ice cream. "I don't know if you noticed," he said, "but they changed the name of the place from Capşa to Bucharest. It's as good as it's ever been, and everybody is calling it by the old name. Only now, instead of the old aristocrats, the Party bosses dine here."

Clara looked at the red velvet chairs, the walnut tables, and the heavy velvet drapes hanging at the windows. Most patrons were men in business suits and ties. "You're right. The place itself feels frozen in time, yet the clientele is entirely new." Clara took her first bite of the Joffre. "This is good, but I have to watch my weight."

"What are you talking about? You're the most beautiful woman I know."

"Thank you, Eugene, but that's exactly the problem with you. If you weren't my husband's best friend, and if I didn't know you as well as I do, I could easily misinterpret your words. You have to be more careful when you speak and especially with what you do. Follow the rules."

"Clara, I always liked you."

"See? Is this a come-on, or what? You did the same thing with Vera, and things got out of control. Now she's devastated because of it."

"I love Vera."

"I thought it was over between you."

"It's not that simple."

"You're married," Clara said in an even tone, as if sympathizing with him. But she wasn't. She didn't think, like Kostea, that Eugene had wanted her to find out about the affair, and she felt angry with him on the inside, disappointed. "And Vera is married too. I thought happily. Until now. Because now she's talking about a divorce, which is your doing."

"Clara, she's an adult, and it takes two to tango."

"I know. But you are the man. You need to think before you act. Grow up. Be responsible."

"Clara, why are talking to me like this?"

"I'm your friend."

"You're not. You and Kostea, you think you are special. But you don't have the moral high ground on anybody. And Kostea, your Kostea, is not the saint you might think he is."

Clara moved her spoon around the collapsed Joffre on her plate. She remembered how once during the war Eugene had felt the need to confess to her about a night he and Kostea had spent in a brothel. His intent, then and now, couldn't be to spread suspicion. Or was it? "Eugene," she asked, "what are you saying?"

He started eating his ice cream. The waiter brought the coffee and left. A mother and her small daughter went silently by.

"Do you know something I don't?" Clara insisted. Her voice was clear, although a measure of doubt rang in it.

Eugene looked at her with innocent eyes. "I got angry. Forgive me."

It was too late. That afternoon Clara left the coffee shop with uncertainty in her heart which she tried to suppress but carried within her for days, months, and years.

CHAPTER 10

His Moscow Man

1955

Kostea yearned for praise and recognition. Professor Dinescu kept the complex and interesting medical cases for himself and assigned the other doctors the routine ones. How could Kostea do broader research and stand out in the operating room, especially as a newly named assistant professor? That assistantship had been in recognition of Kostea's skills as a doctor, but it required him to work longer hours and quickly expand his horizons. He needed to see patients with unusual pathologies, which demanded daring surgical interventions, cases he could proudly describe to his students and publish in medical journals. There were barriers to cross, techniques to acquire.

When Kostea's colleagues were favored over him, in his opinion without a good reason, or when a nurse questioned his decisions, his heartbeat accelerated, his blood rushed to his temples, and he found it difficult to control his anger. In those moments, he wasn't who he wanted to be. He yelled and cursed and called people names. Sometimes he was reprimanded for it. He meekly accepted the criticism and readily apologized, but having seen Dinescu behaving in a similar fashion, he asked himself why his boss could lose his temper and he couldn't.

He needed to become the boss—that truth burned in him.

He knew that Clara understood him but wasn't with him one hundred percent. In her opinion—and she had told it to him several times—he had to be more patient. Amicable. Help others. Becoming the big boss was important, but other things were important as well: give himself a real chance to improve, prove himself, grow. Friends were important. Family, too. Kostea loved Clara. His son. Yes, family was important, but somehow family was a given, a constant, sometimes a refuge. If he needed them, all he had to do was reach and they were there, backing him up. And he'd do anything to defend and provide for them.

Among his friends, Eugene was the oldest. Kostea appreciated him. Sometimes he loved him like a brother, and sometimes he despised him a little, because Eugene didn't have what it took, in Kostea's opinion. Igor, also. Eugene and Igor were not too accomplished professionally, and in a mostly silent way, Kostea found that lacking. Kostea had befriended Igor more recently than Eugene. What brought him and Igor together was the background they shared as people from Kishinev who had come to Bucharest after the war. Igor spoke Russian. He liked to drink and sing Russian songs. Kostea liked that also.

Marin was different. There was less emotion in their relationship and more of an understanding, like a marriage of convenience. I do this, you do that, and we move forward together. It was beneficial. First Marin had helped him become a Party member, and with other things as well. In a society, one needed people like that, always.

———————

Marin called Kostea at work. "Your neighbors on the upper floor, the Demetriades, are leaving for Paris. They were given one week to get out of the country."

"Are they leaving for good?"

"What do you think?"

Over the years, Kostea had spoken with the Demetriades a few times. He had used their phone when he didn't have one, and their little daughter, Collette, befriended Toddy. "That's fast," Kostea said. He was surprised the Demetriades were leaving, but more surprised that Marin knew. Even though that was a part of his job, to know as much as possible.

"Might be fast," Marin said, "but that's not the point. Run home right away. Go speak to them and then go and see Voicu. He's the carpenter who lives next door to you, right?"

"Voicu, the carpenter. Yes."

"Tell him and his wife they can move into Demetriade's apartment. It's larger, on an upper floor. Offer them money if you have to, but get them to do it before others find out that their apartment will become available."

Kostea was still confused.

While he waited, Marin continued, "Take over the Voicu apartment. While the Voicus are moving, grab the residence ledger, and write in your parents' names."

"They live in Bistriţa," Kostea said.

"So what? Then take the ledger and a bottle of brandy to my man at the precinct. I'll talk to him, and he will approve it on the spot. If you do this, you justify the larger space, and later, should you ever decide to bring your parents to Bucharest to live with you, their residence would be already established. You know, a Bucharest residence is not a small deal. Then hire some workers, knock down a few walls, and enjoy the extra space."

Kostea finally understood—a version of the Sebastian maneuver, without a cuckolded spouse in the end.

———

Soon, the apartment became a construction site. The furniture was moved into the middle of rooms, the kitchen utensils and household belongings packed in boxes, and a part of the wall separating the adjacent apartments knocked down. Whether he liked it or not, Kostea had to rely on Ina. While he and Clara were at work, and Toddy in kindergarten, Ina was alone with the workers: masons, painters, carpenters, and electricians. They were young men, and Ina knew that the fastest way to their hearts was with food. She fed them breakfast and lunch, and at the end of each day, she sent them off with a healthy shot of plum brandy—one each, to avoid excess.

Over time, the kitchen doubled in size. The new living room extended the width of the villa, and a set of French doors opened onto a large balcony with a view of the neighboring woods. The foyer was converted into a pantry with deep shelves. "Make sure to leave space for a refrigerator," Kostea said. "I will buy you a Penguin 100 when I get sent to Moscow, as I hope." He expected his promise to please Ina, and for her to regard it as compensation for her role with the workers.

There were two new bedrooms for Ina and Toddy, and a study for Kostea to work from home.

"What do you need a study for?" Ina asked him.

"To write my papers and finish my postgraduate work."

"You've been at it for years! Why does it take so long?"

Kostea did not respond. In the past, he had often come home with piles of medical records and professional books in his arms. "Mama, keep quiet. I have to work," he would say. He would draw the bedroom door closed until Clara came home. The few times Ina entered his room, she found him stretched out on the bed, a cigarette dangling from his lips, uncomfortably writing in his notebooks, X-rays and journals spread all around. Kostea wouldn't look up. But if Toddy ran in, he'd immediately stop, hug the boy, and play with him for as long as it took.

———————

Ina went out on the new balcony facing the woods. Kostea joined her.

"Our apartment looks like one in an American movie," she said.

Kostea felt good about her statement. Proud. Behind them, cool and shady, the mature poplars, beeches, and oaks were a part of the formal royal summer residence that was repurposed as the Pioneers' Palace after the king's exile. The Pioneers, schoolchildren between the ages of eight and fourteen, wore red kerchiefs around their necks and participated in after-school activities meant to educate a young contingent of communists-in-waiting.

Kostea rested his elbows on the handrail and said, "Time flies. In three years, Toddy will become a Pioneer. I'll teach him tennis by then. We'll go swimming together. My boy."

Dinescu made Kostea his Moscow man and had him travel repeatedly to the Soviet Union to attend conferences and acquire medical supplies and equipment for the hospital. Uniquely qualified because he spoke Russian fluently, Kostea accepted the assignment as a badge of honor. Once his official business was completed, he shopped for his family. A refrigerator was too large to take on the plane, so instead, he bought a highly prized Russian vacuum cleaner and a TV set.

While he was away, Clara furnished his study. It was impossible to find a fine-quality desk in the stores, so she bought a used one from a family leaving the country.

"My beautiful, brilliant wife!" Kostea said when he saw his new study and whistled happily. He lifted Clara up and twirled around the room with her, then sat her on his new desk and kissed her.

He brought home anthologies, medical books, and journals from the hospital and from the university library. His bookshelves filled up.

Madam Potzi, a typist recommended by the medical school for her speed and accuracy, came to Kostea's apartment to work on his research papers. They kept the door closed to his study. All Ina could hear was

Kostea's voice and the continuous sputter of the typewriter. Madam Potzi was neither young nor pretty. Otherwise, Ina would have been suspicious. Sometimes, when she overheard Kostea yelling, she brought her ear close to the door and listened. A period of silence usually followed Kostea's verbal assaults. Then the clatter of typing resumed.

One afternoon, after Kostea's irritated voice had resonated through the entire apartment, Potzi emerged from the study, eyes red behind her thick lenses, her peach-gray straight hair in disarray as if she had pulled at it. The tips of her fingers were black from the carbon paper. Her nails were cut short.

Ina was in the kitchen with Dora, her sister-in-law. She offered Potzi a glass of water. "You don't have to put up with this," Ina said.

"I need the money," Potzi said.

Kostea stormed out after her. Potzi saw him, sighed, and passed him on her way back. He walked into the kitchen, dark circles under his eyes. "Dora, how are you?" he said. "How are Leo and Toni?" He turned to Ina without waiting for a response. "Mama, I had a terrible night. Make me some coffee, all right?"

"We're out of coffee."

"How come?"

"You drank it," she said to him, her gaze on her sister-in-law.

Kostea rolled his eyes. "Then buy some."

"We have no more money until the end of the month."

At the kitchen table, Dora tried to remain as inconspicuous as possible.

"Nonsense," Kostea said and rolled his eyes one more time. "If you need money, say so. Don't I give you enough?"

"Clara gives me the money."

"Clara and I," Kostea corrected her. He stuck his hand in his pocket, took out a wad of cash, and handed Ina two large bills. "Here, take this and go buy some coffee."

"I can't go right now." Ina lit up a cigarette to show him she was there to stay. "Dora and I are talking. I'll make you some tea."

"I don't want any tea." Kostea left, slamming the kitchen door.

"That's what I get every day," Ina told Dora.

"You're trapped," Dora said.

"Clara needs me. And Toddy. I love them too much." Ina took another drag from her cigarette and added, "But I know I can always return to my room in your apartment. It's reassuring to have a refuge. A place."

Dora's narrow face darkened. "Now Toni is older. He uses that room all the time. Honestly, it's not like you paid rent for that room. Ina, find a better solution."

———————

At the end of each month, Ina and Clara worked out their budget. They put the bills in envelopes labeled *rent, utilities, groceries,* and *miscellaneous.* Food was the largest expense.

Kostea did not have such concerns. Clara kept the daily worries away from him and allowed him to focus on the hospital and his teaching. From time to time, a patient would stop by and shyly offer a basket with wine bottles, a roast, or a turkey to thank the good doctor for the care he had provided. Occasionally, a plain envelope was slipped under their front door or offered furtively in the doctor's office. The gifts he quietly received from his patients helped a great deal.

"He never asks for money from his patients," Clara insisted to her friends. "It's illegal, and he's not one of those."

Ina thought otherwise.

———————

Mimi called Kostea to tell him Aneta had died. She sobbed on the phone. Kostea remembered Aneta and his trip to Odessa more than ten years ago. His grandmother, a dear old lady, how sad! There was another thing to remember about that time, but he didn't let his thoughts wander. No reason for it.

"She died alone," Mimi said. "We haven't seen her since 1921. What can I tell you? I'm happy you did." And then she proceeded with telling Kostea a tale he knew very well. How in Odessa, Kostea's father had been unjustly accused of misappropriating funds given to him by the Red Cross; how Mimi had wanted to fight the accusers and Aneta had disagreed; how she had given them money to pay for a ship bound to Constantinople. "Do you expect us to leave you here?" Mimi had asked her mother. "Yes," her mother had said. "I have Mila here, my wonderful niece. And your father's tomb is here, and my parents' resting place. I'll survive."

A month later, Mimi called again. This time, she had something else on her mind. "I'm worried about your father," she said. "He complains of chest pains. Last week, at the hospital, they had diagnosed him with angina pectoris and had kept him overnight."

"You should have told me," Kostea said. It was a reproach.

"My mother had just died. Besides, what could you do?"

"Mama, I'm a doctor. You and father should move to Bucharest, where I can help."

"Hmph. That's your standard answer. No matter what, you ask us to move. But we don't want to. Not yet. And if we were to come, where would we live?"

"With me. I have a larger apartment now." His new place was his doing, and he wanted his mother to know.

"No, Kostea. It's not that simple. I'm still working, even though I decided to retire this fall. My eyesight is deteriorating. But Kostea, your father is ten years older than me. Help me convince him it's time for him to retire as well. And don't tell him I asked you. He'd be upset."

"All right, Mother, I'll try."

Mimi breathed hard into the phone. "Last week at the hospital they gave him morphine. For chest pains. I think we should have some at home, not to depend on the hospital or the ambulance service if this happens again. I was told no one is allowed to keep morphine at home. Your father could probably get some, but you know how he is. Everything has to be by the book. Can you help?"

"I'll grab a few vials and find somebody to bring them to you," Kostea said. "Or I'll bring them myself."

———

"What shall I do with you, Kostea?" Dinescu asked. "As always, you're a pain in my side."

Kostea shrugged. After all these years, he knew Dinescu didn't mean what he said.

"Ileana!" Dinescu yelled. He ordered her to bring the controlled substance log and asked Kostea for the name of the last prostate cancer patient who had died in their care. Then he wrote the name in the log. And a directive: "Two doses of morphine to be administered every eight hours as needed for pain." He backdated the order, signed it, and had Kostea sign it as well. He ripped the page from the log, retaining the carbon copy. "Have the nurse run to the hospital pharmacy with this," he said, handing the page to Kostea.

That's how it was done. Power in action, Kostea thought. One day he would reach the level allowing him to do things like that.

CHAPTER 11

What's Immortality?

1958

On Sunday, while Ina was in church and Kostea was doing his morning rounds at the hospital, Clara cuddled in bed with Toddy. She was enjoying her son's embrace. She felt his love and hoped that he felt hers. "When did you get so big?" she asked him.

He pretended to be small, pulling his knees up to his chin. "I'm a baby, a little baby," he said, laughing.

She kissed his forehead and pushed his dark hair to the right. "I like a clean forehead. It's the sign of an intelligent person." She stretched out her palm and he pushed his against hers, comparing sizes, hers still a little larger than his. "You have slender fingers and elegant, oval nails. I don't like short fingers with stubby nails," Clara said.

He was an affectionate boy, with fine features that preserved the fresh, innocent look of a child. Clara picked up a book and read to him her favorite poem by Eminescu:

In times when fairy tales begin,
In times with magic laden,
There lived, of high and noble kin,
A most enchanting maiden.

"The Evening Star" had ninety-eight stanzas. Clara allowed herself to be carried away by its musicality, reading verses that she had memorized. Suddenly she realized her son wasn't paying attention. "You don't like it?" she said.

"I don't understand it."

"Toddy, the evening star symbolizes the genius, an immortal being superior and so different from us that any relationship with regular people is impossible. Yet he is in love with a princess, the enchanting maiden. He begs God to allow him to exchange his immortality for her love. Now, listen to what God says to him."

> Become a man—is this your goal,
> Their likeness to acquire?
> But were mankind to perish whole,
> Others would still aspire.

"What's immortality?" Toddy asked.

"That means you're never going to die," Clara said.

"Are we going to die, Mama?"

"Sure, we will. All of us will, but we don't worry about it. We have a long, long time to live and be happy together. Let me read you another poem that I know you will like better. It's about the king of Walachia, as a part of Romania was called centuries ago. He was a hero who defeated the army of the mighty Ottoman empire."

Clara wondered how she might feel had she had more children, like Kostea had sometimes suggested. Given the hardship of their daily lives and the empty stores immediately after the war, and the many hours of pain and suffering of her first labor and delivery, she didn't want a second baby. Deep inside her, she was convinced Kostea was simply being capricious. She had never assented to his wishes, and he had never insisted. In fact, he had agreed to be careful and was very supportive when on two unfortunate occasions she had to have abortions. She would never forget those abortions, not so much for their cold, clinical aspects as for the emotional weight and moral quandary they caused her. Yet she felt no regret for having had them and taught herself to push those experiences to the back of her mind and never think or talk about them.

Toddy was enough and he filled her life. He was everything Clara wanted: bright, funny, healthy, and well-behaved. He was lovable. Loving. Age eight and still cuddling with his mother, kindred in body and spirit.

Besides, Kostea, too, needed her attention. She comforted him when he had problems at work and when he brought home his medical papers and yelled in frustration or just because he was too tired to be considerate. He often said he would work at taming his temper tantrums, but he never did. Well, life was no picnic, and he was no saint. In many ways, he gave her less than she had expected, and in others, he offered more. Much more. And nothing could ruin their friendship and the trust they had in each other.

Good thing her job was going well, as much as her job contributed to her contentment.

Despite its regulatory reach and importance, the Municipal Public Health Lab was located in a neglected apartment building close to Union Market, twenty-five minutes away by tram. The doctors shared one small office—a former bedroom, they guessed—abutting the lab, while the support personnel of technicians and nurses occupied the second. The lab served a part of their city of a million people, regularly inspecting and testing the cleanliness of the water supply, hospitals, food distribution and restaurants, schools and daycare centers. The work hours were strictly between 7:30 and 3:30, and Clara enjoyed the predictability of her schedule.

At work, in the morning, Clara donned her gloves and protective glasses and approached the cultures assigned to her, unraveling a universe invisible to the naked eye: squiggly life forms, good and bad bacteria known by Latin names to only a few people. The array of tasks that she needed to perform agreed with her personality. She learned to be fond of the rigorous lab procedures needed to keep the equipment sterile and at her fingertips: the test tubes and other glassware, the incubator and petri dishes, the spatulas and the litmus paper. When Clara worked, Ina, Kostea, Toddy, the crowds in the city, and her lingering financial worries shifted into a remote background, waiting to reappear only at the end of the day, often with renewed urgency.

CHAPTER 12

Everything Proceeded Perfectly

1959

"Are you sure you want to go through with this?" Dr. Max asked Kostea the morning of the surgery. It was ten minutes to seven, and they were in the doctors' locker room.

Kostea was scrubbing in. "Why not?" He seemed more jovial and self-assured than usual. "I've done this surgery many times. Besides, you'll keep me under control."

"He's your relative," Max said.

"He's my wife's uncle, not mine, and he asked me to do it. I said yes, and I don't even like him that much."

Max smiled. "That doesn't matter. It's against the rules, and Dinescu will crucify you."

Kostea knew it, but he wanted to do the surgery. To prove himself to his family. To impress others. Besides, an older score had to be settled. "Years ago, Dinescu stopped me from operating on Toddy. This time, he's out of the country." Water dripped off his elbows onto the floor.

"You're a bit of an asshole," Max said, looking at the water trail. "I don't know why people put up with you."

"Because I'm good," said Kostea. "My wife's uncle's *my* patient, buddy. I promised to show my students how to do a suprapubic prostatectomy."

"How many students do you have?"

"Five. Two girls and three boys."

"Full house," said Max.

"Funny."

"Who's the anesthesiologist?"

"Dr. Marcu."

"He's very reliable. How about the scrub nurse?"

"I wanted Greta, but she's out for the week. All I could get was Lily."

"Lily Berciu?"

"Is there another Lily?"

"Oh, boy." Max shook his head.

Just then, the circulating nurse came in and told them the patient was ready.

"Was he shaved?" Kostea asked.

"Above the pubic bone."

Kostea made a face. "I said everywhere."

The nurse shrugged and turned around. The doctors followed her.

"They shaved enough," Max whispered.

"Perhaps," Kostea said. "But they should do what I tell them."

Lily, already scrubbed and sterile, helped the two of them into sterile gowns and gloves.

Uncle Leo lay on the operating table. He was on his back, his entire body covered by a white sheet. An intravenous line in his left arm was connected to a bottle of fluid hanging from a pole at the head of the table. When he saw Kostea, he raised his right hand in an attempt to salute, the gap in between his fingers showing. He was glad that Kostea had agreed to be his surgeon. He trusted him, even though he had hesitated to speak to Kostea directly. So, Dora had approached Ina, Ina had spoken to Clara, and finally Clara had asked Kostea to examine her uncle's prostate. Kostea had determined that surgery was necessary.

Dr. Marcu stood behind Leo's head. The students, three men and only one woman, were lined up against the wall. They wore scrubs, surgical caps, and masks. In unison, they uttered a weak good morning.

"Good morning," Kostea replied. "I thought there would be five of you." One student mumbled an explanation, but Kostea didn't listen. He approached his patient and started talking in a soft voice. "Uncle Leo, how are you feeling this morning?" Again, he didn't wait for an answer. "This will be quick and painless. I guess a little over an hour. When you wake up, you'll have a catheter. Actually, two. One, you know where, to help you pee. The other will drain through your abdomen. In a few days, you'll be as good as new, and we'll let you go home. I promise. Dora is in the waiting room, so as soon as I'm done here, I'll go out and talk to her." Kostea pointed at the anesthesiologist. "Let this nice man perform his miracle on you, and don't worry about anything, Uncle Leo. Trust me, he's the best we have in this hospital."

Dr. Marcu leaned forward and spoke into Leo's ear. "Close your eyes and count backward from ten, slowly." He adjusted a dial on the IV and pressed a mask to Leo's face. Leo went under before he reached number six.

As soon as the circulating nurse finished cleaning and sterilizing the operative site, she uncovered and positioned the instrument table in front of Lily. Max took his spot by the operating table across from Kostea. Lily moved to his left.

"Ready," Dr. Marcu said.

"Students," Kostea ordered. "Move forward. Scalpel," he said next, and Lily slapped the scalpel into his gloved hand. "I'll start with an incision straight across, about ten centimeters. Watch." He brought the scalpel to the skin and cut without hesitation. "The abdominal wall has nine layers, and we're now down to the subcutaneous fatty layer." He snickered. "Seems Uncle Leo has led a good life. There is a lot of fat tissue." The students laughed also.

As the surgery proceeded, Kostea became more focused. "Scissors," he told Lily. When she handed them to him, he shook his head. "Not these. The blunt ones from that corner." The surgical mask covered his face. Under his white cap, his eyes shone blue like daggers. He exchanged a quick glance with Max, who nodded in agreement. This nurse was trouble.

"I'm cutting deeper now. I'll be reaching the muscle," Kostea announced and looked again at Lily. "Come behind me and mop up the blood. Good, now pass me the retractor."

Lily continued swabbing around the incision.

"Retractor," Kostea ordered again. "Nurse, I need you to move faster."

She handed him the instrument, and he gave it to Max to hold the incision open.

"Students, get closer," Kostea continued. "I'm going to cut an opening in the bladder to reach the top of the prostate. Lily, follow me closely with suction."

Max cauterized and tied off bleeders.

Kostea proceeded through the following steps with speed and dexterity. "We only remove the inside of the prostate, a little like removing the inside of an orange and leaving the skin. Then we reposition the retractor. We do this to prevent tissue damage."

The students nodded and watched silently.

Max relaxed and took his hands off the retractor. As Kostea repositioned it, he touched a vessel. Blood spurted out and instantly filled the opening. Lily tried suction again.

"What are you doing?" Kostea yelled. "Clamp! Quickly!"

She straightened up, turned toward the instrument table, and froze.

Inside Leo's abdomen, Kostea tried to stop the blood flow with his fingers. "Clamp!" he yelled again without looking at the nurse.

Lily grabbed the first clamp she reached and gave it to Kostea. He glanced at it and threw it away. "This is for ligaments, nurse. Get out of here. Idiot! Now!"

Max reached in front of Lily and grabbed a hemostat and passed it to Kostea. Lily took a step back, her hands up in the air. It seemed as if she wanted to leave the room but didn't dare. The female student leaned heavily on the arm of the male student standing next to her. The other two froze, their arms across their chests like mummies.

It took Kostea several seconds to stop the bleeding, the longest seconds in his life.

"I'll take it from here," Max said, and Kostea nodded. He stepped back and wiped his gloved palms on his scrubs. His hands were shaking.

Max took his time repairing the damaged vessel.

"Except for a little bleeding, everything proceeded perfectly," Kostea told Dora. He had changed, and his scrubs were spotless. "Another week and you'll get him back home to love and to cherish."

Dora clasped her hands in front of her chest. "Thank you, oh, thank you so much, Kostea."

Uncle Leo recovered quickly. They removed his catheter after four days and discharged him the next Sunday. The results of his biopsy came in negative, confirming Kostea's diagnosis.

Lily Berciu lodged a complaint against Kostea. She stated he had operated on a relative against hospital policy and, consequently, had displayed abnormal anxiety during the surgery. Not only had he placed the well-being of the patient in jeopardy, but he had behaved in a nonprofessional manner with her, a scrub nurse with many years of experience, yelling at her for no reason and calling her an idiot. She also claimed that the students witnessing the procedure were appalled. Even though a nurse was hierarchically lower in rank than a doctor, her complaint went on, she was still a human being and a Party member dedicated to serving the hospital and the fatherland. In fact, she noted, similar unjustified aggressive behavior by Comrade Assistant Professor Bardu had been reported on several previous occasions.

Kostea was reprimanded and suspended from working with students for an undetermined period of time. He saw his dreams go up in smoke and felt devastated. He couldn't sleep at night and talked to himself. For several days he stopped eating. Clara encouraged him to contest the punishment, while secretly she hoped he would learn his lesson. Professor Dinescu, after he returned from his trip, gave Kostea a mouthful and said that the matter was out of his hands. Kostea had to wait, work hard, and one day he might be reinstated. Marin agreed with Dinescu.

BOOK II

THE IRON CURTAIN

Mostly Bucharest, the 1960s and 1970s

CHAPTER 13

This Never Happens in Germany

Spring 1962

Kostea decided to buy a Fiat 600 as soon as the restriction on owning private vehicles was lifted. It wasn't the cheapest option, but it was an economical first car with a good reputation. Kostea and Clara had to borrow money from Kostea's parents and Uncle Leo. Marius Selivanov taught Kostea to drive. He was a friend of Uncle Leo's who had worked as a trucker at Red Grivița and now for TIR, Romanian International Transport. TIR employed a distinct group of drivers who hauled Romanian agricultural products to East Germany and beyond and returned with full loads of consumer goods from the West. Given their exposure and responsibility, these men provided certain services for the Security Police—the Securitate—and had ample opportunities for contraband, which explained why Marius owned a secondhand Opel purchased in West Germany.

Marius drove Kostea to pick up his car at the vehicle distribution center, about one hundred kilometers outside Bucharest. Igor volunteered to come along for the ride.

After Vera left him, Igor got depressed and lost his job at the restaurant—and the privilege of using the restaurant truck. Not many people owned cars or knew how to drive in Romania.

As they were leaving the dusty, pedestrian-filled streets of Bucharest, Kostea admired how Marius maneuvered his Opel with calm dexterity. Driving, Kostea concluded, was like surgery. One needed undivided attention, reliable equipment, and the ability to react promptly.

"Always glance in the rearview mirror and know who's behind you," Marius suggested.

"As if the Securitate were following you," Igor joked from the back seat.

Marius kept only two fingers of his right hand on the wheel, while unbuttoning the cuff of his shirtsleeve with his left. "One mistake rookies make," he continued, "is forgetting to check the air pressure in their spare tire, and when they need it, they're screwed." He scratched the skin on his bony arm under the rolled-up sleeve.

Kostea pictured Marius changing heavy tires, loading and unloading his truck, and driving for hours through the night. He thought of rest stations in the middle of nowhere, where sometimes, he imagined, one would have to be able to hold one's own. For a truck driver, those arms were definitely too thin.

He looked out the streaky windshield at the clouds that had gathered in the sky. It started to rain. A peasant trudging along the side of the road next to his horse and open cart sought refuge under a tree and blocked their lane. The oncoming cars caused Marius to stop. He beeped and told Kostea to open his window. "What are you doing, you moron, you!" he yelled at the peasant while leaning over Kostea. The peasant made an obscene gesture with his right arm.

Kostea rolled his window back up.

"This never happens in Germany," Marius said. "Not on the autobahn."

"They drive fast on the autobahn," Igor said, like a person who knew a few things about driving.

"At least twice as fast as here," Marius said and accelerated. "And mind you, in Germany I'm driving a truck. In fact, they don't have any speed limits. No matter how fast I go, there is always somebody driving faster. I think they are nuts, but the roads are perfect. Horse-drawn carts, farm animals, bicyclists, and pedestrians are not allowed on the autobahn."

The green fields were soaking in the rain.

Marius and Igor, the experienced drivers, were now bombarding Kostea with well-meaning advice. A gasoline can in the trunk was a great idea for when the gas stations ran out of gas, as happened from time to time. Also, a jug of drinking water, a few chocolate bars, basic medical supplies, a raincoat, a blanket, and a flashlight, and always pay attention in the rain because the roads get slick and muddy.

"I don't see any mud," said Kostea.

"That's the problem," Marius said with a self-satisfied smile. "You don't see it."

Soon, Kostea thought, he'd possess his very first car, and goose bumps formed on his skin.

"Marius, tell us more about how it is over there," Igor asked. "I mean, in West Germany."

"It's great, and none of that anti-capitalist bullshit with people being oppressed. Some are less fortunate, true, but everyone is doing quite well. How can I put it? Like when you open the window and . . . suddenly you can breathe. When you walk in the streets of Bucharest and see the foreigners at the Lido and the Continental Hotel—you spot them immediately, not only because they are well-dressed but also because they smile when they speak, and they smell good. In Germany, the stores are so full, you can hardly imagine!"

"People have money, don't they?"

"More than we do. For us, everything there's expensive. Not for them. Even the unemployed—for they have some of those—receive more money from the state than we get in salary. My partner and I bring along our own food, so we can spend our hard currency allowance on household items and clothes for our families. Sometimes we bring Romanian cognac with us to sell. That's how I made the money to buy the Opel."

That sounded incredible, Kostea thought. How many bottles of cognac could skinny Marius have sold, and who would have wanted to buy so much Romanian brandy?

A flock of sheep blocked the road. Marius stopped the car on the shoulder. They listened in silence to the sheep baaing and the barking of dogs. The shepherd came over and hit the roof of the car with his fist, his signal to move it.

"Son of a bitch," Marius cursed. "This is my car. Don't bang it!" He inhaled deeply. "I'd love to take my wife and my daughter once on the road with me. But they don't let me. They hold my family hostage to keep me from defecting."

A short silence followed as if Igor and Kostea were letting this statement sink in.

"Marius," Igor asked after some time, "how do you explain that they have it so good?"

"In the West? The Americans helped them. After the war, we got stuck with the Russians. Now, things are changing a little. I mean, since Buddy decided to follow a more independent political trajectory." Buddy was what people called Gheorghiu-Dej, the first secretary of the Communist Party. "He convinced Khrushchev to pull out his troops from Romania, and here I am, driving back and forth, delivering lettuce, carrots, and grain to the Germans. There, people are free. The harder they work, the more they get paid, so they pour their hearts into it."

"I work hard," Kostea said. "But my salary stays the same, equal to all the other physicians. They say communism achieved equality by making everyone poor."

"As a doctor, people respect you. I'm a truck driver."

Igor jumped in. "Marius, I had my own business. I mean, a restaurant that belonged to my family. The state took it. For a while I still managed it and was able to make a few bucks under the table. No need to tell that, all of us do it. Ask our doctor friend about the envelopes he receives from his patients. But Marius, if they let you take your family, would you come back?"

Marius didn't seem surprised by the question. "I don't think too much about it, but my guess is I wouldn't," he said.

The rain stopped, and the sun broke through the clouds. Marius reached under the dashboard and handed Kostea a piece of buckskin. "You should always have a buckskin. Please, wipe my windshield."

———————————

Their shoulders were touching as Kostea drove his new Fiat on his way back, with Igor in the passenger seat. They spoke about Marius and how it might be to live in the West. Kostea had doubts. Ever since he remembered, his parents had migrated from place to place, his mother complaining they had never found a true home. There was peace, war, and then peace again. Sasha and Mimi had stayed the same, but the places where they lived changed. Where one language was spoken, another language replaced it. Governments changed, borders were redrawn, farms seized, factories and restaurants nationalized. And his parents rode the merry-go-round of their times. Driving seemed the same way. The perception of space changed, and everything was on the move. Trees, telephone poles, fields, and houses passed as if you were still, while the world shifted around you. Toddy was older now. Maybe Ina could move back in with Leo, and he could ask his parents to retire and come live with them.

"Do you think Marius works for the Securitate?" Igor asked.

"I do, but I can't be sure."

"He spoke openly about defecting and about how much better it is over there."

"Counterintuitive, isn't it?"

Igor fell asleep at the spot where the sheep had crossed the highway. There was nothing special about that spot, and the sheep were gone. True or false, Marius had implied he would never defect without his family. Given the opportunity, Kostea wouldn't defect without Clara and Toddy either. Nor would he leave his parents, or even Ina, behind. His family was his balance in life, while medicine was his passion.

With Igor asleep, Kostea continued to ponder. After the debacle with Uncle Leo, he had struggled for a while. A full year, to be exact. Not being allowed to teach students was hard. Demeaning, in so many ways, a barrier in his academic career, a slap in the face. Why continue to study, why do research? On some level he considered himself lucky. At least, he could still be a doctor. Operate. Do his job. But when he felt most depressed, he could imagine the other shoe dropping. Doctor Bardu, he heard this voice in his head, you are reassigned. Go to a hamlet in Northern Moldova. To Dobruja. To some other place. Leave your family here or take them with you. Your choice. He didn't even know why he was being punished. Was it because he yelled at a nurse? Professor Dinescu did it. Other surgeons did it. Why him? Or maybe it was because he operated on Leo, a relative of his wife's. Or because Leo almost bled to death. Well, he saved him. Wasn't that telling how good he was?

In the end, the students saved Kostea, and more than anything, made him proud. Unbeknownst to him, the ones who attended the surgery were asked to provide statements. The scrub nurse had been derelict in her duties, they said. Assistant Professor Bardu might have overreacted, but he was great. As a surgeon and as a teacher. And they wanted him back. Professor Dinescu called him to his office.

"I apologize," Kostea said. "I screwed up and I learned a hard lesson. It won't happen again. I'll be better, more even-handed, controlled, at work and at home."

"You're being reinstated," Dinescu said. "Nurse Berciu is being transferred to Municipal Hospital. It's better this way."

Kostea sniffed the new-car smell. Not many people could afford to buy a car. Material possessions might not be everything, yet this one was one of a kind. He succeeded. In this new world order, where he was to be even-handed and everyone was supposed to be equal to everyone else, some were better than others, and he was definitely on the upswing.

Straight poplar trees with their trunks whitewashed flanked the winding two-lane road, long parallel shadows like piano keys painting the ground. Igor was lightly snoring, his head leaning against the door. His friend trusted his driving—and this was a good sign. Kostea smiled and imagined Clara observing him sitting behind the wheel.

Kostea parked in front of his house and studied the dashboard, his owner's manual at the ready. Igor ran in to announce their arrival. There were no other cars in the street.

The first to emerge was Ina, waving her arms high in the air, followed by their neighbor, Ana Voicu. The children came next, Toddy and two other boys, sprinting from the backyard, then two more from across the street and two more from the building at the corner. They surrounded the car but kept a respectful distance. Clara hurried down the front steps, and Igor opened the front passenger door for her, bowing and making an inviting grand gesture.

Clara nodded with a radiant smile, walked around the car, and wiped a speck of dirt from one of the fenders. "Nice color," she said, noting the car's gray hue. "Very practical."

Ana Voicu agreed, and the children took a step forward.

"Come, I'll take you all out for a spin," said Kostea. "Clara, you sit up front, but first let Toddy and two more kids get in the back. Here, let me show you." He folded down the passenger seat and slid it a few inches forward. Toddy squeezed in, followed by two other eager boys.

"Mama, he'll take you next time, and three other children," Igor told Ina.

"No need," Ina said.

Kostea drove to the end of his street, where he took a left on a wider street called Marinescu, past elegant, turn-of-the-century villas, to the massive wooden gate of the Pioneers' Palace. There, he turned right and drove under the shade of old chestnuts on Medical Heroes and by the school of medicine, his alma mater; then he took another right, on Avenue of the Heroes, the large boulevard where overcrowded city buses rumbled all day long, to the towering military academy. He made a U-turn in front of the wide plaza, veered left, and drove back home, all in maybe ten minutes. On foot, that same tour would have taken the best part of an hour.

He invited more children for a second ride and then a third. Toddy accompanied his friends each time, now proudly occupying the passenger seat. After his third round, the excitement died down, and Kostea parked the car in his backyard, negotiating the stone posts of the narrow double gates with careful guidance from Igor.

CHAPTER 14

Happiness Came at a Price

Summer 1965

On a flat rock by the side of the jetty, Kostea and Toddy were getting ready to jump in the sea. The lifeguards approached them—two young men in blue swim trunks, strongly built but timid somehow.

"We're not bothering anybody," Kostea said.

"We're not saying you are," the lifeguard who looked slightly older replied, glancing at the sea. "Swimming off the rocks is forbidden. There is a sign at the base of the jetty."

"I didn't see it."

"Well," the other lifeguard interjected softly, "it is there."

"All right, maybe it is. We'll be in the water only for a few seconds. We'll cool off and get out of your hair," Kostea insisted.

"Comrade, you can't do that," the older lifeguard said and took a step forward. He faced Kostea, although his eyes kept shifting to the sea. "If you want to cool off, go swimming like everybody else, from the beach, and stay within the limits indicated by the red buoys."

"It's too crowded," scoffed Kostea. "Look, this morning I drove all the way from Bucharest dreaming about this moment. I'm a doctor, and I had a hard week, with many emergencies. My wife is a doctor also, in charge of the entire medical system here in Eforie. And my son is a champion swimmer." Kostea turned to Toddy and grabbed him proudly by his shoulders. "He swims for the Army Club, butterfly, and he is among the fastest in the country."

"In my age group," Toddy clarified. He felt embarrassed and wished his father would stop boasting and arguing, even though parts of what he was saying were true. Toddy was on the swim team and his father had driven that morning, like he did every weekend since Clara worked for the summer as a public health doctor for that Black Sea resort. She was allocated a room in a villa and had brought Toddy and Ina along to spend time at the beach. But Toddy and Kostea had seen the huge signs on both sides of the jetty saying no swimming.

The two lifeguards were just a little older than Toddy, doing nothing but their job.

By now, a small crowd of onlookers had gathered around them. "Go swim!" a man yelled. "This place is full of interdictions."

"That's exactly the point," the older lifeguard said. "You jump in, and others will follow. You're endangering them. They might not swim as well as you do."

"That's not my problem," said Kostea.

"It is, if you're truly a doctor."

"Now I'm a liar? You rascal! Try and stop me. I'm going in." Kostea stepped sideways over his pile of clothes and stood on the edge of the rock. "Toddy, you're coming?"

Toddy didn't move.

Kostea jumped in the water, and a few people applauded.

"Grab his clothes," the older lifeguard said to the other one. "Take them into the office."

When Kostea came out of the water, the lifeguards and his clothes were gone. "Why did you let them take my things?" Kostea yelled at Toddy. "They took my wallet, my license, my keys."

"They went to the office, in the former casino building," somebody said.

Kostea shook, his eyes stormy. "My God, sometimes you're such a pushover, son." He started running toward the casino.

Toddy followed him off the jetty, reached the beach, and sat in the sand. He heard voices, the waves, and felt the salt of his tears. He was too old to cry, yet the world and his father could be unfair sometimes. He looked at the surf and started counting. Wave number one, number two, number three . . . Ina had taught him. The ninth wave was always the strongest. Find a big wave, start counting, and see.

After the ninth wave, he counted anew.

"Let's go." His father's voice stopped his daydreaming. He had his shirt on and was holding the car keys in one hand and his shorts in the other.

Toddy rose.

"They gave me a citation. Peanuts," Kostea said jovially. He grabbed Toddy by his shoulder and started walking away from the sea. "You and I, we have to stick together. Always, buddy." He continued speaking fast as if trying to make himself feel better. "They wasted their time. I bet you, if someone had drowned, they would have had no idea how to react. Instead of watching the beach, what do they do? They give me a citation. I'll call Marin and get it suspended. Fools, that's what they are. They didn't want to call their boss, this Comrade Paul, who was at the bar upstairs, most probably getting smashed."

The next weekend, after he arrived, Kostea took Toddy and Clara to see the lifeguards.

An older man in a faded shirt and a cotton cap sat on a folding chair by the office door, smoking in the shade of a long balcony above him.

"Comrade Doctor, I was expecting you, and you, Mrs. Doctor, what a pleasure," the man said, jumping to his feet.

They shook hands. The door was closed, and one could see through a large window that the office was empty.

Kostea measured the man from head to toe then opened his bag and took out a stack of booklets. "I brought these for your people. Instructions for the resuscitation of drowning victims. I hope you won't mind me doing this, Comrade . . . Paul?"

"Thank you. Yes, Paul Pârvu, that's my name. I don't mind, Comrade Doctor."

"Good. I wrote them last year, with the help of my son's swim coach. The Ministry of Health had them published." Kostea patted Toddy's head and ruffled his hair. "My son swims for the Army Club in Bucharest, and he knows everything about safety. The booklets are for general consumption, and I hope they'll come in handy."

"I'm sure they will. All of us will be happy to read them. Honestly, Comrade Doctor, you didn't have to go to the chief of police with that silly business of a citation. You and I would have sorted it out on the spot, I'm sure. I regret I wasn't available last week. Sometimes my young men can be a little too zealous. And Mrs. Doctor, excuse me, Comrade Doctor, one more time, it's an honor to meet you and thank you for what you do for our town and our community."

"And thank you for watching over *my* boys and making sure they don't do anything rash or stupid," Clara said with the light touch of an angel.

Comrade Paul seemed to be melting.

"I have something for you, Comrade Paul," Kostea said. He reached in his bag again and produced a one-liter bottle of vodka and six shot glasses. "Do you think your boys would have a drink with us and bury the past? It's the end of their shift."

"It is buried already, Comrade Doctor." Comrade Paul stepped onto the sand and blew his whistle. "Doctor," he said leaning toward Kostea, "jump off the rocks any time you feel like it, as long as it's after five."

―――――――

Where the jetty widened into a *T*, several bare-chested boys fished for gobies. Sitting next to his mother and father, Toddy watched them from a flat rock on the side. Long past its zenith, the sun cast the skewed shadow of the old casino over the sand. By now, most beachgoers had retreated, as had the lifeguards. Their rowboats lay upside down on the sand close to the water's edge.

"It's peaceful when the crowds are gone," Clara said, looking thoughtfully across the beach. Her dark-brown hair was tied up in a bun, and her eyes reflected the green of the sea.

"I'm going in," Toddy said. He stepped to the edge of the rock and jumped into the sea headfirst. As he came to the surface, he broke into a fast crawl, advanced a few yards, and flipped. "Hey," he yelled at his father, raising his head and a hand above the water. "Coming?"

"In a minute," Kostea responded.

"Go." Clara prodded him. "I love watching you two."

"You do?" Kostea asked without moving. It felt strange to be totally still while everything around him was in motion—the waves, the fluffy clouds, the seagulls cackling and floating in the air, his son swimming and splashing. "How long will this last?" he asked.

"What? Me loving the two of you?"

"No. Him asking me to go swimming with him."

"Forever," Clara said.

Kostea shook his head and got up slowly. A well-built man, a little heavier around the waist than a decade ago, he was still taller than Toddy, perhaps by two or three inches. Like his son, he took a step forward and balanced himself on the edge of the rock. "When I was his age, I had very little to do with my father," he said.

"You worked in his hospital," Clara said.

"That was later." Kostea propelled himself forward and landed in the water with a bit of a splash.

Droplets fell on Clara, who shivered. Her boys. When they jumped off the rocks, people drew together to see them swim, marveling at Toddy's agility and expert swimming styles. "Look at that little boy," they said, although Toddy was no longer that little. He was fifteen. In the fall, he'd be going to high school—a teenager through and through, still close to his mother and father.

The water was clear. Kostea came slowly up to the surface, breathed, and floated with his head submerged and hands stretched forward. Toddy jumped on him and pushed him down. Kostea let himself drop to the bottom, exhaled, and emerged next to Toddy. "C'mon, I'll race you." He knew his son was a faster swimmer, but he didn't care. This was their time, with the sea as their friend, warm and inviting.

Kostea loved the water and had taught Toddy to love it also. He had explained how to check the sea bottom in new places before jumping in, especially when the water was murky, how to use the waves to climb back on the rocks, allowing the swellings to lift you over the sharp edges, the shells and the barnacles, how to fold your clothes in a pile and tuck your valuables—keys, money, what have you—inside one of your sneakers and hide them from the many gawkers who walked up and down on the jetty.

Now he swam, freestyle, side by side with Toddy, trying hard not to fall behind, looking at his son each time he turned his head to breathe. He stopped. Toddy stopped too and waved at Clara. Then they dove, turning around each other like dolphins dancing underwater, reaching the sandy bottom and crouching on it, their foreheads touching, eyes locked, blue and green, enlarged by the sea water, air bubbling to the surface. When they came back up, Toddy rested his hand on Kostea's shoulder, like he used to do when he was younger and needed the rest and reassurance. No matter how aggravating Kostea could sometimes be, Toddy still liked to feel, through the water, the cool touch of his father's sunburned skin and the reliability of that shoulder, trusting that no matter what, it would be there, always. He also liked to see his father's prematurely white hair fan out around his head on the surface like a halo, silky and longer than his own dark hair. Toddy wanted his own hair to be longer, more stylish, but that was prohibited during the school year, and he had let it grow out since the beginning of summer.

"Hey," he yelled at Clara, "are you joining us, Mama?"

"I am, I am," Clara said and moved forward tentatively. She stepped on a submersed rock, carefully holding her balance with her hands on the dry boulders. The water came to her chest, and she pushed herself forward and swam in their direction in a soft breaststroke, smiling happily and making sure to keep her head above water.

Clara introduced Toddy to Dana, the daughter of a doctor who also worked for the summer at the resort. Dana had recently arrived and was happy to meet Toddy and accept him as companion and guide. In the water, Toddy swam circles around her, his proficiency on display. At the old casino they shared a vanilla ice cream and a lemonade. They talked about books.

Dana was a year older and a couple of inches shorter than Toddy. She was blond, had blue eyes and a beautiful face. Toddy was reading when she got up from her beach towel to rearrange her swimsuit. She wiped the sand off her arms and thighs and passed her index fingers along the hem of her bikini bottom, from the back to the crotch, slightly lifting the material off her sunbaked skin. Toddy, who looked up at that very moment, noticed the shadow between her legs. The glance lasted a fraction of a second, but it had such a profound effect on him that he remained silent for the rest of the day. Unable to erase the lure of that glimpse, he decided he was in love with Dana.

Late afternoon, after work, Clara came to the beach to join her son. From the high edge of the shore, she saw Toddy and Dana below. They were reading, side by side. They weren't touching or kissing or talking to each other. Yet something in their frozen nearness was so intimate, so moving and telling, that Clara couldn't help but be surprised. Their silence was like the serene peak of an iceberg floating on the ocean. She realized that what truly mattered was what loomed beneath. She watched them for a while and decided to walk away. Her son was crossing into the beautiful years between childhood and adulthood, when the world would become his stage. Conflict and fulfillment would mark that path. As Clara's understanding of that moment grew in her heart, a youthful spring developed in her departing step.

Kostea arrived Saturday evening. He had driven two hundred kilometers to be with them, and the next evening, he had to drive back. Clara cherished her time with him and their son, but Sunday morning she was called in to work.

"Don't worry," Kostea whispered to her. "Dr. Max happens to be in Constanța, only twenty minutes from here. While you're at work, I'll visit with him. I'll be back before you know it. Toddy can go to the beach, and we will join him in the afternoon and go swimming together."

Clara returned from work, but Kostea wasn't there. Ina had gone to the market, had come back, and now Clara helped her unpack. That new car, along with all the benefits, was a reason for worries. She imagined the tiny Fiat, smashed like a raisin on the side of the road.

Toddy was at the beach.

Then Kostea returned, relaxed and happy. "We had a fabulous morning. Talked politics and I lost track of time."

"You knew I'd be worried," Clara said.

"Oh?" Kostea exclaimed, surprised. "We discussed Paris. There is a conference there next spring. We want to go and wonder if they'll grant us permission."

Clara said, "No."

"Things are changing. Getting approvals is easier."

"Your husband's a dreamer," Ina chimed in. "I live in the real world."

"I'm so glad you have an opinion," Kostea said.

His condescending tone rubbed Clara the wrong way. She was tired and had witnessed the back-and-forth between her husband and mother for years. It was sudden, but somehow enough was enough. "You go to Paris. I'm going back to work," she said and left.

———————

Toddy gathered his towel, his shirt, and his sneakers and slowly walked home, surprised that his parents hadn't shown up.

He found Ina bent over a small makeshift stove they had in their room and Kostea seemingly sleeping, fully dressed, and facing the wall.

"Where is Mom?" Toddy whispered.

"At work," Ina said.

Hearing Toddy, Kostea turned. "Want to go to the jetty and jump off the rocks?"

"I waited for you," Toddy said.

"He forgot," Ina said. She snatched the skillet off the burner, causing oil to spill onto it, and a tall, yellow flame shot straight up.

"You'll set the house on fire," Kostea said.

"I know what I'm doing." Ina looked at Toddy. "Your father was late, and your mother was worried sick. She thought he had a car accident. When he arrived, with that smug smile on his face, she got angry and went back to work."

"I'm glad you're explaining this to my son as if I'm not here. It will do all of us a bundle of good." Kostea's voice cut through the air like ice.

Ina switched the gas off, and the aroma of fried chicken filled the room. "Toddy, sit down. Time to eat."

Toddy sat.

"When you were delayed, you could have phoned Clara," Ina told Kostea and squinted at him.

"I called her at work, and there was no answer." Kostea sat up in bed.

"You could have called our super. You've done that before."

They had no phone in the room, but the building super had one in his office. The tenants, most of whom worked for the resort, used it to talk to their families at home and in case of emergency.

"I didn't have the number on me."

"That's your fault," Ina said. She plopped a piece of chicken and some potatoes on a plate and passed it to Toddy. "Eat!"

Toddy made a long face.

"Don't start with me," Ina said. "I spent the whole morning shopping and cooking for you."

"If the child doesn't like it, he doesn't have to eat," Kostea said.

"Now you're an expert in children's nutrition, aren't you?"

"Yes, when it comes to my son."

Toddy hated when Kostea argued with his grandmother and always took her side. He started eating.

Ina nodded and pointed at him. "See? He likes it!" She wiped her hand on her apron and arranged her white hair. She asked Kostea, "Why were you so late?"

"You know why. We talked about going to Paris."

"Is that a good reason to get Clara upset?"

"It's exciting," he said.

"And your wife isn't?"

The look on Kostea's face turned indolent. If his wife had walked out that day, so could he. "I don't have to take this," he announced. He stood, walked calmly to the door, and opened it. "You know what? I'm leaving. I'm driving to Bucharest. Tell Clara to call me tonight if she thinks we should talk."

"You call her at the super," Ina said.

Kostea pulled the door shut after him.

"Dad!" Toddy yelled.

"Go to hell," Ina mumbled under her breath.

———————

"Grandma told him to go to hell," Toddy said when his mother walked in the door.

The look in Clara's eyes was stormy. "I would have said the same thing." She saw Toddy's lips tighten, and she regretted her words. "Maybe not," she whispered to him. After all, their squabble that morning had not been such a big deal. "Mama," she asked later, nervously extinguishing her cigarette, "what time is it?"

Ina checked her wristwatch. "Almost six."

"It's been hardly three hours. He needs at least four to get home. I think I might have overreacted. Don't you?"

"You didn't. He was his usual self."

"Mama, don't be like this." Clara crossed her arms and went to the window. No matter what, Ina would take her side. That wasn't always all right, and a thought crept ever so slowly into her mind. She pushed the thought aside, but it persisted. If Ina couldn't be more accommodating, perhaps it was time for her to move out. In truth, now that Toddy had grown and could be left on his own, they could manage quite well without her.

She turned around to the room. Look at Toddy, her boy! He was tall, strong, and sunburned. His hair was thick from the salt in the sea. And he seemed in love.

Still, Clara felt more at peace with Ina at home with Toddy. Teenage years were complicated. But Ina was suffering too, was she not? Perhaps she'd be happier in her own place, without Kostea's constant nagging. She had lived alone before. In Kishinev. Toddy could visit her. She would come to their apartment from time to time, for a nice lunch or dinner.

Be a guest for a change. They could buy her a studio in one of the high-rise buildings that had cropped up in the new neighborhoods all around Bucharest. And she could take a cat or a dog—an old lady with a pet.

Clara gave Ina a quick, guilty look, as if Ina could read her mind. She felt ashamed. Her mother had dedicated years of her life to raising Toddy and had cooked and cleaned for them. How ugly to think in terms of her usefulness. How unjust.

She took a step forward and caught Ina's hand. "I hope he isn't speeding," she said. "People speed when they're angry, you know."

Toddy looked up from his book. "He wasn't angry," he said.

Clara smiled at him. "Come here. Come here, baby. I'm sorry we ruined your day."

"It's all right," Toddy said and dropped his book on the bed. He didn't like being called a baby. Yet he came closer to Clara and his grandmother and pulled them both to his chest. He stayed glued to them in his embrace, taking in the slight hint of tobacco and their warmth. "I'll go for a walk," he said.

Outside, Toddy took a big breath and let the air out slowly. He felt the tension subside. His mother and father loved each other and loved him very much. He was the apple of their eyes. His dad had a difficult temperament, and Clara had always tried to help Toddy understand his father better. Work at the hospital caused stress, and Kostea's outbursts were a reaction to all the pressure and responsibility he had for his patients' health. His gentle, tender mother was good at finding excuses for Kostea and cushioning the severity of his tantrums. That happened a lot.

By the time Toddy reached the old casino, its shadow extended all the way over the beach and the jetty. In front of Belona Hotel, there was a small lake. The water mirrored the blue-gray evening sky. A few seagulls floated on it. Never before had his father left because of a fight.

Toddy walked along the side streets where the locals lived. Small houses were tucked in the back of fenced-in yards full of blooming woodland tobacco flowers that filled the air with the unmistakable fragrance of night. His parents would make up if for no other reason than because they loved him so much. He understood. He was no longer a kid, and Dana was not his first girlfriend. Last year, in middle school, he had fallen for Giorgiana, a girl with a soft body like Dana's and captivating golden-brown doe eyes. She had flirted with him and touched his face with her cold hands. Honest hands, she had said. With Dana, he was more direct. They had gone to the open-air cinema to see *In Ginocchio da Te*, a love story with Gianni Morandi, and he had kissed Dana on the lips.

When Toddy returned, Ina was alone, and the transistor radio was on.

"Your mother's upstairs, visiting with the Pascu sisters," she said.

Like Clara, the Pascu sisters worked at the resort for the season.

Toddy was falling asleep when Clara walked in. He didn't open his eyes but overheard his mother spill out in a happy and somewhat mangled fashion that she had called Kostea several times and that he had arrived home all right. He had apologized and promised they would have a wonderful time together the next time he came down. She then said the sisters had offered her cognac. To quell her worries, they had said. The three of them had finished the bottle, and she was really drunk. By the silence that followed, Toddy guessed Ina didn't approve. Then Clara said, "I'm sick," and rushed down the hall to the bathroom they shared with the other tenants on their floor.

Such was life, Toddy concluded. Happiness came at a price.

CHAPTER 15

They Had No Idea

1965 to 1967

Driving home, Kostea made a conscientious effort not to think about Clara and his mother-in-law. The prospect of going to Paris loomed large in his mind. He had traveled to Moscow and Leningrad, but a trip to the City of Lights would be different. Romanians dreamed about visiting Paris, their cultural Mecca. They learned French, cooked French food, and shed secret tears looking at photographs of the Louvre, Notre-Dame, and the Eiffel Tower.

Romania was changing, and the moment seemed ripe. Lately, at Kostea's Party meetings, the secretary used language like "the principle of noninterference in the domestic affairs of our country" and "autonomous foreign policy." The words were meant to show a break from Soviet dominance. A decade after the Hungarian uprising when Romania had acted in lockstep with the Soviet Union, the servile nature of its relationship with the larger and more powerful sister in the East had decreased to almost nonexistence. The former president, Gheorghe Gheorghiu-Dej, had championed the new approach. Upon his death, among thousands of his countrymen, Kostea had watched as Gheorghiu-Dej's funeral procession moved at a snail's pace up the hill and across the plaza in front of the military academy. Surrounded by white chrysanthemums, the immobile face of the deceased leader suggested the impotence of the dead rather than the idea of a new and independent era in the history of Romania. His successor, Nicolae Ceaușescu, continued and enhanced the policy of independence, to the delight of the West and the majority of Romanians who hated the Russians.

Kostea didn't hate the Russians. He disliked their bureaucracy and politics, but he loved the people, their songs, and their exuberant drinking habits. His ability to speak the language flawlessly brought their troubled, yearning souls closer to his own. He admired the majesty of Moscow and Leningrad, the cities he had visited, and appreciated his friendships with his Russian colleagues and the valuable professional exchanges.

Kostea's conversation earlier that day with Dr. Max had reflected his ambivalence, and together they had wondered whether the political changes were real or simply the strategy of a new leader trying to play both sides, the East and the West. The openness of their conversation was something new. Suddenly people voiced their opinions more freely and were less afraid to oppose the Party line.

"Ceaușescu is just a figurehead," Max had said, sipping his coffee from a chipped porcelain cup. "He is ruthless and cunning, but his policies have no philosophical underpinning. The Party elders elected him as a placeholder until they settle their power shuffle after the death of Gheorghiu-Dej. The new independence from the Russians is not real. We are their marionettes. They need a so-called maverick to keep communication open with the West. And while the likes of you and me should remain skeptical, I see no reason why we shouldn't enjoy the benefits of this political change."

"And go to a conference in Paris," Kostea had jumped in.

"Absolutely," Max had said. "The country is opening. They released most of the political prisoners. Look at what's happening in literature. For the first time in decades, they're publishing Kafka, Proust, and Camus. They're translating Freud and Sartre. They even published some of your beloved Russians that none of us had read before, like Bulgakov and Babel. New books are coming out at a frenetic pace, as if we were trying to catch up to history."

A few books rarely changed anything, Kostea had thought, except, maybe, the thin crust of intellectuals at the top, but if there were freedom to publish, then freedom to travel must come next, and Paris had become suddenly real, worth dreaming about.

Paris overwhelmed Kostea: the people, the stately avenues and twisted medieval lanes, the traffic. He wanted to touch, taste, and discover. He wished Clara were there to share his joy. Yet everywhere he went, especially when in the company of other doctors participating in the conference—French, German, Swiss—he experienced an uncharacteristic shyness and a distinct sense of inferiority. He kept telling himself that he was their equal. He was a medical doctor just like them, as accomplished as they were, maybe more accomplished. Like a layer of grime, the lack of money sullied his enjoyment and made him feel like a second-rate citizen.

His presentation at the conference focused on his research. It was translated into several languages as he spoke, and it garnered many compliments. Speranța was a small hospital, but the approach developed by Dinescu allowed his doctors to reach a level of expertise their Western colleagues admired. The number of case studies Kostea reviewed was surprisingly large and varied, giving strong credence to his conclusions. "We are more narrowly specialized," the doctors told Kostea after his presentation and offered him their business cards. Kostea didn't have any and supplied his address and phone number by writing them on cocktail napkins or the back page of the conference brochure.

His father's brother, Uncle Misha, lived in Paris. Kostea was hoping blood would turn out to be thicker than water. A monetary gift from his uncle—any amount—would be very helpful. The conference concluded on Thursday, his return flight was on Sunday, and midday Friday, Kostea met Uncle Misha at a bistro near the railway station.

When they had spoken on the phone—in Russian—his uncle had sounded a lot like Kostea's father. But he had not invited Kostea to his home, and Kostea took it as a bad sign.

Kostea arrived early. He told the waiter he was expecting someone and refused to accept even a glass of water. His father and Uncle Misha hadn't seen each other in almost fifty years—complete strangers to each other, really. Misha was six years younger than Sasha, a huge difference growing up, which meant, most likely, they had never been close.

When Misha walked through the door, Kostea was shocked. Misha's physical resemblance to Sasha was uncanny, and in certain ways soothing: the tall forehead, thinning hair, and brown eyes, the straight Bardu nose, and the same stature. Perhaps Misha was slightly shorter and slimmer. In a jovial mood—he was a stockbroker and had had a good month at the stock exchange, according to his own admission—Misha displayed from the very beginning an unguarded and accepting attitude, much warmer than Kostea had expected. Even his clothes were in the same style as his brother's: a plaid shirt, a sleeveless knitted vest, loose brown trousers hanging low over his well-worn loafers.

They talked about family, politics, and many other things. It was an easy conversation, and time went by quickly. They drank a few glasses of wine and ate a delicious coq au vin with crusty fresh bread. The similarity between the two brothers washed over Kostea like a warm bath.

"I'm sorry I didn't invite you to dinner at my place," Misha said. "Liliana Vasilievna has a cold, and she's in no mood for cooking." He had never been married and did not have children. He had met Liliana at an age when loneliness could be devastating. Sex was no longer the main issue, and they had been together for the last five years.

Kostea detected a subtle regret in his uncle's voice, but he couldn't be sure.

"We'll have you over next time," Misha added. "Because there will be a next time. Correct, dear Kostea?"

"Without a doubt," Kostea said enthusiastically.

"There is something else," Misha continued. "I wanted to buy you and my brother a gift, but I didn't know what to get. And since I'm a practical man and I know how things are in Romania, I decided to offer you money. It's not much, five hundred new francs for you and the same for Sasha. I hope you'll be able to put the money to good use in Paris, for both of you. Or buy something for yourself and give my brother his half in cash if you think it is better." Kostea thanked him, and they hugged and kissed once on each cheek, Russian style, French style.

There had been two brothers, Kostea thought. Two boys growing up in the Crimea. His father, Sasha, had become a doctor. He had gotten married and had cared for his family as best he could. His entire life, he had fled the Soviet menace and had now reached, perhaps, the last stretch of that road. Uncle Misha had fled to Paris. He simply went there, along with many other Russian emigrees, at a time when it was still possible, while the rest of his family, trapped in Romania, envied and admired him from afar, oblivious of the loneliness he was experiencing, the loneliness of the immigrant, unassimilated and without a purpose—a good day at the stock exchange, a bad one. Misha had found someone with whom to share his loneliness, not a French person to help him immerse himself in his new country but a Russian woman who ate borscht for lunch and understood his jokes.

Was his munificent gift to Kostea the result of his generosity or of a desire to be liked and accepted back into a long-lost family? There was no way of telling, except that the amount seemed astonishing. A thousand francs exceeded Kostea's wildest expectations. It was more than the allowance he had received for meals, hotel, and miscellaneous expenses.

He couldn't return with hard currency to Romania. He would have to declare it, explain its source, and be forced to exchange it at the ridiculous official rate. No, he would spend it all here, enjoy it, and offer Sasha the equivalent in Romanian currency for his part of the gift. His father would most likely reply, with his typical bonhomie, "Keep the money; you need it more than I do."

Emboldened by the extra cash, Kostea invited Dr. Max to Moulin Rouge that night. They knew their male friends at home would ask if they had been there. When the waiter handed him the menu, Kostea realized that his fortune was not quite as large as he had perceived it to be. They ordered a Dubonnet au citron and some peanuts and nursed their drinks throughout the show, which was both provocative and disappointing. But they could not have enjoyed it at home. The arts and all forms of entertainment under the communists had been censored and sanitized of anything erotic or daring. No Moulin Rouge could exist in Bucharest.

At the guesthouse where they stayed, they opened a bottle of Romanian brandy and burned their throats toasting the City of Lights. In the morning, Kostea bought a few shirts for Toddy, a beautiful silver-and-pearl bracelet for Clara, and cashmere sweaters for Mimi and Sasha.

Kostea returned to Paris eight months later. Having been permitted to travel once to the West and having returned, obtaining permission to travel again was easier. Kostea presented another paper at a medical conference, and Misha invited him to his apartment for dinner. Liliana Vasilievna was a pleasant lady in her seventies. There were also four older Russian exiles with titles of nobility, who slurped their soup and spoke briefly about how Leonid Brezhnev had taken the power from Nikita Khrushchev without killing him, then spent the rest of the evening debating the role of the Tsarist cavalry prior to the October Revolution. After dinner, Liliana took

Kostea to her closet and handed him her slightly worn mink coat: "For Clara," she said. "I'm too old to wear it."

A few months later, Kostea presented a paper in Toulouse, and then he was invited again, this time to attend a conference in Zurich, Switzerland. He decided to drive, so Clara could accompany him.

The Securitate officer in charge of their passport applications wondered if they might defect and sent their applications to his superior, who sent them further up for approval. A certain Colonel Spițeru, three levels up, declared emphatically: "There is nothing to worry about. We have their son."

The Bardus drove into Switzerland from Austria and were getting ready to cross the Alps' Flüela Pass when a trucker warned them to be careful at an elevation of 2,300 meters in such a small vehicle. Kostea ignored the advice and looked at his Fiat with pride.

The weather cooperated, and after they made it across without problems, they stopped in Davos to pick up bottled water and snacks. Kostea waited in the car. Clara entered a supermarket for the first time in her life and burst into tears. "It wasn't the mountains that impressed me in Switzerland," she later told her friends. "And it wasn't the cathedrals or the architecture. What I liked best was the supermarket. It was the small, everyday things—the way they packaged a chicken breast, the freshness of the parsley, the shiny radishes, and the beautiful mushrooms. The cleanliness. The way they displayed their fresh seafood on glittering ice."

Their travels changed Clara and Kostea in subtle and not-so-subtle ways. They dressed better and showed more confidence in themselves. Clara was always comparing the puny, half-empty stores she entered on her way home from work to the shiny, clean, and well-stocked Swiss supermarket. In Kostea's case, the change also brought about a new arrogance. When he talked to car owners, he began his conversations with a statement about "the time I drove across the Flüela Pass in Switzerland," and his interlocutors shrugged in wonder. When he talked to his students

146

or to younger doctors, he made sure to mention the research he had presented abroad.

Maximilian Negru, known to most people as Dr. Max, applied for and received permission in a record five months to leave Romania for Israel with his family. Lucky, Kostea thought. Yet he was saddened and surprised by the news, which he found out at the awkward meeting where they voted to strip Dr. Max of his Party membership. The procedure was swift. The secretary announced the topic as a footnote to an otherwise long and boring agenda and asked those opposed to Dr. Max's losing his membership to raise their hand. Nobody did. Dr. Max was the only doctor at Speranța whom Kostea considered a friend. He had known him the longest, had spent many evenings together with him, and had relied on his professional advice on many occasions. He knew Max was Jewish but had forgotten he had changed his last name from Schwartz (*black* in German) to Negru (*black* in Romanian). Kostea guessed it had been their trip to Paris that had caused Max to decide it was time to seek a better life on the other side of the Iron Curtain. Max had not shared his emigration plans with Kostea—people rarely did, even among friends—and now he'd be gone, leaving Kostea with nice memories and a void.

Dr. Max's action was a sure sign that borders and walls, be they political, cultural, or physical, were becoming porous.

Clara had heard through the grapevine that Vera, Igor's former wife with whom they had lost contact, had married a Swabian man and immigrated to West Germany. The Swab had two sons from a previous marriage. In the future, Kostea and Clara might want to visit them, so Kostea urged Clara to get Vera's new address and keep in touch.

People whispered that the Americans paid Ceaușescu dollars under the table for every person or family allowed to leave, Jews and Germans especially. Human rights and free emigration were the topic of the day. It was the mid-1960s, and nobody in Romania genuinely believed in communism anymore. Nobody in the world did, for that matter. It was all about dominance. The Russians and the Americans. Propaganda. Equilibrium.

When the subject of leaving the country came up in conversations, given his travels and experience, Kostea offered a diplomatic answer. Yes, he could see himself living over there. As a doctor, he would make a lot of money. He'd learn the language and adjust to the customs of the new country. But he would always remain a transplant with superficial roots. Retain his accent. Like his parents, who spoke Romanian with a Russian accent. No matter how hard he'd try, he would possess a hidden duality, with the permanent imprint of his origin on the inside. He had seen his uncle, a man he held in the highest esteem, now approaching the end of his life in a country like France, in a city like Paris, surrounded by émigrés like himself and discussing the events of fifty years ago as if they had occurred yesterday. As if they still mattered! Hell, what was an immigrant then but a person with his legs in two countries and his heart riven?

———————

After his conference ended, Kostea and Clara took the ferry to Capri, visited the village of Anacapri, and by late afternoon, descended to the port to find a rowboat for Grotta Azzurra. The crowds were gone, and the skippers were pulling their rowboats to safety. The sea was pounding the white cliffs. A chalkboard announced a fare that seemed excessive.

Kostea approached a skipper who stood smoking by himself, hoping for a late customer. "How much will you charge us?"

The skipper indicated with his head the price on the chalkboard.

"Could you give us a discount? I'm a doctor from Romania, and I don't have that much money," Kostea said in stilted Italian that resembled in many ways his native language.

"You're a Dottore and you don't have money?" probed the skipper with incredulity.

"Yes," Kostea answered. "We are from *un paese comunista*." The truth was they had some money they had borrowed from a man who was the Italian relative of an acquaintance of theirs in Bucharest. But it was for a gas water heater they intended to buy, tie to the roof rack of their car, and take back to Romania. Tudor Voicu, their neighbor, had promised to install it in the cellar to supply hot water for their entire building. Kostea knew there wasn't enough to pay for a boat ride to the grotto as well.

"Un paese comunista," the skipper repeated thoughtfully, took a long drag from his cigarette, and blew the smoke into the air.

"We want to see your beautiful grotto. Let me row the boat," Kostea insisted.

"No," said the skipper. "*Niente soldi, niente grotta.*"

"Then we'll swim," Kostea threatened.

"Maybe you will," Clara muttered.

The skipper threw his cigarette onto the cliffs and walked away. Kostea turned and saw a path between the rocks descending to the sea. It was steep, but Kostea didn't hesitate. Silently Clara followed him. Kostea undressed and eased himself into the water.

"Be careful," Clara said.

The sea felt silky, warm. A few hundred yards across the bay, the opening of the grotto appeared and disappeared under the swells like the mouth of a monster. Kostea would have liked to have Toddy along. The farther he swam from Clara, the less secure he felt. Inside the grotto, the waves splashed against the walls and resonated like voices in a cathedral. He heard his heartbeat and the rush of his breathing. Like an iridescent veil, the beautiful, incredible blue light delighted him and strangled him at the same time. He swam out into the open. He needed air.

They drove back to Rome the next morning and spent the day walking through the streets of the city. As they stood holding each other on

Ponte Vittorio Emanuele looking at Castel Sant'Angelo, the sun lowered itself over the river.

"This is so beautiful. I think I could live here," Clara said.

"Are you serious?" They advanced a few steps and stopped again. Kostea looked at her. "What about Toddy?"

Clara laughed. "It was just a thought. I was daydreaming."

"You know, if we decide to defect and stay in Italy, we should be able to get him out through one of those humanitarian organizations in Helsinki or Geneva."

"Would you ever take such a risk? We might need years," Clara said.

"You brought it up. You know, other people have done it."

"Yes, but they were desperate. We're not. We have everything we need. We have our parents there, and as far as I am concerned, our lives are getting better. I am sure defecting crossed your mind in France and Switzerland, but you came home, to your family."

"Are you saying you love your life with me, Clara?"

"I do." She lingered and looked at the water. "Kostea, if Toddy would ever want to live in the West, would you consider it?"

"That would change everything, and I'd follow him to the end of the world."

"I feel the same, and I love you."

And that was it—their talk on defecting. They bought the boiler, strapped it to the roof rack like hunters bringing home their venison and drove back through Yugoslavia. Never before had they been more satisfied going home than on that occasion. The future looked bright and crystal clear, as if Kostea had captured the sunrays reflected inside the blue grotto. In other words, their lives were about to change, and they had no idea.

CHAPTER 16

A Man at the Peak

Spring 1968

Kostea was impressed and happy when his boss, Professor Dinescu, was appointed by Ceaușescu as the new minister of health. Dinescu's influence grew, and so, Kostea hoped, would his own. Dinescu had to grapple with the country's immense health system problems, and he led the medical team in charge of Ceaușescu's family. He continued to hold his position as director of Speranța Hospital and his professorship at the Bucharest School of Medicine. And he promoted Kostea to lecturer.

A wood-paneled office suite and two secretaries were permanently at Dinescu's disposal on the fourth floor of the Council of Ministers Building in Victoria Square. His official car was now a shiny black Mercedes. He arrived at the hospital early in the morning and left at about ten to be driven to the Ministry. Ileana, his assistant and longtime mistress, was always by his side. His wife accepted her with proud resignation. His new cruel joke was that now that he had finally made it and could commandeer any young woman he wanted, he was stuck with his old lover. Ileana was twenty years his junior. The professor liked to take a noon break at her apartment. The doctors would sometimes ask if he planned to return to the hospital for the afternoon rounds. He would look at Ileana knowingly and answer, "If I can, I won't. If I can't, I will." His statement would be rewarded with an obsequious outburst of laughter. The professor was now a man in his sixties, afflicted by a benign oversized prostate, a condition well understood in a hospital that specialized in urology.

Kostea laughed with the others and subscribed loudly to the idea that a true man must philander, while he was telling himself that he was just going along with the gang, in no way condoning such behavior. His previous reflections on the issue impressed upon him that, unless he was smarter than everybody, sleeping around had consequences. He loved Clara too much to risk causing her pain, and he knew that, unlike the professor's wife, Clara wouldn't take such betrayal silently if she found out about it. She would be devastated, and he had no doubt that she would end their marriage.

After his promotion to lecturer, Kostea was also assigned a new office at the school of medicine, across the alley from the main study hall. He let his hand linger on the impressive antique-style desk and chair, two of the few surviving original pieces of furniture acquired by Carol Davila, who had founded the school in the second half of the nineteenth century. Against the wall there was a tall bookcase. A large brown sofa and two deep leather armchairs were across the room, framing a Persian rug. Once closed and, if necessary, locked, the solid oak door was an impenetrable barrier separating the office on one side and the hallway, bursting with eager and often unrestrained students, on the other side. Through two high windows shaded by old poplar trees, Kostea could see the red clay of the nearby tennis courts and the back corner of the garden full of white, yellow, and red rosebushes. It was in that same spot that he had unexpectedly run into Clara at the beginning of the Second World War, almost a quarter of a century earlier.

Kostea had turned forty-six. As he liked to say, he was a man at the peak of his powers. He had written and presented over a hundred medical papers, had published two books under his name and several in collaboration with others, and had performed thousands of surgeries. Under his guidance, hundreds of students passed through the difficult fourth and fifth years of medical school on their way to becoming doctors. Recently, he committed to producing an exhaustive study, a full-length book tentatively entitled *The Pathology of the Ureter*. That, everybody understood, would entail a major effort.

To the list of conferences he had attended, he added Warsaw, Prague, and Baku. He went for the fourth time to Paris, and then for a fifth time.

———————

The Pathology took up most of Kostea's energy and attention. He worked on it in the mornings before going to the hospital and during the day after surgery and before his afternoon rounds. He wrote chapters at school after seminars and lectures and then at home in the evenings.

Clara tried to help him on Sundays and on weekdays after dinner. He was irritable and distant.

"I'm dead tired," Kostea told Clara one day after his afternoon rounds at the hospital. "I need to rest. Wake me in twenty minutes."

"Go sleep," said Clara.

"In the meantime, since you can read my handwriting, take these scribbles, and type them neatly. It's not much, only three pages. We'll have to check them over against this article from Professor Nekrasov, whom I met in Moscow."

The typewriter sat on the floor in Kostea's study, and every level surface was buried under papers.

"What shall I do with all this?" asked Clara.

"Move them around. What do I care?" He watched Clara remove a pile of documents from his chair, shuffle other piles on his desk, and lift the bulky typewriter. Then she sat down and put on her glasses. He knew she thought the glasses made her look older. He left, and from the other room he overheard her tentative typing, with two fingers. There were some pauses in between, and he guessed she was either reading what she had typed or smoking. He got undressed but couldn't fall asleep. Too much to do, too many work-related worries. He tiptoed back into the study and stood silently in his white underwear behind Clara.

She must have sensed his presence because she pointed at two pages she had finished. He picked them up and threw them back at her. "It's useless."

"What's wrong?" she mumbled and laid her palms on the keyboard. The fingers of her right hand were stained by nicotine.

"Four typos in the first paragraph and all these other corrections. Plus, we type everything with a carbon copy."

"You didn't say anything about a carbon copy," Clara said softly.

Her voice irritated him, always calm and accommodating, meant to exhaust his ire. "I can't believe you didn't know. I've been working at this for a year."

"It's a pigsty in here. You're making a mess everywhere, and you're being difficult," Clara said.

"Oh yeah? And you're becoming your mother."

"Leave my mother out of this! You terrify her, and she tries to clean up after you without making a fuss. So, stop it."

Kostea stretched, indifference imprinted on his face, then slid his right hand under the elastic of his underwear and scratched himself.

Clara sighed. "I'll retype this. I want to help you, not start an argument."

"Forget it," he said. "I'll give the notes to Madam Potzi tomorrow. She's better."

"Splash some water on your face and put on your pants," Clara said. "I'll make you some coffee." She pushed the chair back and walked toward the kitchen.

He noticed she was on the verge of tears, felt bad about it, and decided to follow her in order to continue to explain his mood to her. And apologize, if necessary.

"Was he yelling at you?" he heard Ina ask and stopped behind the open kitchen door. Normally he would barge right in, but not this time. Better to overhear what his wife and mother-in-law were saying. In fact, he had surreptitiously listened to what Ina had said about him at least once before.

"No, Mama," he heard Clara's voice. "He is passionate about his work, and this is how he comes across, like yelling."

"Yeah," Ina said. "He thinks he's God."

There was a pause, the water running in the sink, the coffee pot hitting the burner.

"Maybe some other doctors think they're God. Not Kostea. He cares about his patients. He is a good doctor, and he is working hard to become a professor."

"I understand his ambitions," Ina said, "but trust me, he has changed. You say he cares. If he does, it's only about himself. Don't pretend you don't see it, Clara."

"I don't like it when you talk this way, Mama."

Another short pause was followed by the sound of a striking match. Someone was smoking.

"What can I do?" he heard Ina say. "He leaves his things all over. God forbid I touch them. Madam Potzi hangs on by the skin of her teeth. Have you seen the mess in his car lately?"

"It's just a phase."

"It's worse. He thinks he is so special."

Curiosity kept Kostea in his spot. And yes, he was that special. With Dinescu the minister of health, and him working directly for Dinescu, hierarchically speaking he was high up, important. No time to clean up after himself, worry about minutiae. He'd always been impulsive, choleric even. He knew it, and they knew it. It was hard enough to control himself at work. Couldn't he be himself at home, with his own family? And he had guts. He didn't hesitate to break the rules and take his chances. That's why he operated on Leo the way he did, or drove across the Alps, swam to the Grotto. Just look at what he did for them, his family. Look at this apartment, at his car. The beach, his trips abroad, the benefits they were enjoying.

"I've been thinking, Mama," he heard Clara say. "We have more money now, and Toddy has grown. You can't go back to Leo, but maybe it's time for me to buy you a studio apartment. You could live there and come be with us every day if you want, but not have to deal with Kostea."

That was unexpected and Kostea stepped forward.

The ash at the tip of Ina's cigarette was long. She didn't see Kostea and brought the cigarette to her lips. Her hand shook. "So, you want me to go," she said softly.

Kostea didn't think it was fair, but life rarely was. He understood what Ina represented to Clara and appreciated all she had done for them and for Toddy. In general, he wanted the best for her, but truth be told, she had been a constant irritation in his life. He couldn't come home and relax, be himself. His mother-in-law was always there, and he always needed to be on his toes. With her gone, he would have a chance at controlling his moods better. And he wanted his parents to come live with him. Especially now, given his father's heart condition. When they came, they could move into Ina's room. The fact that Clara understood this was genius. Practical. And it wasn't as if they were kicking Ina out. On the contrary, they were rewarding her for her sacrifice. And they would stay in touch, perhaps closer than ever.

The one other time he had eavesdropped on Ina she was talking to Toddy. "Now that you are almost an adult, your father wants to be with you because he wants to have fun," she said. "You are entertainment to him. In your presence, he feels younger, and he can do things. But he wouldn't sacrifice anything for you, because all he wants is to have you for himself."

Overhearing this sent Kostea's mind spinning. Wasn't that a mean thing to say to his son? And not true. Kostea would make any sacrifice for Toddy. And yes, he wanted Toddy for himself. How else does one love another human being? Your wife, your son? How, if not for yourself? If not *through* yourself? Everything exists through what one perceives and sees. *I* and *me* are at the center of everything. Without *me* as a being, there is nothing. Those who say otherwise are lying. What is jealousy, if not the desire to keep the loved one for oneself?

Still, Kostea was feeling guilty when it came to Toddy. With his work and travel, Kostea didn't give Toddy enough of his time. Each morning, Kostea left before Toddy was up and returned late, when Toddy was doing his homework or was out roaming the neighborhood with his buddies. Whenever he could, he tried to engage Toddy, though mostly in activities Kostea favored, like tennis. Or he took Toddy with him on errands he had to run anyway.

Sometimes Kostea would show up unexpectedly in the afternoon. If Toddy were home, he would summon him. "C'mon, Toddy, the weather is great. Let's go play tennis," or, "Come with me to the service station. I need an oil change, and we can talk while we're waiting." Toddy looked for reasons to say no, and if he couldn't find one, he would follow his father, sulking.

Kostea would notice and would not understand.

"I'd rather be with my friends," Toddy told him one day. "Why is this so hard to comprehend?"

"You will have many friends in your lifetime, and only one father who loves you."

"But this has nothing to do with love," said Toddy.

CHAPTER 17

She Complicated His Life

Kostea's new office at the school of medicine was as messy as his study at home. But there it didn't bother anybody. Like most people who didn't keep things orderly, Kostea could always find whatever he was looking for very quickly. He knew in which pile and how deep in the pile this or that document was buried. On the rare occasions he failed, and especially in the presence of others, he exploded, toppling his piles, papers and office supplies flying into the air.

His students came to his office, sorted his papers for him, organized his files, and indexed his reference materials—an opportunity for them to forge a closer relationship with a successful doctor. He enjoyed their presence and burst with pride when they addressed him as Professor.

In his presence, at school or at the hospital, the female students tended to drift closer to each other and giggle. Kostea's youthful demeanor and his tanned face stood in surprising contrast with his prematurely white hair and his academic position. His blue eyes looked like scalpel steel when he was in surgery, but otherwise they were playful and friendly. When he talked to them about subjects outside medicine or joked around, they could almost forget who he was, were it not for the leonine white mane that reminded them to maintain a respectful distance. The students admired his self-confidence and his ability to focus. Even his occasional outbursts were revealing to them, and they excused them, whether they were aimed at the medical staff or his disciples. They recognized his passion and thought it was worth emulating him, because he was showing them his humanity.

He relied most on Mircea Popescu and Maya Merinde to keep his paperwork in order. Mircea was a studious fourth-year student. He had played tennis in high school, and Kostea, who had gained a few pounds over the years, loved playing tennis with him.

Maya, also in her fourth year, was older by almost a decade than her colleagues. She had worked as a nurse before applying to medical school and had been married to a naval officer. She had a daughter.

Kostea hadn't asked for her help, but she volunteered. Capable and diligent, she worked with imperturbable effectiveness. When Kostea threw one of his temper tantrums, she waited it out with the restraint of a benevolent parent.

Maya was beautiful, with a determined look in her eyes, an intelligent face, and features that Kostea thought were aristocratic. Despite her upcoming divorce, she had kept her former husband's last name. He wondered about her family history, which the personnel files he had access to did not disclose. She had long fingers and long limbs and a body impossible to ignore, along with a tendency to stay close to people and linger.

When she was in his group of students, Kostea pretended not to see her. He locked eyes with the others. When they did their rounds, he kept as far away from Maya as the narrow, whitewashed hallways and the small hospital rooms allowed him.

Some of the female students were rumored to have crushes on him. He responded to those rumors with a self-satisfied, righteous banter, understanding there was nothing serious there or, if there were, that he wouldn't be interested. Maya was different. When in her presence, the book he was writing, the patient in his hospital bed, the women he had loved or had fantasized about, like Katya, Clara even, all disappeared. Yet he wasn't concerned that he would be overcome by the attraction he was feeling, convinced that at the right moment he would know how to handle himself.

Then it happened. He was in his office one evening, reading. Most students were gone, and the hallways were silent. Through the open window, the wind blew in the delicate fragrance of flowers. Someone knocked on the door.

"Yes?" he said without looking up.

"I see you are working tonight. Can I help you, Professor?"

He recognized the voice. "I had a hard day," he answered.

"Professor, the mess in your office is truly romantic," Maya said. She lifted the piles of documents from the sofa and placed them on the floor. Then she walked back to the door and locked it.

———————————

She complicated his life, causing him to feel torn between allegiance and lust, yet rarely did he feel a real sense of guilt. He had the social status for such a relationship and the good looks and the selfishness to think it was his right. He was smart and, yeah, he knew he was selfish. He slept with Maya because he could, even though he had enough self-awareness to be worried.

In other words, he had no love to return. Only lust. Early in the mornings and at the end of long days, the lust came over him: her image, the feel of her embrace. He didn't invite those feelings—they simply materialized. He'd go to a mirror and look at himself. He'd touch his jaw, purse his lips, and push his chest out. He'd feel willing and strong, entitled to her breasts, her buttocks. He lay in bed next to Clara and thought about Maya. Good thing thoughts roamed silent and free!

Sometimes he despised himself and considered himself weak.

He and Maya followed a routine. After their first time on his office sofa, he sent her a note: *Tomorrow, at four, at the North Hotel.* Kostea reserved a room in the newly opened hotel near the North Railway Station, a building that looked like an ugly block of concrete. When he arrived to check in, Maya was already waiting. Trying to blend in, her back was glued against a granite column in the lobby, her pleated dress soft around her bare knees. Their gaze met for a fraction of a second. He got the key to the room, and as he walked to the elevator, he felt her moving silently in his direction and stopping at a safe distance behind him. A few crumbled pieces of paper were lying in a corner of the elevator floor. As soon as he closed the door, he pulled her in and kissed her. The papers rustled under his feet. Like a small animal, her tongue darted in and out of his mouth. He reached down between her legs and lifted her skirt. She moaned. They scrambled into the hallway and to their room. He came before she fell face up on the bed.

The receptionist at the North Hotel had learned his name. He found another hotel downtown and then another, in the old part of the city. The room was small, and a sculpted, old-fashioned walnut armoire stood next to the bed. Two full-length mirrors covered its doors. If she positioned herself on her hands and knees and he angled his back away from the mirrors, he could watch Maya and himself. He saw everything, in all of the salacious details, his excitement reaching a peak.

"Do you like watching yourself?" she asked.

"I like watching you."

"Oh yeah? And what do you like best?" Her voice had the detachment of someone who knew.

He felt compelled to talk dirty. "Your tits swinging back and forth."

"Are they large enough for you?"

"When they hang down they are."

He would never use such language with Clara. With Maya, he was a different man, coarser, more adventurous, and freer of inhibitions and constraints.

After Maya's divorce was finalized, she and her daughter moved in with her parents in a small house at the periphery of Bucharest. Maya's parents turned a blind eye to the affair. Her young daughter was in school. Still, Kostea felt awkward in that house, and he took Maya on overnight trips. They went to small inns and guesthouses outside Bucharest. They drove to the mountains or the Black Sea where the probability of chance encounters with friends or colleagues was reduced.

Kostea took full advantage of Clara's trust, hiding these excursions behind his conferences and meetings. He could afford it. He derived a salary from the hospital and another from the school of medicine. He also received cash, gifts, and favors from patients and royalties for his articles. He had finished writing *The Pathology of the Ureter*, which benefited from an impressive initial print run and resulted in a one-time payment equaling his average yearly income. He could call himself rich.

Maya brought her daughter along when they went to Sinaia. "I want my little girl to breathe the fresh mountain air," she had said. He couldn't say no. The little girl had the spunk of her mother and, he guessed, her father's penetrating dark eyes. She was too young to understand Kostea's role in their lives, yet her presence complicated things. He realized he enjoyed spending time with Maya and Simona together. In his way, he cared for both of them. He didn't love them, but wanted to shelter them from the world and, surprisingly, from himself. Maya shared a room with Simona. Kostea was in a room next door. Late at night, after Simona fell asleep, Maya joined him and had sex with him while nervously listening for any noise from the other room.

In Sinaia, they ran into Professor Dinescu who was dining with Ileana at the ritzy Palace Hotel restaurant. Kostea hoped that having little Simona with them made their encounter less incriminating. Dinescu never mentioned it afterward, either jokingly at work or in private. That made Kostea even more nervous.

Maya graduated from medical school, and Kostea used his connections to help her get a good job. It was the least he could do. He had helped other young doctors in their careers, and in that context, intervening on Maya's behalf was not at all unusual.

Once at Capşa, where they had stopped for coffee and pastries, Kostea noticed Marin in the main restaurant, and they quickly left. Another time, they bumped into Dr. Moraru, an oncologist Kostea knew. He stopped to exchange pleasantries with the doctor while Maya waited silently a few steps away.

CHAPTER 18

It Will Be a Very Long Trip

August 1968

Kostea and Clara talked sometimes about visiting Kishinev. The magic strings of their childhood pulled at them.

"While at it," Kostea said, "we could go to Aunt Mila in Odessa and see the house where my grandmother lived." Every time he thought about the trip, Kostea experienced a strange, almost painful desire to revisit Odessa, but he had to be careful not to accidentally disclose his long-buried memories of Katya, of which Clara knew nothing. He added, "And we could drive all the way to Yalta. The Russian tsars spent their summers there. That's how beautiful that place is."

"Do you want to drive?" Clara asked, surprised. Simply put, it wasn't done. Most pleasure trips to the Soviet Union were by train or plane to Moscow, Leningrad, and Kiev, in groups under the auspices of the National Tourist Office, carefully supervised.

"Yes, drive," Kostea said. "Why not? In my new car." They had recently replaced the Fiat 600 with a larger and more comfortable French-made Renault Gordini, which Kostea liked to think of as his own. Letting Clara borrow it—he stressed the word *borrow*—was generally an inconvenience to him.

"We should take Toddy along," Clara said.

"Of course." Kostea smiled. "The Soviet Union is as communist as we are. They'll let the three of us go together. No chance of defecting. None."

Toddy responded with annoyed ambivalence to his parents' invitation. On one hand, he wanted to travel, especially to a foreign country—a rarity in those times. On the other, his heart was someplace else. It was August, and some of his friends were planning a vacation to the beaches near Constanța. There was a girl in his class, Maria, whom he liked at the moment, and she was going as well. "If you came, you and I could play in the sand," she had teased him when they talked about it, and she kissed him, her lower lip filling his mouth with a touch of sulkiness. In the end, Toddy swallowed hard and went with his parents.

Kishinev seemed provincial to him. In Odessa they stayed with Aunt Mila and her husband, Yura, visited a few landmarks, and stopped for a few minutes in front of the house where Aneta had lived. The drive from Odessa to Yalta took a whole day. Everywhere they stopped, people surrounded the Gordini and looked at it with curiosity, as if the car had dropped there directly from Mars.

Mila and Yura came with them. Yura was an engineer by trade and spoke mostly of his younger brother, dead since the Great Patriotic War. Squeezed in the back seat of the Gordini in between Mila and Yura, Toddy couldn't care less about what had happened twenty-five years earlier to people he didn't know. All he could think was that Yalta was on the same parallel as Constanța where his buddies and Maria were spending *their* vacation without their parents and their parents' friends.

———————

On their second and last morning in Yalta, Toddy went for a swim. Clara came down to the beach to look for him.

The water stretched like blue crystal, sunrays dancing on it. Toddy swam to a cluster of cliffs, dove and looked at the dark barnacles and green moss at close range. Small, silvery fish moved in circles, catching the light. Back at the surface, he heard the waves break. His mother paced at the water's edge. She waved at him.

He wanted to swim a little longer but turned and broke into a fast crawl.

"I'm glad I found you," Clara said, walking into the shallow breakers as he came out of the sea. She held his towel.

"What's the rush?" he asked, water dripping off his black hair and tanned body. The whites of his eyes had a tinge of red.

"We packed our tents, and they all went to eat," she said. "Here, dry yourself, and let's go."

"I don't need the towel. I'll dry in the sun."

"Toddy, there is no time. After breakfast, we'll drive into the mountains to the Fountain of Bakhchisarai. From there, we have another eight hours to get back to Odessa. We talked about it."

"Maybe *you* did."

"You were there," she said. "Go. Your shirt is on the blanket. Get dressed."

"I'm wet," Toddy said.

Aggravated, Clara turned and took a few steps away from the water.

"Why do we have to go to the fountain?" he yelled after her.

She counted to five. "They say it's a beautiful place, from the times of the Tatars. Pushkin wrote a famous poem about it. Remember when you were little, and your grandma read Pushkin to you?"

"Of course I remember. I'm not stupid," he said.

She ignored his tone. "There is a famous ballet."

"I don't care about ballet. I like certain things, and you like others. I really wanted to swim."

"I understand, but Mila and Yura have to go to work tomorrow, so we have to leave now."

Toddy picked up his sneakers and shirt and strode ahead.

Clara put on her sandals. She shook the sand off the blanket, folded it, and placed it under her arm. "When you reach the stairs, take a right," she yelled after him. "The cafeteria is next to the campground."

They spoke Romanian, and the people on the beach followed them curiously with their eyes.

"I know where it is," Toddy grumbled. "And I'm not hungry."

The stairs went up a steep hill to another hill, taller and covered in wildflowers and rich evergreens. In between the greenery there were villas and hotels—tiled roofs, white walls, and onion-shaped gilded church steeples. Behind them rose the gray mountain range they would be driving through to arrive at Bakhchisarai. In the distance, to the south, stood the romantic Swallow's Nest, a castle built on a rocky outpost jutting into the blue sea. That, Toddy knew, was the edge of the city of Yalta. Sevastopol came much farther to the east. He stepped into his sneakers like one would do with slippers and put on his shirt.

Clara caught up to him. "Button your shirt, please."

"I'm hot," said Toddy, annoyed.

"That's too bad. I don't want you to look like a hoodlum." A wind gust lifted sand from the beach and blew it toward them. She squinted and turned her back to the sea. The sun had warmed her face and caused a few freckles to appear high on her cheekbones. As she squinted, thin dry lines formed around her eyes.

"Why do you care how I look?" Toddy asked.

"Actually, I care very much."

"Like hell you do," he said and started up the steps.

"The cafeteria's the other way. Toddy, what's the matter with you?"

"I'm tired of all of you."

"You're going to get lost."

"That would be fun, wouldn't it?"

Clara sighed. She wasn't going to climb the steps after him. Where would he go? He'll calm down, get thirsty, and return. Let him have his space. He had turned eighteen a few months earlier. She wondered whether she had ever been such a pain as a teenager, and figured she probably had.

———————

Toddy appeared in the door of the cafeteria as his family was finishing breakfast. Their conversation stopped, giving Toddy the distinct impression that they had been talking about him.

"You're here," Kostea said. "Great. Let's go!"

"Wait, Kostea darling," Aunt Mila said. "Let the boy eat something. Honey, come and sit down."

"I'm not hungry," Toddy snapped. His shirt was buttoned up.

Clara looked away.

"One hundred and twenty thousand Russians perished during the Siege of Sevastopol," Yura said.

Kostea stood up, and Yura followed suit. Toddy turned on his heels and walked out of the cafeteria.

Clara grabbed a roll and a few pieces of cheese and wrapped them in a napkin. "He'll eat later," she said, placing the small package in her beach bag.

Mila nodded. "He'll be fine, Clarushka. That's the way my son Vasik behaved at this age."

The road through the mountains was treacherous. In places, the asphalt was cracked or totally washed away by the rain. The old town of Bakhchisarai looked quaint and dilapidated. They walked through streets with uneven pavement and through the sixteenth-century Khan's Palace.

"During the war, Stalin forcibly moved over two hundred thousand Tatars to Uzbekistan," Yura said.

"The place reminds me of the Esmahan minaret in Mangalia," Kostea said, glancing at Clara with an insinuating smile. Here she was, his wife, the love of his life. The other woman seemed as far away as Bucharest, where she was waiting for him.

"All minarets look the same to me," Toddy said.

On a wall, he found an inscription etched on a metal plaque with the legend of the Fountain of Bakhchisarai. It was the story of Giray Khan's love and grief for his young wife Maria, stabbed by jealous Zarema, one of his other wives. In memory of Maria, he built the marble fountain of eternal tears. The marble was to weep forever, like Giray Khan himself. Toddy tried to imagine the beauty of the slain wife. He liked her name, Maria, like his classmate who was now at the beach with his friends. His grandmother Mimi, she was a Maria too. He had never studied religion and did not attach a sacred meaning to the name, which struck him as both pure and fragile. Mimi and Sasha had moved down from Bistriţa and came to live with them. Ina moved out. That was a fact he tried to think little about.

He wondered how old Khan's Maria had been. Fourteen? Seventeen? What counted as young in those days? How young had Khan been? He had killed Vaslav, the Polish nobleman who was supposed to marry Maria, and had abducted her. Toddy, still a virgin, marveled at what it would be like to have a harem.

The white marble fountain, with delicate carvings and water gurgling into a catch basin below, was not much larger than the ceramic tile stove they had at home before they installed central heating. Pushkin's bust stood on a pedestal nearby.

———————

They left the Crimean Mountains and drove across a wide plateau to the little town of Armiansk. At the traffic circle, where they were supposed to go left toward Kherson, a policeman stopped them. On his chest he had a badge with GAI inscribed over a red background.

"Where're you going?" he asked and looked them over, trying to assess if they understood Russian. He raised his hand to the window. "Your marshroute." This was the required preapproved itinerary for foreigners traveling through the Soviet Union. Kostea had one from the border with Romania to Odessa but not to Crimea. In truth, once in Odessa, he and Yura had stopped at the police station and requested one. They were told: "It's complicated. Leave the passports and your application here, and we'll get back with you in two weeks." The Bardus had one week left before they had to return. They kept their passports and took their chances.

"I don't have a marshroute, nor did I know that I needed one," Kostea responded in perfect Russian. "Officer, all we did was drive to Yalta and Bakhchisarai for a day. My wife, my son, and I are visiting from Romania, and we wanted to see these beautiful places. And these are our relatives from Odessa. If necessary, they'll vouch for us."

"No vouching is needed," the GAI officer said. "But you can't drive this way back to Odessa, not through Kherson. The road is closed. There is major construction, and no private car is allowed. Unfortunately, the only way is to loop around via Moscow and return that way. It will be a detour, I know, but you'll conform to the law. And I'll be happy to give you the marshroute that you need."

"Officer," Mila said. "Moscow is one thousand kilometers away."

"Fourteen hundred, to be precise."

"I'm a doctor, a surgeon at a major university hospital in Bucharest, and next Monday I have to be back," Kostea said, eager to explain who he was. "I've been to Moscow on a professional basis many times. I know Professor Nekrasov there, and Dr. Putil, and other important doctors as well. It's not that I don't want to go to Moscow or that I don't want to drive. Believe me—I have driven from Bucharest all the way to Switzerland and across the Flüela Pass. But we don't have the time. Besides, we came on the Kherson road the other day. There was no construction in sight."

"Doctor, I don't know what to say." Visibly impressed, the GAI officer shrugged. He seemed a nice enough Russian man—young, with blue eyes and a healthy clump of blond hair escaping his uniform cap. "Maybe they started construction yesterday or this morning. I do what I'm told, and the road is closed. You don't have a choice. Please show me your passport and your registration, and I'll get you on your way as soon as I can."

Kostea complied. The officer checked the documents and returned them. "These are all right." He pulled a notebook from his pocket and wrote in it. Then he ripped out the page and handed it to Kostea. "Here, keep this with you at all times."

Kostea had a hard time deciphering the handwriting and gave the note to Mila. "'Marshroute,'" she read aloud. "'From current position in Armiansk to Moscow, and from Moscow to Odessa. Follow the shortest roads available at all times. No detours allowed. Signed: Lieutenant Zverev, GAI, City of Armiansk.'"

"Thank you, Lieutenant Zverev," Kostea said.

"You're welcome, and have a safe drive."

They departed in silence, exiting the traffic circle to proceed straight ahead as instructed. A gas station was on the left and then a long low warehouse.

"What are we going to do?" Clara asked.

Kostea looked in the rearview mirror. The traffic circle was out of sight.

"I have to be at work tomorrow morning," Yura said. "Stop in Armiansk, and Mila and I will catch the bus."

"There'll be no bus if the road is closed," Mila said.

"The road can't be closed," Toddy said. His voice sounded shrill, like the chirp of a little bird.

An unpaved street opened up behind the warehouse, and without any warning, Kostea took a left turn. He drove on the uneven surface, slowly, avoiding the bumps.

"You'll get us arrested," Clara said.

Kostea didn't say anything. He felt the tension in the car and clenched the steering wheel.

A second even narrower street intersected the first. Kostea veered again to the left. They reached the main two-way highway leading to Kherson, with no policeman in sight.

"Amen," Mila said.

In silence, Kostea checked the rearview mirror every few seconds. The sun was in his eyes. Large pools of water glistened on the side of the road.

"These are the Azov Sea desalinization ponds," Mila said.

"Don't be silly. The Azov Sea is behind us," Yura said.

There were no other cars on the road. Kostea tried hard not to exceed one hundred kilometers per hour. In the distance, he saw a shadow. Soon he distinguished the khaki tarp of a military truck. It was moving slowly, and for a while he drove behind the truck. Ahead of them was a long convoy of military vehicles. A few times he moved to the left and saw no oncoming traffic. He swallowed hard and passed the first truck, the second, the third. Everyone in the car held their breath. They looked straight ahead. From the left lane, Kostea waved at the soldier drivers, who waved back. It seemed an eternity, but eventually Kostea passed the entire convoy and changed back into the right lane. He pushed the accelerator and reached one hundred again.

"That was strange," Toddy said.

"There must be military exercises," Yura said. "That's why they told us the road was closed."

Soon they caught up to another convoy and passed it as well. Then another convoy, and another. The sun was setting when they crossed the Dnieper River and drove around Kherson. One hour later they reached Mykolaiv. At a traffic junction, a policeman on a motorcycle started after them. He followed them for a few hundred yards and turned his flashing lights on.

They stopped.

The policeman introduced himself and asked for their identification documents—all five of them. "Where are you coming from?"

Kostea told him.

"That's more than two hundred kilometers away. Nobody stopped you until now?"

"Nobody," Kostea lied. "Why would they?"

The policeman looked surprised, and their conversation proceeded along the lines of the one they'd had with GAI lieutenant in Armiansk, except for the part about the road being under construction. Again, Kostea introduced himself as a doctor from Bucharest on vacation with his family.

This policeman was a captain, clearly not a traffic cop. "Well," he said, "you can't be on this road. You've been spotted outside Kherson with your foreign car, and I've been radioed to intercept you. I'll keep the passports, and you follow me."

"Where to?" Kostea asked.

"The police station, Doctor. Where else?"

It was already dark. The captain rode his motorcycle fast and stopped in front of a one-story building with a *Police* sign in red letters above the entrance illuminated by an electric bulb. The glass protecting the sign was cracked. He drove his bike onto the sidewalk, released the stand with his foot, and indicated to Kostea to park his car by the curb behind a police cruiser. The street was deserted.

"Doctor," he said, "you come with me. The rest of you, wait in the car."

"Can my son join me?" Kostea asked.

The officer thought for a second. "Why not."

Without a word, Toddy got out of the back seat.

"Why do you need Toddy?" Clara asked.

"We'll be all right," Kostea said. "He's eighteen, and I want a witness."

Clara sighed, and Yura shook his head.

"I'll do the talking," Kostea whispered to Toddy in Romanian as they entered the building behind the officer. "You listen and don't say anything. If anyone asks, you don't speak any Russian, all right?"

Toddy felt good to be at his father's side, but he was scared. No question they were in trouble, not sure how much. He had heard many stories about people who went inside police stations in the Soviet Union never to be heard of again. Of course, this couldn't happen to them. Or could it? No, not with them being Romanians, his mother waiting outside in the car, and his father acting so calmly. He acted as if he was in control.

The room they entered was windowless, with cracked, whitewashed walls, illuminated by an electric bulb protected by a large wire cage hanging from the ceiling. Black flies and other bugs circled the light and produced a slight and persistent buzz. The cement floor was littered with mud and cigarette butts. Several wooden benches occupied the middle. Two youngsters, not much older than Toddy, sat on one of them. They were both in white undershirts, had matching tattoos on their arms, and their ankles were shackled.

"Doctor, sit down here and let me first deal with these two young men," the captain said. "When I'm done, I'll be back with you." He turned to one of the two youngsters and ordered, "You, come with me."

The youngster rose and followed the captain as fast as he could with his shackled legs through a door into an adjacent office. Another door at the back of the waiting room stood ajar, leading to a dark corridor.

Kostea sat on the bench behind the second youth, and Toddy sat next to him.

"Doctor?" the remaining youth sneered, as if doubting Kostea's title. He lifted his shackled legs over the bench and turned to face them.

"Yes, doctor," Kostea said. "You don't believe me, or what?"

Toddy placed his hand on his father's arm.

The youth noticed the gesture. "The two of you are a couple?" He laughed loudly and addressed Toddy. "Hey, pass me a cigarette, will you?"

Toddy didn't reply.

"What's the matter with you, asshole?"

"He doesn't speak Russian," Kostea said.

"Why? Is he thick in the head?" the youth asked. He paused, then added as if surprised by a sudden thought, "Is he American?"

Kostea got to his feet, and Toddy suddenly feared he would strike the youth. To avert his father from making any hasty moves, he rose as well. They took a few paces together in the small room, and Kostea lit a cigarette.

"Doctor, don't be fucking with me," the youth snarled and turned to Toddy. "Listen, faggot, I know what you like. When we get out of this shithole, meet me at the Kamchatka Square behind the cinema, and I'll get you a real nice piece of ass. Much better than this old man, trust me. Just throw me one of his cigarettes now."

Toddy didn't respond, and the youth cursed and spit on the floor.

The other young thug emerged handcuffed, escorted by a regular policeman, not by the captain. He looked at his friend as if about to say something, but the policeman pushed him from behind. He tripped over his shackles, recovered, and moved with small steps into the dark corridor, where they disappeared. Toddy heard a door slam shut and lock. The policeman returned and told the second youth to come with him to the office. With a menacing glance at Toddy, the youngster got up and followed the policeman.

An eerie quiet settled in the waiting room, and a fly buzzed and hit the cage around the electric bulb a few times. Kostea finished his cigarette and crushed it under his shoe.

A few minutes later, the second youth was escorted out of the office and down the corridor. Toddy guessed the two had been taken to a holding cell.

"Doctor, come in," the captain called from the office. He was seated at a large desk with two black telephones on it. Behind him on the wall hung a poster with a hammer and sickle and a map of the city. Pins and little red flags marked different points of interest on the map. "Comrade Gorsky will be back in an instant," he began. "He'll write a report on what happened because he has beautiful handwriting, whereas if I write anything, nobody can read it. All you'll have to do is sign it, and you'll be free to go."

Kostea smiled. Toddy kept his face stern.

Comrade Gorsky returned, pulled up a chair, took the passports from the captain, and began writing in a ledger with a large fountain pen.

"You're not allowed to continue on this road to Odessa," the captain said. "You'll have to turn around and drive to Moscow. I know it's a detour, but that's just the way it is."

"Captain, Moscow is too far," Kostea pleaded. "I have to be back in Romania, at work, in forty-eight hours. You know, duty calls. What's wrong with the way we were going? We drove on that road the other day."

"Sorry, I don't make the rules." The captain exchanged a glance with Gorsky and gave a short laugh as if expecting Kostea to protest some more. When Kostea didn't, he continued in a softer tone. "My advice is you stay overnight at the Agricultural Workers' Hotel, the only one around here. It's too late to go to Moscow tonight."

"I understand," Kostea said.

"It's easy to find the hotel. I mean, start driving in the direction your car is facing right now and take the first right on Kusnetska, a major street. Go less than a kilometer, and the hotel will be on your right. You'll see carts and maybe some horses out in front. All the peasants from the neighboring villages who come for the Sunday market stay there. Can't miss it. Tell them I sent you, and they'll treat you like royalty."

Gorsky finished writing.

"Sign here," the captain said.

Kostea read the so-called report, a single long and convoluted sentence stating that the people listed below had been apprehended for driving on a road closed to private vehicular traffic, apparently without realizing it.

Their five names and passport numbers followed, along with the date and Comrade Gorsky's signature. Kostea reached for the fountain pen, when a long and penetrating scream resounded through the police station. For a few seconds, the bugs stopped bumping into the caged lights.

"It's the hooligans," the captain said. "Gorsky, go and see what's happening."

Gorsky left.

"It gets worse every year," the captain complained. "Believe me, by comparison, the likes of you are no problem at all." He shook his head and watched Kostea sign the register. "Thank you, Doctor." He got up and shook Kostea's hand and then Toddy's. "I assume that tomorrow, after a good night's sleep, you'll start early."

"We have to. It will be a very long trip," Kostea said.

"Tomorrow morning, drive back on Kusnetska and you'll get to the Mykolaiv crossing where I waited for you this evening." The captain showed them the road on the map. "At the crossing, take a left to Kherson and follow the road signs to Moscow." He opened the outside door to let Kostea and Toddy walk to the car. They were alone. In a quiet voice, he said, "Doctor, our regular shift starts at six, so, if you get there earlier, chances are that nobody will see you. And if we don't see you and you take a quick right to Odessa, nobody will ever know. If we don't know it, it won't hurt anybody. What do you think?"

———

Very early the next morning they took a right at the Mykolaiv crossing, and two hours later they deposited Yura and Mila at their home in Odessa. Toddy admired Kostea for being a such daredevil, but Kostea had had enough. They immediately left for Kishinev and crossed into Romania that evening.

A few days later, the Soviets invaded Czechoslovakia.

CHAPTER 19

I Wanted to Live in America

May 1969

Clara came into Toddy's room, surprising him as he finished getting ready for his high school graduation dance. He was in a navy-blue suit, tailor-made out of a length of worsted wool Kostea had brought him from Paris.

"You look nice," Clara said, feeling proud. "Let me see you. Turn around. Button your jacket."

Hesitantly, Toddy obliged.

"Nice," she said again. "The tailor did a good job."

"I'm hot," Toddy complained, took off the jacket, and threw it on the bed. "I'd rather be wearing blue jeans and a T-shirt."

Clara knew better than argue.

"After the dance," Toddy said, "there'll be a bunch of parties. Please, don't wait for me and don't worry."

Clara couldn't stop herself from passing her fingers through his hair, trying to free his forehead.

He moved away.

"I won't wait for you," she said, laughing, "but you'll have to promise me something as well."

"What?"

"That you won't overdo it."

"Mama, you know I'm careful."

"I know," Clara said, "but tonight will be special." She leaned forward and quickly kissed him on his cheek. "You're such a handsome young man. Have a nice time. I love you."

———————

Clara woke up with a start. Toddy! She listened. Besides Kostea's regular breathing next to her, she couldn't hear anything. Toddy might have returned home quietly and gone to bed, but she didn't think so. No matter how carefully he moved through the apartment, she always sensed his presence: the door, the brief flickering of lights, his light steps in the hallway. It didn't bother her, and it brought her comfort. That subconscious extension of her senses she had developed as a mother.

She closed her eyes and tried to fall asleep again but couldn't. The day was breaking. The long shadows from the trees fell through the window and moved across the floor like premonitions. She went to Toddy's room and quietly opened the door. His bed was empty. His blue jeans were on the floor by his desk where he had dropped them the previous evening while changing. She cast her mind back to his smart new suit, which fit him so well, the kiss she had planted on his cheek before he left, and his promise to be careful. On his desk, the phosphorescent hands of the clock indicated five thirty in the morning.

Sasha and Mimi now slept in Ina's old room. Clara prayed Ina was at peace in her studio all by herself. If she were here, she'd be awake, worried as well. Clara went to the kitchen and placed the coffeepot on the stove. Smoking a cigarette, she waited for the water to boil, hoping to hear Toddy walk in the front door. He looked so distinguished last night, so grown-up, but he was at an age when his friends had only to prompt him and he'd follow, happy to be with them. Young men were stupid.

She remembered herself at that age—her and Kostea. They were in medical school already, more mature, the war taking hold everywhere around them. With Kostea, she had been the evenhanded one, rational and sensible, while he had been demanding, impulsive. He was like that to this day, still quick to let himself go, to lose control.

Toddy was different. He had inherited his father's best qualities and was also soft and compassionate—a good soul, a thoughtful soul—like his mother. She smiled, thinking of him: still just a boy. She loved him so much, and the mere idea that anything bad might happen to him sent chills through her body. She couldn't prevent those thoughts. They were like physical pangs.

He had said there were parties after the school dance, but it was morning already. Where was he? What if there had been an accident when he and his buddies tried to jump on a tram? His hand could have slipped on the wet door handle, and he could have fallen. He could have cracked his head, broken his leg, been run over. He might be in a hospital, unconscious, dying. Someone would have telephoned the house by now, but one could never be sure. He might need his mother. And what if he got drunk and was retching in a cold bathroom somewhere? Or was robbed or, worse, beaten, like Kostea had been, long ago, on the beach in Mangalia? What if Toddy was lying in a pool of blood on a sidewalk?

What if he got a girl pregnant?

The image of her son in bed with a beautiful young woman flashed in front of her eyes. Yeah, that was possible. Such an outcome, though, would imply he had a girlfriend, and as far as she knew, unlike his friend Cristi, he didn't. Which made Clara think of calling Cristi's house across the street to ask about Toddy. The two boys had attended the same high school and had gone to the same graduation party. But it was too early, unless she wanted to wake and alert Cristi's entire family.

Being with a woman would be all right, Clara thought. Love was a beautiful feeling. Sex was beautiful also, although a pregnancy would be undesirable now. Toddy was way too young. His college admittance exams were in the next two weeks, and he had no profession or income. Unlike when Clara was young, a recently issued decree outlawed abortions, and the violators, when caught, were punished with jail time—long sentences, to both providers and patients. To top it off, all forms of birth control had disappeared from the market. It wasn't a question of religion or morality but rather a push to increase the country's workforce at the confused and perhaps megalomaniacal whim of the man at the top, Ceaușescu. With one hand he had begun his policies of political relaxation while with the other had turned the screws on the young people. At forty-seven, Clara, no longer able to conceive in any case, fell outside the age limits of the new law, while the boys and girls of her son's generation lived through an unnatural, practical nightmare.

She remembered the pregnancies she had terminated. Would she be less nervous if she'd had more children?

She took a sip from her coffee and then a deep breath to calm her nerves and went to get dressed. Kostea was snoring, his nose buried in his pillow, his mouth slightly open. Sunday rounds at the hospital were at seven. She'd borrow the car and bring it back by then. No sense in getting him agitated.

She drove the car slowly, reconnoitering like a detective. Her son and his buddies had to be somewhere near. There was no traffic, and the sidewalks were empty. She took a left at the corner, moved along the tall garden wall of the Pioneers' Palace, then veered right past the medical school. A deserted bus station was a few hundred yards farther. At the next corner, she turned right toward the military academy, exploring the large plaza in front of the massive gray building. She drove to the top of the hill and surveyed the other bus station that Toddy could be using. Nobody. She drove around the military academy, cut across the plaza, and came back to her street from the opposite end, and suddenly she saw him. He was in one piece, walking slowly, his jacket thrown negligently over one shoulder. She caught up to him, stopped at the curb, and opened the passenger door. "Hop in," she told him.

"Mom, what are you doing here?"

"Nothing," she said, relieved, and started laughing. "Just taking a morning drive through the neighborhood."

"Mom, you weren't looking for me, were you?"

"So what if I was," she answered. "You know, I got worried. It is morning."

In the two minutes it took Clara to drive home and park the car in front of the house, Toddy told her he had spent the entire evening with a girl, Lydia, from his class. He had danced only with her, and then they went to a party, then to another one, and finally they walked to Herăstrău Park to watch the sunrise over the lake. "You actually know her mother," he added. "She used to work with you at the Municipal Public Health Lab. The girl's name is Lydia Faur, and her mother's last name is Malamed. Lydia's dad died when she was little, and her mother remarried."

"Oh, Dr. Malamed. Tina, at the headquarters. All right, go and rest now. I bet you're tired."

"I'm not tired at all." Toddy followed Clara into the kitchen. "I'll have a cup of coffee with you. Mom, I'm very excited. Lydia was in my English class, but we never talked before. She is really smart, and she said that her family is considering emigrating to Israel. I told her I wanted to live in America."

"Since when do you want to live in America?"

"Since, like . . . always."

"That's news to me. What about college?"

"College first, of course." Toddy laughed. "It goes without saying."

"Good," Clara said and poured coffee into two mugs. "Let me tell you. Tina Malamed is a smart doctor and a very hard worker. I'm surprised they are talking about Israel. She's quite involved with the Party."

"Dad is in the Party, but he doesn't really believe in it, does he?"

"No, he does not. Lydia's late father, though, had been a big shot Party newspaperman." Clara hesitated, as if wondering whether to continue. "You should know this," she said. "Her father took his own life, and I believe her mother never told Lydia the truth. I guess she wanted to protect her. Don't bring it up when you talk to her, Toddy."

CHAPTER 20

Everyone Wore Invisible Shackles

June 1969

"Besides being my top Moscow man, you're traveling to conferences all over Europe and beyond. Your presentations are well received, aren't they, Kostea?"

"I hope so, with your help, Professor. Or shall I say, Minister Dinescu?"

"You don't have to kiss up to me. You know I like you."

Kostea waited, his experience telling him more was coming.

"You're a very good doctor and surgeon, and I don't care that you're short-tempered sometimes. Tell me, how many times have you been to Paris?"

"Five times for conferences, if I don't count my trip to Toulouse, when I had to transit through Paris."

"And now you're going to Frankfurt. I hear they'll publish your paper in Germany."

"They will," Kostea said.

"Well, you're famous, and I have a favor to ask." Dinescu sighed. "Take Dr. Nuda with you. He could benefit from your experience."

Nuda was a new addition to the staff, brought over by Dinescu from a provincial hospital in Râmnicu Vâlcea. It was obvious that Dinescu thought highly of him. Kostea did not. Together with the other doctors, he poked fun at Nuda, especially because of his tendency to ingratiate himself with Dinescu.

"Minister, you know the rules," Kostea said. "You're either invited to present a paper, like I am, or you have to pay all costs yourself. And the way we are always short on hard currency, I don't see how Nuda would get the participation fees and travel costs approved."

"Kostea, do this for me, and I'll cover his expenses. And by the way, since I'm the health minister now, our people at the embassy insist that you visit with them."

"I'm going to Frankfurt, not Bonn."

"They'll have a car at your disposal."

———

In Frankfurt, a man from the presidium approached Kostea after he finished his presentation. "Congratulations," the man said in French. "Very impressive. I'm Dr. Jean Caron from Toulouse. We met last year in Paris."

Generally good at remembering people, Kostea was unable to place this man.

"We are opening a new urology section in our hospital," Dr. Caron continued, "and I would like to talk to you about a professional exchange opportunity. Maybe we could have a glass of wine later?"

Kostea felt dizzy. If the Romanians were to get even a hint that he was being offered a job, he'd be a compromised man. Yet his curiosity was piqued. From the stage, he looked at the audience of over two hundred participants to where Nuda was seated. Nuda wasn't watching Kostea but was talking with the person seated next to him. An embassy representative was supposed to stay at their hotel that evening and drive them to Bonn the next morning to meet the ambassador for lunch. "I'm here with a colleague," Kostea said, mostly to give himself a small breather.

"We want to talk to *you*, Dr. Bardu," Dr. Caron insisted. "But if you must, you could ask your colleague to join us."

"No," Kostea said. "I'll come alone, except . . . I'm not sure about my schedule."

"I understand. You are busy. Here is my business card. I wrote the telephone number of my hotel on the back. Call me as soon as you know, and we'll get together."

That evening after dinner, Nuda and the embassy representative decided to take a stroll through downtown. Kostea excused himself, saying that he needed to rest. From the lobby of the hotel, he called Dr. Caron, agreed on a place to meet, and left surreptitiously, suddenly wondering if this whole thing could be trap, a setup.

The restaurant looked expensive. They each ordered a drink, Kostea following Dr. Caron's lead for a whiskey. Dr. Caron described his hospital, its location and history, the number of beds. He said they were creating a senior visiting position to lead a new urology section. Four or five younger doctors would work there and learn. He kept repeating how impressed he was with Kostea's international reputation and suggested a salary that in Kostea's opinion was out of this world. Because of visa limitations, the assignment was for up to six months.

Dr. Caron's demeanor and voice felt genuine. If this were a trap, someone had to have gone to great lengths to arrange it. Find a real Frenchman. Come up with details about a French hospital. Not spare expenses. To what end? Just to compromise Kostea? Nonsense.

Kostea had a hard time finding his words. "What happens afterward?" he finally asked.

"We assume you'll want to go home."

"And if not?"

"Then you'll stay." Dr. Caron smiled. "We'll help you resolve your visa. But listen, we'll reevaluate then. Together. Who knows what the future might bring? Maybe the hospital will make this position permanent, or maybe you'll want to go work someplace else. A man with your reputation could teach medicine in Paris or move to the Unites States. Everything will be on the table."

Kostea felt flattered. "Can I bring my family?"

"That's entirely up to you. Sure."

"So, you're saying I should come with you to Toulouse?"

Dr. Caron seemed taken aback. "You could, but I'm not suggesting that. To be honest, I thought that should you consider my offer seriously, you'd go back to Romania, talk to your family, to your employer, take a leave of absence, and then come."

This man had no idea that in Romania everyone wore invisible shackles. Things didn't work that way. "Do I have a few hours to think?" asked Kostea.

"Absolutely. I imagine you'd need a couple of months to put your affairs in order, but I was hoping to get a yes or a no much sooner."

"What if I gave you an answer tomorrow afternoon?"

"That would be great," Dr. Caron responded.

Kostea rushed back to the hotel where he and Nuda shared a room. Dinescu's generosity with foreign currency went only so far. He hoped Nuda had not returned, but he was prepared to tell him he went out to buy a last-minute gift for Clara. Just in case, he purchased an inexpensive cologne from the hotel souvenir shop.

When Nuda returned, Kostea pretended to be asleep. He heard Nuda getting undressed, smoking a cigarette, sighing, and leafing through a hotel magazine. Then Nuda switched his nightstand light off, and soon his peaceful breathing filled the room. Thoughts swirled around in Kostea's head. At about one in the morning, he went to the bathroom. Nuda shifted, rearranged his pillow, and started snoring. Back in bed, Kostea kept his gaze on the ceiling. An electric light from outside danced across it. Tree branches caused it to shift, fuzzy, stronger sometimes, weaker some other times, at one point taking the undefined shape of a sea creature. Kostea's future seemed that way. Blurry. If he accepted the offer, he would need to work harder than ever before. It was imperative that after six months, the hospital and Dr. Caron would want him to stay. He would have to learn French to perfection, always smile and be polite. Forget about ever going back to Romania. If he decided, he had to go now to Toulouse, and once he defected, returning home was not in the cards. Forever. Toddy was still young, but how would Clara react? In Rome they had talked about defecting and agreed it wasn't a good idea. But that was then, and this was now. Now he had a true offer. Concrete. Attractive. How long would it take him to bring his family out? Would the Romanians let Toddy, Clara, and his parents join him? And if he failed at his work? What if a patient bled to death on his watch, as had nearly happened with Leo?

Kostea tried to stop thinking. He had the whole day tomorrow to decide. Nuda's snoring bothered him, and he had to go to the bathroom again.

Toward morning, he fell asleep and had a bad dream. They were in the hotel lobby. Kostea was nervously playing with a bunch of pfennigs he held in his hand.

The man from the embassy smiled. "There is a public phone on that wall," he told Kostea. "Go and call Dr. Caron, if you have to."

"How do you know?" Kostea asked.

"That's his job," said Nuda.

"Nuda, you stay out of it," the man from the embassy said, breathing heavily. "If you take the job, Comrade Bardu, in four months, you'll be out in the street. I guarantee it. You might think you're on a pedestal now, that you are chosen. But you're not. France is a capitalist country, as rough as they come. They'll use you and discard you like an old jacket. In France, you'll be a foreigner all your life. Remember your own Uncle Misha."

"I don't know what you're talking about," said Kostea.

"Sure you do." The man from the embassy got even more agitated. "Comrade, if you defect on my watch, this will be a blemish on my career, and I'll make sure you won't see your family ever again. Neither Clara, nor Toddy, nor your parents. Not Ina, whom you kicked out of your house."

If this were a setup, Kostea thought in his dream, he'd wait for me to accept.

"I'll let Clara know about Maya," Nuda said.

Kostea woke up with a shiver. It was morning, and the room was bathed in sunshine.

Nuda was packing his suitcase, a white towel wrapped around his waist. He looked relaxed. "Kostea, you need to hurry."

After their lunch in Bonn, the embassy driver took them back to the Frankfurt airport. At the ticket counter, his travel bag still on his shoulder, Kostea told Nuda he needed to look for a bathroom. With a pocket full of change and his heart beating fast, he turned the corner and stopped in front of a battery of shiny public phones. The busy concourse stretched into the distance, lined with restaurants and shops, clean and efficient. All he had to do was keep walking. He hesitated, picked up the receiver, and brought it to his ear. The receiver was cold. He spoke briefly to Dr. Caron's assistant and hung up. Then he threw Dr. Caron's business card into the wastebasket and, with the rest of his pfennigs, bought himself a pack of Hanuta wafers from a refreshment stand.

CHAPTER 21

Guns Are for Hunting

July 1969

Igor waited for Kostea in the street. He looked out of place, if not downright ridiculous, in his green fatigues and knee-high dark rubber boots, his double-barreled rifle on one shoulder and his guitar and a bulging backpack on the other. They had decided to go on a spur-of-the-moment hunting trip, and Kostea was picking him up in front of the building where Igor now lived with Aida, his second wife, in the apartment he had once shared with Vera. Uncle Sebastian had passed, and now a young couple occupied the attic. Igor still didn't have a clue what role Eugene had played in precipitating his divorce. Affairs of the heart should die in secret, Kostea thought with an odd degree of satisfaction as he pulled up to the curb. Opening the passenger door, he yelled, "Quickly, Igor, get in before someone sees you and calls the police."

"Why would anybody do that?" Igor asked innocently, throwing his guitar, his bag, and his gun on the back seat.

"Have you looked at yourself in the mirror? You look like a character from James Fenimore Cooper."

Igor inspected his friend's attire from head to toe. "You're laughing at me, and you're going hunting in your street clothes."

"I came straight from the hospital," Kostea said, stretching his arms on the steering wheel and glancing down at his dark-gray dress pants. "I brought a change of clothes in my bag, and Marin said he has a pair of hunting boots for me. And a windbreaker. He said it can get cold at night."

"It's July. You won't need a windbreaker. Does he have a weapon for you?"

"That too," Kostea said.

They had to drive for a couple of hours to a hamlet on the shore of the Danube, where they were meeting Marin and two of his associates from the Securitate, "my boys" as Marin liked to call them. Marin and the boys were riding there in a modified jeep with special license plates.

"I'm sure his boys have the best weapons," Igor said. "No matter the prey."

"You are so perceptive."

Igor took a cigarette from his pocket and lit up. "How was Frankfurt?"

Kostea cracked open the window to let the smoke get out. He didn't feel like talking about his trip. He wouldn't share what transpired with Dr. Caron with anybody, not even Clara. "Great!" he said, knowing that this was the expected answer.

"Sure. But what did you do?"

"Work, like each time I go to a conference."

"You know," Igor said. "Vera now lives in West Germany. One day, I'd love to see Frankfurt. And Paris."

"Do it," said Kostea.

"I won't get permission to travel."

"You don't know that. Igor, you have to be more assertive."

"I'm assertive enough," Igor said. "With a former wife in West Germany, I have no chance. Unless, of course, I agree to kiss ass."

"I see," Kostea said. "You don't kiss ass, but I do."

"Maybe. But I admire you and the way you manage to always come out on top."

"Like your brother, you mean. Igor, why can't *you* be more like your brother?"

Igor looked hurt. "My brother is dead."

Kostea regretted his words. Igor's younger and only sibling had been a brilliant man who had died suddenly of a stroke. He had been an excellent student, and later he had navigated the communist bureaucracy with skill, gaining recognition in his field, making good money, and taking care of his wife and mentally disabled son. He had helped their aging mother financially and had stood by Igor during his divorce and depression, when Igor couldn't work and lost his job at the Garden. After his brother's death, the burden of supporting his family had fallen on Igor, and he barely kept afloat.

"Sorry. I didn't mean to offend," Kostea said.

They were out of the city and moving at higher speed. Up ahead, several horse-driven wagons loaded high with bales of hay had entered the highway from the fields, leaving behind a double trail of brown mud and blocking the lane. Kostea slammed the brakes too late. They hit the mud. The car skidded to the right and came to a complete stop with one front wheel in the ditch. The engine stalled.

Kostea restarted the car, redirected it, and pushed the accelerator slowly. The wheels caught, and they moved forward. His hands shook. "Fuck!" he yelled as they passed by the wagons. As if in response, one horse bolted and neighed.

Igor opened his window all the way and inhaled deeply. "We could have been killed."

Kostea ignored Igor's comment. "You should ask them tonight," he said. "Ask what?"

"To approve your passport application, if you really want to travel. That's one thing the boys do in their department."

"When they don't harass people."

"Nobody's harassing you, Igor."

"They harassed Uncle Sebastian."

"That was almost two decades ago. Today we are hunting together."

"So that's how you're getting your permission to travel?" Igor asked. "By being in cahoots with the boys?"

"Don't be an ass. Understand what is what. And don't compare yourself to me. I'm a doctor. They send me out to show the world what terrific science a communist country can do."

Igor passed his fingers through his hair and for a second seemed lost. "So what? You're a doctor, and I'm a dimwit?"

"I didn't call you a dimwit. Have a few drinks with one of them, take him aside, and say, 'Buddy, I want to visit Paris. Put a good word in for me at the passport office. I'll bring you a nice present, and my wife will stay here, as guarantee for my return.'"

"All right. Let's say I leave Aida behind. Where will I find the money? You can't even begin to imagine the obligations I have."

"Borrow some. I can help."

"Of course," Igor said as if he expected Kostea to make such an offer. "And if I defect?"

"I don't know." Kostea felt irritated. That was the problem with people like Igor—they kept twisting their arguments to justify their failures. No wonder Vera had cheated on him and left. Yes, in this life you kiss ass, and you lie and cajole, and you fight. You grab and hold what you get. But you also know your limitations and say no when required. "You know what?" Kostea said. "Defect to West Germany. Look for Vera. Maybe she'll kick out her new husband and take you back."

Igor tensed up. "Because we change women like we change underwear."

Kostea grinned. The wound over Vera was still raw. As if his hunting had started, he went for the kill. "Some of us do."

"I've heard rumors," Igor said.

———

They met in the shadow of the old railroad bridge over the Danube, built by engineer Anghel Saligny at the end of the nineteenth century. There, the mighty river split into two, surrounded by marshy terrain. Their plan was to shoot geese the first afternoon and go after deer and wild boar in the morning. The president of the local cooperative and the county chief of police welcomed the vice mayor of Bucharest, the famous urologist, and their friends with open arms.

They had prepared five small rooms for their visitors at the cooperative guesthouse. A long wooden table laid out with cold cuts, breads, wine, and plum brandy waited for them on the enclosed porch, which served as a summer extension of the main dining room.

"Get settled, everyone," Marin said. "Let's meet back here in five, have a drink and a snack, and be going. We still have daylight for a while, and I would like to earn my dinner."

"We have plenty of food, Comrade Vice Mayor," the cooperative president said. "No need to go hunting if any of you are tired and would rather sit on the porch and enjoy the sunset."

"Thank you, Comrade." Marin smiled. "But we're men of action, aren't we, boys?"

Marin knocked on Kostea's door and handed him a pair of rubber boots and a Remington 870. "You'll like it," he said. "It's American, the best gun for waterfowl."

"The windbreaker?" Kostea asked.

"You won't need it. It's warm."

Kostea nodded. Still thinking about Igor, he changed into khaki pants and a flannel shirt and put on the rubber boots. What rumors had Igor heard? The question bothered him a great deal. The left boot bothered him too, rubbing against his toe, but just a little.

They gathered in front of the guesthouse. One of the boys brought the jeep around, and the guests and the chief of police got in. The head of the cooperative and several local men followed in a truck. They took a dirt road that soon disappeared among the tall grasses, reeds, and cattails. The ground was saturated with water, and the mud was ankle-deep. They walked to a row of young poplars on the shore of a small pond. The sun played on its surface like fire.

"That's our spot," the chief said. "Get ready. The beaters will cause the geese to fly toward us along the shore."

Kostea observed his companions spread out and load their guns.

Igor came close. "How you doing? Let me see your gun."

Kostea handed his gun to him.

"Nice," Igor said.

"Igor, back in the car, when you said you heard rumors, what did you mean?"

"Nothing."

"Did anyone tell you I'm cheating on Clara?"

"No, buddy, nobody said anything. Let's focus on hunting. Stick by me, and I'll help."

"I don't need your help."

"As you wish." Igor laughed. "Just mind the recoil."

Kostea loaded his gun. Soon, a skein of geese like strands of long hair darkened the sky. He rushed to take aim and pull the trigger. He stumbled back from the recoil. A sharp whistle pierced his ears. He didn't reload but looked around, expecting people to be laughing at him, but they were all busy. Igor's gun cracked—bang-bang—two distinct shots, one after the other, and two birds fell from the sky. Igor reloaded. He had lied. He knew about Maya, Kostea was certain of that. Everybody around him was shooting, and the geese were a dream.

The mosquitos started to bite. Somebody yelled that the beaters would collect the birds, and it was time to go. Kostea's left boot bothered him more than before.

Back in his room, he pulled off his boots and his socks and wiped some of the mud off his pants. He had a blister on his left toe. Frustrated, he stretched out on the narrow bed and closed his eyes, thinking of Frankfurt.

As they say, the bird in hand is worth two in the bush. No matter how many birds chirped in Frankfurt or in Toulouse, his life at home wasn't half bad. He had done the right thing. Could Dr. Caron boast of an experience like this hunting trip with friends and a special welcome from officials showing respect? Kostea wasn't so sure. Igor had gotten on his nerves, but he loved Igor. And Marin, such a reliable friend. One could meet new people, but one couldn't replace one's old friends. Forty-seven was still young for a man. They all lived in a maze-like system of favors and bribes and connections and traps, and he navigated it well. He used it to his advantage. And he made money. That's how he was able to keep his mistress and afford a new studio apartment for his mother-in-law. Bring his parents. Who says he wasn't a generous man? A professional at the top, ready to collect the spoils in his country of birth, a somewhat backward country that lately seemed to have embarked on a more progressive path.

He had not brought home any gifts from Frankfurt except for the cologne bottle he gave Maya. Their relationship, more intense in the beginning, had lasted for more than a year now, on and off, since he feared being exposed. Each time he said he would end it, she accepted his decision, no questions and no complaints. "I won't steal a man from another woman," she said. "Only you know what's in your heart." When he came back to her, she welcomed him as if he was a repentant, boisterous teenager who had needed some space. She was more than ten years younger than Kostea, yet she seemed the one in control. One time she had threatened to take their affair public, in a furious and desperate voice. He panicked. She later laughed and apologized.

Hunting was not Kostea's thing. Drinking was. He left his room barefooted and met the police chief and two beaters on the porch. They reported their group had shot two dozen geese, a slaughter of sorts. Enough to eat that night and for each to take two geese home.

Kostea had a glass of plum brandy with the chief and ate a slice of dark bread with hard salami. The alcohol warmed his belly. The sun was setting behind the building, the water mirroring the purple sky and the dark silhouettes of the poplars.

The cook came out and started the fire in a pit in the backyard. "You'll need your shoes," the police chief said. "Once it gets dark, the mosquitoes go away, and we will eat by the fire, where it's muddy."

Kostea nodded and went back to his room. He crossed paths with Marin and Igor. "Be right out," he shouted to his friends, happily pointing at his feet as if he had just committed the silliest of pranks.

"Za rodinu!" Marin shouted after him, both thumbs in the air.

On his shoulder, Igor carried his guitar. "Just watch for the recoil," he had told Kostea earlier, but it wasn't the gun he had been talking about. Kostea needed to decide what to do with Maya. The longer he waited, the harder the recoil might be.

―――――――――――

After many more shots of brandy and several bottles of the local Murfatlar wine, after the geese had been roasted over the fire and the charred fat had sizzled, Igor started to sing. The men kept the rhythm by hitting the backs of pots with their forks and accompanied him with their husky voices, some better than others.

On a break, Igor went inside to get more cigarettes.

"Comrade Igor has a good voice," the cook said.

"He's our lark," Marin said.

"Yes, our lark *and* our nightingale," Kostea added ironically.

"Good thing he's not a goose," the chief of police joked.

"He sings as well as he shoots," one of the Securitate guys added in an admiring tone.

"He's truly a great shot," the other one agreed.

"Better than you, boys?" Marin asked.

"Probably not," the Securitate agent said. "Comrade Marin, we should take him target shooting."

Igor returned, a freshly lit cigarette between his lips.

"Hey, Igor, you're being challenged to go target shooting, you and the boys," Marin said.

"You're brave," Igor said. "Let's have one more drink. My aim gets better with alcohol."

"Igor, make sure you take your gun with you," Kostea yelled, annoyed at Igor being the center of attention. "The good one."

"I only have one weapon," Igor said.

"You have two," Kostea said. "The hunting gun and the one in your pants." Someone laughed.

"You know, the one that's too short," Kostea added. At that moment, he didn't care what Igor felt.

Igor looked at him and shook his head. "Doctor, I think the gun in my pants is all right."

"I heard *rumors* that's not what your former wife said." In the light of the fire, he saw Igor's face.

The others saw it as well.

"Guys, guns are for hunting," the president of the cooperative said in a mellow tone. "Big or small, let's keep our wives out of it."

No one sang after that.

Kostea slept poorly and woke up with a massive headache. His shoes were muddy. He sat on his bed, rubbing his head, waiting for his turn to use the bathroom. When he finally walked onto the porch to eat breakfast, he saw Igor and Marin sitting next to each other.

Marin answered his greeting, but Igor looked away.

"Good morning, Igor," Kostea said one more time.

"Shut up. I'm pissed at you," Igor said.

"Why are you pissed? Last night? It was a joke."

"A very bad joke," Igor said.

Kostea wasn't in the mood to apologize. "You're too sensitive," he said. "Anyway, I decided against hunting today. Marin, I'll return the boots and the gun and take off. Igor, you can ride home with Marin."

CHAPTER 22

Dad, I'm Out of Here

December 1969 to January 1970

It was late December, still dark outside, and a light snow was falling. Kostea pulled the choke and started the two-stroke engine. While his new white Wartburg was warming up and the windshield defrosting, he returned to the apartment to finish getting dressed and drink his morning coffee.

"You went outside without a coat," Mimi scolded him in the kitchen.

The apartment was quiet. Sasha was in the bathroom, and Clara and Toddy were still asleep.

"Yes, Mother, but I'm not cold. How many times must I tell you?"

"I don't believe you."

Kostea shrugged. "Where is my coffee?"

"It just came to a boil," Mimi said, pointing to the steaming kettle on the gas stove.

He extended his cup, and she poured, her hand trembling slightly. The coffee spilled.

"Oh, Mother, look what you're doing!" he yelled, shaking his fingers scalded by the hot liquid. Immediately he felt contrite. She was getting older. His father also. And Toddy was almost twenty.

Toddy. He had studied hard for his finals in early December. Kostea was impressed with him and had offered to take him out to a restaurant to celebrate his success, but Toddy had had other plans. He had left town for a week to go skiing. Kostea had never skied but had heard it was fun. In three years, he'd be turning fifty. A young fifty. He had his work, his friends, his parents, his wife and Maya, who increasingly was a complication. But that wasn't all. How many more years did he have left with Toddy? Five, perhaps ten, if he were lucky. This was his time to enjoy his son, no doubt about it.

He and Clara were invited to welcome the New Year at Marin's new large apartment near Herăstrău Park, where the Party leadership lived. In Romania, the government barely acknowledged Christmas, but New Year's Eve celebrations were great affairs, with strings of lights, posters, and decorations everywhere. People had two days off. Kostea looked forward to the party at his friend's place and wanted Toddy to join. He would proudly parade him in front of everybody—his son, a young man, smart, sparkling, good looking. The three of them, he, Toddy, and Clara together, surrounded by elegant, noisy people. A well-stocked buffet, dancing, and drinking.

In his underwear and undershirt, Kostea entered his son's room without knocking. "Tonight's New Year's Eve, and we're getting ready. I hope you're coming with us."

"Dad, I can't. I told Mother already." Toddy sat on his bed, also in his underwear. Kostea noticed the slim and well-formed body of his son and sucked in his belly.

"Told her what?"

"That I'm going to Lydia's."

Kostea paused for a second, feeling disappointed. "Look, Toddy. I would like you to spend this evening with us. It's important."

"Why?" Toddy stood up and put on his black pants.

Kostea crossed his hands over his chest. "Because I'm asking you, son. That's why it's important."

"I don't remember you asking me to join you last year or the year before."

"This year is different. You're a student now, an adult, and I want you to meet some people. Influential people. You never know when in life they might turn out to be helpful." The chair in front of Toddy's desk was piled high with clothes. Kostea pushed the clothes to the floor and sat. He took a cigarette from the pack on the desk. "Give me a light, will you?" He was not going to take no for an answer.

Toddy grabbed the lighter off his nightstand and threw it to Kostea. "I'm not interested in your people. Lydia is having a party at her place with all our friends, and I'm going there. I'm in love with her."

"Of course you are," Kostea said, looking at Toddy sideways, his sarcasm obvious.

Toddy said, "Dad, I know what I'm feeling."

"Listen, Toddy. Girls come and go. What's the saying? Like buses. But you only have one mom and one dad, and if from time to time they ask you to do something for them, you do it."

"Dad," Toddy said, "why tonight? I'll spend the evening with you tomorrow."

"No, go to Lydia's tomorrow and spend tonight with us. Or . . . you know what, let's compromise. Stay with us until midnight and go to Lydia afterward. I'm sure your friends will be partying the whole night, and I'll give you money for a taxi."

"Dad, you don't understand. I convinced Lydia to throw this party. Her parents are going out, and all our friends are coming. I spent yesterday and today helping Lydia with shopping and decorations. I need to be there early."

"Toddy, I ask you to reconsider."

Blood rushed to Toddy's face. His father was being obstinate, pushy. Toddy paused, picked up his white shirt, freshly ironed by Clara, and put it on. A small mirror stood on the top shelf of his bookcase. "No, Dad, *you* need to reconsider," he said, looking at himself in the mirror and combing his hair. "I've told you why, and I explained it to Mother. *She* agrees."

"I don't care that your mother agrees," Kostea interrupted. "She'll agree with you and always take your side. But there comes a time when you need to understand that a firm handshake from your father is worth more than a hundred hugs and kisses from your mother. That time is now."

"Dad, you're being ridiculous," Toddy said. He put on his shoes, grabbed the tie he had chosen, and tried to tie it in a fashionably large knot.

Kostea crushed his cigarette in the ashtray and rose. He came closer and reached out with his hands to help Toddy.

Toddy jumped. "Don't touch me."

"All right, son, you do it. But you're coming tonight. Is that clear?"

"No, Dad, it is not. I'm not coming!"

"Listen, I've always been there for you."

"So?" Toddy said and grabbed his sweater. "Dad, I'm out of here."

Kostea's face changed. "You stay!"

"You can't order me, Dad. I'm no longer a baby."

"You're doing this for a woman?" Kostea sighed. "Do you know how many others there will be in your life?"

"Dad."

"Don't come to me when she leaves you for someone else or goes to Israel without you."

"Don't worry, Dad, she won't leave me. But *I'm leaving*. Now. This minute. And I'm not coming back if you don't want me to. So, Dad, have a nice New Year and a great life."

Toddy stormed out of his room, grabbed his winter jacket off the coat hanger in the foyer, and left.

At Marin's party, Kostea couldn't stop thinking about Toddy. As much as he tried to be loud and jovial, he hurt on the inside. The well-stocked bar and buffet didn't appeal to him. Around him, people seemed noisy. Clara didn't say much, but he could see that she, too, was saddened and upset. He did it, didn't he? Again.

Have a nice life, were Toddy's parting words. While a student, Toddy depended on his parents, didn't have a job, lived at home, and used public transportation. That's how it was in Romania, and while Kostea didn't take Toddy literally, the implied threat was real. Sooner or later. When parents fight with their children, they're always losing. Besides, he had not been fair with Toddy. He had not listened to him, had not tried to understand him, and had only worried about himself and his own desires, which were not always the most important.

Kostea saw Igor in a corner of the room. He had not seen or spoken to him since that ill-fated hunting trip in the summer. When their eyes met, Igor looked away and whispered to Aida. She nodded. Kostea filled two glasses with wine and advanced slowly. He offered one to Igor. "Na zdarovye," he said in Russian and raised his glass.

Igor's face opened up. "Za rodinu!"

Kostea said, "I'm sorry."

Igor nodded. "I'm sorry also."

The two friends kissed on both cheeks and drank bruderschaft, each bringing to his lips the wine, golden like the sunset. Next to them, Aida's face reflected contentment.

Shortly after midnight Kostea grabbed his winter jacket and approached Igor for a second time. "Come with me," he said.

"Where? Why?" Igor asked.

"I'll tell you outside."

Watching from a distance, Clara understood. The others couldn't care less or didn't notice.

———————

Loud music and voices came through the apartment door. Kostea turned to Igor. "This must be it," he said.

Igor pulled a piece of paper from his pocket and confirmed the apartment number. He smiled. "The people in this building must be very tolerant."

"Hey, it's New Year's Eve," Kostea said, ringing the bell. Nobody answered. He tried the doorknob, to no avail, and started knocking. Just then, the door sprang open, and a young couple flew out. Their faces were flushed, and they were laughing and holding hands. The noise from the apartment followed them like a wave. Seeing Kostea and Igor, the woman released her partner's hand and stepped back toward the apartment door. She was very pretty, wearing a black sequined miniskirt. The young man took a few quick steps forward, then pirouetted at the top of the stairs. A cigarette dangled from his lips.

"Can I help you?" he asked, trying to keep a straight face before he succumbed to a peel of uncontrollable laughter.

"We're looking for Lydia Faur," Kostea said, ignoring the man and addressing the woman.

"You're in the right place," she said. "Who are you?"

"I'm Doctor Bardu, and this is my friend Igor," Kostea replied. "Do you know Toddy? I'm his father."

The young woman nodded and disappeared, pulling the door shut in Kostea's face. Breathing heavily, the young man, his black hair sweaty, retreated a few steps and looked down into the barely lit stairway. His white dress shirt, bulging over his waist, was stained at the armpits.

"You and Toddy are friends?" Kostea asked.

"I know Toddy," the young man said.

"Seems like you're having a lot of fun," Kostea continued.

The young man took a drag of his cigarette. "Uh-huh."

The door opened again, and the young woman reappeared, accompanied by another woman in a long gown, her brown eyes sparkling under a mop of short dark hair.

Shyly, she stretched her hand out to Kostea. "Hello, I'm Lydia Faur."

"Happy New Year, Lydia," Kostea said. "I'm Toddy's dad."

"I heard," Lydia said. "Happy New Year, and please come in. Toddy's in the dining room at the buffet." She smiled. "His favorite place in the house."

In the living room the carpets had been rolled away, and the furniture was pushed against the walls to clear the floor for dancing. Beatles songs blasted from a tape recorder. A green branch of mistletoe hung from the ceiling light. The doors to the balcony and to an adjacent bedroom were open. There were about twenty young people in the room and more in the bedroom. Food and drinks were arranged on a table decorated with tinsel and confetti. Kostea found Toddy next to a tray of pigs-in-a-blanket, eating and talking to Cristi. When he saw his father, Toddy froze. "Dad, what are you doing here?"

"I came to wish you a Happy New Year."

"Where is Mom?"

"At Marin's party," Kostea said.

Curious, the young people gathered around them. Somebody stopped the music.

"And why are you here?"

Suddenly, Kostea became aware of how out of place he and Igor looked. "You know—"

"Dad, did you drive?"

"We took a taxi."

"Well, Happy New Year, Dad," Toddy said, suddenly enlivened. "And, Igor, Happy New Year to you."

"Happy New Year, Toddy," Igor said.

The room echoed with good wishes, and Cristi popped open another champagne bottle. Toddy kissed Igor on both cheeks and then kissed his father.

"I'm sorry," Kostea whispered.

"Me too," said Toddy.

———————

"Wow, that was your dad?" somebody said to Toddy after Kostea and Igor left. "What a nice man!"

Toddy kissed Lydia. They danced. When the song ended, she came very close.

"That's how he's always been," Toddy told her. "First he hurts you, and then he feels sorry."

"But are you glad he came to apologize?"

"Very glad," Toddy answered.

CHAPTER 23

We're Out of Morphine

February 1971

As a member of an official Party delegation, Kostea traveled to Cuba, a country lovingly stroked by the sun at the other end of the world. February was dreary in Bucharest.

Clara was the first to wake up in the morning and late for work every day. There were so many things to do before leaving. She fixed breakfast for everybody, made grocery lists, checked on her father-in-law, and left instructions for Marcela, the housekeeper, who usually arrived after eight. She called Ina each morning. With all his connections, it had taken Kostea three years to get Ina a phone.

In addition, Clara was worried for Toddy. Since Lydia's departure to Israel, her son had stayed shut in his room. He only spoke to Cristi, who had stopped by several times. There was no letter from Lydia, nor a quick call stating she was all right. Toddy didn't complain, but Clara could feel his pain. That was the role of the mother—to ache.

Mimi and Sasha were aware that something was amiss, but Clara didn't talk to them much and they did not ask. She appreciated their discretion. She had mentioned her worries to Ina, who had listened to Clara with an impassive face. Days later, Ina surprised Clara by saying she had dreamed about a huge iron bird that had swooped up Toddy and carried him to a remote, undefined land.

Clara wondered if she had gone too far when she had told Lydia to follow her parents to Israel. Lydia and Toddy could have ignored her advice, but they were sad and confused. Impressionable.

Her advice made good sense. Didn't it?

She remembered the moment, late in the day. She had walked into Toddy's room and Lydia was crying.

"Mom, Lydia and her parents have received permission to leave for Israel," Toddy said.

Clara didn't know how to react in the moment and pretended not to sense her son's anguish. "Congratulations. That's what your family wanted," she said to Lydia, guessing it was true.

"Maybe *they* wanted it," Lydia said.

"Mom," Toddy said. "What should we do?"

"Lydia goes to Israel, and you guys grow up. It's exciting. She'll experience a new country and a new life."

"We love each other."

"Do you want to get married right now?"

Toddy looked at Lydia as her eyes opened wide. Neither of them said anything.

"That's what I thought," Clara said. "You're too young."

"Romeo and Juliet were young," Toddy said.

"Did they live happily ever after?" Clara looked at the window. "Listen to me. Give life a chance. Let Lydia follow her family. If your love won't last, maybe it wasn't meant to be. But you love each other, and you have to trust that your love will survive. You'll stay in touch. Write. Lydia can visit from time to time. Finish college and get married when the time is right. You'll know when that is."

"You think Lydia will return to Romania?"

"Maybe. Or together, you'll go someplace else. A lot of young people are leaving Romania, you know. And time goes by very fast. I was your age during the war when your father went to the front with his medical unit. He could have been killed. Almost two years I waited, but I trusted him fully, and he came back to me."

After that, Toddy spent all his time with Lydia until she left. Friends came to her apartment to help pack up her books and ship them in ten-pound parcels to Lydia's relatives in Israel. He watched her family gather the clothes and personal items they were allowed to take with them. Neighbors and total strangers came to buy their furniture and everything else they had. The apartment emptied out bit by bit. The beds were the last to go.

Lydia and Toddy went to Herăstrău Park and quietly watched the swans.

Sometimes Clara entertained a happy illusion: Had Lydia decided to stay, she would have had two beautiful children instead of one.

But Toddy was no longer a child. Clara realized that if she were to keep watch over him, she had to do it discreetly, with innocuous questions and furtive glances. "Toddy, what are you doing for fun?" she would ask, meaning, "I hope you're all right." Or, "Toddy, will you be home for dinner?" implying that he should go out with his friends.

Usually considerate with his mother, Toddy snapped a few times. "Stop pestering me."

"Don't say anything if you can't be polite," she responded and turned away, hurt.

Cuba or not, Kostea had left at the worst possible moment. He had said, "Let our boy be a boy," and had walked away, leaving her unsure of what he meant. Was there something mothers didn't know about boys growing up to be men?

Then an airmail letter arrived. Dated one day after Lydia's departure for Israel, the two crinkly onionskin pages, covered by Lydia's neat handwriting, were the harbinger of a sunny place from a different world. Toddy dashed out the door to look for Cristi, but his friend wasn't home. He read the letter again and called Clara at work. "Mom, Lydia's all right. I have a letter from her! She wrote it on her second day in Israel, and it took almost four weeks to get here."

Clara exhaled, lowered herself onto the high stool by her tiled lab counter, and before she had a chance to respond, Toddy started reading to her:

My dear Toddy,

A whole day went by without you. Maybe writing to you will bring us together. I love you.

Yesterday we were welcomed at the Lod airport in Tel Aviv by Aunt Larissa and her family. You don't know her, but I'm sure you remember her name, from all those books we shipped to her. Larissa's husband, Simon, was there as well, as were their son, Andy, and Andy's wife, Alice. Andy is only five years older than I am, but he is married already.

Toddy read on and on . . .

———————

Kostea returned from Cuba with a straw hat on his head and a chewed cigar in his mouth. When he climbed on the bathroom scale, the needle moved to over a hundred kilos.

"How was it?" Mimi asked while she nervously twisted her hands.

"How was what?"

"Your trip."

"Oh, it was great. You know, Cuba's a beautiful country, and the gulf is so blue."

"What gulf are you talking about?"

"The Gulf of Mexico, Mama. What world do you live in?"

"Excuse me . . ." Mimi said.

"We sailed on the gulf. They told us there could be sharks in the water, but some of us went in anyway."

"You swam with the sharks?"

"No, the water was shallow, and our steward kept watch. At the banquet, we were supposed to meet Fidel Castro, but he never showed up. In Havana, there is nothing to buy. Our stores look much better, if you know what I mean."

"I never go out," Mimi said.

"That's too bad." Kostea pushed his plate away. "Where is Dad?"

"Your dad is not feeling well."

Kostea took Sasha's pulse and urged him to get up, wash his face, and walk around the apartment a bit. Later, as he was getting ready to leave for his afternoon rounds, he found Sasha on the living room couch.

"Hey, what are you doing here, old man?" he asked in a jovial tone.

"Waiting for you," Sasha said.

"Oh?"

"I want you to promise me something, right now."

"What is it, Dad? Quickly. I have to go." Kostea sat next to Sasha. It had to be something important. They rarely talked.

"Kostea, I don't have too long."

"Nonsense, Dad."

"Kostea, listen to me." Sasha's eyelids were thin, his cloudy eyes deep in their sockets and the white skin on his face peeling and dry. "I've seen death all my life. Hospitals too. When my time comes, don't rush me to the hospital. Please."

"All right, Dad, I will take good care of you right here at home. But you're not dying, you know." Kostea smiled and patted his father's leg. "We'll talk some more when I'm back."

"Please promise me, Kostea. I want Mimi to be here with me. And you."

"I promise you, Dad."

That evening, they ate in the dining room. Sasha was feeling all right.

"There was really nothing to buy," Kostea said, speaking again about Cuba. He handed Clara a coral necklace wrapped in white tissue paper. "Besides this, I only bought two liters of rum."

They had changed planes in Casablanca, where their luggage got mixed up. "I had to step out on the tarmac and find my own suitcase," Kostea said. "It felt like a sauna out there next to the roaring plane."

"It was cold and raining in Bucharest," Mimi said.

"There was a second plane next to ours, and those people came out as well. They were bound for the States."

"You should have jumped ship," Toddy said, snickering.

Toddy came home early and found Sasha lying on the couch. White foam was drying at the corners of his mouth. Bent over him, Mimi was trying to give him his nitroglycerine pill.

"Sashenka, stick your tongue out. Please, make an effort for me."

"Mimi, what's going on?" Toddy asked.

"He can't breathe," Marcela said.

"Did anybody call Dad?"

"Mrs. Marie tried, but she couldn't get through."

Toddy dialed the hospital and asked the switchboard operator to tell Dr. Bardu to come home right away. When Kostea arrived, Sasha was wheezing. His body shook each time he took a breath.

"I can't place his pill under his tongue," Mimi said.

"Forget it. I'll give him morphine. Marcela, boil the syringe," Kostea said.

Mimi tensed. "We're out of morphine."

"Mama, how can this be?"

Mimi rolled her eyes. "You used the last vial the last time he had an angina attack."

"And you didn't say anything? Oh, Mother, what's wrong with you?"

"I was sure you knew."

Kostea controlled his displeasure. He pulled a chair over and sat by his dad. He took his hand. "Dad, how are you doing?"

Sasha tried to smile in response.

"Listen, hang in there, and we'll get you through this. I'll run to the pharmacy and be right back."

"Shall I call Mom?" Toddy asked as he followed Kostea into the hallway.

"Yes, Toddy, please. And watch over Mimi, all right?"

February 12, 1971, Bucharest

Dear Lydia,

I am sad. My grandfather died four days ago. He complained that he didn't feel well, and then, puff—he was gone. Just like that, in an instant. Like a light you switch off.

Grandpa Sasha, that nice, generous man, is no longer with us. He used to come to my room every evening as I was doing my homework, silently kiss the top of my head, and place a piece of chocolate on my desk. He was always serene and evenhanded, in striking and direct contrast to my father, who, as you know, can behave like a summer storm.

When my grandparents came to live with us, I resented them— actually, not them as much as our family situation at the time.

I felt like Grandmother Ina was being pushed out of our apartment to make room for them. And I felt sorry for Ina. She always said that my mother and I were the light of her life, and now she was going to live alone in that ugly building where people crawled around like ants. That was my father's fault. He never respected Ina, and in our family, when my father wants something—anything—he gets it.

With time, I grew much closer to Mimi and Sasha, and I realized that Ina is better off living on her own, away from my father's mood swings. Now it's Mimi, his own mother, who has to deal with his temperament. When that happens and I am home, I take her side.

I can't imagine Mimi without Grandpa. It's good she is living with us. They've been through so much together: a revolution, wars, resettlements, and regime change. As Mimi often says, her life has been a sequence of twenties—the first twenty years spent in Odessa, the next in Kishinev, then Bistriţa, and now Bucharest. As soon as she grows roots in a place, there comes a compelling reason to leave.

Lydia, I wonder what life has in store for us.

Grandpa was eighty-four. He lived a good, hard, full life.

His funeral was this morning, at the Mărcuţa Cemetery, in a part of Bucharest where I have never set foot before. Father Daniel performed the funeral service. I didn't know him—a large man, bald, with expressive brown eyes and a deep voice. He was my parents' religion teacher in high school. They taught religion in school in those days. After the war, he was deported to Siberia. He survived, came back, and took charge of the Mărcuţa Parish, with its small but beautiful Orthodox church next to the cemetery. His son went on a trip to Austria two years ago and never returned. Father

Daniel helped my parents purchase a double burial plot at this cemetery. Even a plot for the dead is hard to come by.

It was cold, and most of the service was inside the church. The actual burial didn't last long. Father Daniel said a prayer. The gravediggers lowered the casket. Some of us stepped forward and threw in fistfuls of dirt. Mimi cried in my mother's embrace.

Afterward they all came to the house. Cristi was here, which helped me a lot. I'm embarrassed to admit that I watched with some amusement how my father and Grandmother Ina avoided each other, as if, even in pain, their discord persisted. I guess some feelings are stronger than death. And I pondered the meaning of death, how everything changes and how everything stays the same.

Like Mimi, my father is very affected, maybe even more than she is. It is wrong to grade pain, as it is wrong to grade love, but since Grandpa died, Dad seems a changed man. He is subdued. I feel sorry for him, even as I wonder how long this change will last. When people are around, he puts on a brave face, but when he's alone, I can see his sadness. And he is tortured by guilt. We were out of morphine, which could have saved Grandfather's life. He should have called an ambulance and rushed Grandpa to the hospital. Instead, he left and drove around like a madman looking for morphine.

When he returned forty-five minutes later, Grandpa was dead. So, dad suffered because he had been negligent with the medication and because he had missed Grandpa's last moments.

How does one prepare for death? Eminescu writes that it isn't death that we fear, but the permanence of it. My love, you make me happy to be alive. I don't mean to upset you with this letter. Let's enjoy what we have, even if ultimately it all turns to dust.

I am delighted that you will be here during your spring vacation and in the summer as well. I am counting the days!

I started my second semester and find college life (without you) dreary. The rainy, chilly weather doesn't help.

I love you,

Toddy

———————

His chest felt locked in a vise, and he could hardly breathe. The pain was overbearing. He wanted to scream, but nothing came out. Maybe turning in bed would help. He couldn't. Quickly, he needed to administer himself a shot of morphine for the pain to be gone. Morphine was a miracle drug. Even in the darkness, the medicine cabinet was visible through the open door to the bathroom, a few steps away. There, on the second shelf on the left there should have been three small vials. He could imagine them in their thin, breakable glass with their golden-brown sheen. And the syringe would be on the right. Normally, he would boil the syringe, but there was no time. He needed the shot right away. The chance of infection from the needle that he had used on his father wasn't as bad as his pain.

He rolled out of bed and crawled forward. He stood up. In front of him was not a door, but a solid wall. He had pulled himself up by the edge of the bookshelf. To get to the bathroom, he'd have to cross the bedroom and walk down the corridor—too far and too late. He exhaled at the horror of that thought, and a scream left his chest.

"Kostea, wake up!" Clara was shaking him hard. Her long hair covered half of her face as she leaned over his shoulder. "You're having a nightmare."

He took several long heavy breaths. After a few minutes his pulse quieted, and they went back to sleep.

"I'm obsessed," he told Clara in the morning before driving to work.

"I'm going to do whatever it takes to bring home some morphine. It's too late for my father, but what if I need it one day?" Then he added, "Or my mother, or you?"

The morphine weighed on his mind. He had failed his father—that much he knew. He remembered the common adage that when your parents die, there is no one left between you and your own mortality. Only his mother, with her small form and wrinkled face, stood between him and death. His time was not running out, but he felt the dull pain of his loss. He was determined to wear it like a badge of honor, a measure of love—the love for his father.

He didn't know how to cope with his guilt. Dinescu and other doctors had reassured him the morphine wouldn't have made a difference, but he knew. Better than all. He should have been ready. One wasted moment, one small mistake.

His father was looking at him from above—those brown eyes, that large forehead, those thick lips. He wore his white coat. Kostea was still a schoolboy spending his afternoons at the hospital in Kishinev, and his father was teaching him about pain. When you make a mistake, you remember and learn. There'll be a next time. Until there'll be none.

CHAPTER 24

The Way He Loved Clara

July 1971

Kostea had injured his ankle playing tennis. His orthopedist had put it in a brace that allowed him to walk, drive, and even stand for a long time while performing surgeries. It hurt, but it got better each day. On Sunday morning, stretching his leg under the kitchen table, he told Clara, "Let's join the kids in the mountains. Get our backpacks, and I'll pick you up after my rounds, at about eleven."

Mimi was silently drinking her coffee and smoking her cigarette.

"Do you think it's a good idea?" Clara said. "Lydia has just arrived from Israel. We should give them some space, the children."

"They have all the space in the world," Kostea said. "They are in the mountains," he added and grinned, convinced his joke with the space and the mountains was funny.

Clara didn't relent. "Remember when we were young? Did you want your father with us?"

Sorrow crossed Kostea's face very quickly. It had been five months since Sasha's death, and like the pain in his leg, that pain was also getting better. "Toddy and I are good friends," he said. "It's different."

"They're staying at Curmătura, going on daily hikes. It's a hut, nothing fancy," Clara said. She too wanted to be with the children.

219

"Good. We'll go hiking with them."

"With your leg?"

Kostea's pant leg was split around the brace. "My ankle is better, thank you very much, and a little pain is always useful." He turned to Mimi. "Mama, we'll be gone for three days."

"Go," Mimi said. "I'm not a child. I don't need a sitter." She stubbed her cigarette in the ashtray. The burning tip broke off and rolled over the rim.

"Careful," Kostea said. "You're burning the tablecloth."

"Where?" Mimi asked, continuing her stubbing motion and throwing an innocent gaze at Kostea. Thin blood vessels traversed the white of her eyes, and fragile blue veins, like a river's delta, stood out on the back of her hands.

"You don't see what you're doing."

"Sure," she snapped. "Call me blind."

"Nobody's calling you anything, Mama. I just don't want you to set our house on fire."

"And I do," Mimi said.

Clara placed her hand on Mimi's trembling fingers. She lifted the burning cigarette tip with a spoon and threw it in the sink. "Here we go."

Kostea pulled his right leg closer to his chair and pushed himself up. Clara walked with him to the door. "I'll ask Marcela to stay with her."

"This is as close as we can get by car," Kostea told Clara. "I'll drop you off at the general store, and I'll go look for parking. Get something to eat."

Kostea drove through the little village until he found a friendly local who allowed him to park in his backyard for a fee and agreed to drive them to the trailhead in his pickup truck. They found Clara in the village square staring at a bulletin board. Her backpack rested at her feet.

Behind the red-roof houses, the mountain rose like a wall, two thousand meters into the air. The sun was past the zenith, its rays skipping off the bare, craggy peaks and causing a deep shadow to fall over half the square.

"Hop in," Kostea said through the open window of the truck and slid closer to the driver.

Clara crossed from sun to shade and shivered. It felt as if the mountain wrapped her in its breath, and the temperature dropped a few degrees.

"What is it?" Kostea asked. "You look forlorn."

"Nothing," she said and got in. "I bought buffalo cheese, a can of liver pâté, and a loaf of white bread."

"They bake the bread fresh every morning," the driver said.

"How long will it take to reach Curmătura?" Kostea asked.

"Oh, about three to four hours, depending on how fast you hike. Although, with that leg . . ."

"My leg is fine," Kostea said. "What time does it get dark?"

"After eight. You have plenty of time."

At the trailhead, the driver turned his truck around. "Happy trekking," he said. "And enjoy the time with your son."

The path led uphill through the forest. The air was velvety and fragrant, the light borrowing a green hue from the trees. Kostea walked ahead. As the incline increased, so did the distance between him and Clara.

Kostea stopped, breathing heavily, and Clara caught up to him.

"So," Clara said, pointing at his ankle, "how is it?"

"Not bad." He was in his blue shorts, white tennis shoes, and an unbuttoned flannel shirt, the sleeves rolled up to his elbows. His legs were taut. The brace caused his ankle to look thick and sluggish. "This walk is good for me. I might lose half a kilo or so." He patted his belly and smiled.

A light wind stirred the oaks and the beeches.

"It's nice here," Clara said.

The light changed to blue as they left the foothills and stepped into the shade of the mountain. The slope increased.

"It's an eight-hundred-meter elevation difference to Curmătura," Kostea said, panting heavily. "This is going to be quite a hike, and it takes us only halfway to the top. But we'll worry about it tomorrow. I mean, if we're going to climb to the peak."

"On that bulletin board," Clara said, "I read about a hiker who slipped and fell six hundred meters to his death. That's how steep the last portion is. Six hundred meters, straight down."

"You don't need to fall six hundred meters to die," Kostea said. He didn't seem too impressed.

She stopped. "It's not a joke."

"You're right." He placed his hands on her shoulders.

"The man who died was twenty-two years old," Clara said.

Toddy was twenty-one.

"Toddy will be all right," Kostea said.

"Lydia has a fear of heights."

"That's good. They won't climb to the ridge."

She looked straight at him, her eyes the color of the forest. "I worry," she said.

"Don't worry. Just look around."

Pines and spruces mixed with the beeches of the lower trail. A carpet of dead leaves and pine needles covered the ground. Chalky rocks smoothed by wind and water pierced through. Blue bell-shaped flowers grew in small patches, brightening the forest's carpet like the morning dew. Light danced through tree branches. The path snaked upward, without end.

Clara pointed to a fallen trunk. "Let's sit and have some pâté."

He pulled out his pocketknife and sliced the bread. Then he used it to open the can. They drank water from his metal jug, one after the other, him wiping the neck with his hand. Suddenly he thought about Maya, and he made an effort to stop. "Say you're enjoying this moment," he said.

"I do."

"Do you love me?"

"I do . . . when you are nice."

He stood. He was handsome and tall, his hair a crown of soft silver. "When was the last time I wasn't nice?"

"This morning with your mother."

"She was about to set our house on fire," he said. "It's not easy seeing her grow old."

"We are no longer young ourselves. I, too, see my mother grow old every day. And she is alone."

"We are different. You always think about others. My question was simple. When was I nasty to *you*?"

"I don't remember. Kostea, we don't live in a bubble. You hurt me when you assail other people—your mother, my mother, Igor, the people at work. Toddy. You always argue with Toddy. Why?"

"I love my son. We never argue."

"Ask him if you don't believe me."

Kostea wiped his forehead with his sleeve. "I want to be his best friend. I only think of his happiness."

"You don't own him," Clara said.

A branch fell from a tree. Leaves rustled.

"This trip," Kostea said. "Do you think it's a bad idea? Should we turn back?"

"We are here now." Clara stood up and lifted her backpack. "There is something else. You're always busy, and I hardly see you at all."

"I'll make time. When Dad died, I decided to do my best to control my outbursts."

"I love you," she said.

———

As Clara and Kostea emerged from the woods, they stopped to catch their breath and look around. A two-story log hut with a pitched roof of red shingles and red geraniums in the windows looked cozy and welcoming. There were people sitting around tables on the spacious deck, too far away for Clara and Kostea to see if Toddy was among them. Some of the people waved, and Kostea waved back.

"Dr. Bardu, Mrs. Bardu, is that you?" Cristi yelled from a distance as he ran toward them. "What a surprise! Toddy didn't say you were coming." He seemed taller and slimmer than they remembered.

"Cristi, he doesn't know," Kostea said as soon as he recognized his son's friend. "We wanted to surprise him."

"Where is he?" Clara asked.

"Inside. He and Lydia will be very happy to see you. I'll let them know right away. We're getting ready to eat dinner on the deck. Mrs. Bardu, please let me take your backpack."

Clara removed her backpack and rewarded him with the warm smile of a mother. She straightened her shoulders and smoothed her shirt. "To be honest," she said, "I'm glad we've made it." She pointed to Kostea's brace.

"Oh my God," exclaimed Cristi as he picked up Clara's backpack with the wide sweep of a giant. "What happened to your ankle, Dr. Bardu?"

"Just a strain, nothing really," Kostea shrugged.

"And you hiked on it all the way up here."

"I couldn't leave my foot behind," Kostea joked.

"Of course not, even though you are a surgeon," Cristi joked in return.

He led them to a table where his friends were. "Hey, everybody, say hello to Toddy's parents," he announced.

"Hey, Toddy's parents, come and sit down," said a girl who patted the empty space next to her and moved closer to the others to make more room for them. "You look exhausted. You really do."

"Good day. It's a pleasure," joined in a slim man of about thirty who spoke with an accent.

"Thank you," Kostea said. "Clara, you can stay with the children while I go inside and see about our accommodations."

There was a somewhat amused and loud protest at his calling them children, while Clara shrugged and sat down.

"Mrs. Bardu, I'm Nadia, Lydia's best friend from high school," the girl said. "I don't know if you remember me. I'm so happy Lydia is back here from Israel for the summer. She and Toddy are wonderful together."

"That they are," answered Clara and looked around the table, feeling slightly out of place alone with the young people. Sweaty from the hike, she touched her face and moved her hand across her forehead. She felt a chill. The sky was cloudless, but the sun had long since gone behind the crest. She reached for the bottle of mineral water on the table. "May I?"

"Of course." Nadia pushed a glass in Clara's direction. "This is my boyfriend, Hans," she added, pointing at the slim man who had spoken earlier. "He's from Switzerland."

"It's a pleasure," Hans repeated his earlier words, clearly some of the very few he knew in Romanian.

Clara nodded and drank her mineral water. There were three other young men at the table, Toddy's schoolmates from the Polytechnic Institute. Clara scrutinized their faces, wondering if she had met any of them before, and concluded she hadn't. What might they be thinking of Toddy's mother following him up the mountain? A gust of wind raised a fine dust into the air. She closed her eyes. When she opened them again, she saw Toddy walking toward their table, holding hands with Lydia. Cristi followed closely behind them.

"Mom," Toddy said. "What are you doing here?" He looked sunburned and relaxed. There was a grin on his face that Clara took for a slight embarrassment at his parents' unexpected appearance.

"We came to see you," she said. "Out of boundless parental devotion. Or, no, call it paternal devotion, because it was your father's idea. He's inside getting us a room."

"There are no private rooms here, Mother. Everyone sleeps on bunks."

"They have a few cabins in the back, but they're very expensive," said Cristi, his tone implying that choosing one would be outlandish.

Lydia hugged Clara. "Wow!" she said. "This is quite unexpected. You came all the way up here, and Dr. Bardu, with his twisted ankle." She turned to Nadia. "He twisted it playing tennis and had the brace fitted the day I arrived."

"And now he's OK," Kostea said, appearing out of nowhere. "Don't worry about Dr. Bardu." He held a large carafe of red wine in one hand and three glasses in the other. "Great to see you, son. And you, too, Lydia. Now, Toddy, be a good sport and go inside and bring us some more glasses."

"There are glasses on the table," said one of the students. "We used them for water."

"All right, then," Kostea said. "Here is wine for everybody. Bottoms up!"

The youngsters cheered. There was a larger group at the nearby table, and those people cheered as well.

"They are from Brașov," Cristi told Kostea, pointing at them discreetly, as if divulging a secret. "And they act like they own the place."

Kostea waved his hand in a general salute at the larger group. "Well, what do you expect?" he told Cristi. "Brașov is only thirty kilometers away, so they are at home."

"Kostea, did you make the arrangements?" Clara asked, anxious over the cacophony of voices.

"Yes, I did. I got us a cabin."

"Let's go, then."

"Let me finish this wine. It's good stuff," he said. When there was nothing left in his glass, he smacked it down on the table. "Toddy, while your mother and I are changing, get us another carafe on my account. And one for that other table, will you?"

"Happy to oblige," Toddy said.

"By the way, Toddy, they have empty cabins," Kostea said, loud enough for everybody to hear. "Why don't you and Lydia take one of them?"

Lydia blushed, and Toddy looked at the ground. "No, Dad. Thanks, it's expensive."

"C'mon, Toddy." Kostea laughed. "Your father is here now. Take a cabin. I'll pay."

"Dad, we're fine where we are."

"I thought you'd value a little privacy." Kostea poured some more wine for himself and turned to the other table. "Here, young people of Brașov, cheers!"

The response was enthusiastic. The hikers banged their knives and forks on the table, and one man raised his glass in return. "This one is for you, Doc. Too bad it is empty."

"My son will take care of that," Kostea said and nodded at Toddy. "How did you know I'm a doctor?"

"We, the good people of Brașov, have good hearing."

The laughter that rose off the deck reached the wall of the hut and reverberated. Clara marveled at her husband. In no time, he had managed to become the center of attention. With him, she would be at home everywhere, even though he didn't realize that in his silliness he had just embarrassed his son, and Lydia as well.

Well, they'd get over it. He didn't mean to embarrass any of them. He just didn't know better, and Toddy was used to his father, his prancing and strutting and occasional gaffes.

———

Holding hands, Clara and Kostea went to their log cabin. On their way, they stopped by the little creek where the path widened, and a stream gurgled cold mountain water over a rock like a faucet stuck open forever.

The cabin was adequate: two narrow beds mounted on opposite walls and covered with gray woolen blankets, with just enough room between them for a small nightstand that held a kerosene lamp and a vase of wildflowers. The voices from the deck reached them like a murmur. They changed into warm sweatsuits, left their backpacks on the beds, and returned to their dining table.

While they ate, Kostea kept the wine coming. He sent carafes to the other table as well. There was no moon and no city lights, and the sky was high and starry. A kerosene lamp burned in the middle of each table. Soon, the people from Brașov rearranged the benches and pushed the tables together. Somebody passed around a plate of homemade cheese pie cut into small squares. Everybody smoked, and several loud conversations went on at the same time. Nadia and Hans were kissing in a corner.

A sheepdog came out from the kitchen, sniffed, and lay down at Clara's feet. She gave him a piece of bread, and the dog swallowed it without chewing. "Good boy," Clara said. It felt like a storybook picture, the crisp air, the dog, and the flickering flame.

"How about a song?" someone said.

The group's guide from Brașov was a tall man with a pronounced chin, in a light-blue windbreaker. He took his hands out of his pockets, lifted one finger, and started singing a popular song about a young college student in a tattered coat who didn't have money to pay his rent. His voice grew stronger as he went, and soon the people around the table locked arms, swaying with the tune, and sang along. Cristi, Lydia, and Toddy joined in. Prompted by Kostea, they next sang "Iupaidia," the so-called anthem of the medical students. The song was happy, simple-minded, and full of sexual innuendos and puns, causing some girls to laugh, embarrassed, and some of the men to yelp and bang the table.

The guide began a new song, and everyone clapped.

Cobori Doamne pe pământu
Să vezi Stalin ce-o făcutu
C-o făcut din capră vacă
Și țiganca deputată
C-o făcut din cal măgaru
Și țiganu' secretaru

Nadia leaned into Hans and translated:

Come to Earth, oh God Almighty
To see Stalin's doing
He made a cow out of a goat
And a Party deputy out of the Gypsy wife
He turned the horse into a donkey
And the Gypsy man into our Party secretary

Without fully grasping the bite and irony of the words, Hans laughed, enjoying the contagious camaraderie of the others. "Aren't you afraid to sing this in public?" he asked Nadia in German when the song ended.

She grinned. "Why would we be afraid? Everybody knows what's going on in this country. Especially us, the young people. All we want is to get out of here." Then she translated what she said into Romanian, to the delight of the crowd.

Kostea gave Toddy more money. "Get us another carafe, for the road."

Toddy went inside with Cristi, who looked at him with admiration. "Your dad hiked up here with his injured leg just to be with you. He loves you so much."

"Whatever," Toddy said.

Clara and Kostea walked back to their cabin, and the dog followed them. Once inside, Kostea lit the kerosene lamp. Clara rummaged through her backpack, found the buffalo cheese and the bread, and fed them to the dog. Kostea sat on his bed, humming. As she squeezed by him, she felt his hands on her hips. He guided her down to his lap and kissed her. She kissed him back, her hands around his neck. Then she bent over her backpack, looking for her nightshirt. He reached for the lamp on the table and switched the flame off.

"Hey, I was doing something," she said, her arched back toward him.

"I love you," he said.

It was pitch dark in the room. They fell on one of the beds, pushing aside the woolen blanket.

Later, they draped themselves in the blankets and stepped outside. The dog was still there.

"Go home, dog," Clara said. The dog whimpered and moved a few feet away.

The sky was bright with stars. Their multitude pressed down, and the silence was like a crystal canopy. "Listen," Kostea whispered, and recited a stanza from "The Evening Star," Clara's favorite poem by Eminescu.

My immortality recall,
Extinguish my eyes' fire,
And give me, in exchange of all,
One hour of desire.

She sighed: One hour of desire.

He stepped away and glanced to the west, looking for a blinking star, the fourth in a cluster. The mountain obscured the sky, and all he saw was a patch of darkness. No one would know what he was searching for. He smiled. Nobody needed to know because he didn't love anybody the way he loved Clara.

CHAPTER 25

The Boy Will Come Back

Late summer 1971 and winter 1972

A raindrop touched Lydia's forehead and rolled down her eyelid. She wiped it away with the back of her hand. She was with Toddy at the beach, but she would be returning to Israel in a week.

"What if I visit *you* next?" Toddy asked. It was one of those crazy ideas that come out of nowhere and qualify as a dream. Who in Romania would allow him to travel to Israel, a young, unattached man?

Feeling mellow and downcast, Lydia played along. "Do come. I would be very happy. My parents too. You would stay with us, and we would tour the country. Go to Jerusalem, Eilat, Sharm El Sheikh."

Weeks later, Toddy received a letter from Lydia, along with an official invitation to be submitted to the Romanian State Department. It stated that Lydia's family, Ben and Tina Malamed, would provide Toddy with room and board for the length of his stay. That was the way it was done.

Toddy looked at the invitation and shook his head. This could never happen—he wasn't naive.

He showed it to his mom and dad.

"Will you come back?" Kostea asked.

"I will."

"Then file your passport application. I'll see what I can do."

"Can you really help?" Clara asked Kostea later that day.

"I don't know," Kostea said.

He traveled with a group of doctors to Mongolia, where they visited hospitals in Ulaanbaatar and a nomadic settlement in the steppe. He spent a few days in Moscow on his way there and back. Then he attended a conference in Sofia and one in Braşov. He tended to his patients, taught his students, and coauthored a paper with Minister Dinescu on the treatment results of one hundred men with prostate cancer at Speranţa Hospital. Once the paper was submitted for publication, Kostea brought up Toddy.

The minister rolled his eyes. "Kids. They bother you when they're little, and they bug you when they're grown. I still remember removing his appendix. He was three or four years old."

Kostea nodded.

"Find somebody to talk to at the Ministry of Internal Affairs," Dinescu said, "and tell them that I consent."

In early January, Kostea went to dinner with Marin at the Garden, which was now called the White Brook.

"See Nicu Spiţeru. He's the general in charge," Marin said. "Ask for an audience."

"Do you know him? Will you call him beforehand?"

"I will."

"And you think he'll let Toddy go?"

"Saying no to passport applications is what he does." Marin grinned. "Be charming."

"The boy will come back," Kostea said.

"I know."

Kostea asked for an audience. Two days later in the afternoon, he walked up the stairs to the monumental entrance of the Ministry of Internal Affairs. An armed guard escorted him to the general's office and knocked at the door. Kostea buttoned his suit.

Spițeru was at his desk. "Dr. Bardu, a pleasure to meet you," he said and stood up, showing off his perfectly ironed uniform.

"General," Kostea said.

They shook hands.

"Tea, coffee, Coca-Cola?" Spițeru offered. "No alcohol on the job."

A drop of sweat rolled under Kostea's collar. He opted for tea.

"Two cups of tea, lemon and sugar," Spițeru said to the guard, who clicked his heels and withdrew.

Kostea thought that the general looked tired.

"Comrade Sabac called. But tell me what brings you here in your own words," Spițeru started.

Kostea had thought about what he wanted to say, yet he found it hard to begin. He closed his eyes, coughed in his fist, and said he was there on account of his son, Alexander. He said Alexander and Lydia had met in high school. They were good, serious young people who studied hard. "My son studies engineering," he specified.

"Why not medicine?" Spițeru asked. "I thought you would want him to become a doctor in keeping with your family tradition. Did you not?"

"No," Kostea said. "Being a doctor is hard." He raised his eyes at Ceaușescu's portrait on the opposite wall, and the familiar face caused him to pause. Spițeru was a bureaucrat, no different from any other, and he, Kostea, had no reason to feel intimidated. Not many parents in his shoes could do what he was doing for Toddy. "Lydia is Jewish," he continued. "Two years ago, she and her family left for Israel. Since then, she visited us several times."

"I know that," Spițeru said.

A woman walked in with a tray and placed it on the general's desk. Spițeru took out his cigarettes and offered one to Kostea.

Kostea declined.

Spițeru put his cigarettes down. "I, too, am cutting back. Sugar?" he asked.

"One spoon."

Spițeru complied.

Kostea smiled. "Now Alexander wants to go to Israel for several weeks." He considered assuring Spițeru that his son would come back and decided against it. Why bring the topic up? "I look at his trip as a great opportunity," he said, "and I've encouraged him to go. Minister Dinescu, who is my boss, agrees with me. My son will see new things and learn about the world. He and Lydia, they love each other a lot."

"They are still very young," Spițeru said. "I, too, have a son. He didn't go to college, and he recently got himself into trouble with a girl and the company he keeps. Honestly, it's my wife's fault. She spoiled him. She did everything for him when he was little. Now he thinks he's the center of the world, and I have to set him straight, which is difficult."

"I'm sorry," Kostea said, surprised at the unsolicited confession.

"Consider yourself lucky. Alexander has met a good girl."

"That's right."

"Doctor, you mentioned Minister Dinescu. I heard you are being considered for a full professorship."

Kostea took a long sip of his tea. It was obvious that after Marin's call, the general had had him investigated. And the news about the professorship was a surprise. Of all the colleagues at the hospital, Kostea was most guarded with Dr. Nuda, who had been recently promoted to chief surgeon over his ward and whose competition Kostea feared the most. While Nuda was a good doctor, Kostea was sure that he was the better one. And now, this news! Dinescu must have revealed something Kostea didn't know about, but the Securitate did.

Spițeru waited for an answer and when none came, he added, "If you ask me, from everything I have heard, you've earned it."

Suddenly, Kostea felt on top of the world. He was sitting properly in his chair in front of the general, still and upright, but in his heart, he was dancing. He was running down the steps of the Ministry, skipping two and three steps at a time. There was nothing he couldn't achieve. Nothing. "General," he said, trying to keep his voice calm. "You are busy, and I don't want to abuse your time. Can I count on your help?"

Spițeru leaned back in his chair and brought both hands behind his head, pushing his double chin forward. In that position, his face seemed bloated. His jacket strained at the seams. "Doctor, tell your son that expensive French cognac is my favorite drink."

───────────

Toddy surrendered his identity card at the police station and received his brand-new passport. He was handed a permit stating that he was authorized to purchase hard currency in the value of ten US dollars at the National Bank. He also needed to purchase an airline ticket and obtain an entry visa from the Israeli Embassy.

Kostea gave him the money for the ticket, no questions asked. While doing his errands, Cristi kept Toddy company, despite the gloomy January weather. They took buses and cabs, stood in long lines, and ate quick, cold lunches at smoke-filled snack bars. At the embassy, Toddy entered alone, while Cristi waited by the security booth in the street and smoked two cigarettes. Toddy's passport made a crackling sound when the Israeli consul opened it flat to apply his stamp. Waiting in the elegant, wood-paneled office of the embassy, Toddy felt part of a rarefied elite. He and Cristi went to the bank three times on three different days, to find out the hourly schedule, to file the request, and finally, to collect the cash. Toddy was handed a crisp ten-dollar bill. At home, they passed it to each other, awestruck.

"Are you coming back?" Cristi asked.

"I have to, for my father."

"But you want to leave."

"You know I do."

"One day, I'll leave, also."

Ina's small studio was full of stuff. Her dead husband's photograph stood on her chest of drawers, next to her precious ebony-black telephone and an alphabet-tabbed notebook with phone numbers. In a housecoat and brown leather slippers, Ina looked old. Her braided white hair pinned at the top of her head had acquired a yellowish tint. She had dark circles under her eyes.

Ina moved a hat and a scarf from a chair to make room for Toddy to sit. Toddy tried to cheer her up with details about his trip and told her how much he looked forward to it. His flight was the next day. She responded with a sad smile. He talked about flying for the first time in his life. Like him, Ina had never been on a plane.

"I hope I will see you again," she said.

He stood up to leave and gave her a kiss. "Don't worry, Grandma—I'll be back."

"I love you," she said.

At home, Mimi was playing solitaire at the dining room table. She had a hard time seeing the cards.

"Mimi, what shall I bring you from Israel?" Toddy asked.

She flicked her cigarette. "Yourself."

Clara and Kostea drove him to the airport. They didn't say much. Kostea suggested the best place to buy cognac was the duty-free store prior to boarding his flight back.

As Toddy walked through customs and waited for his luggage to be checked in, he looked back. His parents were far away in the waiting area, his mother's face buried in his dad's overcoat.

CHAPTER 26

We Need to Talk

April 1972

"We need to talk," Maya said. "I hope you won't overreact."

Kostea laughed. "Don't worry. I'm in my postcoital bliss." He rolled out of bed, picked up his boxer shorts from the floor, and pulled them up. He moved his hand to his stomach and pressed in. "I need to go on a diet," he said.

"You do," Maya said.

"Speaking of diets, let's go eat." He winked. "*You* make me hungry." When he returned from the bathroom, Maya was dressed. "What do you want to tell me?" he asked, buttoning his white shirt.

"Let's talk over dinner," she said.

The dining room at Malul Alb, a small inn on the outskirts of Râmnicu Vâlcea, was empty. Large windows faced the Olt River. The white tablecloths were set with crystal wineglasses and candles.

That morning, Maya and Kostea had attended a medical conference in town. To avoid any suspicion, they had traveled to the conference separately, Maya by train and Kostea by car. He had reserved a room for the night at the inn. When they left the conference together early, nobody saw them—Kostea made sure of that.

Now raindrops were drumming against the windows. On the

riverbank, two blooming apple trees were swaying in the wind. White petals covered the ground. Because of the clouds, dusk came early, and the innkeeper lit the tall white candles on the table. They ordered bread with smoked pork belly and plum brandy to start, pan-roasted partridge and a chicory salad and white wine for the main course, and the multilayered Doboș torte for dessert.

"I suggest we get up early tomorrow and drive to Bucharest via Rucăr," Kostea said. "If it's sunny, we'll go on a short hike. Toddy and I hiked the other side of the mountain last summer, after I busted my ankle."

Maya took a sip of her brandy. "Ouch. It's strong. How was his trip to Israel?"

"Toddy's? Fine. It was actually more than fine. When he returned, I took him to see Spițeru. Toddy gave him the cognac himself. I want the youngster to learn how it's done."

"You're smart." Irony twinkled in Maya's eyes. "I'm impressed he came back."

Kostea gulped down his brandy and reached for the bottle. "Of course he came back. He's my son and he would never betray me."

"You must know some very powerful people. We are not allowed to move from one town to another without special permission, and you got your son a passport to travel to Israel. How many people can claim such an achievement? I can count them on my fingers."

The innkeeper brought the main course and poured the wine.

Kostea sat up straight, chest out. Life had treated him well, and he did well by Toddy. "To your health," he said. "I'm glad we'll have tomorrow, because I'll be busy for the next few weeks."

"What are you saying?" Maya leaned over her plate and started eating. The candles flickered.

Kostea took a few bites. "Hmm, this is good." Then he added, "I'm saying, I don't know when I'll be able to see you again." His schedule had interfered with their affair before, but this was different. This time he was lying. Their affair had lasted much longer than he had ever expected, and this was part of his plan to let her go slowly, give her time to adjust.

"That's all right," Maya said. "Remember, I had something to tell you as well."

"Yes," Kostea said.

Maya looked around. "Are you still in your state of bliss?"

"That depends." He lined up his utensils on his plate and faced her. She was beautiful, even more so in the candlelight.

"I met somebody," she said. "A young man. I like him."

"A *young* man?"

"Yes, he's my age."

"You mean not an old man like me."

"I didn't say that."

"You didn't." Kostea emptied his glass of wine. "Does he like you as well?"

"He does."

"Did you sleep with him?"

"Kostea, that's rude."

"It's a good question."

"Well, you sleep with your wife."

"Yes, I do. It's part of the deal we have had from the very beginning. This guy is not."

"He wasn't, but now he is. We want to get married."

"How beautiful," Kostea said, his sarcasm as obvious as his pain. "So, you did sleep with him?"

She lowered her eyes. "Yes."

"Was he good?"

"Kostea, I think we should go."

"We'll go when I say we go." He had been feeling proud. Not anymore. Stay calm, he said to himself. This is good. He had wanted an end without tears and without obligations, and she was making it easy for him. Yet his blood was boiling, and his temples hurt. He poured himself more wine, drank it, and pressed the cold glass against his forehead. She was his. He didn't want to let go. Not on her terms. "Hey," he said. "Let's spend the night here, all right? Let's have one last fairytale screw."

"You're being a jerk."

"I'm a jerk, and you are a whore."

The innkeeper came out of the kitchen. "Is everything all right?"

"We're sorry," Maya responded calmly, looking straight at Kostea, her fingers curled into fists. "We have to leave—an unexpected change in plans."

"I understand, but at least finish your dinner," the innkeeper said.

"That's all right," Maya said.

"It is not." Kostea huffed.

The innkeeper ignored him and addressed Maya. "Should I pack the Doboş torte for you?"

"Very nice of you to offer, but no."

"I'll have to charge you for it anyway, and I'll have to charge you for the room as well."

Maya pointed at Kostea. "He'll pay. He's a doctor, and he can afford it." She got up abruptly and added. "I'm going upstairs to pack."

By the time Kostea finished his wine, Maya returned, the bags in her hands. "I have your things and your windbreaker," she said.

"What would men do without their wives?" the innkeeper said with a smile.

"Right," Kostea said. He took the windbreaker from Maya and gave her the car keys. "The luggage goes in the trunk. I'll pay and be right out."

"Doctor, I hope everything is all right," the innkeeper said.

"Don't worry about it," Kostea said.

Maya was waiting in the front seat. When he opened the door, he saw the luggage piled in the back. He wiped the rain off his face, turned on the engine, and switched on the low beams. The rain was pelting the car.

"There is no visibility," he said and added, "I asked you to put the luggage in the trunk." His soft white hair was glued to his forehead, yet somehow he looked like a child.

For a second, she felt the impulse to caress his face. "It was raining too hard."

He backed out of his parking space and hesitated. "Which way, left or right?"

"I have no idea."

"Of course." There were no cars in the street, and he decided to go right. "You had to do it," he said.

"Do what?"

"Tell the owner that I'm a doctor, that's what."

"What difference does it make?"

"Now he has my name *and* profession. He knows everything about me."

"You're being absurd."

"No. I'm married," he said.

"Kostea, I'm not going with you to Bucharest. Take me to the train station, please."

"Great idea," he said and accelerated, leaning over the steering wheel.

"Do you know where you're going?"

"I'll figure it out." He took a left and a left. The wheels screeched. The lights of the city were ahead of them.

"You have no right to be upset," Maya said and touched his hand on the wheel. "You don't love me. You'll never leave your wife."

He pulled his hand back. "I see. You took advantage of me while you were my student. Then, I guess, married or not, I was all right."

"You were charming," she said. "A force."

"Yes, and when I arranged your job for you, that was all right too."

"Kostea, please."

"The fun trips we went on together. The gifts."

They came to a crossing with a larger street. He stared at a sign on a post. "I can't see. What's written there?" he asked.

"The town center is to the left."

He turned. A truck came from the other side and honked.

"Shut up!" he screamed at the truck.

"I have a daughter and my whole life to think of," Maya said. "Admit it. For me, you are a dead end."

"Oh yeah?"

"My new boyfriend is nice."

He glanced at her angrily. "Don't talk to me about him."

"Kostea, watch out!"

It was too late. The red light swung widely in the wind. They flew through the intersection. A car hit them from the left, sending them spinning across the road. Instinctively he slammed on the brakes, propelling himself and Maya forward. The luggage came tumbling over them. A third car appeared out of nowhere, blew its horn, and veered drastically, managing to avoid another crash. When Kostea's car stopped moving, they were on the opposite side of the road, two wheels in a ditch. The engine stalled. The traffic light was green.

His forehead hurt. Next to him, Maya breathed hard. She's breathing, he thought. He was still mad at her and didn't want to say anything. What the hell! He opened his door and stepped out. The middle of his car was crumpled inward.

The driver of the car that hit him rushed toward him. He was furious, but otherwise all right. "You idiot!" he screamed. "What did you do?"

Enraged, Kostea turned to face him. The world spun.

When he came to, he was on his back. People were milling around. They were like cutouts against the dark. Maya was leaning over him. The rain was coming down in cold sheets.

He tried to stand, and Maya stopped him midway. "Don't move."

"Don't tell me what to do," he blurted but remained on the ground. His windbreaker was twisted around his torso, and his shirt was wet. His chest hurt. He felt blood on his lips.

Farther away, someone with a flashlight directed traffic. The other car, its front side crumpled above the wheel, was parked next to his.

He was still down when the police arrived. Two officers came out and started asking questions. The crowd formed a horseshoe around them. Kostea pushed himself up, his right hand against the fender of his car. This time, Maya didn't object. The policemen checked his papers and had him wipe the blood off his face and take an alcohol-level test. Kostea tried to resist, to no avail.

The other driver was tested too.

The longer this dragged on, the bigger a problem it would become, Kostea thought. His dizziness had subsided, and he feared his alcohol level was high. Worse, Maya was involved, and Clara could find out. Somehow or another, he needed to make this go away.

The other driver seemed distraught. Kostea took a step toward him and said, "No worries, friend. I'll pay."

"Friend? You bet your ass you'll pay. This is my wife's father's car. Brand-new. You stupid man, you're drunk! Just wait for the police report."

Kostea took the older policeman aside. "I'm a surgeon at the Speranța Hospital in Bucharest, and I work directly for the minister of health. I was here for a medical conference." He paused to take in as much air as he could. "It's paramount that I make it back to Bucharest tonight. It was raining, and there was no visibility. The accident was my fault. I assume full responsibility. Is there anything I could do for you, personally, to speed this thing along and be on my way?"

"Sir, you're not going anywhere," the policeman said. "You've been hit and possibly injured. An ambulance is on its way. You'll be taken to the hospital to be checked out. And your wife, too."

Kostea let the comment about the wife go. "Comrade, you don't understand. I'm an experienced doctor, and I'm telling you there is nothing wrong with me."

"Doctor, you've been drinking. Even if your car is drivable, I can't let you drive. I'm suspending your license for two months. It's the law."

"Two months?" Kostea exclaimed. "I had only one drink. You're kidding, right?"

"I'm not."

"What happens to my car?"

"I guess you'll have it towed tomorrow morning. It's too late now." The policeman offered a resigned look, pulled the bill of his cap over his eyes, and slowly walked back to his car.

By the time the ambulance arrived, the police report was done. The other driver took his copy and waved it at Kostea. "It's all here, you scum," he said menacingly before driving away, his fender rubbing against the wheel.

The small crowd that had gathered in the intersection dispersed.

Maya pulled their luggage out of the car, and Kostea locked the doors. The paramedic took the luggage, helped Kostea climb in the back of the ambulance, and had him stretch out on the gurney. "Normally, it's ladies first, but your husband looks more banged up than you do," he said to Maya with a smirk.

"He's not my husband," she said.

"Whoever he is, you were in the car with him."

"True. We are both doctors returning from a medical conference in town. Could you drop me at the train station, perhaps?"

The paramedic was clearly taken with her looks. "Sorry, we have our marching orders. But if you really feel all right, go up front and sit next to the driver, madam."

"It's Dr. Merinde," Maya said.

"I'm Vincent, Dr. Merinde," he said.

"I don't want to leave my car here," Kostea said from the stretcher. The paramedic had cleaned him up and helped him take off his windbreaker and place it on top of his bag. His shirt was stained with blood and clinging to his chest.

"Is it drivable?" Vincent asked.

"I think so."

"Look, if you don't mind, I'll drive your car to the hospital for you." Vincent winked. "Just give me the keys and slip me a little something, as much as you think."

———————

At the hospital, Kostea made sure they knew who he was. He told the intake nurse he had chest pains and insisted on seeing the doctor on call. Maya waited, standing a few feet away from him.

"I'm Dr. Zaharia." A bald man in a white coat looked Kostea and Maya up and down. "Boy," he said to Kostea, "you're pretty banged up."

"It looks worse than it is," Kostea said.

Dr. Zaharia took the chart from the nurse and reviewed it. "Your chest hurts?"

"If I inhale deeply, it does. I might have a broken rib."

"Your last name is Bardu, and you're a doctor? I worked with a Dr. Clara Bardu one summer in Eforie, ages ago."

"She's my wife," Kostea said.

"Oh?" Zaharia said and gave Maya a long look. "And you visited your wife on the weekends, did you not? Your son and my daughter were friends. I think I met you back then."

Maya stepped in. "Excuse me. This is all very interesting, but I would like to go home."

Dr. Zaharia checked the paperwork one more time and smiled. "Dr. Merinde, your charming demeanor tells me you're OK."

"I am fine."

"But you were in the car accident with Dr. Bardu?"

"That's right. He was driving. When he slammed the brakes, I flew forward, and the luggage came tumbling onto me. Luckily, I didn't get hurt."

"We were at the medical conference, for only one day," Kostea explained. "I offered Dr. Merinde a ride back to Bucharest. It beats the train."

"Of course," Dr. Zaharia said. "The conference was a big deal for our town. I almost signed up myself."

"After the conference, we stopped for a bite," Maya said.

"At Malul Alb," Kostea clarified. He wanted to sound like someone who had nothing to hide.

"The inn on the Olt," Dr. Zaharia said. "I hear their food is very good."

"I see Dr. Bardu is in good hands, and I am fine. Can I leave?" Maya asked. "Nurse, would you please call me a cab? And maybe you have a train schedule. I want to get home."

"Nurse Helga," Zaharia said, "take Dr. Bardu to the examination room and help him out of his shirt. In the meantime, I'll help Dr. Merinde, and I'll join you as soon as I can."

———————

"Your chest, as you said, is nothing big," Dr. Zaharia confirmed. "A bruised rib, maybe two. I'll give you a painkiller, and you'll sleep it off. I insist you stay here tonight, just in case. If the pain persists, take an X-ray once you're back home."

"It's from the stupid steering wheel," Kostea said.

"Stupid or not, you've been lucky. And Dr. Merinde too."

"I know," Kostea said and added quickly, "She's getting married. It's good she'll have nothing broken or bruised to ruin her day." Kostea had

246

had years of practice and was good with his lies. The notion of Maya getting married should dispel any ideas Zaharia might entertain about the relationship between the two.

Indeed, Zaharia smiled. "Her future husband's a lucky bastard," he said. "She's quite a beauty, you know."

"I feel bad about the accident. I never expected to put her in any danger. Did she say anything before she left?"

"She wished you the best."

Good, Kostea thought. At least Maya had been discreet. "Doctor, could I use your phone?" he asked.

Zaharia took him to his office and left.

Kostea called Marin first.

Marin laughed. "You have to stop drinking," he said. It was late, but he promised to do what he could. "I'll call if I have anything."

Kostea called Clara next. "It's minor," he said. "A cut on my face, maybe a bruised rib. I'll spend the night at the hospital and be home tomorrow midday."

"You'll miss the second day of the conference," Clara said.

"I don't care. It was boring, not worth my time. I was on my way home. I thought I'd return early to be with you." He paused. "By the way, I offered Dr. Merinde a ride, so she was in the accident with me. You might have met her before."

"I don't think so," Clara said.

"Whatever. After the accident, she took the train. Imagine if something had happened to her, how bad I would feel."

The hospital bed was narrow and uncomfortable. His chest hurt. He rolled from one side to the other. A sharp pain crossed his face as a corner of the pillow touched the spot where the cut was. Marin had not called back. That wasn't a good sign. If Marin were unable to quash the police report and retrieve Kostea's driver's license, the whole thing could come to light. So far, Clara didn't have any reason to suspect anything, but Kostea worried about what would happen if she found out about the affair. It wasn't the first time he had imagined the moment. He had rehearsed his responses and had decided that his relationship with Maya had lasted too long for him to confess. He couldn't.

Years earlier in Odessa, Katya had said, "Do not tell." Katya was right. His only choice was to deny and pray that Clara still loved him and would choose to believe him, possibly for her own protection.

CHAPTER 27

Why Did You Tell Her?

June to October 1972

Kostea returned home by train. His car was towed to a body shop on the outskirts of Bucharest. Clara asked him a million health questions but displayed no suspicion at all. Two weeks went by. Marin had promised to get his license reinstated very soon, which, in fact, didn't matter too much, since the car was still in the shop. Then Dinescu told Kostea he had received a complaint. It had to do with his drinking and driving and his affair with Dr. Merinde. Dinescu said the author was highly connected in Vâlcea County, where Malul Alb was located and the car accident had taken place. If he were to give Kostea the name of the complainer, Kostea would immediately know who it was. It sounded like a tease. Then he added that sadly he had no choice but to curtail Kostea's professional growth, not clear how as of yet. Nobody else was in the office when Dinescu said all of that.

For the first time in his life, Kostea was less concerned with his career than afraid that Clara would find out about the complaint. Not knowing where else to turn, he ran again to Marin. As mayor of Bucharest, Marin had access to other levels of power than the minister of health. They met at his house in the evening. Eugene was there by chance. The three of them talked, Kostea denied his affair with Maya, and they joked about pretty women. They drank a bottle of wine.

"I'm angry with you," Clara said.

"I'm sure I deserve it," Kostea answered, hoping it was a joke.

"I mean it," she said.

"Of course you do."

There used to be a childish game they engaged in from time to time, when one made up a phony reason for being upset, followed by tender reconciliation and recognition of their deep love. We could never be cross with each other, their conclusion invariably went. Instinctively, Kostea sensed this was different. He became tense.

"You cheated on me."

He looked up. Two silent tears rolled down her cheeks.

"What are you saying?" he asked. The cut on his face was healing nicely. He sat in his armchair and bent forward to take off his shoes. They were getting ready for bed.

"That woman who was with you."

"Which woman are we talking about?" Kostea stayed calm on the outside, while inside he felt tangled up in knots. He couldn't say his dalliance with Maya had been a momentary lapse that didn't mean anything. He couldn't blame Maya's looks, the wine, or his colleagues at work who held fooling around in such high esteem. It'd been too long. Clara would ask and probe and find out he had lied again and again.

"Kostea, please . . . don't pretend you don't know."

"Clara, you are crying and accusing me of being unfaithful, which is hurtful enough. Tell me what you think happened, so I can prove to you it's not true."

"Maya Merinde. You were with her in the car."

"Are you talking about the car accident? God, Clara, we both could have died."

Clara sat on the bed as far away from him as she could, as if the distance reflected her pain or her hate. Or her love.

"Clara," he said. "Nothing happened between me and Maya Merinde. I swear to you."

"You took her to a hotel, Malul Alb." She looked at him. There was hope in her eyes.

He guessed she wanted to hope. He loved that look and those eyes, even though he had lied to them. Sometimes he had lied when he said he was going to work, or to meet with a friend, or to a conference out of town. He had lied coming home when he said he was tired, and she thought he was tired from work. Now, he needed to lie one more time, because he needed Clara to hope.

"We went there to eat," he said. "Nothing else, and I told you about it myself."

"No, you only said she was with you in the car."

"I don't remember. But would I have mentioned Maya Merinde to you if I were sleeping with her?"

"You are cunning," she said.

"Clara, you know me better than that. Have you spoken to Maya?"

"I have no intention of speaking to her."

"Why not?"

"I'd be ashamed. Oh, you don't get it, how much it hurts."

"You're hurting me too. We've always trusted each other, and the fact that you are accusing me is . . . is . . . I don't even know what to say. If I didn't mention Malul Alb to you, tell me who did."

She hesitated. "It's in the complaint."

"What complaint?"

"What difference does it make? What matters is that I know."

Kostea stood, went to the window, and looked outside. A light in an apartment across the street went out.

"She was your student four years ago," Clara said.

"You think I've been cheating on you for that long? That's absurd."

"I've had my suspicions." She turned on her side, pulled up her knees, and rolled up in a ball.

He climbed on the bed next to her and put his arm around her. "Clara?"

She shook off his embrace.

He persisted, moving closer and whispering to her. "Clara, there is a police report about the accident and a complaint, filed separately and addressed to Dinescu. The complaint is full of lies by somebody who is trying to derail my career. Dinescu only told me about it the other day."

She didn't react. He held her. Her pillow was wet.

"Clara, I love you. How did you find out?"

She turned around slowly and looked at him. Hair clung to her face. Her eyes were deep in their sockets, her swollen lids almost shut. "You told me the conference would last for two days."

Talking was good. He rushed to respond. "That's right."

"But it didn't. It ended on the day of the accident, at two in the afternoon."

"I left early. I didn't know."

"You booked your conference, and you didn't know the schedule?"

"I didn't book it. The minister sent me. He told Ileana to book it for me."

"And what did you do before the accident? How much wine did you drink? Were you planning on staying the night?"

He swallowed.

"I used to love you," she said.

Every time he wanted to talk, she walked away. When there were other people around, they behaved as if nothing had happened, but as soon as they were alone, an ice curtain dropped between them. He tried to come to her at night, and she rejected him. He tried again and again.

One morning, feeling spiteful and stupidly courageous, he asked her, "What, do you want a divorce?"

She answered coldly, "What do you want?"

He had no words. Without her, his life made no sense. She had been with him through it all. She had stood by him, helped him, calmed him down, encouraged and loved him. This was one relationship he had needed to guard and cherish—Clara—and he had failed. What choice did he have now? He didn't want a divorce. He had denied the affair, and he couldn't back down. What if she decided to leave him? What then? He couldn't imagine himself separated from Clara. Clara, the love of his life. His career could go to hell, but he needed Clara. She was his. And on a practical level, what? Move to a different place? Do his own shopping? Clean the apartment? Cook for himself? What would his mother say? Would she move in with him? Ina would take Clara's side, but Toddy, who was almost an independent adult? His son, Toddy, would be so hurt.

He understood that even if Clara would not divorce him, she would never forgive. Still, as if to drive home the point in the absurdity of the situation, he decided to sleep for one night on the sofa in the living room. It was self-flagellation and meant as an alarm signal for Clara at the same time. Clara didn't react. Mimi walked in before dawn and woke him by bumping into the furniture she couldn't see.

"Mama, what are doing up so early?" he asked, feeling embarrassed.

"Why are *you* sleeping here?" she asked.

Kostea had a suspicion about how Clara had found out about the complaint. Before work, he drove to the small house in which Eugene and his family occupied the main floor. A garage stood in the backyard where, years earlier, Uncle Sebastian had buried his golden coins. Kostea hid behind the garage. Laundry was drying on a clothesline stretched between the garage and the house. Through the kitchen window, he saw shadows moving back and forth.

The first to leave was Elvira, Eugene's daughter. She crossed the yard, went into the street, and disappeared. A year older than Toddy, she had graduated college and now worked in an office downtown.

Then Norma came out, touched one of the shirts on the clothesline, shook her head, and followed in her daughter's footsteps.

Eugene was last, a cigarette between his lips and a briefcase in his hand.

Kostea stepped forward and pushed him with both hands in the chest.

"Kostea!" Eugene yelled. "What the hell?"

Kostea pushed him again, harder this time.

Eugene's cigarette fell. "Kostea, what's wrong with you?"

"You know what's wrong. Why did you tell her? Why?"

"What are you talking about?"

Kostea punched him in the face. Eugene lost his balance and stumbled back a few steps. A thread of blood appeared under his nostril.

"I don't want to ever see you again," Kostea said and walked out of the yard.

In a few days, Lydia was arriving to spend her vacation with Toddy. Clara accepted Kostea's suggestion to take Toddy to dinner at a small restaurant with a beautiful garden. There wasn't much Kostea could do to win Clara back, but when she agreed to his suggestion, he took it as a good sign.

The evening was clear, and the air smelled of linden.

"What are your intentions toward Lydia?" Kostea asked Toddy suddenly during dinner.

"What do you mean?" Toddy said.

Clara smiled.

"Don't keep a girl waiting like this," Kostea said. "You love her. It's time you proposed."

Toddy looked radiant. He nodded. He was meeting friends later and left quickly after dessert.

Clara followed him with her gaze. "What a handsome young man!"

"That he is."

"We both want him to be happy," Clara said. "He's still very young and I don't want to hurt him. For him, for our son, I'll stay in the marriage. You understand?" There was a pause.

"Clara, you make me happy," he said.

"Don't kid yourself. It won't be like before."

———————

Bucharest was a fortress surrounded by invisible walls. There were a million inhabitants in the city, but if you lived there long enough and belonged to the same social strata, it was impossible to avoid bumping into the people you knew, whether you liked it or not. The downtown area was small. They all went to the same parties, movie houses, and theater shows. People loved and hated each other, spied on each other, and went on with their lives. They worked for bosses who worked for fewer bosses who all worked for one man. His huge portraits hung all over town.

If Kostea and Eugene met someplace or another, they pretended everything was all right. Their wives, of course, didn't know that Kostea had punched Eugene in the nose. The two men talked past each other, avoiding each other's eyes. One evening, at the dinner party of a common acquaintance, Kostea walked out on the balcony.

Eugene followed him and offered him a cigarette. "I read in the paper that Dr. Nuda was promoted to a full professorship, not you. I'm sorry," he said.

Kostea made sure to hide his feelings. He had taken Nuda's promotion as a personal insult and a consequence of the complaint. He was jealous of Nuda and angry and disappointed with Dinescu. But his concern over Clara overshadowed the changes at work, no matter how bad they were. He had hurt her, he knew, and getting over the affair was his focus. He understood there was nothing specific he could do at the moment except wait. Give time a chance. And be patient and kind. Watch her and accept.

Besides, of all the people in the world, Eugene was the last he would confide in.

"I was sorry as well," Kostea said, "although, honestly, Dr. Nuda deserves it. He's a very good doctor, and I'll have plenty of other opportunities."

"The article mentioned Dr. Nuda grew up in Râmnicu Vâlcea."

"So what? You think Dr. Nuda lodged the complaint because he's from the area and had found out about the accident?" Kostea decided to lie. "Listen to me, Eugenius. I spoke to Dinescu at length. Contrary to what you may suspect, it wasn't the complaint that hurt me. You see, Toddy, your godson, has proposed to Lydia, and he has filed an application with the state department for permission to marry an Israeli citizen."

"Congratulations, Kostea! These kids have been patient for a long time. I'm happy for them."

"I'm sure you are. But remember how the people in charge look at Romanians marrying foreigners. It's a sensitive matter. I can no longer be trusted. I'm a marked man."

"That's stupid."

"Whatever you say, Lydia is an Israeli citizen, and that's how things work over here."

"Where are they going to live?"

"In Romania."

"You're saying she's coming back?"

Kostea took a long drag of his cigarette. "That's the only way for them to get the approval quickly. Toddy's not ready to leave the country."

"Quite a sacrifice she is making."

"She loves him. All she wants is to be with him. I'd do the same thing." Kostea looked over the railing. There was something he wasn't saying. Toddy and Lydia were young, and the young people who could left Romania. Once married, Toddy might ask permission to emigrate. Kostea hoped he would take his time. "It was their application that stopped my promotion," he continued to lie. "Dinescu said so himself. That's another reason why you had no business telling Clara about the complaint. You were uninspired and mean."

Eugene leaned forward and looked over the railing too, as if trying to follow Kostea's gaze somewhere far below. "I wanted to protect her."

"Protect her? Clara is my concern. She is *my* wife. You hurt both of us deeply and I hate you for it."

"*You* hurt her. I didn't. And don't fool yourself. She already knew."

"What did she know?"

"She had suspected all along you were having an affair."

"Well, the affair didn't happen. I talked to her, and she understands. We trust each other. And by the way, when you cheated on your wife with Vera, I kept your secret," Kostea said.

"You told Igor."

"I didn't."

"Norma and I are not like you and Clara," Eugene said, his face dark as he stepped out of the light coming from the apartment. The summer wind blew through the branches, and the roof rattled. "You married an angel, the most beautiful and desirable woman I know. But you don't value her. Truly, Kostea, I watched you over the years. You're squandering your treasure."

"You're an idiot," Kostea said.

"So are you. Stop taking Clara for granted."

"And you stop loving my wife." Kostea threw his cigarette over the railing and went back to the party.

CHAPTER 28

Her Cross to Carry

1974

Clara left work early and stopped at Union Market. To her surprise, the line at the butcher shop was reasonable. After only twenty minutes, she walked out with a chicken and a kilo of pork chops wrapped in brown paper. She was happy and proud, like a hunter bringing home a trophy. Lydia and Toddy were visiting. They now lived in Făgăraş, a small Transylvanian town, and were going back that evening on the last train. Clara could send them off with food for a few days. Finding food, especially meat, was much more challenging in Făgăraş than in Bucharest, and every time the young couple came, they left loaded up with provisions. Clara would ask Marcela to roast the meat so that it wouldn't go bad during the train journey.

On the tram home, Clara found a seat by the window. She placed her shopping bag on the floor and balanced it with her foot. A man sat next to her. She turned away from him, looked outside, and started dreaming.

A justice of the peace had married Lydia and Toddy a few months earlier that fall. The rather austere ceremony was followed by a wild party at the Bardu residence with food, drinks, dancing, gifts, and well wishes.

Three black-and-white photographs captured, perhaps, the essence of the celebration. The first showed the happy couple—Toddy in a dark gray suit, his beard neatly trimmed, looking youthful and mature at the same time, and Lydia, her face raised to him, dressed in white silk shantung bell-bottom pants and a matching sleeveless top, like a spring flower foreshadowing a bright and unpredictable future. The second picture captured Kostea delivering his nuptial speech, standing at the head of the sumptuous table, while Lydia's mother, Tina, who had traveled from Haifa to Bucharest for the occasion, sat on his left and looked up at him as if questioning the intentions and boundaries of her new extended family. The last picture was of Clara, her head tilted backward, while a laughing Kostea was pretending to pour wine out of a demijohn straight into her mouth through a narrow funnel. To what degree that moment of extravagance was reflective of real happiness and how much it was meant to hide the recent dark undertones pulling Clara and Kostea apart, Clara couldn't say.

After the wedding, Toddy reported to his place of work in Făgăraș, a chemical plant, a state-owned monstrosity employing a quarter of the town's inhabitants. That place had been designated to him upon graduating the engineering school. Kostea wanted to intervene and find work for Toddy in Bucharest. "Live with us in our apartment," he said. "Why move to that god-forsaken town, five hours by train, and drag Lydia with you. Just say the word, and I'll make a few phone calls."

"No, Dad. It's time for us to have our own place and our own life. Lydia is OK with living in a small town."

Kostea told Clara he felt rejected and was convinced that sooner or later Toddy's youthful pride would wear off, and he would want to return, tail between his legs.

Clara understood Toddy moved to Făgăraș to get out of his father's shadow. He knew what to expect of Kostea, how to deal with him and how to forgive. Now he had to shelter Lydia from him. Life in Bucharest would have been easier, but if the price for their peace and independence was a drab provincial town, so be it. Her son didn't have to explain. Clara had hoped for a mellowing of Kostea's character, more wisdom and less turbulence as they advanced in age. But as Kostea himself had said, people rarely change, and she had resigned herself to accepting him the way he was. The way he had always been.

Still, Kostea had done something to help his son. One of the master welders at Toddy's plant had a urological problem, and Kostea took care of it. He did it quickly and efficiently. As a consequence, Toddy's manager approved Toddy's request for a transfer from production planning to external coordination, a role that involved frequent trips to Bucharest.

As Clara's tram ran along the Dâmbovița River, the late-fall dusk, the people rushing home in their dark coats, and the bare trees cast an aura of gloom over the city. Unexpectedly, Clara felt sorry for Kostea. He must still feel deeply hurt by Letitia Banu's husband, who months earlier had accused him of malpractice and had called him a butcher. Kostea had arranged for Letitia to undergo a mastectomy at Speranța Hospital, at Toddy's request. Letitia was Maria's mother—a girl Toddy knew from high school. The surgery was performed by Dr. Moraru, the oncologist who worked from time to time at Speranța. Because he had arranged it, Kostea had been a part of the team. Whether the mastectomy was unnecessary, as the husband pretended, and whether Kostea had been the surgeon or not, a butcher Kostea was not. He was an excellent doctor, and Clara would defend his reputation and argue with whomever might say otherwise.

Whether Eugene's story about Maya was true or not didn't matter as much anymore. In deciding to overlook Kostea's possible dalliance, she did so for Toddy. She had felt betrayed and jealous and had realized she didn't love Kostea that much any longer. Rather, she loved him differently. When it happened, they were both skilled enough to hide it from Toddy. Kostea slept on the sofa just once.

Life was a game of chess. You did your best with the pieces you had until someone came, knocked the board over, and sent all the pieces flying. One had to be practical. It was easier to live with the status quo than start anew. Clara was trapped. Kostea was her fate, for better and for worse, her cross to carry.

Not Toddy's.

Clara got off at Elefterie Station and walked on the wide bridge over the river. The muddy water in the deep riverbed moved slowly onward. On the left stood the new Saint Elefterie Church. Its copper onion domes amplified the last rays of the setting sun. Her shopping bag cut deep into her right palm; her purse pressed into her aching left shoulder. She tried to imagine Lydia walking the streets of Făgăraș, looking for whatever food she could find in the empty stores. That was the price Lydia was willing to pay for her love. She had left behind the land of milk and honey, following Toddy to what seemed like the end of the world. A small town where water and electricity were sporadic, food was available by accident, and people got eggs from the hens in their yards. A supermarket in Haifa had to be as plentiful as the one that had brought Clara to tears in Switzerland. There were no supermarkets in Făgăraș.

Clara admired Lydia. The young woman had shown more independence and resilience than Toddy. She had come to see him every year and had waited determinedly to marry him. Her friends and family in Israel must have tried to discourage her. Going back to Romania is madness, they must have said. Yet here she was with her husband, her love. Once, Clara had loved Kostea like that. She had chosen him over others, had waited for him, had trusted him, and had been ready to follow him anywhere.

Clara stopped at the old Saint Elefterie Church, where Toddy was baptized twenty-four years earlier. It seemed yesterday. Much smaller than the new church, it was intimate and quaint. That was the beauty of time. Looking ahead, it was unlimited. Looking back, twenty-four years compressed into an eye blink. She had loved Kostea for all of these twenty-four years and longer, a time span erased in a flash. The months since Eugene had told her about Maya felt like a lifetime. Her anger came and went.

Toddy would never betray Lydia the way Kostea had betrayed her. Yet how much patience was ensconced in one's love? Lydia must know she and Toddy could live a happier life elsewhere, in a place with nice supermarkets and palm trees by the sea. When was enough enough? Six weeks, six months, one year? When would Lydia take Toddy aside and tell him it was time to pack their suitcases?

Before the wedding, Clara had hoped to talk to Tina about their children's future, but Tina said that Lydia and Toddy were adults and needed to decide on their own. She and her husband didn't want to interfere. Maybe Tina was disappointed Lydia had returned to Romania or maybe it was something else. All Tina talked about was her work. She and Clara had been colleagues once and she expected Clara would be interested. She didn't say a word about her husband, or about her feelings or friends, nor the Arabs or the weather in Israel.

Unlike Tina, Clara was thinking of retirement. Her work was convenient but monotonous, and she needed a change. Germs didn't change. Her green petri dishes bloomed with the same cultures, day after day. Her work no longer excited her the way it once had, when her discovery of a pathogen would save people from infection and illness. Staying home appealed to her. Maybe Lydia and Toddy would have a baby soon.

"Where are the children?" Clara asked, placing her shopping bag on the kitchen table.

"Getting ready," Marcela said.

"And Kostea?"

"He said he'd be late."

Toddy walked into the kitchen. "Mom, you're here."

Clara smiled. "I took off work early and look what I found." She pointed at her shopping bag.

"Mom, Lydia and I want to tell you something. Come to the living room, please."

Clara couldn't read Toddy's bearded face, but she knew this was serious. She didn't like his beard. It made him look older and harsher and less *her* child. His eyes were the same: *her* eyes. "Sure. Let me change, and I'll be there in a minute," she said.

When she walked into the living room, Toddy and Lydia were whispering to each other and holding hands.

"All right. What's the matter?" Clara asked, trying to look unconcerned.

"Mother, sit down. I'll get Mimi," Toddy said.

Clara pulled up a chair. She looked at Lydia and smiled. "He's very serious, your husband," she said.

Toddy returned with Mimi. "Here, sit next to me," he told her. "And here is an ashtray for you." He leaned forward. "Lydia and I have decided, and today I applied—"

Immediately, Clara knew what he meant.

Mimi interrupted, "Sorry, I don't understand."

Clara was glad for her comment. She needed the few extra seconds to collect herself. She was glad she wasn't the only one getting the news.

"This morning I filed the papers asking permission to leave for Israel," Toddy said. He exchanged a quick glance with Lydia and added, "For good."

"I thought you had an assignment this morning for work," Clara said, again to gain time.

"I went to the Ministry of Internal Affairs after work. It didn't take long."

The world was divided: East and West. Once you crossed over *for good*, you belonged to the other side. Or so the theory went. There were those who came back for a visit, or, like Lydia, for longer, but the fracture was unavoidable. Much different than moving to Făgăraș.

"You did it without talking to us," Clara said, her voice trailing off. She looked at him and his wife.

"Mom, I didn't tell you because I didn't want you to worry and try to delay us. More importantly, I didn't want Dad to know before I applied."

"You do know I'll tell him tonight."

"Of course," Toddy said. "And I'm sorry to put this on you. Trust me, I didn't plan it this way. I wanted to tell you and Dad and Mimi, the three of you at the same time. Mom, he'll yell at you, I'm sure of it."

Mimi sighed. "He'll be sad." She looked like a withered dandelion.

"Well, at least you won't see him react," Clara said.

Toddy shook his head. "You know, we decided this a long time ago, when I visited Lydia in Israel. Now we are just executing the plan. There was a lot of paperwork and a lot of red tape. Not easy. Not easy at all. Every time we came to Bucharest, I did a small part, passport photographs, copies of certificates and diplomas, proof I don't owe money to the state, and unreturned library books. I paid all the fees and completed the application. Today I finished. Lydia said we should wait until the next time we are here to tell Dad. I disagreed. Mom, Mimi, I feel bad, but it's done. There is no turning back."

"Clara, Mimi, I know it hurts," Lydia said. "It hurt when I left Bucharest five years ago, and it pains us today to cause you this anguish. But after we leave, we'll come back and visit, and you'll visit us. It's easier to travel today than before." She looked out the large windows overlooking the trees. "I hope you agree that leaving Romania makes sense for us."

Clara took a cigarette from Mimi's pack. She took the matches and waited. Her hands shook.

Toddy saw her frown and her lips tighten and thought she would cry. He reached over, grabbed the matches, and lit her cigarette. She inhaled. He held her hand. "Mom."

"It's all right," Clara said. "I'll be all right. We talked about this a lot. I mean, your father and I. We knew this would happen, but we were hoping you'd take more time."

"I knew it too," Mimi said.

"Mimi, I'm sorry," Toddy said.

"What's done is done," Clara said. She knew they were right. They didn't mean to hurt anybody, and proceeding in secret had saved arguments and frayed nerves. It was the best way . . . the only way. She would have done the same thing.

Now she needed to take their side. With Kostea, it was only his mouth. He loved Toddy. Of all people, he'd understand. How many times had he talked about leaving? He had not had the courage to do it, not alone, without his family. Troubled times might be coming. The ministry could deny Toddy's request. Toddy could lose his job. Kostea could be reprimanded and demoted. Clara raised her eyes and looked at Toddy. "Don't worry about your father. I'll tell him. He'll be all right, and I don't care if he yells at me."

CHAPTER 29

You Betrayed Me

"Today Toddy has applied for his definitive departure," Clara told Kostea as soon as he entered the apartment, using the official term for Toddy's application. Kostea walked into the bedroom without saying a word.

He took off his shoes, then his sweater, then he slowly unbuttoned his shirt. He did it mechanically, trying to think while walking in and out of the bedroom, throwing his clothes on the floor. It wasn't happening. Not Toddy. Not now. His son couldn't do this to him.

He came back to the living room where Clara and Mimi were silently waiting, as if ready to receive their punishment. He walked past them, turned around, and kicked one of the chairs with his bare foot, his mouth twisting in pain. "How could he do this behind my back?"

As if expecting his question, Clara said, "He didn't want you to stop him."

"You're right. I would have stopped him because he made a mistake. Stupid, stupid, that's what this is."

"It's not stupid. Risky perhaps, but we expected this, didn't we?"

"I didn't." He stopped pacing and looked directly at Clara. A thought occurred to him, and he became suspicious on the spot. "Did you know about this?"

"No."

"Clara, did you help him? Did you hide this from me?"

"No. I'm as heartbroken and worried as you are."

He sat down, feeling exhausted. The chest hair above the opening of his undershirt was turning white. "Don't lie to me. You know I'll find out."

Clara scoffed. "This is not the time to be threatening me."

He stood up. "I'm driving there right now."

"Where? To Făgăraş? It's five hours away."

"I don't care. What time was the train? I'll be there before midnight."

Clara buried her face in her hands.

"I know exactly what happened," he said, pacing again. "It's Lydia, this devious, conniving girl. She wants him with her in Israel. She has completely twisted his mind."

"Kostea, don't talk like that," Mimi said.

"Mama, stay out of it."

"You are tired and angry," Clara said. "Five hours is a long time. If you're going, I'm coming with you."

"You are? Why? You want to be there and act as a shield? You think I'm out of control and want to protect your precious angels from me?"

"I want to protect you," Clara said. "From yourself."

He got to the door and turned. She was right. He was losing control. He knew he needed to think and calm down, but his pain was too big. "After everything I did for him. I gave him all a father could give. I gave him my life. I put my reputation and career on the line when I helped him go visit her."

"He came back," Clara said.

"Sure, he did. Lydia's family didn't want him there. That's why."

"And now they do?"

"Lydia does."

"He came back because he loves you," Mimi said.

"No, Mama, you don't understand. Do you think I enjoyed begging Securitate officers to let Toddy go? Or when I used my connections to get Lydia her resident status? People will laugh at me. I fought for Lydia and lost my son. And I operated on his friend's mother and ended up being called a butcher. At least the master welder from Toddy's plant didn't complain after I cured him." He paused and looked up, cold sparks flying at Clara. "Are you coming?"

"Give me a minute. I'll ask Marcela to stay with Mimi until we come back."

In the car, Kostea's anger came and went like the wind. They smoked a lot. Clara cried. When he yelled, she yelled back. "You know this is my way," he said regretfully at one point. "Yelling gets the pain off my chest."

"We talked before about the possibility of them leaving," she said.

"Maybe, once or twice."

"We talked about it when Toddy went to Israel, and earlier, when Lydia left with her family. Also, before they got married. It was obvious all along. Let's be honest. We considered defecting ourselves. I specifically remember our discussion in Rome."

"That was different. We were adults."

"Toddy is an adult."

"Is he? Age-wise maybe, but mentally not. Do you think it is perfect on the other side? Is the West waiting for him with open arms? No. You know it, I know it, and that's why when we had the opportunity, we didn't take it."

"We were without our son and didn't want to leave him behind," Clara said.

"We didn't, of course we didn't, and look at him now. He did it without telling us. Without telling me. I don't matter to him."

"He was remorseful today."

"Was he? Good actor. I bet you he learned from his wife."

"You can be offensive all you want, but when we get there, I want you to think what you say," Clara said. "Be careful. Don't hurt her, all right?"

"Why? Is she a porcelain doll?" Kostea asked. He was ready to fight the whole world. It was his fault. He should have defected in Frankfurt and taken that post at Caron's hospital. At that time, he was well known. People wanted his expertise. He would have brought his family out—his entire family. Now his family was torn apart. He'd been a coward and had no one to blame but himself. Clara didn't trust him anymore, and somehow, because of that, he didn't trust her. They were together, and yet they were not.

Clara lit a cigarette. "To him, she is a porcelain doll," she responded. "We are his parents, and it's our obligation to protect him and take care of him, not the other way around. He doesn't owe us anything, no matter how upsetting or unfair that seems. Kostea, you should be happy for him."

"Happy? No. I can't be an angel like you, always thinking about others. Clara, we are his family—the least he could do is keep us informed. Have the courage to tell it to *my* face. Now I'm mad. I'm outraged, and surprised you are so forgiving. Unless, as I said, you knew about it all along."

"I told you, I didn't."

"You don't trust me," Kostea said, his voice low. "Ever since Eugene filled your head with his lies."

Clara was very calm. "Are you saying I conspired with Toddy as payback, because you slept with another woman? Do I get this right?"

"That's what I'm saying." Kostea was doubling down.

"And my revenge is to send my own son away? You must be out of your mind."

———————

Toddy and Lydia lived on the ninth floor. The elevator was broken. Kostea and Clara took the stairs, Clara stopping on each landing to think and to catch her breath. When he arrived, Kostea waited for her in front of the door.

"What are you going to say to them?" she whispered.

His eyes gleamed. The five hours in the car evaporated like after an accident when one doesn't remember a thing. What was it that she wanted from him? He was losing his son. He had already lost his father, but he could live without parents. He could even live without Clara. Look at her, pale and distraught. He didn't want to live without her, but he could. Without Toddy, he couldn't imagine his life. He wouldn't be guarded when talking to him. Considerate. Understanding. Polite. What a joke! He was hurting, and if he hurt Toddy, the others, well, that's the way it would be. "Everything," he said to Clara and knocked as hard as he could. He heard shuffling and knocked again. "Open up."

"Dad?"

"Yes, it's me."

Toddy opened the door ever so slightly.

Kostea pushed his way through. It was dark, the only light coming from the stairway. "What, you didn't expect I'd show up?" As asked, his question implied the other half of his thought—he had been left with no choice.

Clara followed him timidly into the small studio apartment. Lydia was under the covers and just then switched on the hourglass-shaped bedside lamp. She squinted while the room filled with a soft yellow light. She was in a sleeveless nightgown. Toddy stood facing his father. They were the same height, but Kostea was massive, especially with his mane of white hair and his winter coat on. Toddy's clothes were on the back of a chair, his shoes next to it. He stood there, vulnerable, in his white undershorts.

Clara closed the door.

"Toddy, pass me my robe," Lydia said.

"Dad, turn away," Toddy said.

"Why?" Kostea's voice was dismissive. "Do you think she has something I haven't seen before?" But he turned.

Toddy ignored his father's comment. "Mom, please come in and sit down," he said, pointing at the chairs by the table. "Dad, you too."

"I prefer to stand," Kostea said.

"At least give me your coats."

"Would you like something to drink? I could make you some tea," Lydia offered and stepped forward.

"How polite," Kostea said.

"I'll have some." Clara smiled at Lydia and caught her hand. "Thank you."

Lydia walked into the kitchenette and turned on one of the burners.

"Dad, why are you here?" Toddy asked and put his shirt on.

"You don't know?"

"No. I don't." It seemed like he said it deliberately, and he held his dad's gaze while buttoning his shirt.

"You did something very stupid today. I want you to come back with me to Bucharest and withdraw your application," Kostea said. "We'll do it tomorrow morning, first thing. I know people, and we'll withdraw it without a trace."

"Dad, I'm not doing that."

"Yes, you are."

"I thought about this long and hard. I always wanted to leave, and this is as good a moment as any. I'm not changing my mind." Toddy yanked his jeans off the back of the chair and put them on. He leaned over and picked up his socks. "Mom, give me a cigarette, please."

Clara handed him her pack.

"Why did you do it behind my back?" Kostea asked.

"I didn't tell you or Mom. I didn't want you to try and stop me. Like what you're doing right now."

The teakettle whistled, and Lydia pulled it off the stove.

"I'll have a cup of tea also," Toddy said and sat next to Clara.

Kostea couldn't stop the fog in his brain. "You didn't tell your mother?" he asked, sounding like an interrogator.

"I didn't," Toddy said.

"You swear?"

"Kostea, we talked about this," Clara said. "What's the matter with you? Are you jealous?"

"Maybe I am."

Toddy faced Kostea. "Dad, this is insane."

"Insane?" Kostea repeated. "I'll tell you what's insane: you having applied to leave the country without our knowledge. I can block your application. I can tell the authorities I don't agree, and you'd be stuck here for good."

"You'd never do something like that," Clara said, shaking her head.

"You don't know me," Kostea said. Besides hurting, threatening was all he had left. He wanted his son to stay there forever, next to him. Because he loved him so much.

"I do," Clara said, sounding certain. And cold.

"All right," Kostea said. "Never mind what his application does to me, to my career. You're right that I'll never harm him. But what will he do if his request is denied?"

"I'll fight the decision," Toddy said.

"Really? How? Will you bribe somebody? Will you ask me to help and to intervene? Will you talk to me then? And what if they kick you out of your job? How will you live?"

"We'll write to American congressmen," Lydia said. She placed three steaming cups of tea on the table. "We'll go to Radio Free Europe and the Voice of America if we have to."

"Now that's an idea," Kostea said sarcastically. "Do you think they'll help?"

"They've helped others," Lydia said.

"And how will you do that?"

"We'll write."

"Because you speak English, of course." Kostea came near the table. "Your letters will never get through."

"Then I'll go back to Israel and do it from there," Lydia said.

"I thought you wanted to be next to your husband," Kostea said. "That's why you needed me to help you become a resident, isn't it?"

"It may take more than a year for Toddy to get the permission to leave. That's why I needed to be a resident."

"I know. Because it's so hard over here, isn't it? You have to come to Bucharest to do your shopping, let our housekeeper cook for you, and have us pay for your wedding and all."

"Kostea, stop!" Clara said.

"Stop? What did I say that's not true?"

"You know full well why they want to leave."

"I'm sorry. I must have misunderstood."

"Israel is a free country," Lydia said.

"Yes, a country at war."

"I don't think we need to fear the war."

"Oh, you don't? And if they send Toddy to fight, that's all right. He can do it. He's young. You know, I had this suspicion all along. You persuaded him to apply, and if he gets rejected, you go back to Israel and get him out. Brilliant, if it were as easy as that. Young lady, let me assure you, it is not. Some people have waited for years and have gone to prison over this, in case you don't know. So, spare me your magic, all right? We opened our home to you, and you played us like fools. He fell into your trap, but I will not. I know who you are: a manipulator. Deceitful, cowardly, and stingy, like the whole nation of you. And those who dare call you out are accused of being anti-Semites."

"Dad!" Toddy yelled and got up.

"What?" Kostea said. "You betrayed me. I'm losing my mind seeing how everything I have worked for is being destroyed."

"I don't know what you mean, but you can't hurt people like that. Lydia doesn't owe you anything, Dad, and neither do I. Apologize to her right away, or get out!"

"I'm sorry," Kostea said, sounding fake.

Lydia walked away from the table and lay down on the bed, facing the wall.

"You do what's right for you. Don't think about us," Clara told Toddy. She looked like a ghost.

"Don't listen to her," Kostea said.

They started again. Toddy yelled. Kostea yelled because yelling was Kostea's way. Lydia cried, sometimes silently and sometimes her whole body shaking. Clara smoked. She swirled the cold tea in her cup. Father and son repeated themselves. At some point, they quit out of exhaustion. It was three in the morning, or four.

Toddy found a blanket and threw it down on the floor. There was no other place. Kostea stretched on it fully dressed, covered himself with his winter coat, and fell asleep in an instant. He snored.

"That's your father," Clara said.

Toddy nodded. He sat next to Lydia on the bed and looked for her hand. Clara sat next to him. Their shoulders touched.

When Toddy awoke in the morning, his parents were gone.

––––––––––––

Toddy had expected a reaction from his father for keeping his plans secret but not as brutal as it had been. He had taken the easy way out, and his mother and wife had paid the price. "Hopefully, you'll forgive him one day," he told Lydia the next morning as he was getting ready to go to work. Anguish and tiredness were pressing on him.

She rose on the bed, resting her back against the bare wall. Her nightgown was glued to her skin. "He's your father. What choice do I have but to forgive?"

"As wound up as he gets, when he's over it, he's clean and fresh as if nothing had happened. And he doesn't carry a grudge."

"*He* doesn't carry a grudge," Lydia repeated and smiled. "Because people around him pretend to forget it ever happened. Because they are trapped."

"You won't have to see him for a while."

Late that day, Clara called Toddy at work. "We made it home safe. He's calmed down."

"I'm glad," Toddy said.

"I was wondering. Are you coming any time soon?"

"No, Mom, I think not."

After that, each time Toddy went to Bucharest on business, he went alone. He arrived on the morning train and made sure to leave the same day. Once he stopped in to see Ina. She had no idea what was going on.

Clara called him at work every week. "Do you need anything? I could get you some canned sardines, ham, and smoked fish. I can meet you somewhere in town."

"Thanks, no. We are doing all right."

Kostea called. It was March already, early in the afternoon. "Your birthday is coming up."

"I know, Dad."

"You should stop by the house."

"Maybe. If I have the time."

"Both of you," Kostea said.

"You would think."

"Listen. I overreacted. I'd take it back if I could."

"This time, it's not me you need to worry about." Toddy knew an apology wouldn't erase Lydia's pain. She'd do whatever he'd ask her to do.

"Unless I drive over there, I have no way of talking to Lydia," Kostea said. "Shall I write her a letter, you think?"

"Don't do anything," Toddy said.

Toddy and Lydia showed up at his parents' on the eve of Toddy's birthday and stayed for three nights. Lydia and Kostea talked very little—just hello, good morning, goodbye. On Saturday evening, the Bardus threw Toddy a party, with their friends and some of Toddy's as well. Ina was invited and came. As a gift, Mimi gave Toddy a framed black-and-white photograph of Sasha as a young man wearing a military uniform. "He was as handsome as you are today," she said. Toddy wondered how much of that picture she remembered and how much she was able to see. Before they departed on Sunday afternoon, Clara presented them with an envelope full of cash. Kostea gave Toddy a bottle of whiskey—father to son. Then he stepped toward Lydia and gave her a light kiss on the cheek.

"Welcome to the Bardu family emotional roller coaster," Toddy told Lydia on the train.

On the surface, the wound had healed.

CHAPTER 30

Take Good Care of Him

December 1974 to January 1975

"I'm happy to inform you that Alexander's passport is ready. By mutual agreement, the Romanians send the passports to us once approved for departure, to allow us to perform our security checks," the Israeli consul explained to Lydia. She had been invited to come to the embassy and meet with him. "Since he is not Jewish and he is keeping his Romanian citizenship, we can grant him an Israeli visa to join you only after you fly back to Eretz Israel. You have to be there ahead of your husband."

Several weeks later, Toddy received the official confirmation that his definitive departure request had been approved. He resigned his position in Făgăraş, effective the end of the year, and purchased an airline ticket for January. Lydia left at the beginning of December.

At work, there were no accusations of disloyalty, no envy, no Party meetings, and no comments behind his back. His direct boss and the master welder took him aside one morning and showed him how to handle a welding rod. "To get good, you need to do it day in and day out, so you can get a job over there, wherever you're going to end up," Toddy's boss said. "Now, at least, you know the difference between MIG and TIG. I have an uncle in Cleveland, Ohio. He makes good money. America is a great place."

After Christmas, Toddy traveled with his parents to Sinaia—a last vacation together in the beautiful mountain resort. Igor and Aida came to Sinaia as well. Toddy skied during the day. Kostea and Clara took endless walks along the snowy paths. Toddy didn't want to think or guess what his parents were talking about. Every night, they played bridge. Aida, who didn't play cards, served drinks and emptied the ashtrays.

Igor and Aida returned to Bucharest early. The Bardus saw them to the train station and waited with them in the waiting room. It was early afternoon.

"It's stuffy in here," Kostea said to Toddy. They walked on the platform along the rail tracks. There were two pairs of tracks, shiny and black and frozen, dirty snow in between. Another platform ran along the opposite side. A cold wind blew from the plains toward the mountains.

"I've been thinking," Kostea said. "You're doing what I should have done." He let a few moments pass. "I should have left Romania years ago, but I didn't have the guts."

"It's not a matter of guts," Toddy said. "You had everything going for you. You had your house here, your possessions, and your family. You had your career. You still do. I'm starting fresh. You couldn't just leave us and go. I can."

"Still, we are a family, are we not? Families do everything to stay together."

Toddy didn't say anything. The guilt for leaving his family behind was a heavy burden. They reached the end of the platform and turned. The wind caught their faces. Toddy leaned forward and zipped his ski jacket all the way to his chin.

Kostea ignored the cold. "Son, you go. Grow your roots wherever you choose. When you're settled, you give me a sign, and I promise you, we'll be ready. We'll come and live near you. Being with you again will become my life's purpose."

Dreams instantly filled Toddy's mind. He stopped. "Dad, give me two years, tops."

"Let's say five," Kostea said.

"Five? That's forever."

"Trust me. You'll need the time." They hugged. "This will be our secret. We'll call it the Sinaia Accord."

The wind was blasting, and Kostea's eyes were filled with tears.

January 1, 1975, Bucharest

Dear Lydia,

You must be surprised to receive a letter from your mother-in-law, but feelings that are very private are better expressed this way.

We had a New Year's Eve party last night, with friends, good food, and a glass of champagne at midnight. Igor delighted us with his guitar. Toddy stayed home, and Cristi stopped over.

Underneath it all, melancholy took over our gathering like a shadow, spreading and enveloping us in the midst of all the good wishes, resolutions, and laughter.

Now, I feel tired and a little hung over. My head hurts. Maybe I smoked too much. Kostea is somewhere in the house. Mimi too. Toddy is still asleep. He needs the rest.

In a few days, he will be joining you. He's nervous and excited. I know he can't wait. I am sure you are eager to see him and hold him in your arms. I'm very happy for you. You love and deserve each other. Both of you showed a great deal of maturity and determination. You succeeded in spite of the odds. Your life is ahead of you, and I wish you the best.

I must confess that besides being happy for you, I am also sad. In order for you to hold Toddy in your arms, I must open mine. Toddy, my son, my only child, is leaving me. Leaving us.

He'll be here for several more days, and then there will be an irredeemable void. His room will stay the same. He will be leaving behind most of his winter clothes, his skiing equipment, his books, and a shoebox filled with your letters. I prepared for this moment from the time he was born. I want to be strong and say it is bittersweet, but it's not sweet at all. I left my mother behind in the time of war. Only now do I understand what I did to her. Lydia, when you and Toddy have children of your own, you will understand what I'm feeling. Whether your children are little or full-grown adults, you worry for them all the same. And now I have two children to worry about.

We don't know what the future will bring, but there is something very important I want to tell you. Toddy and his father have an agreement to reunite our family once you settle down. As much as I want us to be close, I don't want us to share a house. If or when we come, find a place for us that is not your own. In my experience, living with your in-laws is a mistake, especially with a man like Kostea. He has hurt you, and you forgave him for Toddy's sake. I love him, and I forgave him also, but I'm asking you now—don't plan to live together with us.

Today it is possible to cross the iron curtain. But I remember a time when it was not. Political winds blow any which way, and I am afraid. Will things change? Can it happen that we'll never see each other again?

I shouldn't entertain such thoughts. In my life, I tried to be pragmatic, restrained, and hope for the best. I've always been fatalistic. By fighting one's destiny, one could end up worse.

You and Toddy are a family now. You are everything to each other—lovers, best friends, husband and wife. You trust and protect each other. The further you travel, the stronger the bond between you. Take good care of him. I love you, and I rely on you.

Clara

Nothing Else Mattered

1975 to 1986

Everything became quiet. Too quiet. Quiet as if nothing else mattered. As if he had fallen and was badly hurt. Time passed him by, day after day. Monday, Tuesday, Wednesday . . . then, Monday again. He only felt alive during surgery, when holding someone else's life in his hands. Then his training took over and he was as cold as steel. He excelled at his profession. He no longer yelled and didn't throw things around.

He knew Clara's pain was strong as well, but he saw that she managed it better somehow. She seemed almost serene. As planned, she retired several weeks after Toddy departed and tried her best to stay occupied. She took care of the mothers, both of them. She wrote letters to Lydia and Toddy, bought groceries, spent time in the kitchen with Marcela, talked to friends. He couldn't do any of it. Nor did he want to.

Each time he couldn't bear his pain, he found solace in talking to Clara.

"Be patient," she told him. "We'll go when the time is ripe. Remember your Sinaia Accord. He said two years. You told him five." She thought her answer was strategic. Five years was a reasonable buffer of time.

He didn't know she was of two minds. On one hand, like him, she wanted more than anything to be closer to Toddy, whom she missed very much. Close to her children. On the other hand, she was afraid that if she and Kostea were to join them, in a new country where they wouldn't have anyone else, Kostea would destroy their lives. Less Toddy's than Lydia's, whom he'd harass and attack the way he had harassed and attacked Clara's mom. She didn't care that Kostea, with his difficult personality, had compromised his potentially brilliant career at work. That was his problem. And it was too late, anyhow. Her problem, the real tragedy of her life, was what he had done at home. Therefore, if they went, under no circumstance would she agree to live with Toddy and Lydia in the same house. She had said this to Toddy, and she had written to Lydia. And yes, she had told it to Kostea as well. Many times. But he just looked as if she was speaking a foreign language, and he did not understand.

Often, when they talked, he would say he was the victim of what Toddy did. Then he'd switch it around and say it was all his fault. He should have foreseen it, prepared for it. He should have been the one to leave Romania. Had he done it earlier, he wouldn't have lost his son. Tears ran down his face.

He stressed the word "lost." He liked to say it because it sounded painful and permanent, like a deep wound in the heart. "He's my son," he would tell her. "My raison d'être. We need to go live with him."

"Near him," Clara corrected.

He smiled and nodded. He said he and Clara were becoming good friends.

"We've always been friends," she said.

"Yes. You are right."

Clara thought the longing that united them now caused her to forgive everything he had done.

In the winter he decided to go skiing with Cristi. It seemed odd given the age difference and since he had never tried skiing before, but Clara didn't object. She welcomed the opportunity to be alone for a while. In addition, she understood his attempt to resurrect the memory of their son.

In March, a major earthquake shook Bucharest. People died and many buildings were destroyed. Kostea was skiing for the second time that year and was recalled by the hospital. He spent days and nights working, patching wounds. Every day, Clara traversed the devastated city looking at the rubble, shaking her head. She wore a dark kerchief tied around her hair, dust settling on it.

As it was getting increasingly difficult for Ina to live by herself, Clara brought her home to stay in Toddy's old room. Kostea didn't object.

Later that summer, Toddy informed them in a letter that Lydia was pregnant and that his company was transferring them from Israel to the United States.

Kostea said, "That is a big deal. America has always been Toddy's dream." His face broadened in a huge smile. He hugged and kissed Clara, lifting her off the floor.

Clara thought Lydia's pregnancy was the big deal and wondered again how different she and Kostea were.

The letters they received from Lydia and Toddy kept them informed of their children's lives. They read each letter aloud to each other, analyzed it, sniffed it, tried to guess at anything ambiguous, and otherwise filled in the gaps. Sometimes Clara remembered how Toddy and Lydia wrote to each other every day during the almost five-year period they were apart. But those, Clara knew, were love letters, and she couldn't expect the children to write as often to them. Still, when in her opinion a letter was late, Clara worried. Kostea did too, while trying to pretend otherwise. When the children telephoned, their crystal-clear voices were full of fun. Their calls from Israel came on special occasions—birthdays, New Year's Day—and were limited to three minutes. After they moved to America, their phone calls became longer and more frequent. From America, calling was cheap. Everyone had a phone in America. They worked only five days a week, not six, and everyone drove. They stuck their dirty dishes into dishwashers and watched color TV.

Clara understood that America had just become Kostea's dream. With this realization and the clear goal ahead of him, she became concerned. "If we go to America, life might prove to be difficult for us."

He disagreed. They debated for days on end after that. In actuality, he talked, and she listened. Once or twice, she managed to express her concerns: language barrier, unfamiliar places. Culture shock.

"Don't get me wrong," she said. "I want to go, but in Bucharest, we're at home."

"I've had it with Bucharest," Kostea said. "Now we go, we see, and we conquer." He was a changed man. A war was waiting for him, and he was getting ready to win.

———————

Walking out of the medical school one afternoon, Kostea noticed a young woman on the other side of the street. Although far, he immediately recognized Toddy's schoolmate Maria, and his heart skipped. She reminded him of the operation he had performed on her mother, after which Maria's father had accused Kostea of butchering his wife. His first thought was to walk on, but she waved and came running. "Dr. Bardu! Dr. Bardu!" she called.

She hugged him. "How nice to see you," she said. "My mom and I talk about you all the time."

Thinking of Maria's father, he was surprised by that unbounded affection, but curiosity took over. "How is she?" he asked.

"Oh, she is doing quite well. You saved her life, Dr. Bardu. You really did."

Modestly, he leaned his head to one side and wondered whether to remind her that her father didn't think the same way.

As if guessing his thought, Maria said, "My father left us half a year after the operation. He had the gall to tell us he couldn't stand my mom's mutilated body. An idiot, what can I say."

Nothing, thought Kostea, taking her statement as absolution. He nodded for no reason at all. "I had no idea," he muttered.

"Forget him. How are Toddy and Lydia? In my book, their love story is the most powerful in the world."

"They moved to America."

"From Israel? Wow! This is great news. Dr. Bardu, I'm sure you're going to join them."

He was surprised, one more time. She was straightforward, so unrestrained. No fear of the Securitate, of being overheard. It used to be different when he was young. While wanting to be honest with Maria, his son's friend, he decided to be measured in his response. "It's not that simple. I have a situation here. A home. And I don't speak English," he said.

"C'mon, Dr. Bardu, we all know how much you love Toddy. Cristi said you climbed a whole mountain with a broken ankle just to be near him." She didn't wait for his answer. A wrought-iron fence with a solid concrete base separated the grounds of the medical school from the sidewalk. Red and white roses peeked behind it. She rested her foot on the base of the fence, ripped a page from a small notebook she had in her purse, placed it on her knee, and wrote on it. "Here," she said, handing the note to him. "She's a very good teacher of English, my friend. She'll help you." She smiled. "For a fee."

———————

Clara objected to the idea of taking English lessons, but Kostea insisted and, as always, prevailed. Once they started, Clara did her homework, diligently writing down the new words and expressions, testing her pronunciation in front of the mirror, and doing the exercises assigned by the teacher. Kostea did not. He spoke French since childhood, Russian, and a little German, and he relied on his memory, picking up most of it on the fly. Speaking English, he displayed less inhibition than Clara and thought he was doing very well. At least until he took the ECFMG—the equivalency exam required to allow foreign graduates to practice medicine in the United States. The first time.

He took it at the American Embassy in Bucharest. Marin said he was crazy. Just because it was possible didn't mean there would be no repercussions. America was still the enemy, and the Securitate kept the embassy under surveillance. But Minister Dinescu had just died, and Kostea's career wasn't going anywhere. His interest in professional recognition and advancement had vanished since Toddy left. He had accomplished enough, and consequences be damned. Now, more than anything, he wanted to be with his son in America and work in the States as a doctor. Fulfill his daring Sinaia Accord. He signed up for the exam and, as he had done many times in the past, studied general medicine for months, evening after evening. But he failed, on account of the English comprehension test.

In America, Toddy's daughter was born, followed two years later by his son. Kostea decided to visit them. He was barely sixty, still working and hoping to try the ECFMG test again. He asked for a leave of absence from the hospital and planned for a two-month stay. He practiced his English more seriously than last time.

"No matter what happens, you're going to come back," Clara made sure driving him to the airport.

"Of course," he said. He was full of hope, and she was happy for him.

Toddy's house in Columbia, Maryland, was busy with a toddler and a newborn. While staying with them and driving them crazy studying for the exam, he met, through friends of friends, a urologist, Dr. Claudius, at Howard County General Hospital. Dr. Claudius invited Kostea to witness two back-to-back prostate surgeries. "Wow," Kostea told Toddy at the end of that day. "The equipment they have is unbelievable. Their abilities are not. If we had in Bucharest what they have in this hospital, we would be gods."

He then took the test, did well on the clinical part, and failed the English again. Their loss, he tried to console himself. The offer he had received decades earlier from Dr. Caron in Toulouse loomed in his mind. He wouldn't have needed to take a test in order to work in France. The French doctors had appreciated his skill. Not so the Americans. Anybody could learn English, while being a great surgeon was a different story entirely. Just take this doctor, Claudius, a native speaker of English and a mediocrity. In his place Kostea would do so much. It would have been nice to pass the test, but he had only come for a visit and needed to return. His hospital, Clara, and the mothers were waiting for him. He would have other chances, try again and again, and in Bucharest he would study English some more.

In the late '70s and early '80s, life became difficult in Romania, very difficult, and not just for Kostea and Clara but for everybody. The stores were empty like during the war, and gas for heating and cooking was rationed. It was cold in the winter, dirty and ugly. Kostea and Clara had plenty of money and nothing to spend it on. But Kostea had social status. People still bowed to him, opened doors, and rolled out the red carpet for him.

Toddy and his family moved to Copenhagen on a two-year work assignment. Kostea and Clara went for a visit. They traveled by train, via East Berlin. In his suitcase, under his white cotton briefs, Kostea had hidden a plastic box filled with morphine—thirty vials, snapped into their molded cardboard slots like lead soldiers. He gave it to Toddy. "Take it back with you to America. We'll join you there after our mothers are gone."

Toddy shrugged.

"I don't want to end up like my father, begging for morphine," Kostea said.

"It's a controlled substance, Dad," Toddy said. "I can't take it."

"Sure you can. You'll do it for me."

Ina and Mimi passed away quietly, one after the other, one year apart. They had kept Kostea and Clara pinned down like two rusty anchors, but now Kostea's ship was ready to sail. No stopping him any longer. He had risen to the top before, and he'd prove himself once again. America, near Toddy, here we go!

One month before they left, Clara and Kostea went to the Black Sea. It was a goodbye trip to a place they had loved, with a mild autumn sun and the water stretching ahead of them to infinity. Kostea arranged for them to stay at Europa, a fancy new hotel built for Western tourists. Once in America, they intended to defect, but they couldn't make their plans known. Kostea pretended to be interested in a professorship position that had recently opened in Timişoara. They sold Ina's studio and spent lavishly in restaurants. In their dreams, America was like home, only better.

When they returned to Bucharest, Kostea went back to work for the remaining weeks, and the last-minute preparations fell on Clara. She invented a story to tell buyers and advertised the car for sale in the paper. The large pieces of furniture were easy. This one would go to this friend, that one to the other. Clara taped labels to them to make sure they'd know. Sometimes, when she walked through the apartment alone and saw the labels, sadness hit. She cried. *Goodbye, friends. Take good care of our armoires and dressers and sofas and love them the way you loved us. Remember us, Clara and Kostea.*

The small stuff was more complicated. She had Marcela take their mothers' shoes and clothing. Then there was china, bedding, books, and pictures. There was bric-a-brac, drafts of old medical papers and letters. Everything was staying behind.

Clara spent a day and a half creating an inventory. She gave up. Let their friends take what they want, and if not, so be it. It was clear to Clara and Kostea that when their exit visas expired and the authorities realized they had defected, they would requisition the apartment and give it to one of the Party's trusted people.

The plan was to leave a key with Eugene and Norma and then send them a postcard from the US and tell them to go to the apartment. They would find a letter on Kostea's desk, read it, and understand. The labels on the furniture would make the rest clear.

Kostea went out on a last walk through the neighborhood. Clara finished packing the suitcases. She sat on the kitchen floor with a metal washbasin and Lydia's letters to Toddy in front of her. She read a few letters, entering a forbidden space and wiping the tears that were dripping off her cheeks. There were about five hundred letters, written over five years. When Toddy had emigrated, he had given them to her—people leaving the country for good were prohibited from taking with them documents or letters of any kind. Now, Clara couldn't put them in her suitcase and risk being found out in customs. She and Kostea were traveling for a visit, weren't they? Why would she take the letters along? And the letters were too personal to be given to any of their friends for safekeeping or to be left in the apartment.

Slowly, Clara burned them one by one, like embers in the night— envelopes, postcards, pressed flowers and all.

In the evening, she cried again. They both cried, out of fear and hope. The held hands and they cried for the lives they were leaving behind.

BOOK III

AMERICA

Maryland, the late 1980s and early 1990s

CHAPTER 32

Will You Be My Patient?

Fall 1988

The passenger door was locked, and Clara knocked hard on the window. Kostea sighed, leaned across the front bench of his Chevy Impala, and pulled up the door lock.

"I told you to always have a key on you," he said.

"My back hurts." Clara didn't have to say anything else.

Kostea felt a lump in his throat and started the engine. "Watch my left, Clara."

She gently stretched her neck to look behind Kostea. "It's free." Kostea switched from neutral to reverse, and the car inched backward.

It was a beautiful fall morning. The air was warm, and the trees, still full of leaves, were green and luscious. Children were back in school, their grandchildren included. Kostea had scheduled Clara's doctor's appointment early in the day so as not to interfere with their duties minding the grandchildren after school. When it came to talking on the phone, Clara hesitated. Kostea didn't speak English much better, but he was daring. He had to be. He was the man in the family. It bothered him that he, a former doctor of a certain standing and reputation, couldn't just go and see a doctor, a colleague of his, at the drop of a hat. He had to wait in line with the other people. That's the way it was over here—he was like everyone else.

Kostea remembered Dr. Claudius, whom he had met during his visit to the States before he and Clara defected. Eager to prove to himself he could still get things moving, he leafed through his old notebook, found the phone number, and spent the next forty minutes on the phone trying to get through to the doctor. Eventually he gave up, drove to the hospital, and returned in time to pick up his grandchildren at the bus stop. He had a piece of paper with Clara's appointment time in his hand.

Clara's lower back had been bothering her for several weeks despite the remedies Kostea had recommended: stretching, hot showers, and lying flat on the floor. Over-the-counter painkillers helped, but they were not a solution. Plus, there were so many to choose from, some rather expensive, and Clara didn't want to spend money. In America, Clara and Kostea had to relearn how to live on a budget. Clara wanted to read the labels, but Kostea was impatient and rushed her. They avoided salespeople because they didn't speak English well. Clara asked Lydia to suggest a headache medication. Her daughter-in-law breathlessly covered the gamut: Tylenol, Aleve, Motrin, Advil, Excedrin, aspirin, and so on. Clara remembered aspirin, but the other names escaped her. She yearned for the lost familiarity of Bucharest. Over there, they had Algocalmin in vials or pills, Fenacod, and Antinevralgic. Over there, she would have known.

Then Clara saw blood in her urine. Kostea assaulted her with questions. Was it the first time, was it red or dark brown, was it clear or murky. Itchy? Painful? Did it burn?

"I don't know," Clara said. "I just noticed it when I flushed."

It seemed like she was holding back, which annoyed Kostea. They had been married for forty years, and there was no reason to be bashful. "You don't know if you had a burning sensation?"

In Bucharest, he would ask such questions of his patients every day, and they never hesitated to answer. It was his duty to find out, and nothing was too intimate. As a doctor and a former professor of medicine, he knew many reasons there could be for bleeding. Some were innocuous and some not. It was important to proceed methodically and not alarm the patient. His patient. "You shouldn't have flushed," he told Clara. "Next time, be sure to call me."

Clara nodded, went into the kitchen, and cut a few slices from the bread she had baked the previous evening. No point in arguing with her husband. She was a doctor as well. She had already thought about the possibilities and felt that she could wish the worst ones away by not talking about them.

"I'm sure it's nothing serious." Kostea pressed on through the open door to the kitchen. "I guess this is a urinary tract infection."

An older Korean woman, Mrs. Lili, used to live alone in the apartment across the hallway from their apartment. Like them, she didn't speak English well, and each time they saw each other, they asked, "Mrs. Lili, how you doing?" and she always answered, "Better and better." The last time she said it, she was on a stretcher being carried out by the paramedics.

"You don't think the bleeding is tied to my lower back pain?" Clara asked, unable to keep all her thoughts to herself.

"No," he said. "What you need is an antibiotic. I wish I could prescribe it, but I can't, and we'll have to go see a doctor." He smiled again. "A *real* doctor."

Clara almost said, you are a real doctor, but she didn't. It would only add to his frustration. At times she felt frustrated as well, although not as intensely. This was the price they had to pay for choosing to live close to their children and grandchildren. When Kostea smiled at her, with his shiny white hair, fading blue eyes, and perfect white teeth, he looked peaceful and approachable. But she knew how quickly he could pivot.

"Let's not tell anything to the children," she said. "I don't want them to worry." She placed the bread in a basket. "This one came out very nicely," she added and knocked on the golden crust. "I'm getting better at baking, don't you think? Better and better."

They advanced to the reception desk, and Kostea did the talking. "We have appointment with Dr. Claudius. He is expecting."

"Very good, sir. Please write your name over here." The receptionist pointed to an open register on the counter. "And give me your ID and insurance information."

"Dr. Claudius knows we are here," Kostea added and looked at the receptionist intently.

"I understand. He'll be with you shortly."

"It's my wife." Kostea turned to Clara, who started fumbling in her purse, her hands shaking a little. He entered her information in the register, and she produced her driver's license and Medicaid card.

"Thank you," the receptionist said and made Xerox copies of the documents. "Now, please take a seat and complete these two forms while you're waiting." She handed Clara several sheets of paper on a clipboard.

Clara nodded and took a step back. Kostea followed, after lingering as if debating if he had anything else to tell the receptionist.

The waiting room was clean and pleasant, with rows of blue chairs and teak side tables. About a dozen people were waiting silently, some leafing through old magazines. Clara had the distinct impression of being observed.

The first form was a general medical information questionnaire. Clara entered her personal data at the top of the page in her nice and orderly handwriting.

Kostea watched and after a minute or so whispered to her in Romanian: "This is nonsense. Stop."

"She asked me to do this, and it's not a big deal," Clara said.

"Suit yourself." Kostea picked a magazine from the side table and started turning the pages. He would have smoked, but smoking was not allowed.

Clara filled out her medical history. Checking yes or no on the long list of illnesses and conditions was relatively simple, most of them not being applicable. At the bottom of the second page was a space that asked for the reason of her visit. She wrote a word, crossed it out, and wrote another, unsure how to describe her symptoms in English. She was a doctor, yet she felt awkward, uneducated.

Kostea noticed her hesitation, looked over her shoulder at the form, and said, "Leave it blank. We'll tell the doctor."

Clara signed and dated the sheet and moved to the next one, which was a medical consent form. It asked for the same personal information as the first, plus a next of kin. Clara wrote in Kostea's name. There was text on the page that Clara read and a place for a signature and date at the bottom. This form also asked for her Social Security number. When Clara looked for the card in her purse, a nurse came out and called her name.

Clara and Kostea jumped to their feet, Clara holding her purse and the clipboard in one hand and the pen in the other.

"You're not done with the paperwork," the nurse noticed. "That's OK. Finish it before you leave here."

Kostea beamed. "I told you it's nonsense."

The nurse asked Clara to climb on a scale and took down her weight. Then she measured her height. She led them both to a small room and asked Clara to take a seat on an examination table. There were two more chairs in the room, and the nurse told Kostea to sit on the one farthest from the door.

Kostea did his best to be patient.

The nurse took Clara's temperature, blood pressure, pulse, and oxygen level and wrote them all in a chart. "Dr. Claudius will be with you in a minute," she said.

Kostea asked, "The doctor tell you to take my wife blood pressure?"

"No," the nurse said, "it's standard procedure."

"Yes," Kostea insisted. "I am a doctor. I did surgery with Dr. Claudius. Blood pressure not necessary. My wife has urinary infection."

"Very well, sir. Tell this to Dr. Claudius," the nurse answered and left the room, pulling the door shut after her.

Kostea looked at Clara. "What did I tell you?"

"What?" Clara asked.

"I don't believe this. You come here with a urinary tract infection, and what's the first thing they do? They weigh you and take your blood pressure. No urine sample. Standard procedures, my ass. They're loading it up. Don't you see? That's how they make their money."

Clara closed her eyes and leaned to one side, trying to ease her pain by tightening her back muscles. A crinkling sheet of paper, rolled at one end, covered the examination table. When they had entered the room, the nurse had pulled off the used paper sheet and replaced it with a new one. Everything was so clean, logical, and simple.

"All right," Kostea said. "If you don't want to talk to me, so be it."

It was all about him, Clara thought, and in a way, it was for the better. What sense did it make to talk about her, her fears, and what she might need to do to feel better? They were at the doctor's, weren't they? Whatever disease she might have, if any, she'd find out in a minute, or in a few days.

Kostea was wringing his hands and fidgeting, trying to stay calm while waiting for the doctor.

"If you're tired of waiting, go for a walk. I'll meet you at the car later," Clara said and smiled. She knew he wouldn't want to leave.

He shook his head. "Let's see what happens. I'll wait another five minutes. If he doesn't show up, I'll go find him. This is ridiculous."

"You're not going to look for him. Remember when you saw patients? He might have an emergency."

"I never kept a fellow doctor waiting," Kostea replied.

"Does he know who you are? Do you think he remembers?"

"I'm sure he does."

———————

Dr. Claudius walked in, shook hands with Clara, and introduced himself. He was shorter than Kostea, and his smile was hidden under a handlebar mustache, red like his neatly cropped hair. He turned to Kostea. "You must be her better half."

Kostea wasn't sure he understood. "My name is Dr. Bardu," he said.

"So, you're a doctor. Great. That makes it easier."

"My wife is doctor also."

"Three doctors in one room. Wow! So, tell me, Doctors, how can I help you?"

Clara had anticipated this moment and had prepared a few simple sentences describing her symptoms, but Kostea jumped in.

"Before we tell, I met you, Doctor. You must remember. You operated in hospital, and I witnessed, through Dr. Calin."

Claudius pulled back, squinted, and looked at the ceiling. Then his face opened up and he wagged his index finger. "Yes, now I remember. You were visiting here from Romania. You wanted to tour my hospital and see a surgery performed. Dr. Calin had introduced us."

"Yes, yes," Kostea exclaimed and threw Clara a triumphant look.

"How many years ago was that?"

"Five," specified Kostea.

"No wonder I didn't remember you at first. I think you witnessed an open prostatectomy."

"Two," said Kostea.

"Even better. You must know that poor Dr. Calin passed away, don't you?"

"Yes. He had cancer of the pancreas at age sixty. We went to Bucharest School of Medicine together."

"And now you're here with your wife. Visiting, I presume. Your son lives in the area."

Kostea would have loved to tell his story. He had always tended toward the verbose, the information flowing freely out of him, aspiring to charm his audience, be funny, captivating, the center of attention. He couldn't do that in English. As he spoke, he stumbled often and realized he couldn't be either eloquent or fluent—the vocabulary was lacking, the accent was wrong, the grammar stilted. By necessity, he had learned to replace sentences with words and cut to the essence. "Not visiting," he said. "Immigrated."

"How long ago?" Claudius asked.

"Two years."

"And do you like it here?"

"America is great country," Kostea said.

He and Clara both nodded.

Clara added, "It was hard in the beginning. Now is better and better."

"Better than communism, I hope," said Claudius.

"Yes, better."

"Well, in that case, congratulations and welcome to America. Are you still practicing?"

"What?" Kostea asked. "Practicing?"

"Yes, practicing. Are you working over here as a doctor?"

"Not working." Kostea wondered if he should mention the failed medical equivalency exam, decided against it, and added, "Take care of grandchildren."

"Oh, that's fabulous, isn't it? The true joy of retirement. So, am I to understand that you're staying with your son and his family?"

"No," Kostea said. "We have apartment on Cross Fox, two miles from here."

"Great. It's better this way, believe me. Living with your adult children can be a challenge." His moustache twitched. He looked at both of them, as if wondering if they had understood him. After they nodded, he glanced at the chart in his hand. "So, what brings you here . . . Madam Bardu? I think you are the patient."

"Yes," Clara said at the same time Kostea corrected Claudius: "Dr. Bardu." Clara continued without looking at him. "I saw hematuria." Her pronunciation was better than Kostea's, or maybe the word was simpler, while her voice sounded less secure.

"When did it start? Or, better said, when did you first notice it?" Claudius inquired.

Clara looked at Kostea. "Yesterday," she said. "No, Tuesday."

"OK. It's recent. Any pain or discomfort?"

Clara said, "In back." She brought her hand to her lower back. "Most here."

Claudius came closer as if to make sure he saw exactly the area Clara was indicating.

"Doctor," Kostea interjected, "I think not serious. Urinary tract infection. I treat with penicillin."

"Yes, Dr. Bardu," he said. "Don't worry. I'll prescribe an antibiotic. But I think it would be smart, given Clara's age, to run some tests, to ensure that we don't miss anything. I recommend a simple urine analysis and a CT scan with contrast of the lower lumbar region." He turned and opened the door.

"Doctor," Clara stopped him. "My pain?"

"Until we see the results of your tests, take some Advil, two at a time if necessary. It's over the counter, and the instructions are on the bottle. Listen, my nurse will give you my instructions and set up the testing. Nice seeing you after all these years, and good luck with your new life in America. Enjoy the grandchildren." His mustache lifted, revealing a smile and a row of slightly crooked teeth, and he walked away.

—————

"He's not a doctor," Kostea said as soon as they left the office. "He's a functionary. I saw this five years ago when I watched him operate. What doctor doesn't listen to his patient's lungs and heart, check his skin, touch him?"

"You said yourself it's a urinary infection. Why would he need to examine me?"

"I know what I said." He strode forward and stopped. "Clara, this is my specialty, and I'm good at it. You must trust me. I'll take care of you from now on, if you let me. Will you be my patient?"

"Yes," she said. "I will be your patient."

As they approached the car, he went straight to the passenger door and unlocked it. "My lady," he said, bowing gallantly.

Clara brushed against him as she climbed in. She understood. He still loved her.

Kostea turned the key in the ignition. The windshield wipers started up briskly. He must have touched a lever inadvertently, either now or earlier when he had turned off the engine. "Fuck," he said, bewildered. He stopped the wipers and turned to Clara. "This car. Sometimes I wonder."

Clara let his comment go. He criticized everything, because to him everything was unfamiliar. It was for her too, but she had learned to accept her own ineptitude at how to start the dishwasher or navigate supermarket aisles filled with still unknown products.

Toddy had bought them a secondhand car shortly after their arrival. Clara had driven it only a few times, to go grocery shopping. As in Bucharest, Kostea was the family driver. Even so, and after all this time, the car still bewildered him. It was large, with a soft suspension, automatic transmission, power steering, cruise control, and air-conditioning. Kostea would surprise himself slamming the brakes in the middle of an intersection, nervously searching for the nonexistent clutch. The dashboard, its gray vinyl slightly scorched by the sun, looked like an airplane cockpit.

After failing his doctor's accreditation exam for the third time, Kostea had started working for a courier service. He delivered letters, money, and small packages. His lack of language skills didn't matter, since he spent most of his time driving around on his own, in this car, in Columbia and the surrounding areas. The owner of the business, a man younger than Toddy, handed him typed instructions each morning. He was curt. Kostea preferred his instructions written anyway because he understood written English better. Every night, the owner paid him cash. The pay was meager, barely covering the cost of gas and parking. Kostea got lost on the intimidating highways or in the unfamiliar cities. Impatient as he was, he found maps of little use. Instead, he tried relying on his sense of direction and memorizing the names of the streets, which proved impossible. He came home exhausted, beaten. It was obvious he felt humiliated, but he denied it. Clara, Lydia, and Toddy were worried.

His last assignment had been to deliver a refrigerated AIDS cocktail to an address in Baltimore. He found it after an hour—in a slum, a dark and decrepit wooden shack that reminded him of dwellings he had seen in remote Romanian villages. But in those villages the poverty had been humble. Here, the shack and the dark alleys around it seemed menacing. He felt vulnerable and threatened. He had persevered for months at his job, eager to put behind him his failure at the medical test and to prove that he could adjust to his changed circumstances. But he wasn't suicidal. He quit that same evening.

"Mom, Dad, help us with the kids after school," Toddy said, relieved to know his father had stopped driving for the courier service. "We'd rather pay you than our babysitter. Help the kids with their homework, take them to sports programs, and speak to them in Romanian. Also, Lydia could use some help in the kitchen."

Clara immediately agreed. Kostea thought they should do it without any pay, but eventually accepted the money. They could use it.

CHAPTER 33

Teenage Mutant Ninja Turtles

Clara took two Advil, made Kostea lunch, and stepped onto the porch to feed the parakeet. She had found it injured in the grass next to their apartment building, brought it home, nurtured it to health, and named it Honey. Now she replaced Honey's water and put a few apple slices in the cage feeder. The little blue-and-yellow bird chirped in recognition and looked at Clara with eyes as shiny as polished onyx. Clara's back was still bothering her, but she was less worried than she had been before she had seen the doctor. Rain was coming, and the trees on the other side of the parking lot were swaying in the wind.

When they had moved into this apartment, two years ago in the fall, the leaves were turning shades of red, brown, and gold. On sunny days, the view of the trees from their porch was more colorful than she had ever seen in Romania, even in Sinaia, in the mountains. In the fall in Romania, the trees displayed a monotonous brown color like a shroud drawn at the death of the season, whereas here, the foliage seemed alight with celebratory hues.

The apartment, while smaller than the one in Bucharest, was more than adequate: a nice living room with a dining area, an enclosed porch, a kitchen, two bedrooms, and one and a half bathrooms. A wood-burning fireplace was framed by glass bookshelves, and a washer, dryer, and dishwasher caused a flow of questions and head scratching from Kostea, who insisted that washing dishes by hand was more hygienic. The rent was controlled—Section 8 housing.

On the day they moved in, a truck pulled up in front of their building, loaded with a queen-size bed, two nightstands, a table and chairs, a convertible sofa, and all the other household stuff that they needed, donated by a religious charitable organization. Some items were new and some not, but they all were useable. Two young men spent the better part of two hours carrying everything upstairs. "God bless you," they said when they finished.

"Do we have to join your church?" Clara asked tentatively.

"You don't have to do anything," one of the two young men answered.

Clara didn't know how to interpret such disinterested generosity.

It took Clara two months to get her green card. Kostea received his several months later, delayed on account of his having been a member of the Communist Party. The McCarthy era was long gone, and communism was losing influence everywhere, even in the Soviet Union under Gorbachev. But Kostea had to prove he was not and had never been a communist. He produced two letters from people who knew him from Romania, now US citizens. They vouched that they had firsthand knowledge that he had joined the Party only for professional advancement, not for ideological reasons.

Sometimes Clara felt people watching her at the checkout as she handed over the food stamps. "So what if we're poor and get some benefits?" Kostea said. "We don't buy anything we don't need. We have paid our dues in Romania."

———————

Clara opened the door to Honey's cage. The bird was her new little friend, and the two of them had a connection. She enjoyed allowing the parakeet to fly inside the enclosed porch. The slider to the living room stood mostly open, but Honey rarely ventured into the apartment. Somehow it knew where it belonged, and each time it came out of its cage, it perched on the branches of the potted ficus.

"Well, are you coming out?" Clara asked the bird in Romanian. The bird didn't move. Clara shrugged. "Have it your way."

She went back into the living room, sat on her secondhand floral-patterned love seat, and lit a cigarette. She could lean sideways, put up her feet, and doze off. In the evening, Kostea usually took the armchair, and they watched television.

After his nap, Kostea showed up undressed, looking refreshed and sleepy. He moved friskily, his belly hanging over the elastic of his under-wear. "Ready? The kids will be home from school in twenty minutes."

"Kostea, do you think I am ill?"

"You're fine."

"I don't want to die, Kostea."

———————

Sprawled on the couch, Rudy, Clara's eleven-year-old grandson, was watching TV with his friend Brian. Their miniature apricot poodle, Del, short for Delano, was sleeping next to them.

"Your Mom says no TV," Clara said in English. She spoke Romanian to the grandchildren except when they had friends over, because they said that speaking Romanian was embarrassing. Brian belonged to the Chinese family next door, and the two boys spent a lot of time together. Clara continued, "Not before you doing homework."

"I have no homework," Rudy said without turning his eyes from the TV screen.

"How come?" asked Clara.

"My mother said I can watch until dinner," said Brian.

"Three hours." Clara shook her head. "Too long. What are you watching?"

"*Teenage Mutant Ninja Turtles*," Rudy responded quickly. "We watched it before, remember?"

Clara didn't understand the title and didn't remember. She went to check on Ginny. She found the girl at her desk in her room, bent over a large sketchpad. Her backpack was on the floor, next to clothes, school manuals, and notebooks. Ginny was sketching a butterfly in black pencil, the details in a fine juxtaposition of light and shadow. Clara kissed Ginny on the top of her head and caressed her blond hair. "What is this, my little princess?"

"I'm drawing a swallowtail butterfly, Bunica," Ginny responded in a Romanian loaded with a clear and endearing American accent. The key words in her answer were *swallowtail*, which she said in English, and *bunica*, "grandmother" in Romanian. She turned her head and leaned against Clara's body.

"Beautiful," said Clara.

The pain in her lower back had completely disappeared. Maybe it was the Advil, or maybe there was nothing to worry about. Kostea might be right, and all she needed was the antibiotic. They had turned in the prescription, and Kostea would get the meds for her a little later. She remained standing, feeling her granddaughter's touch, enjoying the moment.

She loved Ginny. She loved Rudy as well, but in a different way. Ginny reminded Clara of her own childhood. Now that Ina was gone, the recollection was even more vivid, like looking through old photo albums. Her relationship with Ina, their love and need for each other, had at times been complicated—such as when they lived in the same crowded apartment and Ina squabbled with Kostea.

With Ginny, there were no fights to be fought, no disagreements even. Lydia ruled, and Clara gladly submitted. She tended to the grandchildren on Lydia's terms, as she often told Kostea.

She loved Ginny's calm yet intense manner, just as she liked her curiosity and desire to listen. The young girl was clearly talented, and she loved to draw and paint. Less than two years older than Rudy, she seemed mature for her age.

"Is your homework all done?" she asked Ginny.

The girl pulled away, focused on her drawing again, erased a line, and drew another. "Almost done," she said. "I have a few math problems left, but I needed a break."

Clara nodded. "Take another half hour, and we'll finish the problems together." She left Ginny and found Kostea reading in the guest room. "Why don't you take care of Rudy?"

"What do you want me to do?" said Kostea.

"You're the grandpa. First walk the dog and then play a game with the boys. They are watching too much TV, and Lydia doesn't like that."

"Lydia, of course," Kostea said and waved his hand but got up. He rearranged his hair with his fingers and pulled at his shirt. "I'll go see," he added. He didn't look happy, but not too unhappy, either. He understood he was the one to walk the dog, and besides, being with his grandson appealed to him greatly.

"Delano," he called. The dog ignored him. "Delano."

Rudy turned. "Call him Del, not Delano." Then he added with a mature self-awareness, "Delano is his formal name, like in Franklin Delano Roosevelt."

Kostea took the leash from its hook. The dog jumped off the sofa and stretched. After walking Del, Kostea and the boys agreed to go fishing. Brian pushed the remote control and Raphael, red mask and sai, fizzled from the screen.

The fishing rods stood in a corner of the garage.

"I have to go ask my mom," Brian said but didn't go anywhere.

"Hand me the tackle box, Bunicu," Rudy said, his request in English except for the word *bunicu*, Romanian for "grandfather." Even Brian called him that.

Kostea seemed lost.

"The tackle box, Bunicu," Rudy repeated and pointed at the shelves on the back wall of the garage. Both cars were gone, the garage was poorly lit, and Rudy's voice sounded hollow. "Look there, on the top shelf. We bought it together in Copenhagen."

"I don't know the box and cannot reach," said Kostea.

"Bunicu's a geezer," said Brian.

Kostea didn't understand the word *geezer*, but he sensed its meaning. In response, his memory flickered to the time in Copenhagen, when he gave the morphine to Toddy. Years later, when Kostea came to America, he asked for it back.

"I didn't bring it," Toddy said. "I agonized over the decision, but I figured that if they caught me, I might end up in prison, so I threw the morphine away."

CHAPTER 34

The Best Possible Option

The CT scan showed an ill-defined and rather large lump in Clara's bladder. Dr. Claudius referred her to Dr. Harris at the University of Maryland Medical Center. "Go see him for a cystoscopy and a biopsy. Dr. Harris is a surgeon, like your husband. You'll like him."

"Necessary?" Clara asked.

"It is. We want to cover all possibilities."

"If this is a teaching hospital, it must be one of the best. A little bit like Speranţa," Kostea assured her.

Dr. Harris was younger than Kostea by more than a decade. He was slim and had a high, slanted forehead and bright, piercing eyes that gave him an intelligent air.

Clara's biopsy took forty minutes. When she came out, her face was the color of butter.

"I like Dr. Harris," said Kostea. "I am sure we speak the same language, and he'll be open with us. He knows that we understand."

The biopsy revealed a high-grade cancer likely to invade the muscular wall of the bladder. Dr. Harris explained that due to its location, a transurethral resection of the tumor was not possible. He made a drawing on his blackboard and started describing the options. Kostea became animated. He advanced to the board and drew a few sketches of his own. Clearly, he knew what he was doing. Clara slumped in her armchair. She was tired. It was her body they were talking about, and her self-defense mechanism took over. She understood her diagnosis and that the surgery was complicated and scary. She had to trust Kostea. Placing herself in his hands was her way. For better or for worse, a lifetime ago she had chosen him as her guardian angel.

Dr. Harris said that a radical cystectomy was the safest option, with the detriment of a permanent urinary diversion to a urostomy bag placed on the abdomen. Clara shuddered and exchanged a meaningful glance with Kostea. Dr. Harris then described a less invasive procedure, removing the tumor through a partial cystectomy. Chances were good, he said, especially since the cancer seemed contained within the bladder.

They agreed Clara and Kostea would think about these options and get back with Dr. Harris in a few days. They were in control—to some degree, at least.

"What a great place," Kostea said as they were driving home. "So many floors, and the parking. And all those wings. If we had such a facility in Bucharest, wow, could you imagine what we would do?" When facing a patient with a difficult diagnosis, it was his habit to try to ease the burden by bringing up something mundane.

But Clara was not just a patient. "We have a decision to make."

Kostea bit his lip and asked for a cigarette.

———

Toddy met them at the hospital early in the morning. They drove separately, Kostea and Clara in their Chevy and Toddy in his Corolla. He wanted to stay with Kostea, but Kostea convinced his son that he was used to waiting in hospitals and would be all right, while Toddy's work was important and his time valuable. Lydia had found a babysitter for the next several weeks until Clara recovered.

When they came to take Clara for the procedure, Toddy gave her a big hug. She was pale and seemed smaller, the wrinkles around her bright eyes more pronounced than ever. Kostea stood to the side. She smiled at them both and whispered to them not to worry, while a tear rolled down her right cheek.

Toddy was getting ready to leave when Dr. Harris came out, accompanied by a man who appeared to be Toddy's age or slightly younger. Dr. Harris introduced him as a recent graduate who was shadowing him. In turn, Kostea introduced Toddy, using his full name, Alexander.

"I'm glad you have your son to wait here with you," said Harris.

"No, he has work to do," said Kostea. "Very important. He come back in the evening."

"All right," Harris said, and looked at Toddy. "What do you do, Alexander?"

"Engineer for very big company," Kostea rushed to answer. "He speaks English perfect." It was obvious he was proud of Toddy. He had stopped a few times at his workplace and had waited for him in the impressive lobby of his building.

Toddy took a step back. His father was unable to hear that he spoke English with a foreign accent, and Toddy felt self-conscious of the unwarranted praise. "Dad is exaggerating. But I have some work to do, and he has convinced me he will be all right by himself. My wife and I will be back here in the afternoon."

"Family support is invaluable," Harris said. The young doctor next to him nodded his agreement. "I have something to tell you," Harris continued, addressing Toddy. "Your parents have opted for a partial cystectomy, to avoid the need for a urinary diversion, which nobody likes. I'll remove the lymph nodes around the bladder and send them to the pathologist. As I told your parents, I want to make sure that you understand that a total cystectomy is the safest available option."

"I do, and so do my parents," said Toddy. "They analyzed the pros and the cons, and this was their decision."

"All right," Harris said. "I didn't want there to be any chance of a misunderstanding because of the language barrier. I'll be out as soon as we're done, in two to three hours, and brief your father on the results." He turned to leave but stopped and added with a smile, "And tell your father he'll be allowed in the recovery room, as long as he refrains from harassing the nurses."

Kostea accompanied Toddy downstairs. "Your mother doesn't need a total, mutilating cystectomy," he said, irritated by the surgeon's insistence for the more radical option. "She and I have discussed this in detail. Whatever life she has left needs to be normal. She wants it to be normal. She understands. She's a doctor. I'm sure there'll be many beautiful years ahead of us, and she doesn't want a bag hanging from her belly. She wants to see people without feeling embarrassed, play with her grandchildren, and travel. And I agree with her." He almost said, *I want that for myself, also,* but he didn't. "Trust me, Toddy. I'm good at this, and I know what I'm doing."

"I know, Dad. I trust you."

"You should know I'm sorry you threw away the morphine I brought you in Copenhagen. It might have been useful to your mother right now, on her way to recovery."

"Don't worry, Dad. Dr. Harris will prescribe what is necessary."

"I hope so," Kostea said, and pushed his chest forward. "Did you see how he came out with his assistant in tow? I bet it was to impress me. In my time, I had a whole group following me around. As many as four to six students. And he'll give me a detailed report afterward because I'm a doctor."

———

In the waiting room, Kostea remembered Letitia Banu and her mastectomy. He could visualize the flat half of her chest and the incision under her nipple. He and Dr. Moraru had to do it, to save Letitia's life. As a thank you, her husband had called him a butcher. How befitting that idiot had divorced Letitia and had left her and their daughter Maria several months after surgery. And how friendly Maria had been that day they had met in the street! Sadly, a few years later, Kostea had found out that Maria, that young woman, had prematurely died of a breast cancer of her own, undoubtedly hereditary. Her mother, on the other hand, was still alive.

Kostea had been right then. He had been a prudent doctor and had the results to show it. Some might say that this time with Clara his emotions might have taken over. But they didn't, and he'd be proven right one more time. Being a doctor was his life's calling, and he was good at it, whether allowed to practice or not.

When he and Clara defected to the US, he was determined to take the medical equivalency exam for the third time. In preparation for it, he enrolled in English classes at the local community college. He had heard that older people had a hard time learning a new language. Maybe, he thought, but not him. He was different. And it wasn't memorizing the words; it was just their pronunciation. Reading was all right, but when people talked to him, he didn't understand them.

Then he failed the third time, and his pain became visceral. And it was English again. How many times can a man bang his head against a brick wall to understand he can go no further? And there was no turning around this time, no plane taking him back to Bucharest.

He held the rejection letter, his hand shaking. He was at Toddy's, in the kitchen. Lydia and Toddy were at work, and he could hear Clara and the grandchildren upstairs. He had picked up the mail, noticed the large envelope from the medical board, and ripped it open. It came to Toddy's address because he had registered for the exam before he and Clara had moved into their apartment.

Looking at the letter he stopped breathing. He had missed the passing grade by three points. His knees buckled.

Clara was coming down the stairs. He folded the envelope and the letter and hid them in his pocket.

"Have you seen a ghost?" Clara asked. "Shall I give you a glass of water?"

"I don't need anything," he said. He opened the door and walked out.

"Kostea," she called after him.

He didn't answer.

There was a path behind the house, through the woods, winding down to a brook. Trees grew on both sides, tall and bare. The path was paved, the soil around it saturated with rainwater. Wet brown and yellow leaves covered the ground. Kostea walked fast, stepping hard on the dead leaves, not caring that they were slippery. He kept his right hand in his pocket, holding onto the envelope and the paper showing his test result. He wanted to take them out, but instead he walked faster and faster. A group of schoolchildren came up the path. Kostea squeezed the papers in his pocket and stepped aside to let the children pass. The children only looked ahead.

He stopped at the narrow wooden bridge over the brook. The water flowed vigorously, swollen by the rain of the previous days. He leaned over the railing and touched the papers in his pocket again. He didn't take them out. Reading the letter one more time would not change the outcome. Crying wouldn't help. Yelling wouldn't help. Blaming somebody else didn't make sense.

The path followed the brook. He saw a fallen tree. The large trunk rested on the mossy shore, still connected to its stump by a few strips of bark. The crown extended into the riverbed, the joyous brook cascading around it through a new channel carved in the moist soil. Two large branches trapped a pool of water, its surface dull between brown leaves.

What flowed past the fallen tree was the life of others. Deprived of his right to practice medicine, Kostea was the trapped pool of water.

When he returned home that afternoon, he told his family about the test results, and they tried showing compassion and understanding. He nodded, not saying much. Clara served him his favorite roast chicken and made him sweet *khrustyky*.

The courier job he took a few days later was his last act of defiance. He didn't know what he was getting into and needed the diversion. Driving alone for ten hours a day every day seemed therapeutic. He, a man who had sought the company of others his entire life, went into hiding. He got lost in the maze of highways and streets, found his way back, and used his wanderings to attempt a tentative peace with his new reality.

The day he quit, he understood. He wasn't a young man any longer.

That's when, at last, he felt disheartened. He longed for his old life in Bucharest. He shed tears shaving in the bathroom mirror of his efficient new American apartment. His blue eyes turned cloudy. He was ashamed to face Clara.

She nurtured him. The children and grandchildren moved around him on tiptoes. They were a constant reminder of his new life's purpose: his family. That was the reason he had come to America. That had always been the reason. Slowly, he recovered from his initial shock and depression. He didn't have a choice. He glossed over the memory of his former self and tried to repress his envy of doctors and the feeling he had been unfairly robbed of his profession.

Brian, Rudy's friend, was wrong: Kostea was not a geezer. Not yet. He could go on strenuous walks, beat Toddy in tennis, and hold his liquor. His memory no longer was what it used to be, but he still had a good head on his shoulders. With the help of his son, he had enough money for a modest but comfortable existence. He could be charming if he needed to be, or at least he thought so. He couldn't work in his profession, but he *was still* a doctor. Clara, his love, his best friend, his wife of over forty years, needed his help. Her ailment was in his specialty, the area of his expertise. Life was ironic this way—what a coincidence! He saw a new clear purpose ahead of him, larger and more important than everything else at this moment: take good care of Clara, guide her steps, and lead her to recovery.

Kostea shifted in his chair and looked at the clock on the wall: 11:25 a.m. He'd been waiting almost four hours. He wished his friend Eugene were sitting with him there in the waiting room, to witness how much he loved Clara.

CHAPTER 35

Better and Better

November and December 1988

"How are you feeling, Bunica?" Ginny asked in a small, caring voice. They were visiting Clara for the first time since she'd returned home from the hospital.

"Thank you, baby. I'm feeling much better."

"Look what I made for you." Ginny handed Clara a drawing—two small silhouettes and a larger one in the middle, holding hands under a colorful rainbow. "You and us, Bunica. Do you like it?"

"I certainly do," said Clara and laid the paper next to her on the sofa. She was looking frail in her blue bath robe.

"I brought you chocolates," said Rudy. "Mom, give Bunica *my* present."

Lydia placed the box of chocolates on the coffee table. "From Rudy," she said, holding a bouquet of delicate flowers in the other hand.

"Thank you, Rudy, and Lydia too. Freesias, they are my favorites! Kostea, get Lydia a vase from the kitchen."

"It's in the cabinet above the stove," Kostea said and took his place on the love seat.

"I'll find it," said Lydia.

Toddy let Del off the leash. The dog ran to the grandchildren, jumped on the sofa, trampled Ginny's drawing, and stepped over Clara's lap, yelping happily.

"Delano," Kostea yelled. "Careful."

"He's just a dog." Rudy apologized for Del, picked him up, and held him against his chest. "Bad dog. Bunica had surgery. You don't want to hurt Bunica." The dog wiggled.

"Let him go," Clara said. "I'm not that fragile."

"So how are you feeling today, really?" asked Toddy.

"Good," Clara said. "Better and better."

Kostea felt the need to explain. "She has almost no pain, and look at her face. Still pale but healthy. She doesn't have to run all the time to the bathroom . . . I mean, not as much as before, because of the bladder. It's expanding, you know, but slowly. You don't force these things, ever. And her urine is clear."

"Kostea, nobody needs to know about my urine."

"Well, I beg to differ. This is a doctor's family, and I think medical details are important. At least more important than 'Ouch, my back is hurting, and I can't play with my kiddies. What will I do? Kissy, kissy.'" He moved his head sideways and made the sound of kissing.

Clara didn't react. Only her eyes were full of sparkle, as always. Her ash-brown hair dropped to her shoulders. To save money, she was coloring her hair herself, using the bathroom mirror. It had been chestnut brown when she was young. Now, two weeks since she had colored it, the white at the roots was showing.

"Mom, you look beautiful," said Toddy.

"Thank you, Toddy. You are nice. And your dad, you'd think he's tough, but if he doesn't get to see you one day, he's a whining, nervous wreck."

"I'm not," said Kostea.

Rudy lowered Del to the floor. The door to the porch was open. The dog walked to the door, sniffed the air, returned, and lay down next to the sofa.

"Good dog," said Rudy.

Ginny put her drawing on the coffee table and tried to straighten it with the back of her hand. "You didn't tell me how much you like my drawing, Bunica."

"I love it, honey."

"Is the bird in her cage, speaking of honey?" asked Toddy, silently pointing at the dog.

"I don't think so," said Clara. "But Honey doesn't fly into the living room, so don't worry about it."

"Where do you want them?" Lydia asked Clara, holding the white porcelain vase with the freesias.

"On the mantelpiece," said Kostea.

"No," Clara said. "Put them in the middle of the table. Kostea, why don't you bring out the pastries?"

"I hope you had dinner already," said Lydia.

"Yeah, we had something," Kostea answered, not very convincingly.

"We had chicken parmesan," Clara said. "It was very good. Kostea made it. Your father has to learn how to cook, with me being sick and not always able to stand on my feet. What will he do if I'm no longer here?"

"What are you talking about?" said Lydia.

"You know what I'm saying." Clara laughed nervously and closed her eyes for a second. "Your father worked hard this afternoon in the kitchen, poor soul, under my supervision."

"Dad, I'm impressed. You in the kitchen," said Toddy.

Kostea shrugged. "Cutting up a chicken is nothing. Remember, I operated on people."

"Bunicu's becoming a chef," said Ginny.

On the wall to one side of the television set, there was a corkboard filled with pieces of paper in Kostea's impossible handwriting—lists, English words, and telephone numbers. In the middle, between the postings, was a shiny "Get well soon!" Hallmark card with a furry gray kitten with dark eyes and a broken paw in a white cast. Below had been added, "Dear Bunica," and the names Rudy, Ginny, Toddy, and Lydia. They had given Clara the card the day she returned from the hospital.

Clara picked up Ginny's drawing. "Ginny, honey, why don't you pin your drawing on the board, over Bunicu's nonsense, near my kitty?" She tried to stand up.

Kostea moved to the table. "Toddy," he said, "help your mother."

Toddy and Lydia each supported Clara by one arm as they slowly walked her to the table. The dog followed.

Clara sat down, stretched her neck, and inhaled deeply. "I can smell the freesias. Kostea, the pastries," she reminded her husband and turned toward Toddy. "They're yummy, with sweet cheese and walnuts."

"They're Danishes."

"Kostea, please bring them, OK?"

"I'm tired," said Kostea. He made a sly face. "Lydia?"

"Sure," Lydia said. "How many plates? Kids, are you eating?"

"I want my chocolates," Rudy said.

"They're Bunica's chocolates," Ginny said.

"Let's share," said Clara.

As Lydia was getting the pastries and the plates, Kostea asked her to bring the bottle of vodka. "It's in the freezer," he said.

Around the table loaded with pastries and shot glasses, everyone was talking and laughing. Kostea, Toddy, and Lydia each had a shot, followed by a second. The vodka was cold. The grandchildren drank milk. Clara drank water. Del became agitated and scratched Kostea's lap with his front paws, begging. Kostea slipped him a piece of Danish.

"Please don't feed the dog from the table," said Lydia.

"You have all these rules. It's amazing," said Kostea.

He poured a third round, and Lydia refused. "I've had enough. Toddy, you drink that, and I'm driving."

"C'mon," Toddy said, "these are tiny shot glasses."

Lydia shook her head. "We have the children in the car."

Kostea rolled his eyes. "Hey," he said, "don't listen to her, and drink this one for your mother."

Toddy looked at Clara and smiled. "To your health. Yes, Mother?"

Kostea fed Del one more piece of pastry, and Lydia smacked her palm on the table.

His grandmother Ina was being replaced by Lydia, Toddy thought. His father was directing demeaning comments at her more frequently than before. One day he would stop his father's nonsense once and for all, but today they were celebrating. This wasn't the moment. It never was, really. "Dad," he said, a gentle smile on his face, "please don't feed the dog. It's not so difficult."

Kostea looked at the dog. "Delano, get down. You hear Toddy."

"If you keep feeding him, he'll learn to beg," explained Rudy.

"Now you have become the expert," Kostea said. "Listen, Rudy. I have a pack of cigarettes on the nightstand in the bedroom. Be a good sport and bring them."

"The doctor said you should refrain from smoking," said Toddy.

"Toddy," Kostea said, "my dad, your grandpa, used to say that smoking a few cigarettes a day calms the nerves and helps with the digestion. Certain ladies see it as a sign of sophistication."

"Oh, Bunicu is concerned with the ladies," said Ginny.

Rudy returned with the cigarettes, and Kostea lit one.

Suddenly, there was a fluttering noise and a chirp. Del came running from the porch, feathers hanging on both sides of his muzzle.

"Delano, no!" Kostea yelled and threw himself to the floor, the miniature poodle disappearing under his large body. Delano growled. "Let go," Kostea yelled and pried the dog's mouth open. It was too late. The bird dropped, flopped on one side, and stopped moving. "You killed her, stupid."

Del jumped to his feet and tried to get to the bird again. Kostea stopped him. "Rudy, take him away."

The dog looked at the boy with his beady dark eyes, confused and scared. As a hunting dog, he had only performed his duty.

Toddy placed the dead bird in a plastic bag and took it downstairs to the garbage bin. When he returned, all of them quietly hugged Clara and Kostea. "I'll get you another parakeet," said Toddy.

Kostea stubbed out his cigarette in the ashtray and shook his head. "Don't bother." He sat at the table next to Clara and emptied his shot glass. His eyes were murky. "This bird is a harbinger of death."

"No," Clara said. "When I found Honey, she was badly wounded. If anything, she taught us survival."

———————

Clara had her hair colored and permed for Lydia and Toddy's New Year's Eve party. She wore a black-and-silver gown, while Kostea donned his dark-gray suit and a freshly ironed white shirt. Two dozen guests, Romanians and Americans, mingled, their voices barely understandable over the dance music blasting from the speakers. A beautiful spread of sarmale, piftie, salade de boeuf, cold cuts, cheeses, olives, smoked fish, and platters of different appetizers stretched over the dining room table among gold and silver leaves and branches, confetti and colored strips of paper, and an arrangement of white candles in crystal holders. Champagne, wine, and mixed drinks were being served in the kitchen. A Christmas tree stood in a corner. On but muted, the TV served as a timekeeper for the ball to drop in Times Square.

Their contemporary-style house was ideally suited for entertainment. An open gallery connecting the upstairs bedrooms overlooked the large living room, giving the home a spacious and elegant feel. Brian, Rudy, and Ginny were allowed to stay up past midnight. When the ball dropped, they ran upstairs to the open gallery and threw down a storm of confetti. People were hugging, dancing, and cheering. Everyone kissed everyone else, twice on both cheeks.

THE LAST PATIENT

Clara held her cigarette in one hand and a champagne flute in the other. She looked radiant. Kostea and Toddy were doing shots in the kitchen.

Nancy, their neighbor from across the street, waved at Clara and patted the place next to her on the living room sofa. Clara approached her, careful not to slip on the confetti covering the hardwood floors. She knew Nancy spoke up a storm in a New York accent that was hard for her to understand. With the music blasting, she didn't expect much of a conversation.

"I understand that you're done with your treatment. Lydia and Toddy worried so much for you. They are wonderful people." Nancy was somewhere in her fifties, on the stocky side. Her children were out of the house, and her husband had left her for a younger woman. In college, she had spent a semester abroad, in Vienna. She had traveled to Prague, Bratislava, and Munich and was proud of her worldly outlook. "Look at these decorations," she continued. "It's so beautiful. I've never attended a New Year's Eve party in a house as festive as this, and with so many people."

Clara nodded vigorously. "In Romania, it's always a big party. Christmas is small and New Year's big. They discourage religion."

Nancy rolled her eyes. "I don't believe it. You don't celebrate Christmas in Romania?"

"We do. But not big, because of the communists."

"Of course." Nancy placed her hand on Clara's arm as if to calm Clara's well-hidden indignation. "Now you are here. You can celebrate any way you want. You must consider yourself very lucky. I'm sure you more than appreciate your freedom."

CHAPTER 36

It Was More Complicated

1989 to 1990

There were many things Clara appreciated in America, freedom among them, although perhaps in a different way than Nancy had meant it. Had she said so at the party, Nancy might have misunderstood her.

It surprised Clara that the Americans she met were convinced she had been unhappy in Romania. It surprised her when they asked her why the Romanian people didn't rebel, as if they didn't understand, as if they, had they lived in Romania, would have changed from regular humans to heroes, unafraid and incorruptible. Things were never that black-and-white, Clara thought, and Romanians certainly had had their heroes. There had been brave souls who had resisted the new regime, and most of them ended up dead or in prison.

There was a system and a way of life in Romania. The Americans had a system as well, and no system was perfect.

She thought often about what life had been like in Romania. There was little to buy in the stores. Most people weren't allowed to travel. Their letters were censored, their telephones tapped, and they couldn't speak freely. Yet they adapted. They took full advantage of an underground economy and acquired the art of bribery. They laughed at themselves and learned the main rule of the game: pretend, be duplicitous when in public.

The truth rarely helped anybody. In the shelter of their homes, they were free to be happy or sad. People were the same everywhere: envious, generous, smart, dumb, trying to make their lives bearable.

Clara liked the new balance in her life in America. She described the advantages to her new friends' delight. The minuses she kept hidden.

She was thankful for the medical care she had received, which, apparently, had ended her ordeal.

The two little parakeets Toddy had gotten her brought her joy, with their morning routine of preening and chirping. One looked exactly like Honey, so she gave it the same name. The one with a white spot on its chest she called Sugar.

When the weather was lousy in the morning, she and Kostea went to the mall. She checked out the shop windows while he waited on the bench near the water fountain, reading or watching people. If he wanted to smoke, he went outside. Clara enjoyed the variety and the beautiful presentation of the store windows. Here shoppers didn't push each other and didn't raise their voices. She never bought anything because she didn't need anything, and because she was used to saying no to temptation. In her mind, she told stories to her friends from back home. Sometimes she felt like a young woman again, and she surprised herself, imagining talking to Eugene's wife, Norma. *Take a look at that leather armchair,* she'd imagine saying. *Notice the switch on the armrest. If you push it, it causes the whole thing to vibrate and massage your body.* Then she'd say, *Norma, let's walk over to the shoe store. There is something I want to show you: see those shoes with thick soles? What do you think of them? They're called platform shoes, and I guess they are very fashionable. And look at that turquoise necklace, it matches your eyes, Norma.*

After a while, Kostea would show signs of impatience.

She and Kostea were good friends now, even though he still had his flare-ups. When these occurred, she walked away, and usually he calmed down and later apologized. He had become more patient and tender. In many ways, he was like an old sweater—not fancy but warm. Comfortable. The sweater had a label on the inside, which, no matter what you did, from time to time irritated your skin. And after all these years, the memory of Maya still irked Clara with the pain of betrayal.

There was an unexpected wound as well, an anxiety both old and new. Clara witnessed verbal skirmishes between Kostea and Lydia, a continuous poking, minor enough to be imperceptible to others but obvious to her and Toddy, both sensitized by their lifelong experience with Kostea. Clara was determined not to allow the clashes to become wars. Whether Kostea was the initiator or not, Clara tried to stop him. After her brush with cancer, she feared that if she were to die, Kostea would destroy the balance in their son's marriage. "If I'm gone before you, promise to never move in with them. Never, all right?" she begged him again and again, while Kostea nodded, wordless.

Every day after lunch, Clara went to the lobby of their apartment building, her heart beating a little faster, and checked their mailbox. It was often filled with fliers and advertisements—junk mail, as everybody dismissively called it—which she nevertheless scrutinized in detail before tossing, eager not to miss any useful information.

Real letters in the mailbox made her very happy. Most were squatty white envelopes, little treasures with dried sap-colored glue oozing out from under the flap as a result of unsubtle censorship and multiple stamps bearing the black postmark with the date and "Romania" printed on them. Clara would calculate the number of days it had taken the letter to get there, run upstairs and read it, then wait for Kostea to wake up from his nap before reading it a second time with him, glancing over his shoulder. Then they would quickly get ready and leave to tend to Rudy and Ginny.

Twice in as many years they had received postcards from Vera, Igor's former wife, who now lived in Karlsruhe. In one, she informed them she was coming with her husband to New York, but only for a few days, and flying to Los Angeles from there. No chance of visiting Columbia.

The letters Clara appreciated most were from their old friends in Bucharest. Some came from Aida, Igor's second wife, others from Toni, who notified them that Uncle Leo had died in his bed, playing chess with himself, his chessboard on a chair.

Norma wrote frequently. Eugene added only one or two lines at the end. Kostea expected more from his childhood friend, but then he himself never wrote back. Norma's letters were full of news about their other friends, snippets of their old, familiar life. With a touch of longing, Clara realized how many people they used to know when they lived in Bucharest.

Norma never complained about her daily life. Clara attributed that to her positive outlook, as well as her fear of censorship. Norma wrote that once, she and Eugene had run into Clara's former neighbors, the Voicus, on Clara's old street and had gone to their place for coffee. *Served in their small, Turkish coffee cups,* Norma wrote, *was a brew of roasted ground chickpeas and oats and a tiny bit of real coffee for aroma. It's what people drink these days because we can't get anything else. With enough sugar, it doesn't taste too bad.* Norma described how Tudor Voicu had hung white Christmas lights throughout the apartment and how he had wired them to a car battery. *A relay turns the battery on automatically each time there is a power failure, and that happens every day. He has aged a lot, but he remains ingenious.* The official Party decree was to keep indoor temperatures low, a maximum twelve degrees Celsius in the winter, to save energy. Things were so bad that the meager living conditions of the '60s and '70s felt now like a luxury.

It felt weird, walking into your former building, stopping for a second or two in front of your apartment door, and then proceeding upstairs to the Voicus, Norma wrote. *The Voicus said a family of Party activists lives in your apartment. They said Marin Sabac was well-acquainted with them.*

Kostea wrote to Marin and asked about the family. His letter was short and was the only one he wrote to Marin. The typed response came quickly. Marin was disappointed in the choices Kostea had made recently and throughout his life. Kostea's strong desire to be with Toddy was understandable, yet the fact that he had opted to live in the West reflected an opportunism and ideology Marin could not condone. He did not provide any information about the family in Kostea's apartment and advised Kostea that he was severing their relationship.

Kostea felt hurt. "What's wrong with him? After everything I've done to help him."

"You mean to say after everything you went through in life together," Clara said.

"He's retired now. There is nobody breathing down his neck."

"You don't know that. Maybe someday you'll find out. Maybe he had to do this."

Just like the letters they used to receive years earlier from their children and which revealed to them a new world at once distant and miraculous, the letters from Norma pulled Clara back into her old life, still familiar and quickly vanishing. The sensation was that of a sudden dip in the ocean, when the water surrounded you, replacing the air and making you weightless. There were places in her past to which she wouldn't have given a second thought when she lived in Bucharest that now returned to her mind filled with meaning: the Capşa restaurant where she once had a talk with Eugene, the Military Circle building illuminated during the German occupation, the room at Leo's place when she was a student. She and Kostea had gone through so many changes in the last several years, whereas everything in her past had stayed the same. Known. Discovered.

She thought about their apartment in Bucharest, not deliberately but because it had become a part of her, like a human being. She remembered its heart and soul: the big rooms, the tall ceilings, the sunny windows, the terrace, and the beautiful neighborhood. There were nooks and crannies in the apartment, dark spaces, wet and ugly, and they were dear to her as well. She understood that time and distance worked like a melancholy filter—only the good parts remained.

She remembered herself young. She remembered Toddy as a child, and her mother.

She thought about their last days. The tears.

No, she didn't come to America for freedom. It was more complicated.

When Clara told Kostea that one day he would understand why Marin wrote the letter he wrote, she didn't imagine it would happen so soon.

Yet a year later, everything changed. It was a good year for the Bardus. Lydia started a new career as a professional recruiter. She had to work longer hours, but the commissions were good. Toddy traveled a lot. He was building new chemical installations all over the States. At home with the grandparents, the children were growing, flourishing.

In the spring, Clara and Kostea went on a short trip to London. They had visited other European capitals but never London, and London had been one of Kostea's wishes.

That summer, they rented a beach house in Rehoboth, Delaware. The grandchildren loved the ocean. In the morning, Kostea took Rudy fishing. They drove to Indian River and parked under the bridge, and Rudy fished off the rocks. He was nimble and quick. Kostea moved with difficulty. He looked at the water breaking against the slippery rocks and the green algae bending with the current. Decades ago, he and Toddy had jumped off such rocks into a sea seven time zones away. By nine o'clock, he and Rudy were back at the beach house, and after a quick breakfast with Clara and Ginny, they all went to the ocean.

One afternoon, on the boardwalk, they ran into Nancy, Lydia's neighbor. "You look tan and relaxed," Nancy told Clara. "Feeling much better, I guess."

"Much better," Clara said.

For Clara's birthday in September, Kostea booked a trip to Mount Hood. They flew to Portland and rented a car. The owner of their bed-and-breakfast had served in Korea. He talked to them about the war. His husky dog, Wolf, was blind in one eye. By the time Clara and Kostea flew back to Maryland, the mountains were covered in snow.

The world as they knew it was undergoing massive changes. What started in the summer of '89 in Poland and Hungary as a popular revolt ended in November with the collapse of the Berlin Wall. In December, the people of Romania violently overthrew the communist government. These were tense moments filled with excitement and hope.

The Bardus exchanged gifts on Christmas Eve as they watched the Romanian revolution unfold on CNN. Clara unwrapped a gray woolen sweater and Kostea tried on a light winter overcoat. They had placed two small packages for Ginny and Rudy under the tree.

In Romania, on Christmas Day, Ceaușescu and his wife were tried and summarily executed. With them gone, it seemed the future of the country was wide open, but in January, doubts started to emerge. It was possible that a coup d'état had taken place under the cover of the so-called popular revolution.

In February, they received an unexpected letter from Marin. He described in detail his life as a recent retiree. He was worried about Miranda's health. His son was finally getting married. Marin never mentioned his earlier letter in which he had announced the end of their friendship.

Kostea understood. In his hand he was holding his friend's apology.

CHAPTER 37

How Would You Like Your Steak Cooked?

April 1992

Kostea put on a crisp white shirt and his dark suit, tailor-made in Romania the year they left. In front of the mirror, he carefully adjusted his yellow silk tie with gold dots. Clara wore comfortable low-heel shoes and an emerald-green dress that matched the color of her eyes. The day before, she had splurged on getting her hair done at the salon. Toddy, Lydia, and the grandchildren, who had been taken out of school for the day, came along. They drove in two cars, Kostea following Toddy. Clara and Kostea had passed their citizenship exam and were being sworn in as US citizens in a large group ceremony at the city hall in downtown Baltimore. Traffic was heavy. Clara smoked two cigarettes in the car, one after the other.

The formal proceedings lasted twenty minutes. Ginny and Rudy, who had waited quietly in the back of the room with their parents and all the other witnesses, ran to their grandparents and hugged them. Everyone shook hands, and Kostea congratulated people on his left and right.

"Son," Kostea said, "now that we get our American passports, do you think it is safe for us to go to Romania?"

Toddy nodded.

"Bunicu, if you go, take me with you," Rudy asked.

"Not this time," Kostea said. "Let Bunicu go and see what is what. Next time, we'll take you and Ginny." He was beaming. The naturalization process had seemed as much a formality to him as any other bureaucratic step he'd had to undertake in his life. While he and Clara could live in the United States as permanent residents, he perceived the citizenship as necessary to acquire a sense of permanence and, more importantly, to be on par with the rest of the population. To be an equal. And although there was no comparison—and he knew it—he even remembered the moment he had become a member of the Romanian Communist Party.

During the swearing ceremony, the people surrounding him, joining him out of their free will in uttering the simple words of the Pledge of Allegiance, became his equals. He was one of them, an American. Blood rushed to his face, he choked, his lips quivered, and he understood he had wanted that as much as he had denied it.

They decided to celebrate with Maryland crab cakes at Phillips in the Inner Harbor. "People travel from all over the place for them," Toddy said.

"Now that you're citizens, you can eat them too," Ginny said with a smirk on her face.

They all laughed. The grandchildren wanted burgers and fries.

The waiter, a young man with a mustache just showing above his upper lip, turned to Kostea. "What would you like to drink?"

"I like many drinks, but my wife is over here," Kostea said, trying to be funny by suggesting that unfortunately his wife watched over and controlled his alcohol intake.

The young man didn't get it. "Sir?" he asked. The nametag on his uniform said Bob.

Toddy came to the rescue. "Bring him a shot of Stoli. Neat."

"Stoli?" Bob repeated.

"Vodka," Toddy explained. "Tell the barman. He'll know."

"Toddy, your father is driving," Clara said.

"I'll help him. I'll have a sip."

"You're driving also." Lydia shook her head.

"This is a celebration," Toddy said.

"Would you like a slice of lemon in your vodka?" Bob asked.

"Lemon, phooey." Kostea made a long face. When it came to the food, he opted for steak.

"Steak, not crab cakes? You don't know what you're missing," Toddy said.

"I'll take a bite of crab cake from your mother," Kostea said.

"How would you like your steak cooked?" Bob asked.

After a short exchange with Kostea, Toddy turned to Bob and said, "Medium rare, please."

Bob wrote it down. "The steak comes with a green salad. What kind of dressing would he like?"

"What are the options?" Toddy asked.

"Ranch, Caesar, elderberry vinaigrette, Russian, blue cheese, or oil and vinegar."

Toddy looked at his father. "Dad?"

It was clear Kostea was uncomfortable and trying to hide it. Because here he was, the newly minted American citizen, former famous Bucharest urologist and assistant professor of medicine, with his immediate family in a touristy place in downtown Baltimore, unable to select which combination of liquids to pour over his greens. He understood the things that made the world tick, but some of these trivial differences were lost on him. What had been and what was weren't aligned. He couldn't accept being like Clara, and simply following Toddy's lead. No, he had to be his own man.

"Take oil and vinegar," Lydia suggested.

"Yes, that," Kostea said to the waiter who jotted it down, nodded, and left.

"Boy! Hey, boy!" Kostea yelled after him. "I want Russian, not vinegar and oil."

Bob stopped in his tracks and turned, slightly surprised, and nodded again.

"Bunicu, *nu e frumos să spui 'boy,'*" Rudy said, which meant it was not nice to call the waiter "boy."

"It can be a racial slur," Toddy explained in Romanian. "Especially in the South."

"I'm not a racist," Kostea said back in Romanian. "The waiter is white. What is he, sixteen, seventeen? To me, he's a boy."

"Then call him Bob," Ginny said.

"In Bucharest, when I entered a restaurant, the waiters stood at attention. They called me Doctor." Nobody said anything. "And here?" Kostea asked, looking at Ginny. "He's Bob, and he calls me Kostea?"

When the crab cakes came, Kostea took a bite from Clara. "It's good," he agreed, "but if you really want seafood, I'd take you to my friend Igor in Bucharest. He's no longer in business, but in the good old days, we had fresh sturgeon there and ate black caviar with the soup spoon."

CHAPTER 38

This Is Where You Belong

Summer 1992

In September they traveled to Bucharest. Igor picked them up at the airport while Aida was getting things ready at the apartment.

"I'm wiped out," Kostea said after they brought the luggage in. "I appreciate the preparations, but I don't know how long I will last."

They had flown through the night and changed planes in Amsterdam. Clara had slept a little, but Kostea, who could usually sleep anywhere, had stayed awake throughout the flight because of nerves and anticipation.

"That's all right," Aida said. "Your room is the quietest, in the back. You go rest whenever you want."

After an early dinner sprinkled with sweet homemade wine, Kostea retired. Clara stayed up a while longer and listened to Igor's stories about the December revolution, the protests, and the shooting in front of the TV headquarters, one block from their apartment. It had happened more than eighteen months earlier, yet the events seemed very fresh in Igor's mind.

That night, Clara slept until three in morning. When she woke up, she found Kostea smoking on the small balcony off their bedroom. The backyard was dark. A dog barked in the distance, and the red light blinked at the top of the TV tower antenna.

"It smells like home," Kostea said.

Clara inhaled and realized that the fall air was different than in Maryland—less humid, less fragrant, thickened with city dust and vehicle exhaust. Clara remembered that smell. She drew closer to Kostea until their shoulders touched, and she reached for his cigarette. "Why can't we sleep?" she wondered.

"Jet lag."

She nodded. "You think we're home?"

"I don't know," Kostea said and took her in his arms.

In the morning, he made a list of people he wanted to call and places to see. Not many: Eugene, of course, who knew they were coming, Marin, Speranța Hospital, their former neighbors, the Voicus, and their old apartment, at least from the outside. Eugene greeted him warmly and confirmed they would be coming to Igor's for dinner that night.

Marin answered on the second ring. "Where are you?" he asked when he recognized Kostea.

"In Bucharest," Kostea said. "We're staying with Igor."

"How long are you staying?"

Kostea told him.

"Miranda was sick," Marin said. "She's recovering in Sinaia right now, and my train leaves in two hours. You should have let me know you were coming." He gave Kostea his telephone number in Sinaia and suggested that if they had the time, they should jump on a train and come visit. Kostea thought about the letter Marin had written to him but didn't say anything.

He called Speranța Hospital next, expecting the old telephone operator to answer. When he heard an unknown woman's voice, he introduced himself and asked to speak to Dr. Nuda.

"Where did you say you're coming from?" the woman asked.

"The United States."

"Professor Nuda passed away last year."

Kostea refilled the shot glasses. They drank up, and for a moment, everything seemed like before. Eugene wheezed and stubbed out his cigarette in an overfilled ashtray. Kostea got to his feet. "To my friends!"

Everybody cheered. Aida went to the kitchen to bring the roast. Clara offered to help.

"No," Norma said. "Clara, you are the guest of honor. You sit. I go."

"They treat you with kid gloves over here," Kostea nodded at Clara and winked.

"Maybe *you* should go to the kitchen," Clara said.

"I'm drinking. That is my job."

"I mean it," Clara pressed on. "Kostea can cook," she added, looking at Igor. "When I came home from the hospital, he learned how to cook, for me."

"We're so glad you're here," Norma told Clara when she returned from the kitchen, smoothing her linen skirt over her knees. And patting her stomach. It was obvious she had put on a few pounds. "Eugene says that without the two of you, Bucharest is no longer the same."

"You're kind, Norma." Clara shook her head. "We, too, miss you." She wasn't just being polite. Eugene had been at times very close and at other times odd and distant, but always there for her, while Norma, shy and introverted, had stayed mostly in the background. Yet Norma's letters had changed that. She had opened a window into the world Clara had left and, in doing so, had become Clara's friend. "Thank you for your letters," Clara added. "They keep us anchored."

"I don't want you to forget us," Norma said. "You have a new life. But we, too, went through big changes, and writing to you helps me put order in my own thoughts."

"In my mind," Clara said, "everything here stayed the same. Except the regime, of course."

"Look at me," Norma said, gently grabbing Clara's hand. "If nothing else, look at how much *we* have aged."

That was true. Clara had noticed Eugene's fingers, yellowed from heavy smoking, his wheezing, and his hairline retreating to the middle of his head. She saw Igor's graying hair and the beginning of a goiter.

"You didn't age," Clara told Norma and shook her head.

"Thank you." Norma smiled. "As I said, we went through a lot. You were lucky. You left. The last years of imposed austerity under Ceaușescu were awful. And now, Elvira has decided to leave the country."

Clara nodded with understanding; at one time, she'd lost her son, so she understood what it was like for Norma to lose her daughter.

"Yes, you know what this means," Norma continued. "Her husband wants to take her and their two daughters, my little darlings, and go. To Brazil."

"But here, things are getting much better."

"Progress is chaotic and slow. The young still want out."

"My theory is," Igor chimed in, "we all saw Ceaușescu as the enemy—the origin of all evil. We were united in thinking that once we got rid of him, we'd become Switzerland overnight. Unfortunately, it's not that simple."

"We know people who regret Ceaușescu's rule," Aida said. "After they shot him, he was interred at Ghencea, and these people bring flowers and pray at his grave. They claim that, even though we were poor, it was better before."

"Ghencea is where my mother was buried and her mother before that," Clara said.

"Let the dead bury the dead. We came here to have fun with the living," Kostea said and raised his glass.

Clara finally smiled. Rested after his afternoon nap, Kostea was again the heart of the party, at least in her eyes.

"Igor," Kostea continued. "Sing us a song."

"Let the man finish his dinner," Norma objected.

"Too much food isn't good. I'm saying this as a doctor."

Igor didn't need a second prompting. He stood, placed his right leg on the chair, and cradled his guitar.

Aida whispered, "Igor, ten minutes, all right?"

"Why ten minutes?" Kostea asked.

"He gets easily tired," Aida said.

———

The week went by very fast. They never caught up with the jet lag. It was like starring in a movie and watching it at the same time. Things were both extremely familiar and slightly off. There was dust everywhere. Many old building facades were crumbling, plaster and debris lying on the pot-holed sidewalks. It felt like the city suffered from an enormous shortage of paint and plaster. Compared to Columbia, with its manicured lawns and trimmed bushes, the grass, weeds, and trees here were out of control. On Victoria Road, in front of a new casino, a shabbily dressed man, evidently a peasant, was mowing a patch of grass with a scythe, unperturbed by the hurried pedestrians.

Everyone was complaining and criticizing everything all the time.

Clara wanted to tell her friends about her surgery, but no one wanted to hear about it. They assumed that if she lived in America, she must be all right. She tried to describe their new apartment, but she was stopped after a sentence or two. She showed them pictures with the grandchildren, but they were not interested. Norma lamented again about her granddaughters possibly moving to Brazil.

On the fourth day of their visit, Toddy called from the States. Kostea held the phone so Clara could hear him as well. Toddy had fed the parakeets, and everything was OK. Then Lydia came to the phone and was drowned out by Ginny and Rudy, who yelled, "Bunica, Bunicu, we miss you! Come home!"

Suddenly, Clara and Kostea had no doubt where home was.

———————

Their old street had not changed. The tree-lined sidewalks were broken by sprawling roots pushing up out of the ground, the gardens behind rusting fences a bit wilder. They paid a visit to the Voicus in their old building. When they left, they slowly negotiated the steps down from the third floor and gathered, all four of them, in front of the door to their old apartment. They reminisced in a hushed tone.

Igor drove Kostea to Speranța Hospital. They stopped by the gate. At the last moment, Kostea decided not to go in. Through the fence, the hospital yard seemed neglected, and the building looked small. A young man in a brown security uniform advanced to the curb and told them they were blocking the entrance.

They left Bucharest early in the morning. Their return flight had its layover in Amsterdam. Clara was tired and relieved to be on her way back. They walked around the airport to stretch their legs. The duty-free store windows sparkled with bottles of liquor, perfumes, watches, and cigarettes. Clara remembered how impressed and intimidated she had been years earlier when she had traveled for the first time to the West. What she saw now was what she expected to see.

On the leg from Amsterdam to Washington, Clara sat by the window, an empty seat between them.

"My back hurts," she said.

Kostea shrugged. "All of them looked so old," he said.

"We do too."

A flight attendant brought them drinks. She was smiling, polite. "Old or young, we are no longer home in that world," Clara said. "In

Columbia, there are many things that are still unfamiliar to us. It's like there's nowhere we truly belong."

Kostea reached over and pulled her across the empty seat. She rested her head on his shoulder and closed her eyes. "Here," he said. "This is where you belong."

CHAPTER 39

Why Did He Choose Me?

Fall 1992 to winter 1993

Clara's cancer returned. It started with a dull pain in her torso, and Clara, who knew how to tolerate pain and was afraid to find out what was wrong, postponed telling Kostea. When she finally did and they went to the doctor, it was stage four, all over her body.

At home, Clara burst into tears. "Why am I being punished? Why me?"

"I don't think it's that bad." Kostea held her. "We beat it before, and we'll beat it again."

"I like your optimism." Clara's answer came across more spitefully than she intended. They both fell silent, aware of his desire to cheat reality, and of the gaping difference between them, the ill one and the healthy one.

Clara dried her tears and went to the porch to feed the parakeets. When she returned to the living room, Kostea was on the sofa holding his open book upside down in his lap, his reading glasses on the coffee table.

"I have to call Toddy," Clara said.

In learning about his mother's condition, Toddy didn't have the presence of mind to say more than "I am sorry." He and Lydia would stop by after work. He asked Clara if she still wanted the grandchildren there that afternoon. Ginny and Rudy's high school was around the corner, and most days, after school, they walked to the grandparents' apartment. They all loved the arrangement. Clara made them sweet khrustyky or other snacks. Sometimes they did their homework or brought their friends. If they had sports or other after-school activities, Kostea drove them. Then their parents picked them up, or Kostea brought them home for dinner.

"Absolutely. I want to see their happy faces," Clara said.

It was late in the year, and the leaves on the trees in front of their apartment matched Clara's feelings: the melancholy of the season with dying leaves, all dun, tawny, and amber. She had chemo twice a week and received the treatment intravenously, each session lasting several hours. They checked her blood periodically for leukocytes. It wasn't painful, but she had weak veins, and soon her arms turned blue below her elbows. Her hair fell out. She never lost it all but stopped coloring it, for lack of energy or purpose.

"This is the end," she said one morning. "I feel it coming."

"No," Kostea said. They were in bed. He took her by her shoulders, turning her to face him. "Clara, my love, please look at me. I am a doctor. It's not the end."

She made a face. "I trust you." Her skin was papery, dry. Her cheeks were sunken. She went to the bathroom and threw up. She wiped her lips. "This life is useless. It goes too fast."

Her thinning hair was turning gray. She cut it in the bathroom mirror as best she could. Kostea, trying to be lighthearted, called her a wet pussycat. She didn't like what he said and sulked for half a day, until she craved some soup and asked him to start cooking.

"Take three onions, two carrots, some celery stalks, and a carton of chicken broth," she told him. "But first, bring me a chair and put it in the doorway to the kitchen."

Kostea complied.

"Take the chicken thighs from the refrigerator," she said.

In the past, Clara had smoked and drunk a glass of wine during their cooking lessons. She had enjoyed those moments, watching her husband, the supreme alpha male who had never in his life worked in the kitchen, acquiring a new skill. It had felt like a tender game between the two of them, in which he was revising the old world order. Now the game was over. They were running out of time.

"Wash the carrots and cut them in three," Clara said.

"What happens if I cut them in four?" he asked, still trying to be funny.

She was dead serious. "It takes too long."

And so it went, and in the end, the soup boiled and simmered. The apartment filled with the comforting smell of cooking.

"Unfair God," she said, not caring how trite this sounded. She had lost weight, and the skin on her arms was flabby. She salted her soup and squeezed in half a lemon. "Why did he choose me? I hate him. When I was a little girl, I decided to be good. I've never hurt anybody my entire life."

She couldn't sleep the nights following the days of her chemo. "It's the steroids in the medication," the nurse had told her. "Read if you can. Don't fight it."

She would lie down with a book and try to read, until her eyes became dry, until the arm supporting her body went numb, until Kostea complained the light was bothering him. Then she'd go to the living room and turn on the TV. She'd keep the volume all the way down and look at the screen without hearing or comprehending. She didn't care. Sometimes she just walked around, whispering to herself, body bent, each step hurting. Through the glass doors, she glanced at the parakeets sleeping side by side in the cage, not bothered by the flashing TV, unquestioning of fate or the future. She'd become thirsty and walk into the kitchen, the chlorinated tap water causing her to gag and the filtered water from the refrigerator too cold, burning her throat. "Next time, I'll leave the filtered water out on the counter," she'd say to herself and forget.

The nights were never-ending and dark. Her thoughts raced through the darkness in all directions. There were good thoughts, memories of happy times and accomplishments, and bad thoughts about dying. "Make it quick, God. Don't let me suffer too much, oh God almighty."

Then she would remember that she didn't believe in God and would try to be rational. As a doctor, she understood very well—no miracles. She was seventy-one now and had hoped she would live a while longer, a decade and a half maybe, like Ina, her mother, into her eighties. Oh, well. That was how it was, an end to that expectation. She had lived her life and had been content. Dying was the expected end for everyone, and so it wasn't a tragedy. But she didn't want her pain and suffering to affect the people who loved her. She'd do everything she could to shield them.

Toward morning, she would go back to bed and fall asleep next to Kostea. Her sleep was light, troubled by dreams and nightmares. She saw black birds, black clouds, and dark forests. She saw her mother in a fog, and her father. She experienced memento mori. She remembered a poem by Eminescu entitled "Mortua est!" She dreamed that her beloved Ginny had applied to several colleges and been rejected by all, without reason. She imagined fifteen-year-old Rudy getting ready for his tennis camp and realized she wouldn't be alive next summer to see him off. She dreamed Kostea had died, and she had gone to his funeral. The grim reaper was waiting behind a headstone at the cemetery. "You took my love away by mistake," Clara yelled at him. "I was supposed to die, you stupid!"

In another dream, she drove the Chevy Impala to the children's house one morning. Lydia greeted her with a wicked smile on her face, a man standing next to her, barefoot. "Where is my son?" Clara asked. "On a business trip," Lydia said. "This is my lover and don't act rudely. Kostea cheated on you, and you forgave him."

Like snow, a pall covered everything she saw in her dreams and while she was awake. That pall was death.

After each chemo treatment and the following sleepless night, Clara felt worse. She vomited, experienced headaches, weakness, and dizziness. Her skin turned into parchment paper. It was so bad that she had no choice but to stay preoccupied with her immediate physical discomfort. She preferred it, in a perverse way, because it blocked out her thoughts of death and her fears.

The grandchildren stopped coming after school. They were taking the bus straight home, and while Clara hated that, she had been the one to request it, not wanting them to see the way she looked and suffered.

The best time was the weekend, when the break after the second weekly chemo session was the longest. They would drive to have dinner with Lydia and Toddy and the grandkids at their house. The fear was still there, but for a few hours, life seemed normal.

Her treatments stopped before Christmas. Her PET scan indicated a mild remission. "We had hoped for much more," the oncologist said. "But listen. You have a healthy heart and strong organs. I recommend one more round of chemo after the holidays. Your leukocytes are low, and we will watch them."

Clara looked at Kostea.

He nodded. What else could he do?

Before taking their citizenship exam, Clara and Kostea had attended an English-as-a-second-language class at the community college. They enjoyed having something structured to do when not busy with the grand-children. They met new people, most of them immigrants. When the class ended, they signed up for the next one. Kostea loved the idea that now, in his old age, he had become a student again. He showed his student ID to everybody. The ID provided him with free access to the gym, where he went to work out without Clara, especially in the winter.

The attendant at the gym, a young dark-skinned man with a shaved head and muscular body, looked him over with a dose of polite suspicion. Kostea showed him his ID and proceeded to recount his life story. "I am student now, and this facility free," he concluded happily. The man smiled and waved Kostea in.

Often, Kostea was the only patron. On those occasions, the attendant would help him adjust the settings on the machines, and they talked while Kostea exercised. His name was Mario, and his parents were Cuban refugees living in Florida. When Kostea told him he had been to Cuba as part of an official Romanian delegation, their relationship grew stronger. Mario took to calling him Professor, which Kostea found ironic. He had worked his entire life to achieve the title and never fully succeeded.

The college campus was on the same block as the hospital and the medical center where Clara was undergoing her chemo. Once, Kostea went to the gym during her treatment. He needed the break. It was a bright winter day, and he thought he'd enjoy his solitary ten-minute walk to the gym and back.

"Will you be all right?" he asked Clara after her drip was connected and she reclined in her seat.

She opened her eyes for a second and nodded.

Mario was glad to see Kostea. "It's been a long time," he said. "I was wondering about you."

There was only one other person in the gym. Kostea monopolized Mario, telling him about Clara, eager to talk about her to someone other than family.

"I feel your pain," Mario said when Kostea finished. "My aunt died of cancer, but it happened in Cuba. The American doctors are better."

"The doctors are good in Cuba," Kostea said, slightly defensive. "Medicine is advanced. I know. I've met them."

Mario shook his head. "No, Professor. Nothing is good in Cuba."

Kostea didn't exercise long. His body was stiff and hurt in places. Guilt ate at him for having left Clara alone. She needed him to hold her hand, to give her a glass of water. To tell her a story.

She had to fight her disease. If she didn't, she would die sooner. It was that simple. He had treated people his entire life and held no illusions. But this was more painful. Clara was the patient and he a bystander. Powerless. As long as the oncologist recommended chemo, there was a chance to prolong her days. Hopefully, the American doctors were better than the Romanian ones or the ones he had met in Cuba.

If he prayed, he would have prayed for a miracle. But he didn't believe in prayer, and he was terrified of a life without Clara.

There were those who thought that a quick death would spare their loved one needless suffering. Not him. He'd give anything, pay any price to keep Clara alive for a little longer! There was nothing on the other side, and besides, *he* was *here*.

Other people claimed they would gladly swap places with the suffering. Would he change places with Clara? Why even entertain such a question?

In his entire life, he had never lived alone. He could vacuum and cook, but loneliness was a curse without cure. Clara had said that he should remarry. Ha, a seventy-one-year-old man looking for a mate. Pathetic! Nobody could replace Clara. Clara didn't think of his remarrying as a betrayal. That was because she wasn't selfish or jealous, as he had been. She was generous, and she didn't want him to go live with Toddy. She had him swear he wouldn't.

Clara was his life, his foundation, his purpose. His friend and lover. He had neglected her for his job. He had made their relationship rough at times, but they had always managed to turn the page and smooth things over. He had cheated on her not because he didn't love her but because he gave in to temptation. That had almost destroyed them. And now, after all these years, he was on the verge of losing Clara, not to another man, as he had sometimes feared, but to a disease he had fought in his patients many times before and that nobody could conquer.

———————

Over the Christmas holiday, Toddy and the grandchildren went skiing in Colorado, without Lydia, who didn't ski. Given the time difference, by the time they came down from the slopes and had dinner, it was late in Maryland. Toddy called every evening and spoke to Kostea.

"How is Mom?" he would ask.

"Resting," Kostea would say.

"Yes, OK, but how is she? Any better?"

"Maybe. All things considered."

One time Clara came to the phone—her voice weak, her speech muffled. She said she was feeling well, and Toddy accepted her answer.

"Hey, kids, good news. Bunica is doing better today," he said to Ginny and Rudy, lying and hoping.

While Toddy and the children were away, Lydia stopped by to see her in-laws, sometimes before work and other times in the early evening. She always brought food over. After getting home each night, she, too, spoke with Toddy by phone.

"She told me she felt better today," Toddy said to Lydia.

"She's protecting you," Lydia said.

Toddy returned from Colorado in time for a New Year's celebration at the house of Romanian friends in Northern Virginia. It was supposed to be an all-night deal, with lots of guests, dinner, and dancing. Everyone was invited. Kostea called to tell Toddy they weren't coming. "It's a long drive," he said. "Your mother is tired."

"Dad," Toddy said, "you don't have to stay late. It will be a nice party. Come for a few hours and have a glass of champagne with us. It will cheer Mom up, make her feel better."

"The two of us, we'll have a glass of champagne at home. You go and don't think about us. Have a wonderful celebration."

Lydia, Toddy, and the children went. The host silently removed the table settings for Clara and Kostea. "We're sorry they couldn't make it," the host said and nodded tactfully. Others approached either Toddy or Lydia to say how much they appreciated Kostea's spunk and Clara's kindness. Ginny and Rudy ate dinner with them. At midnight, people toasted.

Lydia turned to Toddy and raised her glass. "This is for Clara," she said.

The music blasted. The children laughed and threw confetti and streamers over the dancing guests. Mary Hopkin's voice singing "Those Were the Days" sounded on the speakers, and melancholy overwhelmed Toddy. Life goes by, he thought as he listened to the words and remembered the Russian original he had heard so many times in his childhood, *Dorogoi dlinnoyu, pogodoy lunnoyu* . . . He saw Igor hugging his guitar and placing his leg high on a chair, young and handsome, singing his heart out, accompanied by Kostea and many other guests who were old now and belonged to a world that no longer existed. He thought of his mother and father tonight, in their small apartment, in America, in a familiar and yet strange place for them. Tears sprang into his eyes. Goodbye, my mother, he thought, allowing the thought to take over and the tears to run freely down his face, while dancing with his wife in the changing rhythm of the music, alone, surrounded by his friends and his joyful children.

Clara started chemotherapy again in January. Her adverse reaction to the treatment was stronger than before, her physical discomfort accompanied by impatience and bursts of anger. It felt like the world was conspiring against her instead of letting her be.

"I know it's hard," her nurse said at the end of the first session. "What choice do you have? You need to stick with it, honey."

Like hell I do, Clara thought. She got up, and leaning heavily on Kostea's arm, she walked out of the medical center. At home, Kostea sat her in the love seat and covered her with two blankets. He turned the TV on. She didn't want to watch anything. He brought her soup, and she pushed it aside.

"I want mint tea," she said suddenly. "I feel metal in my mouth. It's bitter."

"We don't have mint tea," Kostea said.

"Then go and get some."

He shook his head. "I don't want to leave you alone. I'll make you regular tea and ask Toddy to bring some later."

"I want mint tea," Clara repeated. "Go. I'm not a child. I'll be all right. Just go already."

When Kostea returned, he found Clara seated in a chair that she had pushed in front of the sliding door to the porch, her forehead pressed against the glass, watching the parakeets.

"They're happy birds, aren't they?" asked Kostea.

Clara didn't answer right away. She looked at Kostea sideways, her lips pursed. "Why did you let them out of the cage? See what a mess they're making."

"We always let them fly around during the day," said Kostea.

"Look at the floor. It's all seeds and bird poop and chewed-up ficus leaves. I don't like that."

"It's all right. I'll clean up later."

"No," Clara said. "It's not all right. I don't like these birds anymore. I hate them."

"What are you talking about, Clara? They're Sugar and Honey, and you love them."

"The nurse called me honey today," said Clara. "I didn't like it."

Kostea smiled. "I was right there. I heard her. She just wanted to be nice to you."

"I don't need anybody to be nice to me."

"Of course you do. You're not feeling well, and you're angry. Let me take my coat off, and I'll make you some mint tea, and maybe later we'll watch some TV together." His voice was tender.

Clara's eyes swam in tears. Her face was drawn, and her eyes seemed greener than ever. "I don't want the birds anymore," she said. "Kostea, let them fly away. Let them free. I don't want them."

"It's winter. If we let them go now, they'll freeze to death. I don't think we should do that, Clara."

"I don't care," she snapped back. "They brought death to our house, and I want them gone forever."

"How did they bring us death?"

"You are the one who said it, Kostea."

"You mean when Delano killed that first one?"

"They're all the same." Clara got agitated. "They're dirty. Look at the mess they make. In my dreams, they attack me. I want them out. Understand? Get them out of here."

Kostea hesitated.

"Out!" she yelled. Her mouth looked like a dark wound, lips pale and foam in the corners. "Out, out, out of here!"

It was a small price to pay, and Kostea surrendered. As he stepped onto the porch, the birdseed on the cement floor cracked under his shoes. He pulled the slider shut and threw a glance at Clara, who watched him from behind the glass. He remained motionless, as if figuring out how to cause the little birds to fly away. Then he opened the window and waved his arms, stamped his feet, and turned in circles. Sugar leaped from the ficus tree, flew around Kostea, and entered the cage. Honey followed. Kostea smiled. This was their home, their safety. They didn't know anything else. He looked at Clara one more time, then picked up the cage and brought it to the open window. "Shoo," he said and shook it. This time, the birds flew out, one after the other, up and down through the cold air, across the parking lot, and disappeared in the bare trees.

He took his winter coat off and gently moved Clara from the chair to the love seat, holding her tight against his chest and stroking her thinning hair.

Much later, he vacuumed the porch and took the empty cage down to their storage bin in the basement.

———————————

The doctor stopped Clara's chemo in early February. "She's getting too weak," he said, "and we are reaching the point when the treatment is more damaging than the disease. I want her to recover a little, and then we'll see what else we can do."

"She has pain," Kostea said.

"We'll prescribe her morphine."

"She cannot stand to take shower."

"The nurse will get you in touch with the hospice service. They'll help. They'll deliver a hospital bed. Put a stool in the bathtub."

Clara listened to the conversation and didn't say anything. Her eyes were two torches.

Toddy took the doctor aside. "What happens if she doesn't recover her strength and cannot continue with chemo?"

"The cancer will grow. In two months, she won't be able to breathe, but we'll keep her comfortable."

Lydia and the nurse contacted hospice, and they sent Amber and Laura. At first, Kostea objected, fearing he was losing control, but he slowly relented. In his mind, he was the doctor in charge and the two women were his nurses. He told each one what to do. They listened, they nodded, and then they did what they deemed necessary.

The hospital bed had removable safety rails on both sides. It was on wheels. It came with an electric blanket and a vibrating pad to keep Clara's body from getting sores. The people who delivered the bed moved the furniture in the living room and installed the bed perpendicular to the wall with the fireplace, facing the sliding doors to the porch. "No fires," they told Kostea.

Laura and Amber came each morning at nine. They changed Clara's sheets, made her a light breakfast that she hardly touched, and gave her a sponge bath. They combed her hair and gave her one morphine pill. In less than an hour, Clara was asleep.

Laura handed Kostea a container with twenty-four pills. "Try to give her one every eight hours, depending on how she feels. If she's still in pain, call me. I'll bring more when you need them."

"I know how to give medication," Kostea said.

As he grew more comfortable with the hospice nurses, he went to the supermarket or just walked around the neighborhood to be by himself.

Toddy stopped by every day. Lydia brought Kostea cooked food. The cleaning lady came once a week. Clara hated the noise of the vacuum cleaner. And she hated the hospital bed.

"I want to sleep in my own bed," she told Toddy. "With my husband. Do you have a problem with that? Does anybody?"

"Mom, it's temporary," Toddy said without thinking.

Another evening, Kostea went to the bedroom to smoke a cigarette, and Clara complained to Toddy. "He leaves me alone. Always."

"I am here." Toddy smiled. "Dad went to the bedroom to smoke."

"I want to smoke also."

"First you need to get better."

"Says who?" Clara asked. "Your dad? He comes up with these rules, and I hate him."

"Mom, what are you talking about?"

"Your father cheated on me." Her voice was weak, but it was full of passion. "I never told you. He did. I trusted him, and he slept with another woman."

As the days went by, Clara's pain increased, and so did the quantity of morphine. She slept most of the time. Unless there was somebody else there, Kostea could not leave the room. He spent his nights next to her bed, on the sofa.

The grandchildren came, and Clara made an effort to put up a happy face. She tried to smile, but Ginny and Rudy could see that she was a frail shadow of her former self. While they ate chocolates with Kostea at the table, Toddy lowered the rail of her bed and sat next to Clara. He held her hand. It was smaller than he remembered, and her skin felt loose and soft.

"Mom, you seem happy to see the kiddos," he said.

"I'm very happy," she said. "You know, being here with you is the best thing that happened to me in my life."

"I'm glad to hear this, Mom," Toddy said. "I know it's been hard for you. You're missing your friends, and many things are still unfamiliar."

"They don't matter," she said. "I have more than I've ever had in my life. I love you, and I love America, Toddy. I didn't want to come, but every day I'm thankful."

It was time to go. Driving home and then later, watching TV, Toddy felt a calming spirit descend over him. He knew it was the effect of his mother's words, even while he wondered if she had said them to please him or if they were true.

———————

"You know," Kostea told Toddy, "I've been a doctor my entire life. I believed in my powers, and I cured a lot of people. Now, I'm watching your mother dwindling away, and I can't do anything. What kind of a doctor am I?"

"Dad, don't say that. You're doing all you can."

Kostea smiled. "We have the best times in the morning. Your mother wakes up with the first rays of the sun, and I'm there to greet her, before the nurses arrive, before you or Lydia come over. At that hour, she's rested, and her pain is not bad. She's still under the influence of her medication, but only a little, and we drink tea together and talk, sometimes for almost an hour."

"What do you talk about?"

"Life. Our childhood. You name it. Sometimes we talk about death."

They were in the bedroom, and through the open door to the living room, they could hear Clara's labored breathing.

"Is Mom afraid?"

"Sometimes. We both are, but that's all right. When we are out of things to talk about, I read to her, poetry mostly. She loves it. I wish I had a copy of *Ruslan and Lyudmila*. Do you remember when you used to listen to Pushkin in Russian when you were little?"

"I do. It was magical, sad." Toddy smiled, thinking of Ina.

"Here," Kostea said and handed him a book from his nightstand. It was a collection of Romanian love poems. "Your mother and I are together in this, and nothing will separate us. We have our beautiful routine in the morning and sometimes, when I'm lucky, in the evening as well."

"Dad," said Toddy.

He left for work and thought of the word *routine* that his father had used. It implied a repeated activity along with a measure of permanence. His father needed the illusion of permanence—they all did.

———

Laura, one of the hospice nurses, called Lydia. "There is something I need to tell you. Your father-in-law, I think he's holding back on the morphine. I don't think he gives his wife what she needs."

Lydia waited.

"I brought them the new bottle with medication this morning," Laura continued. "The old one should have been empty or almost empty, but it was half full. We give Clara a tablet each morning, and he should give her at least two more during the day, but obviously he doesn't."

"Have you asked him?"

"I did. He said he's a doctor and knows how to administer painkillers. I didn't think it was my place to argue with him and decided to speak to you. I feel sorry for Clara. She could be in terrible pain."

Lydia told Toddy, who said he would talk to Kostea.

"Trust me," Kostea said. "I know what I'm doing." He was cutting each pill in half or into quarters and administering an amount to Clara according to how he perceived her pain. He was good at gauging her pain, he claimed. He had experience. There was no need to have her numb like a zombie and asleep all the time. That was what the nursing staff wanted because it made their work easy. But in his opinion, a little pain was acceptable, along with a little stimulation—a conversation, an exchange of some kind, a smile, a cup of tea. She was his wife and he wanted her by his side.

Toddy's heart sunk. There was no way for him to know what his mother would prefer. Was his father causing her unnecessary pain? Was he prolonging her life? And was he doing it for his own benefit, or because he loved her so much and couldn't let her go?

CHAPTER 40

The Room Was Quiet

March 1993

Toddy came by in the morning. Clara was sleeping. She didn't open her eyes. There was a rattle in her chest, her breath a harsh noise, a useless struggle. An oxygen bottle lay next to her hospital bed in the middle of the living room. The nurse was supposed to connect it when she came by later. Kostea was asked not to smoke. He didn't like to be told what to do in his own house. When Toddy arrived, Kostea went down to the parking lot to have a cigarette.

Alone, Toddy looked at his mother's body, a knocked-down tree, her legs broken branches sticking out from under her pale blanket and touching the cold metal railing. Her eyes were closed, and the light that always shone in her face was extinguished. Her colorless hair, glued to one side of her forehead, covered her temple and revealed an oversized ear, white like a seashell thrown on the shore by last night's tempest, her breath a harsh noise, a useless struggle.

Lydia was at work, and Ginny and Rudy in school.

When Kostea returned, Toddy left for work. He had to go, and he'd call at lunchtime.

Kostea brought two mugs of tea and set them down on the coffee table near the bed. "Clara."

She didn't answer.

He pulled up a chair, put on his glasses, and opened his poetry book. His foot rested on the oxygen bottle. "You'll like this poem I found last night. It's by Marcel Breslaşu. It doesn't have a title, and it is very short."

Don't fear dying, my dear
Beginnings and endings are one and are near
A short night untangles the engagement between us
Thereafter, death eternal together will bring us.

He set the book in his lap. "This will be our poem, Clara. We are together in this—just us. Two people without a title. Did you like it?"

Her chest rattle continued.

"That's all right," he said. "You'll tell me when you wake up. Now I'll read to you from Eminescu's 'Mortua est!' But only the last few stanzas, the ones we talked about so many times."

For he who is not, even grief can't destroy
And oft is the grieving, and seldom the joy.
To exist! O, what nonsense, what foolish conceit;
Our eyes but deceive us, our ears but cheat,

What this age discovers, the next will deny,
Far better just nothing than naught but a lie.

Kostea skimmed and skipped ahead, then continued reading.

O, what is the meaning? What sense does agree?
The end of such beauty, had that got to be?
Sweet seraph of clay where still lingers life's smile,
Just in order to die did you live for a while?

O, tell me the meaning. This angel or clod?
I find on her forehead no witness of God.

The room was quiet. Clara wasn't breathing, and her eyes were open. His book slipped to the floor. He rose, lowered the bed railing, and sat next to her. He took her hand. It was still warm, but he knew. He had seen it so many times. He leaned forward and slowly closed her eyelids. He didn't cry.

The nurses would be arriving soon. It was ten minutes to nine.

Author's Note

Spi mladienets moi prekrasny
Tolyko krepko spi.
Bayushki bayu...

Sleep my beautiful little baby,
Sleep soundly,
Hush-a-by, hush-a-by...

With these gentle words, my maternal grandmother (Ina in the novel) used to sing me to sleep in a makeshift crib in our subdivided Bucharest apartment in the early 1950s. The lullaby, gleaned from a poem by Lermontov, had spread across Russia, its neighboring territories, and perhaps other parts of the world. A widow before turning thirty, my grandmother raised my mother on her own, and then took care of me as a child. She read Romanian and Russian poetry to me. The deep love and devotion I enjoyed from my parents and grandparents have molded me into who I am today, and I am eternally grateful to them. This novel wouldn't exist without them, and without the stories I heard growing up and the unforgettable moments I witnessed. Behind the Iron Curtain, life was hard but never hopeless, and the people who lived in those times and places were as happy, as accommodating, as skilled, and as fulfilled as people everywhere.

I've always dreamt of turning my family's history into my most important novel. I changed names and created scenes and episodes. The places I describe are the way I remember them or as I imagined them to be. Real people merged to form fictionalized characters fitting the narrative.

In 2016 when I started writing this book, my intent was to meld my family's story and my wife's family's story into one narrative, the way our love had brought our two very different families together. I wanted it to be a compelling and epic novel, a depiction of an entire society, a sweeping tale of the history, love, and survival of these people I cherished. Because of its length, I had to separate the two stories. The first part, based on my family, became The Last Patient, a tribute to my parents and grandparents who are no longer here. The second part became another novel, based on the lives of my wife's parents. While there are a few necessary overlaps between the two works, each is freestanding. The second novel remains unpublished at the time of this writing.

Throughout the years, my wife, Vio, stood by me, encouraged me, put up with my nerves and patiently listened to my rambling about the pain of creation and the difficulty of being true to myself while writing a commercially viable novel. My adult children, Nira and Daniel, and their families and children, my grandchildren, bring balance and meaning to my life.

To my dear friends and beta readers, Marianna and Andrei Roman, Mara and Dan Preoțescu, Mary and Peter Gross, Michael Amster, and my fellow writer and friend, Lawrie Deering: Your support and your comments helped me tremendously.

The encouragement and critiques I received from my novel workshop colleagues motivated me to turn on my desktop computer each morning. Every few weeks they reviewed fifteen-page submissions from my novel and made helpful and creative comments. Thank you to Clark Riley, J. Wynn Rousuck, Lauren Goodsmith, Peter Silverglate, Gregory May, and

Steve Lubs. There were others who participated in our meetings from time to time, too many to mention here. I thank them as well.

I want to thank Dr. David Priver and his wife Rita, and my good friend Dr. Craig Singer for helping me accurately describe medical procedures and use the correct medical terminology.

I benefited from the professional help of two outstanding editors, Zoe Quinton of Santa Cruz, California, and Kristin Thiel of Portland, Oregon, who unscrambled my original writings, helped me develop a more coherent storyline, and provided me with valuable copy editing. With their input, my novel looked and felt more and more like the real thing.

Exposed to Romanian poetry from an early age, and eager to share its beauty with my American readership, I quoted in my novel excerpts from Mihai Eminescu's masterpiece, "The Evening Star," an ode to the love of an immortal genius. Among the many available English translations, I chose the one by Adrian Soncodi, which, in my opinion, is the closest to the original in terms of content, language, rhythmicity, and melody. Adrian has graciously given me permission to use his translation. A second excerpt from "Mortua est" by Mihai Eminescu was translated by Corneliu Popescu, a talented seventeen-year-old, who tragically perished during the 1977 Bucharest earthquake. He was found in the rubble of his building in his dead mother's arms. Finally, I also used my own translation of a short poem by the Romanian poet Marcel Breslaşu. It is a beautiful love poem with words I imagine my father would have wanted to say to my mother as he helplessly watched her slip away on her deathbed. The poem has no title.

My friend Yvonne Kisiel introduced me to my publisher, Boyle & Dalton. Her encouragement and kind words, not to mention her legal experience, were instrumental in allowing me to reach a publishing agreement with this very fine independent publisher.

Special thanks to Heather Shaw, Boyle & Dalton developmental editor. Having gone through two previous editorial reviews, when Heather and I started the process, I was skeptical about the benefit of a new edit.

Heather proved me wrong. There was still much to tighten and strengthen, and after I implemented her suggested changes, I held in my hands an even better version of the original.

With a few good options, choosing a cover design was challenging, and I would like to express my thanks to Clair Fink for her patience, and creativity, as well as for her additional contributions to this book.

Many thanks to publisher Emily Hitchcock for her continuous and friendly involvement, advice, and expertise, and to the other members of the Boyle & Dalton staff, who supported and helped me throughout the various steps of the publishing process.

About the Author

Alex Duvan lives in Columbia, Maryland, and publishes under the pen name Tudor Alexander.

Alex started writing in high school, and enjoyed an early success, publishing many short stories in established literary magazines in Bucharest, Romania. Since he came to the US as a political refugee in 1977, his writing has been informed and inspired by his personal immigration experience. Although writing was his passion, he studied engineering and management to support his family. After the fall of the Berlin wall and the Romanian Revolution in 1989, he published several novels and short story collections in Romania, including *The Runners, Smoke, Planet New York, One Morning and One Afternoon*, and *The Visitor*.

Planet New York, his first novel written in English and published in the US, received an Honorable Mention at the 2007 New York Book Festival. He published his second novel in English, *No Portrait in the Gilded Frame*, in 2016. Alex's short story "Somewhere in the City" received an Honorable Mention at Glimmer Train's Spring 2017 short story contest.

He is a member of the Maryland Writers' Alliance and serves on the board of directors of the *Little Patuxent Review*, a biannual Maryland literary publication.

For more information on his literary activity, please check his website at www.tudoralexander.com or www.alexduvan.com. His blog, at medium.com/@alexduvan, includes short stories and excerpts from his novels.

www.ingramcontent.com/pod-product-compliance
Lightning Source LLC
Chambersburg PA
CBHW021133260626
47169CB00005B/1596